KNIGHT SEEKER

KNIGHT SEEKER

BY
ERIC MANN COOPER

Knight Seeker
Published through Lulu.com

Book Design and Layout by
www.integrativeink.com

TABLE OF CONTENTS

ACKNOWLEDGMENTS

A big thank you to all who have had an effect on this novel and my life.

To the most high Father and the Son, where my strength comes from. To my caring mother who has always been there when I needed her. My main editor Tim Grundmann, who worked so well with me to produce a fun loving story, and characters. My cover artist Bryan Rogers of Orlando, FL, who worked on the main character's image with great enthusiasm. My rough draft editor, Andrew Feindt of N.J. The character Tygron, inspired by Irtiza Naqvi of Hamilton Tws., N.J. The character Paul Sole, inspired by John Monaco of Ewing, N.J. The character James Q. Booker, inspired by Terry Booker of Trenton, N.J. Daniel Chen of Long Island, New York. Appearance actor Ben Yetter, of Iowa. Thomas Chervenak of St. Paul, MN. B. Britt Association.

Knight Seeker Fan-Film recognition, by Blinky Productions: Director, Chris Notarile II of Cranford, N.J. Actor, Lamont Williams of N.Y.C. Actor, Reginald James of N.Y.C. Actor, Shing Ka of N.Y.C. Actor, Tony Dadika of N.J. Actress, Niki Rubin of Central N.J.

Musical inspirations by the group Lesiem of Germany. The character Rev. Squire inspired by the music of Rev. Clay Evans. Missy Elliott, you go girl.

Costume makers: My personal costume maker Tom Sirkot of Philly, PA. Valerie of spandexoutfitters.com. Sarah of IITYWYKM Designs.

Scifi creators: the late Gene Roddenberry, Stan Lee, and George Lucas

PROLOGUE
THE DARK TIMES

"WHAT WILL it be tonight, Little One? A nice story or a scary story?"

The almond-eyed boy thought carefully before making his decision. "A nice story," he told his grandfather.

"Very well. One nice story and off to sleep you go. Once there was a—"

"No! No!" the boy shouted, kicking his feet under the bed covers, "I changed my mind. A scary story!"

A sly smile played on the old man's wizened face. "Are you sure, little sprout? You know your mother does not approve of my telling you such stories." He winked and gave the boy a playful nudge. "But I *might* tell you a scary story if you promise to be brave and not cry out and wake the house like you did the last time—even if you're really really really really REALLY scared? Like this—?"

The old man made claws with his gnarled hands and bared his yellowed teeth. With a flurry of rustling sheets and blankets, the boy quickly hid himself and screamed into his pillow. The old man waited patiently. He knew how the game was played. It was very quiet now, only the sounds the chirping of crickets and the croak of a river frog outside the window. Then the boy giggled and said in a small voice from under the blanket, "Yes, Grandfather."

"Very well," the old man said, pulling back the blanket an inch or two. "But you absolutely have to lie still and not make a fuss. Now, this story happened a very long time ago, during the Dark Times. There was once an army of warriors in Asia known as the Fury. Their leader was the warlord—"

"Sage," the little boy interrupted.

"Ah, you have heard this before. Shall I tell you a nice fairy story instead?"

"No, I like this one," the boy insisted, his eyes blazing with excitement.

"Very well. Now, Sage was a highly-skilled combatant who studied the black arts. Legend has it that he used demonic sorcery to give the Fury the ability to defeat anyone they faced."

"Anyone?" asked the little boy suspiciously.

"Yes, little sprout, anyone. Now, the Warlord Sage forged a sword with black magic. This gave him the power to draw souls from anyone that died by the sword's blade. The sword was thus named the Soul Taker. These captured souls increased Sage's physical strength and kept him youthful, at the same time it gave him all the knowledge and memories from the people he had slain."

The little boy stopped breathing for a long moment. Words like "slain" had that effect on him. So did words like "decapitated," but that would come later in the story.

"In exchange for this evil gift," his grandfather went on, "Sage had to promise his soul and his body to the Netherworld, which he did gladly so that he could conquer whomever and whatever stood in his way. And with these new dark powers he swept across all the territories of Asia, leaving death and destruction in his wake, all the while gaining more minions for his army of dark warriors. Then came—"

"The Mongols," the boy said.

"Yes, the Mongols. They were a particularly ferocious army led by a great warrior named Genghis—"

"Genghis Khan," the boy said in rush.

"That's right, but who's telling the story? Please don't interrupt. Now, when the two armies clashed, the battle lasted for hours. And in the heat of the confrontation Khan challenged Sage to fight him man-to-man. So both armies stopped fighting to take witness of both leaders squaring off in the middle of the bloody battlefield. Both of them fought with the heat of rage, neither one giving ground as both their swords met, clashing and lighting up the heavens."

By a delightful coincidence, thunder and lightning boomed and flashed outside the window at that same moment. It happened often these summer nights in the Pearl River Delta, but the timing could not have been more perfect. The boy gasped in fright but quickly covered his mouth in time.

"That's it, you're a brave soldier, all right. Where was I? Oh yes. Now, Khan lost his sword when it was deflected by Sage. He ran quickly to one of his men as Sage chased after him. But he wasn't running scared, not Khan. He had a plan, you see. It happened that one of his men had a large crossbow at the ready. They just started to develop these weapons and they used them rather well. A standard crossbow arrow would not put Sage down and Khan knew this, so he had a larger one made for himself."

"How big?" the boy asked.

"This big," the old man said, spreading his hands as far as he could. "Then Khan grabbed the crossbow that was tossed to him and he aimed it at Sage, who stopped in his tracks. Khan pulled the trigger and the arrow flew straight into Sage's chest, knocking him down on his back within an instant.

"Then Khan went over to look at his opponent and saw to his shock that he was not yet dead. That is because the regenerative powers of the demon world enabled him to take a fair amount of damage to his body and still survive. So Khan picked up his sword and cut off the head of the Warrior Sage."

The old man paused a moment for effect. He observed that his grandson appeared not to be breathing and that his eyes were double their normal size.

"Sage was dead. All the captured souls in his sword were released and Sage's soul was in damnation. The Fury fled and disbanded, and the Mongols declared victory.

"And now Khan picked up the Soul Taker. What do you think happened? Sage's spirit spoke to him. It said, 'Take this sword and kill another with it, so that I may return from the dead.'

"Khan only laughed. He knew it would be madness to do such a thing! He ordered the removal of Sage's body and the sword; both to be sealed inside a stone coffin. He also instructed the lid of the coffin to be engraved with a warning of the Warlord Sage's power and a curse to whomever dares to disturb his buried remains."

The story had ended. The boy said nothing, his thoughts still lingering on the Warrior Sage entombed in the stone coffin. The old man leaned over and kissed him on his cheek, then picked up the candle and tiptoed to the door.

"Grandfather?"

The old man stopped. "Yes, sprout?"

"Grandfather, where is the stone coffin buried?"

The old man stood still in the shadows for a moment, the candle casting an eerie glow on his face. "Do you really want to know?"

"Yes," came the small voice, sounded very unsure.

When the old man answered it was in a deep voice the boy scarcely recognized. "The coffin," he said, "is buried under your bed."

The little boy screamed into the darkness. It was a scream that awoke his mother and grandmother at once, for their voices could be heard raised in alarm in the next room. The old man cackled quietly to himself as he shuffled back to the boy's bedside.

"Hush, hush, sprout," he murmured, stroking the boy's hair until the trembling and racking sobs stopped. "It is not under your bed. The stone coffin was buried somewhere in the hillsides of the mainland, never to be found again."

"Never? You p-p-promise?" the little boy pleaded.

The old man chuckled softly. "Yes, sprout, I promise."

CHAPTER 1
THE DRAGON FEATHER

AT 5:14 A.M., the Dragon Feather, a cargo freighter out of Hong Kong, was on a straight approach course into New York harbor. The Port Authority had given its clearance and the engines were at one-quarter cruising speed as it eased into port.

It had been an uneventful voyage. Captain Lu-Wan looked forward to a smooth docking and a restful week in New York before setting off back to sea. After six weeks of ship's rations, he especially looked forward to a nice dim sum in Chinatown with his cousin Chang. Now he sipped the dregs of his morning tea as he looked out at the pre-dawn silhouette of the Manhattan skyline. He felt completely at peace.

But then the War Pack arrived and hell was in season.

They came by speedboat in the pre-dawn darkness—ten mercenaries dressed in black and armed with automatic assault weapons. With practiced efficiency, they moored their craft to the Dragon Feather and silently rappelled up the sides of the freighter. One of them disabled the ship's communications systems, the others rounded up the crew and marched them down to the cargo hold. It was all very quick and very efficient. It had to be; they had roughly a half-hour before the ship reached the pier.

Now Captain Lu-Wan fought back tears of anger. He and his crew were on their knees, guns aimed at their heads. It would not be a good time to lose his temper.

"Well, Captain, hmm? I assume you do understand English, and that you do have a name?"

The captain looked up at the War Pack leader. "I am Captain Lu-Wan."

"Pleased to meet you, Captain Lu-Wan. My name is Malice."

1

"My crew and I will not give you any trouble," the captain said. A quick glance at his crew told him that this assurance did nothing to calm their fears.

"What we want is simple, Captain. We want access to the stone coffin of the Warlord Sage."

At first Captain Lu-Wan thought he had simply imagined what the War Pack leader said. Yes, he knew from the ship's manifest that the large crate in the security vault was an archeological artifact, and yes, it might possibly be an ancient coffin. But the legendary stone coffin of the Warlord Sage? Ridiculous!

"No, that is not possible. The Warlord Sage is only an old Chinese folk tale. My grandfather told me the story many times. It cannot be Sage in that coffin."

"Frankly, Captain, I don't care if it's Mickey Mouse in that box. All I know is that some crackpot collector is paying me three million clams for whatever's inside the coffin, not the coffin itself."

The captain's eyebrows rose. "A collector, you say? Ah, but the ship's manifest says its destination is the Museum of Natural History. So it cannot be—"

"Yeah, yeah, I know," Malice said with mounting impatience, "it's supposed to go to the museum for authentication first. Captain, I really don't see you having any choice in the matter. Kindly lead me to the cargo. Or . . ." He left the rest of the sentence unfinished.

Captain Lu-Wan was a man who took his responsibilities seriously. The safety of his cargo was as important to him as the safety of his crew, and so he forgot himself when he answered, "No, I cannot do that."

The War Pack leader looked surprised, then disappointed. "Pity," he said.

For a crazy moment Captain Lu-Wan thought this man and his gang of hoodlums would simply storm off the ship in a sulk. But Malice had something else in mind. He searched the eyes of the captives kneeling before him, looking for the one who looked the most frightened. It happened to be the youngest of the crew, the nineteen year-old ship's mate.

Malice pointed at the young man, his fingers playfully making a pistol shape. "Bang," he said.

Without hesitation, one of the armed men shot the youth in the back of the head, spraying blood and bits of brain everywhere. The screams began.

"Oh God, Lee-Ming, no!" the captain shouted. "You bastards, you killed my nephew! He was just a kid. Just a kid . . ."

"Shut up! Shut up!" Malice violently back-slapped the captain's face to remind him who was in charge. "Shall I pick another, Captain? Or will you give me what I want?"

The captain rubbed his face. The sting of the slap brought the full horror of the situation into a clearer light. "All right," he said, getting up from his knees. He held back his tears for his murdered nephew; there were still the lives of his remaining crew at stake. He had been foolish to resist...

Malice followed Captain Lu-Wan into the darker part of the cargo hold, turning briefly to give his men an order. "Stay here. Keep an eye on the crew. Anybody moves, shoot them. Mayhem, follow me." His accomplice, a very large-built, muscular young man with a disconcerting permanent smile on his face, joined the two, leaving the other eight mercenaries to keep their Glocks trained on the terrified crew.

Captain Lu-Wan ushered Malice and Mayhem to the walk-in security vault at the far end of the hold. It was here where especially valuable and highly insured freight were stored for the duration of the voyage. With a surprisingly steady hand, the captain punched in the access code on the wall-mounted keypad. The huge steel doors opened with the hissing pressure of the working hydraulics.

The vault held only one item: a wooden crate the size and shape of a coffin. Malice's eyes widened as he gazed at the prize that would make him and his team of mercenaries three million dollars richer. "Open it, Captain," he ordered.

Captain Lu-Wan nodded, grabbed the mallet and the chisel hanging on the wall, and went to work on the crate. As he pried the lid open, uprooting the nails that secured the top of the crate, he prayed he wouldn't disturb the spirit within. Not that he believed for a moment in the demonic powers of the Warlord Sage, or even that it *was* the Warlord Sage. But in his culture the dead were to be honored, and disturbing their spirits was bad luck.

Once the lid of the crate was removed, the stone coffin was revealed. It was cold-looking, a deep slate grey, yet elegant in design, with ancient Chinese characters boldly chiseled on the coffin lid. "Impressive," Malice commented as he looked at the ancient encasement. "Open it."

But something on the coffin lid held the captain frozen to the spot. He read the ancient words, he blinked, and he read them again. A dim memory surfaced: a child screaming in the darkness, a grandfather stroking his hair as he murmured, *"Hush, hush, sprout."* Captain Lu-Wan felt the terror once again.

"It says," he said in a tremulous voice, "that a curse will befall anyone who disturbs the spirit of...the Warlord Sage."

"I don't care if it says 'Don't Open Till Christmas'," Malice shouted. "I said, open it! Mayhem, you help him."

The two men did as they were told. The stone coffin lid made a terrible grinding noise as they lifted it, signifying how heavy and thick it was. It was also much heavier than they had realized and made a deafening noise when they half-dropped it to the metal floor of the deck.

Malice stepped forward and peered inside the stone casing. "Oh, now, that is fantastic," he purred.

The remains of the Warlord Sage were mainly skeletal with little or no remaining flesh at all. The decapitated skull rested atop the chest area, attached with an ancient but well-preserved leather strap. The robes were tattered shreds now, its once-brilliant colors long ago faded to a coffin-grey that matched the burial casing. As the men took it all in, the dank, stale smell of centuries-old air and human rot wafted into their nostrils.

Malice did not notice the smell. It was rather the sword known as the Soul Taker that held his attention. It was sheathed, the handle obscured by the skeletal hands that rested in repose upon it.

"Get the sword," Malice ordered.

Mayhem hesitated for a second, not wanting to touch such a disgusting heap of rotting flesh and bones. But he reminded himself that one had to get dirty sometimes, figuratively as well as literally, so he reached for the ancient weapon.

He could not pick it up, not so easily. It seemed to be locked in the warlord's hands. As Malice looked on impatiently, Mayhem tried to pry the hands apart—a harder job than he would have imagined—finally freeing the sword only after breaking a few bones. The crackling sound they made gave him a slight case of goose bumps, but only slight; God knows he had broken many bones before. Once the sword was freed from the dead warlord's grip, Mayhem unsheathed it to reveal the weapon in all its glory.

It was of standard battle length, forged of black metal. Symbols or ancient writing (Malice did not know which, nor did he care) were etched on the handle, surrounding a highly artistic green and gold intertwining vine design with a dragon's mouth that bit at the hilt. The blade itself was unusually wide, narrowing only towards the tip, but its most striking feature was a flat, clear crystal set in the middle of the blade itself. It was strange and magnificent, Mayhem thought; it was a weapon that demanded respect.

Captain Lu-Wan had been watching all this with a rage that built up inside him and threatened to snap. He no longer saw the thieves with the sword; he no longer saw the ancient remains of a childhood horror story come true. He only saw his nephew being shot over and over again, like a nightmarish film loop playing before his eyes. Then he heard a calm voice, as clear as if whispered into his ear: *"They killed your nephew Lee-Ming. They deserve to pay. They deserve to die."*

Startled, the captain jerked his head to look behind him, but there was no one else here, not in this part of the cargo hold.

"Take the sword and drive it into their hearts," the voice went on in a louder, more insistent whisper. *"Make them pay with their lives for what they have done."*

The disembodied voice had the effect of calming the captain. It was a voice to be honored, to be obeyed. "Yes, yes, you are right," the captain whispered back. "I must avenge the death of Lee-Ming. I will kill them. I am going to kill them all."

He approached the two men with a vengeful gleam in his eyes.

Malice was preparing to place the sword in a narrow duffle bag. But it was Mayhem who noticed the sudden movement from behind. The captain jumped towards the two men with the fury and speed of a wild animal. In the same movement he bit the arm of Malice, who screamed out in pain and dropped the sword. Mayhem moved quickly, pulling out his Glock and shooting the captain. But Lu-Wan had unexpectedly bent over to pick up the sword and received only a glancing wound on his shoulder.

Now the captain's vengeful eyes turned on Mayhem.

Mayhem fired another bullet into his right knee. Like a marionette that had one vital string cut, Captain Lu-Wan collapsed to the floor—but that did not deter him from reaching for the sword. But Malice snatched it up before he could reach it.

"Give me the sword so that I may kill you with it," Lu-Wan said in a voice that sounded strangely doubled, as if two were speaking at once—one voice the captain's, the other voice strange and sinister.

Mayhem backed up in surprise. This was something that he was not expecting. This was becoming a bit scary, even for him.

Malice then took out his pistol to shoot the deranged captain and finish him off, but then stopped. He slowly put the gun back in its holster, and then approached the captain with the sword in his hands.

"You want this sword so badly? Then I'll give it to you right here," he said as he swung the sword across the captain's neck. The slicing was so perfect that there was no blood splatter at all.

The captain's head slid off his neck slowly and then rolled to the floor. Then came the blood—a thick, gurgling pool that seemed to boil over his neck and shoulders.

"This sword is wicked! Oh, I do like this," Malice said with childlike glee. He examined it more closely. Before his startled eyes the weapon started to glow red. He noticed something else: a pulsating and neon-bright blue light that seemed to emanate from the captain's decapitated body.

"What the hell—?" he said.

The two mercenaries watched spellbound as the strange light drifted from the headless body into the red-glowing blade of the sword. Malice felt a strange surge of energy coming from the direction of the captain. He dropped the sword, the clatter echoing throughout the cargo hold.

Mayhem laughed incredulously, a laugh of fear. "Man, I am out of here. I've seen enough, that thing is cursed." With a final shudder he rushed out of the security cargo hold.

But Malice stayed, his greed clouding his judgment.

Curse or no curse, you're mine, baby, he thought to himself. *That is, until I trade you in for a cool three million.*

As he picked up the sword to put it into the duffle bag, he felt once again that overwhelming surge of energy. If he understood that it came from the departed captain's soul, it was not a conscious awareness. Malice had only the sketchiest knowledge of the legend; he knew nothing of the properties of the Soul Taker.

Suddenly he heard a movement and the lights in the security cargo hold area went out. He frantically fumbled inside the pockets of his cargo pants for his flashlight. Then came another sound, a strange bone-cracking rattle, as if something was extricating itself from the stone coffin.

It's only a legend, it's only a legend. Just a myth, nothing more. He forced a hollow laugh out of himself, trying to pretend he wasn't becoming more terrified each passing second in the pitch-black cargo hold.

Finally his hand found the flashlight in his right leg pocket. "Okay," he whispered to himself, "when I turn this on, nothing will be there. It's all in my mind."

He switched on the flashlight at the doorway he was facing. Nothing. Absolutely nothing. Malice sighed deeply, suddenly feeling stupid, and he laughed now with relief.

Jeez, I must be a damned moron to think for one minute—

But wait, he remembered with a start—*that sound. What was that—?*

There it was again, that creepy bone-crackling noise right behind him, and this time he dropped the flashlight to the deck floor. Malice froze. Just as suddenly, the sound stopped.

No, it's not happening, he told himself. *It's just a figment of my imagination.*

And yet, as he said it, his shaking hand groped for his gun. He somehow managed to pull it from its holster and aim it into the darkness.

"Go back to hell!" Malice screamed as he readied to fire. But something grabbed his arm with a grip so tight that it made him drop the gun instantly. He stooped quickly to pick it up with his other hand, but it found the dropped flashlight instead. Now he shone the light on the thing had such a mighty grip on his arm.

What he saw was more frightening than death itself. A grotesque, part-skeletal, part-flesh figure stood before him. Malice knew at that moment and without question that it was the warlord Sage and that the curse was indeed true.

"Give me the sword, now," the body of the warlord said in a deep, raspy voice that chilled Malice to the marrow of his bones. Sage tightened his grip, twisting and bending until Malice's right arm seemed ready to snap.

"Take it! Take it," he yelled out in unbearable pain, dropping the duffle bag off his shoulder to the floor.

Sage released his forceful grip. Then the decrepit body reached into the bag to remove his weapon. Sage looked at his precious blade in all its brilliance.

Malice had seen his chance to save his skin. With the flashlight as his guide, he made a mad dash out the vault, cradling his arm as he shouted to his crew, "Everybody outa here! Get off the boat now!"

Malice found another stairway to the upper decks. Hope flickered in his heart as he took a flying leap to the first step, but then came a whooshing sound behind him and he felt something else in his heart. He looked down, surprised to see the tip of the Warlord's sword sticking half way out of his chest. In his shock Malice only marveled that it had cut so cleanly, not even a drop of his own blood on it. Then he fell over to his side.

He did not see the luminescent blue light of his soul leaving his own body because for the moment he was dead. He did not see it flow like thick, ghostly lava into the Warlord's sword, nor did he hear the rattling bones that walked towards him.

Sage pulled the sword from Malice's body and now the light flowed through him, giving him life. He watched as flesh returned to his near-skeletal remains, filling out his hands that gripped the sword, then spreading to his arms, his shoulders and his torso. It felt delicious.

Mayhem was already back on the speedboat, unhitching the rope that moored it to the freighter, when he heard the sounds of the massacre that shook the hull of Dragon Feather: shouting, gunfire, screams. Then all was over and all was quiet again. He looked up for any sign of his team joining his escape, but saw something else. The dusty armor was familiar, but the face was somehow different, younger. But wait, there had been no face before, only shreds of rotted flesh and petrified bones. And now the eyes of this monster were glowing blue, and gazing down at him. Mayhem felt his knees quake.

"Don't go away, Mayhem," the Warlord Sage shouted as he smiled broadly. "Take witness of my wonders!"

Fat chance, Mayhem thought to himself, then put the engine into full throttle and sped away.

Sage watched the speedboat skim across the waters and disappear from sight. Then he saw his hands gripping the deck railing and marveled how fine and strong they looked. He felt his face with his hands, and laughed in giddiness.

"I live again. *I live again!*" He roared with laughter, rejoicing in the sensation of air filling his once-petrified lungs, rejoicing in the new start of the building of a new empire for the demon world, to once again rule the living and extend his immortality.

The Dragon Feather was getting closer to land as dawn approached. As Sage took witness of the mighty structures of the island, overwhelmed by such monumental structures that scraped the sky, he debated whether to swim to shore or simply enjoy the ride aboard the unmanned freighter. He decided on the latter. Why get wet? He hummed contentedly to himself as a voice from the demon world guided him into New York City.

"Dragon Feather, Dragon Feather, this is the New York Port Authority. Cut your engines, you're coming in too fast! Dragon Feather, respond please!"

Getting no response, the Port Authority went on a collision alert. The freighter was only a half-mile from port and still traveling at one-quarter speed.

"Clear the docks! Alert, clear the docks! Level One alert! Clear all docks!" the dock supervisor's voice screamed over the outdoor speakers.

Everyone working on the docks scrambled off as the spotlights beamed on the grayish hull of the Dragon Feather.

Then it happened, what all the dock workers feared. With a sickening crunch, the freighter crashed into the pier, ripping everything in its destructive path. Docks were smashed like sticks, fuel tanks exploded, and dockworkers screamed in the chaos. The ship finally came to a stop when it ran aground and listed to the side.

Soon after, there was a frenzy of reporters and emergency vehicles on the scene. None of the dockhands were hurt, but the Chief of Homicide found a mass murder on his hands when he and his team went aboard the Dragon Feather. They were trying to piece together what had happened and why there were over thirty dead bodies with wounds seemingly inflicted by a very sharp blade or sword. Only one person was dead from a gunshot wound to the back of the head, though there were bullet casings littering much of the outside area of the cargo hold. The investigators figured that the person or persons who killed all of these people had to be an expert swordsman to take down nine armed men.

CHAPTER 2
THE ONCE AND FUTURE SUPERHERO

NYGEL SPINNER blinked. No, it couldn't be nine-thirty, he thought. But when he blinked again the numbers on his clock radio didn't change. "Oh man, I gotta stop pushing that snooze-bar," he groaned.

It was an old habit of his, mumbling to himself when he had overslept.

He dressed in record time, grabbed a protein bar and his car keys and was out the door in a flash. On his way to his car he stopped to admire how nicely the wax job was holding up. Okay, it was only a '94 silver Jetta, nothing to squawk about, but the previous owner had kept it in good shape and now it was his. Well, two more years of payments and it would be, free and clear. That is, if you don't count the never-ending insurance premiums, which was enough money out of his pocket as it was...

Wasting time, he thought, and unlocked the front door and hopped inside.

It was normally a twenty-minute drive from his home in West Trenton, New Jersey to Mercer County College. This morning he made it in fifteen. Better luck, he scored a prime parking spot in front of the Fine Arts Building.

As he raced from his car to his class, Nygel sounded out a few excuses. "Sorry, Professor, but my car wouldn't start."

No, that was last Tuesday . . . A gas leak? And I had to wait for the gas company to come fix it? Hmm, not bad . . .

But by the time he arrived at the lecture hall, sweat pouring off his forehead, Nygel realized it sounded so pathetic that he doubted he'd manage to pull it off. He'd have to try the old sneakeroo.

He snuck a peek inside the lecture hall and immediately realized there were two things running in his favor. One, the lecture hall lights were dimmed because his Fine Arts professor was using the slide projector. And two, Professor Zimmer conveniently had his back to the class as he read some text on the projection screen.

Nygel decided to make his move.

He opened the door just wide enough to get in. Within a few seconds he was able to slide into an empty seat at the rear of the lecture hall with a minimum of noise, then took out his notebook and pen from his book bag and started to jot down information. A few of the students glanced in his direction, but did not pay him too much attention since he was frequently late. But this day he was later than he had ever been before.

Professor Zimmer finally finished his lecture, turned off the projector, and switched on the lights. Just as he was about to begin the usual post-lecture discussion, something—or someone, Nygel feared—caught his eye.

"Well, well, Mr. Spinner, I see that the front desk at the hotel forgot to give you a wake-up call."

A few students laughed, all smiled broadly, but what could Nygel say? He knew that Zimmer had him over a barrel.

"Well, actually, Dr. Zimmer, the hotel kicked me out last night for throwing too many wild parties, so I had to go home and wake up to a whining alarm clock. Only I kept mashing down the snooze-bar till it gave up and went to sleep itself." The class laughed, but his common sense kicked in and whispered in his ear: *Okay, pal, that's enough.* Now give the professor his due. Nygel cleared his throat and said in a conciliatory tone that was both genuine and disarmingly charming, "The truth is, I really have no excuse, sir. It's my own fault I was late to class today. I'm very sorry."

Zimmer nodded, but was not so easily charmed. "Understood, Mr. Spinner. I would like to see you in my office after class."

Nygel sank his head trying to disappear and avoid eye contact with the not-so-subtle stares of his classmates. He already felt doomed as it was; the students did not need to confirm that fact.

An hour later Nygel was waiting in Zimmer's office while the professor tortured him by taking his sweet time looking over some students' reports on Renaissance paintings. In the past whenever Nygel was late to class, Zimmer would overlook it by giving him a cold stare and then turn his attention back to the class. This time he had pushed it. He could see Zimmer's jaw muscles working and it probably didn't have anything to do with some freshman's ramblings on Caravaggio. *Oh boy, he is going to kick my ass into next week.*

To keep his mind off his impending doom, Nygel looked around the office to take in the decor. There were small paintings on the walls and some awesome prints of gothic cathedrals. Nygel always had an affinity for the Dark Ages—he didn't know why. Then he noticed the framed family photo on Zimmer's desk—two young boys, the professor, and his wife. The boys appeared to be about six years old. Zimmer's wife had a nice smile. She looked like a Sheila, he thought. The boys were probably Tad and—

"Tell me something, Mr. Spinner . . ."

Nigel snapped to attention, presenting Professor Zimmer with his best earnest look. "Yes, Professor?"

"How come one of my best students is always late to my class? Do you have no interest in the subject?"

"I—I don't know, sir. I don't mean to be late, it's just that things always seem to come up on the days I have your class . . . and a few other classes as well. But wait, rewind, you consider me one of your best students? I thought that I was more of a . . ."

"An annoyance?" the Professor asked helpfully. "Yes, you are, when you stroll in so late to my class. But then I look at the work you've been handing in and I'm impressed every time. Your research is impeccable. And there's real feeling and passion behind what you write about."

Nygel's heart began to race with excitement. This wasn't at all what he had expected to hear from Zimmer.

"As you know," the professor went on, "I don't give grades out to the class until the end of the semester. You're ahead assignment-wise, but your attendance is causing your high grade to drop. So consider this a piece of friendly advice: get your act together, get to class on time and you'll get a good grade."

It was clearly a warning, but the praise that accompanied it was so unexpected that Nygel felt flushed with pride. " I understand, sir. I'll do my best to get to your class on time, along with my others."

"That's good to hear. I see a lot of potential in you, Mr. Spinner."

"Thank you, sir."

A curious look crossed the professor's face. It was almost as if he were seeing Nygel for the first time. "I don't know what it is you want to do with your life, but I hope whatever it is, you choose it carefully. You've got something—something special, I think. A spark. No, a fire burning bright. I can see it in your eyes. I think perhaps your destiny lies on a different path from most others . . ."

He stopped, seemingly in the middle of a thought. Nygel shifted uncomfortably in his chair. Professor Zimmer broke away, as if embarrassed.

"Forgive my ramblings. You see, I sometimes flatter myself in thinking I'm a good judge of character."

Nygel smiled broadly. "Well, Professor, after all the nice things you've just said about me, I think you're an *excellent* judge of character."

The professor laughed as he stood up from his desk. He gave Nygel a friendly pat on the shoulder and said, "Then you'll think about what I've said, Mr. Spinner?"

"Definitely, yes, sir, I will."

There was a spring in Nygel's step when he left the Fine Arts building. Blame it on the praise Zimmer had heaped upon him, he thought. But it was also his only class that day, so that put a shine on his smile.

He unlocked his car, pausing to check his Star Questers wristwatch. Seventeen minutes before he had to be at work. Or was it twenty-two?

It was a seriously cool-looking, futuristic-style collectible, but it wasn't the easiest timepiece to read. Nygel hadn't considered that fact when he outbid fourteen other Star Questers fanatics in his determination to win the online auction. Still, it almost made up for getting outbid on the Star Questers sheet set and the Limited Edition Star Questers lunch box...

Screw it. He hopped in the car and buckled up, then checked his reflection in the rear-view mirror.

"Nice job," the reflection said.

"Thanks," Nygel said, then started the ignition and pulled out of his parking space. He wasn't crazy. He had these little chats with himself from time to time and was due for another one. "Hey, guess what? Professor Zimmer said I had something special, said I had a spark."

"Yeah, right. You can't even get things completed. You hop from one unfinished project to another."

"Hey, I wrote that book, that Star Questers novel."

"Took you long enough."

"Still, I finished it. Jerry read it, said he thought I was a good writer, said I could probably make a career at it."

"Wait a minute. You finished the book but did they buy it? Did you even submit it to the Star Questers publishers?"

"I'm, uh, waiting to proofread it."

The reflection laughed back at him. *"Sure. Class, can we say, 'Afraid of rejection?' And watch the oncoming traffic."*

Nothing like having your own reflection jeering at you to brighten your day, Nygel thought. He drummed his fingers on the steering wheel as he waited for the SUV barreling down the highway to pass.

"What're you waiting for? An invitation? Go! Go!"

Nygel swore under his breath and pulled into traffic. He drove in silence, deep in thought. It was true, no getting around it—he was his own worst enemy sometimes. Fear of rejection, fear of being laughed at had plagued him since he was a kid. Only back then it was because he was fat.

Well, not exactly fat, he thought; he was never really obese, more, um...

"Pudgy?"

Nygel frowned in the mirror. "I didn't say that out loud."

"I'm you, nimrod. Remember?"

Nygel fumed as he floored the accelerator. "I was thinking 'husky', but thanks for your help."

"Anytime."

Pudgy, husky, fat—same difference . . . "My, he's a big boy now," his relatives would say, and even then he knew that was a euphemism for "Jeez, if you got any bigger you'll have your own zip code." Some things you don't forget. Like the time the Macy's clerk directed him and his mother straight to the husky boys' section . . .

But it was worse at school. He was always last-picked for games and generally left out of things. He didn't know why he didn't have friends; he tried to be nice to everyone he met . . .

"Excuse me," his reflection said. *"You excluded yourself. You didn't think anyone would like you."*

Maybe. His mom would tell him to go outside and play with his friends—which would have been fine if he had had any. But she didn't know that. She was busy working overtime a lot to pay the bills. And when she wasn't working she'd hang out with her friends.

"She's allowed. Plus it showed she trusted you, wanted you to be independent."

"Maybe too independent." Nygel said. "It would've been different if I had a father figure. If they didn't separate when I was three, then maybe—"

"Shoulda woulda coulda. Trust me, that separation wasn't a bad thing."

Yeah, he remembered what his mom once told him: "Honey, the only good thing that came out of that relationship was you."

High school was a little better. It was a Catholic school in Hamilton Township, a nicer atmosphere than his old public schools and he did manage to make some friends. No girlfriends, though—too chicken to ask anyone out. Sure, he had the usual high school crushes but he did nothing about them. The fact was, he was too self-conscious about his weight and too fearful of rejection. The mere thought that a girl he liked might want to go to the beach one day and then see his flabby abs and love handles spilling over his swimming trunks... The mere *thought* of it nearly killed him! It was easier to be lonely and miserable. Grade school and middle school had been bad enough. He did not want to hurt that way again.

So naturally he missed his high school prom.

"You should've asked Nicole Walker," the reflection said. *"I bet she would've said yes. She stayed home prom night, too."*

"Figures," Nygel murmured.

Then after high school, what? A dozen dead-end jobs, a zillion unfinished projects and what did it all add up to? Nothing. Nada. Zip. He was twenty-four years old and had nothing to show for it. And what the hell was he doing with his life now? Not a whole lot. It was already his second year of college, and majoring in Communications wasn't thrilling him any more than driving limos.

Actually, he reflected, driving limos wasn't that bad. Most of the clients were decent and tipped pretty well, but trying to keep my eyes open late at night while driving—that was the hard part.

"Those limo rear-view mirrors were deluxe," the reflection reminisced. *"Chrome frames—not plastic like this dud there. And big? Man, they fit my whole head. Really top-notch."*

And what other crap jobs did he put himself through? Let's see: fast food restaurants, construction sites, even directing traffic. Then there was that job working for the Rides Department at Five Stars Great Amusement Park, and that security company job at an aerospace satellite center in East Windsor...

"Which might have worked out if you hadn't been fired for falling asleep at your post."

"So I just hate boring jobs. Sue me. I get tired really quickly if my brain is idling too long."

"Then I guess you must be tired all the time."

"You got it, friend."

He remembered the rental car company job and man, what a dive that place was. People treated the cars like crap. Dog hair, mud, sand, spilled drinks and half-eaten burgers under the seats, and guess who had to do most of the cleaning?

After that came the sales rep position at the optical retailer job. The pay was good, but he had just started college and his boss wanted him to put in more hours than he could give him. So that was that.

And now this job at Rapid Action News. It paid pretty well and they were flexible enough to let him work around his class schedule. But did he really like being an assistant equipment technician? Okay, it was just a part-time internship position, but was that even the field he wanted to work in? Still, it was something to tide him over till he graduated from college.

"There's another job you forgot about," his reflection said.

Nygel thought a bit. "Waiting tables?"

"Actually, I was thinking about your last job. You know, when you were a superhero."

Nygel gave the mirror an angry glance. "I thought I told you not to bring that up any more. Anyway, it wasn't a job. More of a . . . calling."

And it was over. He had retired from the superhero business, had hung up his costume and helmet long ago. He didn't remember how it even started.

"Yes, you do," his reflection said.

Yes, he did. He just didn't like being reminded of it all the time, and he was fed up with this mirror working his nerves. So he gave it a hard smack with his hand and shouted, "I told you to zip it!"

"Hey! That hurts!"

"Good," Nygel said, twisting the mirror to face the window. He drove the rest of the way in silence. But he couldn't help remembering, damn it.

It started last year. He had been too depressed to apply himself to his studies, so he did just enough work to get by. The only time he felt alive was while watching his favorite show, *Antorian.* He watched it religiously, even spent hours scouring the internet for anything having to do with his favorite superhero.

Nygel smiled. Just thinking about the A-Man cheered him up a little.

He was not only the coolest superhero to walk the face of the earth, he also had a bitchin' alter ego—Ronald Strong. He lived in New Jersey, too, and worked as a car mechanic for the Newark Police Department. He dated a lot of women—played the field, more like it, but was always very respectful to the ladies. True, he never committed to any relationship, but what superhero could? Obviously it would interfere with his crime-fighting duties.

The pilot episode was all about how Ronald got his powers and became Antorian. It started out with his reserve unit serving near the Iraq-Kuwaiti border during Desert Storm. Just one week before the end of his tour of duty, his chopper crashed into a mountain, killing the pilot and the other crew members instantly. Only the mountain wasn't a mountain at all, it was a huge freaking anthill (thinking about it still gave Nygel the heebie-jeebies), and its residents weren't too happy with the unannounced visit. Worse, they weren't cute itty-bitty ants like Ronald had kept in his ant farm when he was a kid. They were mean ol' fire ants with seriously poisonous venom, and they swarmed the wrecked chopper with a vengeance. Ronald was trapped in the wreckage; there was nothing he could do but scream as the ants (millions of 'em!) attacked him savagely. There was probably not one square centimeter on his body where he was not bitten. The last thing he said before slipping into unconsciousness was, "Must be payback for keeping an ant farm..."

A desert shaman came to the rescue. He helped Ronald escape from the wreckage and the ants by tossing handfuls of some powder all over the li'l bastards. (Insecticide, Nygel figured, and wasn't it convenient the shaman just happened to have it on him, but hey, those TV writers were lazy sometimes.)

Anyway, the shaman dude dragged Ronald to a clearing and summoned the desert spirits to heal him. After a night of agonizing torment and delirium, Ronald's fever broke and a rescue team found him the next day. He finished the last week of his army stint recovering in the base hospital with a bevy of cute army nurses drooling over him.

It wasn't until he returned to his job at the Newark Police Department when Ronald noticed that he had, well, powers. But not the usual unbelievable yeah-I'm-sure super-powers like flying and x-ray vision. Ronald's normal human abilities had simply increased. A lot. He had amazing strength, and he could climb walls and jump as if he were on a souped-up trampoline.

Just like a superhero, Ronald thought; except a superhero fights crime and he was just a mechanic. On the other hand (he found himself thinking), maybe it was time for a career change . . .

He went shopping.

As Ronald explained in the pilot's voice-over, he took Home Economics in high school just to meet girls, which explained how he could sew like a demon. So he whipped up a really amazing costume out of dark red spandex and an extremely cool, aerodynamically-designed black helmet. And because he figured that his superpowers were the result of the fire ants' venom (plus a little magic from the desert spirits), he would be . . .

Ant Man!

Ronald said it aloud a few times, decided it sucked, then tried to think of a name with a little more pizzazz.

Ant Guy!

Fire-Ant-Criminal-Fighter-Super-Dude.

Antorian . . .

Antorian! *Yeah!*

Ronald got back to work, constructing an arsenal of weapons at the police garage on the weekends when no one else was around. Some of those weapons were really stylin', like the M.M.C.s. That was the acronym for the mechanical mandible claws that extended twenty-five feet from his wrists and could grab hold of anything (and crush anything, too). And he made Taser darts that launched from his wrists. Needless to say, Ronald Strong really shocked the mess out of the bad boys with those things.

Antorian was not only Nygel's hero; he wanted to *be* Antorian. And was it any wonder? Nobody messed with the A-Man (as his legions of fans called him), or laughed at him or picked him last for dodgeball or called him names. And he wasn't shy with the ladies, either. Nygel didn't need a therapist to tell him why he was obsessed with Antorian. The dude was everything Nygel wanted to be and wasn't.

His obsession remained a secret one—until he found the Antorian fan site on the internet.

It was started by some guy in Germany who was as fierce an Antorian freak as Nygel was, and the fans were right up there with them. They even had custom-made costumes and posted pictures on the website. Simply put, that German site was the bomb!

One guy's picture really caught his eye. Not only was the costume really well-made, the guy looked amazingly like Antorian himself. Nygel messaged him: *Kewl kostume!!!!!* and the next day the guy messaged back. That's how the friendship started.

His name was David Chandler and he worked for Marble World Corp., the company that owns the character of Antorian. He told Nygel that he did appearances at malls and grand openings for the past three years. He said Marble World didn't let him use the company-made costume off company time, so he ended up making his own after a lot of trial and error.

Got your own costume? he asked Nygel at the end of his e-mail. *If so, post away!!*

Yeah, right, Nygel thought. At that time he was tipping the scales at two hundred sixty-five, so the only way he would get into a form-fitting Antorian costume was if someone put a gun to his head. He could imagine the comments the names the fans would post . . . the names, starting with "Fatorian."

So Nygel braced himself and emailed David back. He started out by saying he was way too overweight to wear a superhero costume, and that David would probably not want to get to know someone like him. As he typed Nygel could feel his self-esteem wilting away. He felt as if he had intruded into a place where he did not belong; he felt doubly humiliated having to put it into words. So he told David that he was sorry, but maybe it would be better if they ended their communication then and there.

But David did email Nygel back.

Let me get this straight, he wrote. *You think I wouldn't want to email you because you're overweight?? How shallow do you think I am?? Sorry, pal, but you're way too hard on yourself. And if you feel that bad about the way you look, don't you know you can do anything your heart desires if you want it badly enough? Think about it, okay?*

Nygel did think about it. Then came Christmas dinner at his aunt's house.

After dinner all the family started doing physical challenges. (Whose lame-brained idea was that, he now wondered.) Then it was Nygel's turn to do ten push-ups. Sit-ups he could maybe fake, but with push-ups there was no cheating; you could do them or you couldn't. When he got down on the floor, he prayed he wouldn't fall on his face in front of his whole family—mom, cousins, aunts, uncles, and even friends of the family.

He went down for one, then two. Those were not too bad. The third was a harder and the fourth just about did him in. His strength gave out coming up from the fifth. He collapsed to the floor, and then the laughter started.

It wasn't mocking laughter, more good-natured and even loving, but a sensitive kid doesn't always see it that way. "Better luck next time," someone said.

Humiliation gave way to anger and Nygel stormed out of his aunt's house. He got into his beat-up '87 blue Pontiac and drove off, crying all the way home.

An email from David awaited him on his return home. Nygel stared at the "Merry Christmas!" message and muttered "What's so merry about it…" But he emailed David back and thanked him for his thoughtfulness and friendship. He went to bed.

The next day his Mom told him the entire family felt badly for the way they treated him, especially on Christmas night. "They send their apologies," she said.

"Don't worry," he lied, "I'm over it."

It was that same day he logged onto the German fan site and saw the Halloween costume pics that one fan calling himself "Ant-Fool" posted on the forum page. All the fan site regulars had nicknames like that, he recalled. Nygel's handle was "Antie Maim."

It was those Halloween costume pics that gave Nygel the idea. He e-mailed David: *Okay, here's the plan. I'm gonna do it, I'm starting a crash diet and get myself in shape come hell or high water. But no way can I make my own costume. You know some genius costumer who can custom-make one for me?*

David emailed him back with the name and phone number of a well-regarded costume maker in California. *I knew you had it in you!* he went on to say, *but crash-dieting isn't the way to go—you'll just be a skinny dude in a leotard. Change your diet. High-protein, low-carb is the way to go, and (do this today!) get yourself a gym membership!!!!*

Nygel didn't waste any time. He called the costume maker who told him to send his body measurements along with his money order. After they hung up, Nygel sat down and figured out the measurements he expected to have by summer. He pre-ordered the suit for summer, just in case he still needed more work to do on his body before Halloween. He jotted the measurements down on a note and sent it along with his money order.

One week later, New Year's Day, marked the day of his new life. Nygel changed everything—his diet, a grueling exercise regimen at Man's World Gym, his everyday habits, even the way he thought. If he was watching TV, he didn't sit on the couch with a fist in a bag of corn chips. He did sit-ups, and he followed it with a protein shake. If he was surfing the 'net, he did butt-clenching isometrics. Nygel became a man obsessed.

People laughed as they did before, but he ignored them. He kept his eyes on the goal, and the goal was the costume, nothing more. Eventually the weight started coming off, and by June he had dropped an incredible sixty pounds. That same month his Antorian costume arrived.

He was giddy with excitement as he tore open the package, but it took him a half hour to put the suit on; he was so afraid it might rip if he was not extra-careful. Once he had it on he got a pleasant shock: it was actually a little too big around his waist. So he took the suit to a local tuxedo shop and had alterations made. Then it fit perfectly.

Halloween came and Nygel packed his costume in his gym bag and headed off to Washington Mills Mall. It was one of the biggest malls in the Tri-state area and their Halloween festivities were huge events. Nygel changed quickly in one of the men's room stalls, and when he looked at himself in the mirror, he actually gasped. Was that really him? He couldn't get over the fact that he had exceeded his expectations.

"You did it, bro," he murmured aloud, then took a deep breath, grabbed his gym bag and headed out to face the world.

When he hit the mall floor he was pleased to see there was a nice turnout—people in monster masks, 50s-style clothing—even some folks decked out as Star Questers characters. As he took it all in, he became gradually aware that people started taking notice of *him*. There were a few kids in Antorian costumes (store-bought as well as homemade) and they immediately surrounded Nygel. They called him big brother, said they wanted to be as big as him when they get older. Complete strangers asked him to pose for pictures with their kids. Nygel had brought his digital camera so he asked them to return the favor. People kept asking him if he worked for Marble World. He said he didn't and they insisted that he should. He even got a fanny-pat from a cute lady walking by. Nygel was flattered and stunned. He knew he looked good in his Antorian suit, but that good?

But it didn't matter; he was walking on air. No one laughed at him, no one called him names. He was a hit. He had arrived!

As soon as he got home that night he snuck the suit up to his bedroom and stashed it in his closet. His mom still knew nothing about it and he wanted to keep it that way. He knew she'd think he was crazy or something.

He sat down at his computer and uploaded his digital pics to the fan site forum. And waited. He was proud of his accomplishment, but what would the Antorian fans think?

The response was immediate and overwhelming. *Is that really you in that suit?* one fan asked. *Impressed, to say the least!!* wrote another. One fan said he looked like he was born to wear the Antorian costume. Nygel was beyond pleased with the feedback, but there was one person whose opinion he wanted the most. David e-mailed him very late that same night. *You did a fantastic job and you look great! I'm really impressed with your determination and drive.*

That meant a lot. So did the comments from a few fans who told him he should be doing personal appearances for Marble World. Nygel e-mailed David, asking him for advice on applying for an acting job with Marble World. David wrote back: *All you have to do is get nice and ripped and read up on the Antorian biography to understand more about the character. You can use me as a reference in your application. Good luck!*

Nygel kept working out religiously and the results paid off. People started to take even more notice of his changing body. Even a couple of talent scouts from a modeling agency signed him up after they spotted him shopping in one of the malls.

Finally he felt he was ready to submit his application to Marble World. He attached some digital full-body pics, along with a link to the German website where his Halloween pictures were posted.

The reply he got was not at all what he had expected. It was from a representative in charge of the appearance department, informing him that he was infringing on Marble World's trademark. It further instructed him to remove his pictures from the website and to cease and desist all public appearances wearing his custom-made (and not "officially sanctioned," as the Marble World rep had put it) Antorian costume.

If Nygel felt like crap then, he felt even worse later: he got David into trouble, too. Not only did Marble World demanded that he also take down his pictures from the German website, they further ordered the webmaster to remove *all* the pictures.

None of the website regulars blamed Nygel for causing the trouble. The general consensus was that the Marble World heavies had really, *really* over-reacted.

Come on! one fan posted on the forum, *They're only Halloween pictures. It's not like you're going to your 9-to-5 dressed up as Antorian!*

But the real reason no one was too bummed out was because excitement was building for the much-hyped Antorian movie opening that coming spring. The movie trailers looked fantastic and the fans were really getting psyched. Nygel saw it as an opportunity. He knew that once the movie opened Marble World will need more actors to do appearances as Antorian. So he worked his butt off working out, putting on muscle mass. He even had his suit altered again when he noticed his waistline was getting even slimmer.

Then he got a call from the modeling agency he had signed up with, asking if he wanted to do a charity event as Antorian with a local radio station at one of the biggest movie houses in New Jersey. No money, since it was a benefit, but Nygel was excited and knew it was time to tell his mom and a few friends about his secret identity. They were all supportive, to his relief. "You're full of surprises," his mom told him.

Nygel grinned. Now the only thing he had to do was get permission from Marble World to do the benefit. He figured it was just a formality and they'd appreciate him asking first.

The rep in charge of personal appearances was very nice . . . at first. As soon as Nygel asked about doing the charity event as Antorian, her tone completely changed.

"The short answer? Absolutely not. The long answer is you don't want to open that can of worms. First of all, there are legal issues of you appearing as a Marble World character in an unauthorized costume—"

He managed to get a word in edgewise, saying he had thought it would be okay as long as he asked permission. "So did the other people I've talked to," he said. "That way it would all be totally above-board. Besides, all the money is going to a good cause—"

She then lost her cool. "What 'other people'? Who are these people you're talking to, and who told you doing this would be all right?"

Nygel felt as though a 500-watt interrogation light was shining in his face. She said a lot more, something about "unfair competition," but her aggressive tone had so startled him that he stopped listening. It might as well have been a dog barking on the other end.

When she finished her rant Nygel figured he had nothing else to lose. So he asked her about the other matter he wanted to discuss. "Just switching gears a moment," he said in his carefully-maintained polite tone, "I submitted an application to be an Antorian actor for personal appearances. Can you tell me the status of my application?" Her response was silence. "From the way you got quiet all of a sudden," Nygel went on to say, "I guess that I am best forgotten?"

"I'm afraid you guessed correctly." She further informed him that because his case had been taken up by their legal department, he could never appear as Antorian again.

"I see. Um, is there anything else you need from me, anything else we need to discuss?"

"No."

"Well, in that case, I'll say thank you for your time and—"

But Miss Congeniality had already hung up.

The next two phone calls were even harder to make. The radio station and the movie theater people were understanding about the situation, but Nygel couldn't stop thinking about all the hard work he had put in at the gym, all his expectations now dashed. He had *assumed* he'd be working for Marble World and damn it, he would have done the character justice. Now that door was closed forever.

Both Dave and the Antorian site webmaster told Nygel not to worry about it; he was still a superhero in their eyes. *Even if Marble World doesn't see it that way,* Dave wrote him.

But Nygel was inconsolable. On the afternoon of the movie opening he lay on his bed thinking what-ifs as he stared at his costume hanging limply on its hanger. All that work, and for what? If things had gone according to plan, he'd be out the door now on his way to Oats Bridge Mall in Lawrenceville for the opening.

A cool breeze blew through the open window, rippling his Antorian costume. His eyes misted over as he watched his dream vanish before his eyes.

Then something happened. It was as if a bell went off in his head, or someone had splashed cold water on his face. The pity party was suddenly over. "Screw 'em," Nygel said aloud, "I'm goin'!"

He whipped the costume off its hanger and got dressed. It would be his last hurrah, his last appearance as Antorian, but damn it, he'd be there in costume just as he had planned. And let anybody try to stop him! Better still, he wouldn't pack his costume in his gym bag; he'd head out the door in full costume.

"Honey," his mom said when he headed out the door, "you're not going outside dressed like that—"

"Yeah, I am, Mom," he called back. He checked his watch: it was a twenty-minute drive to Oats Bridge Mall in Lawrenceville and he'd have to put the pedal to the metal. A few drivers did double-takes when they spotted him stopped in traffic. Once they got a gander at him, they honked their horns and gave him a thumbs-up. Nygel thumbed 'em back, grinning ear to ear. This is what it was all about, right? The recognition, the smiles, the friendly shouts of "Yo, Antorian!" and "you've got it, man!" from complete strangers. Name-calling like this he liked!

He got to the theater in time, actually managed to get a decent seat, and the excitement was electric. This was the moment he'd been waiting for!

And when the lights went up again...

Nygel was left with a curiously empty feeling. He thought the movie was good, not great—a bit of a letdown, really. No, the special effects were great, and the story was well-constructed and even riveting at times. Was it something else?

He couldn't put his finger on it, but whatever it was, he felt like taking off the suit. Now.

He stayed in his seat and waited till everyone else cleared out before leaving. On his way out when he realized he had forgotten something. He had promised his friends at the optical shop he'd stop by and show them his costume. It was actually the last thing he felt like doing, but these were old work buddies.

He bit the bullet and headed toward the shop.

He decided to give his friends a real superhero-style greeting. So he took a flying leap from outside and landed inside the store with his arms akimbo, looking heroic as hell in his get-up. "Anyone in danger?" he called out.

His old work buddies burst into howls of delighted laughter and applause. "It's Antorian!" they shouted. Someone ran to another shop to buy a disposable camera and everyone (including a few customers) clamored to have their picture taken with him.

It was a brief visit—he told them truthfully that he had to get to work. And of course he didn't bother regaling them with the long sordid saga of Marble World versus the Antorian pretender. Why dampen the mood with that downer of a story? He kept it short and sweet and everyone was happy.

On his way out the mall exit, a gentleman stopped Nygel and introduced himself as the manager of the mall. "Great costume," he said with a broad smile. "May I ask who do you work for?"

Nygel told him he worked for no one, he was just dressed up to celebrate the release of the new Antorian movie.

"I see," the manager said, his smile changing almost imperceptibly. "In that case, would you please take it off immediately or else leave the mall? We have the official Marble World actors signing autographs over there—"

Nygel glanced over to where the man pointed and sure enough, there they were: Antorian, Ant-gal, and Sharp Claw signing away at a long table as security guards kept the line of fans in order. Nygel thought the Antorian actor looked completely miscast.

"—and we have to protect our costly investment," the manager went on, "so you see . . ."

"Uh-huh, gotcha," Nygel said, and headed out to the parking lot.

Once outside he started to laugh. It figures, he thought. And to think he had actually expected the manager to offer him a job on the spot—a job, of course, that he'd have to refuse. But still, didn't it just figure? It all seemed to be in keeping with some strange cosmic script he would never understand.

Or would he?

Nygel stopped in his tracks. In a blinding flash he now understood why he felt empty after the movie and wanted to take the costume off. He was over it. The costume had helped him get in shape as well as gain a good measure of self-confidence, but it was over. He got some great pics, he'd always have those pics till he was old and gray—but it was over. And all those hassles from Marble World hadn't been the universe conspiring against him; it had all been part of the cosmic script telling him to move on.

But where? he wondered. *Move on to what?*

Maybe . . .

A car blasted its horn at him—he was standing in the middle of the parking lot roadway—then swerved angrily around him. Nygel remained oblivious, lost in thought.

Maybe to create a new superhero, something of my own. A superhero with Antorian's sense of morality, but more of myself. A character like me who overcomes his insecurities when he suits up. Someone with my own attitude—more realistic and down to earth . . .

That's how he would break into the comic book industry. That was the new plan.

CHAPTER 3
CLASH IN THE NIGHT

AND HERE it was six months later, Nygel reflected as he neared the Rapid Action News building, and still only thinking about this as-yet unknown superhero he wanted to create. *I just need time*, he thought, *time to do it properly.*

He pulled into an empty space in the R.A.N. parking lot and checked his watch. Just a hair under a minute late—not too bad. As he readjusted the rear-view mirror back to its normal position, he noticed his reflection had a sheepish look.

"Just so you know," it said, *"I don't think you're a total washout."*

"Well, thanks," Nygel said.

"Maybe half a washout . . ."

Nygel was about to smack the mirror when a voice startled him from outside his open window. "Miracle of miracles, you showed up on time."

It was one of his supervisors, James Quincy Booker—"Q" for short—a young black guy around Nygel's age. Nygel hoped he hadn't heard him jabbering to the mirror, or it would be all over the office tomorrow.

"Hey, Q, what's up?"

"Don't bother getting out. I need you to help me install the equipment over at the hotel."

"No kidding. The station finally got the permit?"

"As of this morning. I clocked you in, so just meet me at the hotel. The equipment is already on site and ready to go." James gave the top of the Jetta a friendly slap and walked off, a spring in his step.

Nygel drove off, pleased at the unexpected break in the work routine. Plans to set up an expansion news studio at the top of the new Chariot Hotel had been in negotiations for months. The change of scenery also explained James' uncommonly good mood, he thought; James was always upbeat whenever he got the chance to get away from the office drudgery and politics.

It was a short drive to the Chariot Hotel. Nygel was shocked at how quickly the building had gone up, though there was still obviously major work left to be done. A parking spot was not easy to find, though, and he regretted not leaving his car back at the main studio lot and walking the piddling four or five blocks.

He met James inside. They stood gawking at the huge lobby for a few moments, taking in the sculpted pillars and polished black marble floor threaded with a gold design—a far cry from the shabby lobby of the network's home building. "Well, it *is* a hotel," James said.

"Still, it's swank," Nygel's said. "We're gonna work here?"

"Who, us peons? Nope, this is for the international news crew. "

"Well, la-dee-dah."

A security guard checked their Rapid Action News I.D.s as they signed in, then they made their way to the elevator bank.

"Hold it!" called Nygel. A construction worker held the elevator doors for them as they raced across the polished marble floor.

It was like riding a cloud. It was also the first time in his life Nygel felt underdressed for an elevator. He took in the dark mahogany paneling inlaid with mosaics of stained glass and mirror chips; he luxuriated in the plush, thick carpeting beneath his feet, and then murmured to James, "I am so unworthy." James grinned, and they both burst out laughing when a sultry female voice purred the floor number at the first stop.

"It's got everything but a karaoke bar," James said.

But there was mellow music ("Supermarket music," James muttered in disdain) playing from hidden speakers. But by the tenth floor that was drowned out by the various sounds of banging, sawing, drilling and shouts of construction workers on different floors getting the hotel in shape for the opening.

"Top floor: Rapid Action News Network. Have a nice day."

When they stepped out the doors they were greeted by an even louder racket. Workers were busy in every corner—

carpenters fitting wood panels and electricians installing light fixtures, both with dueling boom boxes blaring Top 40 and Talk Radio.

"Okay, let's do it," James said.

Nygel started to follow but stopped to take in the view out the window behind the reception desk. As he looked out over downtown Trenton, he thought it would make a much finer picture without the New Jersey Department of Labor building blocking the view.

"Nyge!" James shouted, and Nygel broke away from the window.

They worked through the afternoon and into the early night, taking an hour break for dinner at a Tex-Mex restaurant across the street. As they wolfed down their high-fat, high-carb, artery-clogging dinners they talked about the importance of maintaining a healthy diet. The irony wasn't lost on Nygel, who usually watched every morsel he ate these days, but James was a bad influence whenever they shared a table at lunch or dinner.

"I'll have to go on a three-day fast after this pig-out," Nygel sighed. "How do you do it? Tapeworms?"

James shrugged. "Good metabolism."

In a secret part of his brain Nygel reserved a little contempt for people like James who could eat whatever they wanted and still manage to look buff. Then again, James also played all kinds of sports and lived for his workouts.

It was a relaxing dinner, Nygel thought, and the Mexican beer went down nicely with his artery-clogging enchilada platter. He listened as James talked about his recent engagement and upcoming wedding. There was a spark in his eyes when he spoke of his fiancé, and Nygel knew why; he had met Tasha before and thought she and James were a perfect match.

"She's way too good for me," James concluded, scarfing down a taco.

"Just keep telling her that and you'll have a long and happy marriage."

They gossiped about various newsroom personalities, getting more animated when discussing the on-air talent. "Overpaid drama queens," James called them. But he reserved his special wrath for their boss and station owner, Mike B. Payne. No week was complete without James getting into some completely unnecessary and avoidable scrape with "Payne-in-the-Ass," as James called him.

They both admitted, though grudgingly, that Mike Payne was a media genius. In his short five-year tenure he had transformed a small local television station into the most-watched news station in the Tri-state area. This was due in large part to giving the viewers what they really wanted—sensational news and celebrity gossip all under the guise of "hard-breaking news."

"Didja hear the latest stunt he pulled? You heard about the freighter crash, right?"

"No. What crash?"

"Nygel! A Chinese freighter smashed into New York Harbor! Dragonfly or Dragon's Breath or something. Where've you been?"

Nygel lathered his bean burrito with salsa and shrugged. "School, mostly."

"It's on all the news. Big secret cover-up over something, the police aren't talking. Only Payne-in-the-Ane decided he'd get the real story. So he—get this—he got Marty to pass himself off as a coroner and sneak a minicam past the police cordon."

"You're kidding me. Marty-the-Cameraman-Who-Can't-Shoot-Straight?"

James grinned. "He was the only one willing to risk getting arrested, and Payne promised him a hefty bonus if he came through with the goods. And man, did he come through! He got aboard the freighter and got shots—the whole crew dead, some hacked to pieces."

"What? Jesus." Nygel put down his burrito and took a long sip of beer.

"Then a couple of guys from Museum of Natural History showed up—telling the cops they were there to pick up a stone coffin with a priceless mummy from the freighter. Wanted to check the cargo hold but the cops wouldn't let 'em through. So one of the museum guys started yelling that they had to get the mummy into a climate-controlled environment immediately or some crazy stuff. Said he was a close personal friend of the mayor's and wanted their badge numbers."

"Yeah?"

"The cops called his bluff and told 'em to take a hike. They did. Oh—wait. Back to Marty. He's conned his way inside the freighter, right? He checked out the entire cargo hold. There *was* a stone coffin," James leaned forward and whispered dramatically, "but it was empty."

Nygel shivered. "Q, next camping trip I take, you're coming along to tell ghost stories."

"Only this isn't a ghost story. Marty got tape of the empty coffin, the bodies, everything. The other networks are flogging themselves, wondering how Payne pulled it off."

"Won't he get in trouble, though? Payne, I mean."

"Naw. He'll just say he bought the tape from a freelancer, can't reveal his sources, blah blah."

They went back to the hotel to finish their job. It wasn't exactly how Nygel would have preferred to spend his evening, but James was good company. They worked late into the night installing operating systems, until James finally called it quits. Nygel stayed alone to finish wiring a bank of video monitors in the control room. At ten o'clock a security guard poked his head in and announced he was leaving for the night. Nygel started to pack up but the guard told him he could stick around. "The main doors will be locked, but you can let yourself out the rear lobby exit."

"I'll find it, thanks."

He stuck it out for another hour and a half before deciding to pack it in. He wasn't completely convinced that one of the wall shelving units was strong enough to support the video monitors—it seemed to give a bit, and Nygel suspected it had been mounted on flimsy drywall. But let some inept carpenter take the blame for that one, he thought as he switched off the lights and closed the door. He was beat and wanted to go home.

He stopped en route to the elevator to look out the reception area window. As he gazed on the rooftop of the Department of Labor building, now barely visible in the moonlight, random thoughts came to mind: having to get up early for classes the next morning... the nice things Professor Zimmer had told him in his office... a malicious but funny remark James made at dinner about a colleague...

Then he saw a man on the rooftop, appearing out of nowhere.

Then another man. Two men on the rooftop, seemingly out of thin air. Then it became suddenly darker (a cloud cover, he thought afterwards) and he could see nothing. Had he only imagined it? His mind had wandered but his eyes hadn't moved, he thought.

But he must have looked away, he just didn't remember it. As he walked to the elevator, another possibility occurred to him: he had also been thinking about the superhero character he wanted to create. So maybe what he "saw" was merely an inspiration, a moment of creative madness.

Okay, he thought, what do we got: two characters appear on a rooftop. What could he do with that? He'd think about it on his way home; maybe he'd come up with something.

The elevator arrived but Nygel realized he should hit the john before leaving. So he let the elevator doors close as he headed down to the dark corridor to find the men's room. It was too long a drive home to hold it in.

* * *

When Aracnus (Spyconian Seeker First Class, Protector of the Innocent and Captain of the Space Authority of the Milky Way Galaxy) appeared on the rooftop, he had a splitting headache.

The problem with the Emergency Matter Transporter, he reflected hazily, was that it scrambled your brains a bit. Surely in this day and age someone could have worked out the kinks in that. He stood dazed for a few moments as he tried to get his bearings.

Bits and pieces slowly came back to him: lounging poolside at Space Station Starbright, the high-class resort for interstellar travelers... sharing oxygen cocktails in the Meteor Lounge with a cute Spyconian stewardess who had a thing for leather and space cops . . . an antique weapons convention . . .

Oh, yes, now he remembered. Dracus! How could he have forgotten? He had been after the alien smuggler for over a year, had a sneaking hunch he'd find him at the space station, and sure enough, there he was doing a brisk business selling illegal arms to collectors. But just when Aracnus was about to slap the laser-cuffs on him, the crook bastard bolted out the space station's convention center and into his vehicle. Aracnus followed in his official Space Authority police ship, but Dracus' larger and clunkier space craft was a souped-up, super-charged surprise.

It was a wild ride at light speed. Aracnus fired, blasting holes through the enemy ship's shields, finally scoring a direct hit on the engine's light drives. It worked—Dracus' space craft sputtered and swerved crazily, finally slowing down to sub-light speed.

"Gotcha," the space cop grinned, shifting his gears down to sub-light speed. He thought he had Dracus then and there, but then the alien creep outfoxed him by leading him into the Terran System—absolutely the worst place to be playing cat-and-mouse and strictly forbidden to travelers. The sole inhabitants of this sector were a bunch of dolts who didn't have the technology to travel outside their own system, so if you were stranded here in a damaged craft you were plain out of luck, fella. Maybe the smuggler took that risk figuring the cop wouldn't follow him.

"You figured wrong," Aracnus muttered between clenched teeth. He locked into the enemy craft's ion trail signature and followed—

Straight into the asteroid belt.

"Uh-oh," Aracnus muttered.

The cunning smuggler had led him there, and now the space cop watched helplessly as the enemy craft launched sonic detonation charges into the asteroid field. In a frightening light show, shock waves from the sonic blasts sent fragments of asteroid debris hurtling towards the police ship's shields. Luckily Aracnus had them set at full power, but one look at the control panel told him the ship's sensors had sustained damage.

When he looked up again, the enemy craft was gone.

"Damn," he muttered, but pressed onward, hoping the smuggler would not risk an open space confrontation with his light-speed drive damaged. As he reached the fourth planet from the sun Aracnus still had no confirmation of the smuggler's craft on his tracking screen.

This wasn't good, he thought; without any visual he was in an extremely vulnerable position. He veered his police craft towards the dark side of a moon to keep cover while the automated repair systems finished their job.

But there wasn't time. A whiny voice drawled from the command console: *"Thought you should know, Officer Aracnus, two high-yield missiles are locked on our craft and are approaching rapidly."*

"I thought you were asleep, Goliath," Aracnus murmured, snapping to attention. He fired counter-measures from the rear, then sped away from the incoming missiles.

They exploded on impact, just as he had hoped, but Dracus followed with volleys of laser blast cannons mounted on the wings of his craft. Aracnus returned fire, explosions lighting up the skies as the two crafts pummeled each other. Within seconds the protective shields of both were destroyed.

Aracnus brushed the sweat from his eyes. Already he could feel the searing heat as laser weapons scorched the hull of his craft. Worse, his laser banks had run low and had switched to automatic recharge.

"May I make a suggestion, Officer?" the whiny voice from the command console inquired shyly.

"Yeah, what'ya got, Goliath?"

"Um, ions?"

Sheesh, how could he have forgotten ions?

"Typical," the voice yawned, *"You'd forget your spike-bones and organic webbing if they weren't attached to you."*

"All right, all right," Aracnus muttered, hating it when Goliath gave him attitude. He gritted his teeth and took aim, launching a round of ion cannon fire at the enemy ship's life support systems.

It was a bulls-eye. But Aracnus was not yet in the clear. His enemy had nothing to lose, and now emptied all his sonic charges at the patrol ship. Aracnus could only swerve to avoid fire; with no shields left and defenses running low, one direct hit could blow the police ship to smithereens.

Aracnus waited it out until the last of the sonic charges exploded within a safe range of his craft, then continued his pursuit, following Dracus towards the third planet of the Terran System. He closed in, confident that the smuggler's craft had exhausted its weaponry, but once again he had underestimated the smuggler. A surprise torrent of laser fire shot out from the tail of the enemy craft, blasting a hole through the police craft's hull and frying the navigational systems.

Aracnus could do nothing. He had lost control of his craft and was caught in the tail wind of the enemy ship. He was following too fast and getting closer; a crash was inevitable. Goliath made the same assessment and whined, *"Engaging Emergency Matter Transport."*

Aracnus gulped. "Go with honor, Goliath."

"Likewise, Captain."

The space cop braced himself. He had employed the EMT on a space craft only once before and he had never forgotten the stomach-turning, brain-rattling feeling. *Here we go*, he thought as the dreaded blue and yellow lights enveloped him. He only hoped it would be quick.

He saw and heard the explosion of the two crafts, so he naturally figured he was a goner. But he had forgotten that inexplicable phenomenon of the EMT: it transported the body first while the mind lagged seconds behind. He was already safe on land when—too high above this strange blue planet to be noticed—the two space crafts were extinguished in a brilliant flash of color and light.

So, he now wondered, *where the hell am I?*

He knew the EMT always took the straightest path to dry land. That happened to be the rooftop of the New Jersey Department of Labor building, situated at the edge of downtown Trenton, New Jersey. Of course, Aracnus didn't know the name of the building or the city or even the country. He did know what planet he was on, and was grateful that the EMT sent him to a place where there was clean air to breathe.

It figured that the smuggler's spacecraft had a similar EMT and whisked its survivor to this same spot. And sure enough, there was Dracus appearing on the opposite end of the rooftop. You couldn't miss the ugly bastard in a crowd, Aracnus thought; he looked like a cross between a Terran human and one of their ugly flying nocturnal creatures—what did they call them? Bats.

Aracnus watched Dracus touch something on his wrist. A weapon? But before he could determine that, the smuggler nodded with satisfaction and turned to face Aracnus.

"When I am done killing you," he said as he pulled a laser rifle from its holster strapped to his back, "I will retrieve my priceless merchandise that is coming down from the upper atmosphere."

Aracnus almost laughed. It sounded like a line from an old green-and-white Grade-Z picto-tale, when the villain tells his intended victim his evil plan just before killing him. "Our ships are dust, and so's your crappy cargo, Fang."

Dracus visibly stiffened at this insensitive reference to his toothy visage. He was about to inform Aracnus that the females on his planet found his sharp, protruding teeth extremely sexy, but the space cop would doubtless have a snappy comeback for that. He usually did. "Sorry to disappoint you," he replied with a forced smile, "I sent my cargo into temporary orbit before the collision."

Aracnus shrugged. "Either way, you're coming with me, dead or alive." He touched the onyx device on the forearm of his uniform, forming a dark blue-and-gold full-body suit with an alien script insignia on his chest. Once that was done, a blue translucent shield thirty inches in diameter appeared in front of him.

Just in time, too; as Dracus fired at Aracnus, the combat shield deflected the green laser bolts as it shimmered and glowed.

The problem with the body shield, Aracnus thought as he took the assault, was that it didn't cover your whole body. The smuggler knew that and fired at his feet. Aracnus jumped up to dodge the laser bullets, only he had overestimated this planet's gravity and somersaulted high in the air. Dracus tracked his orbit, and fired at his feet again when he landed. But Aracnus dropped to a crouching position, lowering the shield to the ground where his feet should have been.

It worked. The shield deflected the laser bullets, sending their energy right back to the source—the laser rifle itself. It exploded in the smuggler's hands, doing his armor-protected hands no harm but throwing him backwards.

When the smuggler came to his senses, Aracnus was standing over him.

"Now you just made killing you much more interesting," Dracus smirked. He gave an ear-piercing shriek that released laser-claws from his wrists of his body armor.

The space cop reached for his battle blade. It was just a hilt with no blade, but once he freed it from its magnetic leg attachment, a blade of light expanded and with a blinding flash, became solid metal. Aracnus deactivated the protective shield to give himself full movement.

"Dracus, this chase ends tonight," he said.

The toothy bat-creature smirked. "Fine, then tomorrow I'll pick out a suit for your funeral."

Officer Aracnus leapt forward and slashed his sword at the smuggler's head. Dracus flicked his laser-claws to block the attack, then crouched low on his right leg to sweep Aracnus' feet with his left leg. The space cop executed a graceful jump, neatly avoiding the leg-sweep.

"Not bad," Dracus grudgingly admitted.

"Then you'll love this," Aracnus grunted. As he swung his battle-blade, Dracus jumped backwards, the blade slashing where his head should have been.

They kept at it, exhausting themselves with neither gaining the advantage. Aracnus activated the sonic mode on his sword and fired a small shockwave that missed the smuggler by inches, but blasted a nice chunk off the roof.

"You're losing your grip, Aracnus," laughed Dracus, then jumped off the edge of the building.

The space cop didn't expect that. He went to the edge of the rooftop to see if maybe Dracus was hanging off the side of the building. Peering cautiously over the ledge, he saw no sign of the fugitive.

"Where the hell—?"

His shield device, nicknamed Compass, gave him the answer. *"Right behind you, Captain."* Aracnus spun his head around quickly. Sure enough, the smuggler was gliding towards him from above on bat-like wings. Aracnus gripped his sword and aimed to strike.

But Dracus deflected the weapon easily with a slash of his laser-claws. As the sword clattered to the rooftop he hovered in mid-air, hacking away at Aracnus's right shoulder plating. Aracnus fell to his knees, gasping in pain as he clutched his shoulder wound. The laser claws had cut through the shoulder armor and left a hell of a burn, nothing serious, and he could live with the pain. But where the hell was Dracus?

His eyes followed the likely flight path—off the side of the building to a smaller building a good distance away. Sure enough, there was Dracus, laughing at him from the neighboring rooftop. Aracnus muttered a curse. It was much too far for his sonic sword to be of any use, and he had no wings to glide to the other rooftop. He had to move quickly before he lost track of Dracus. With a sinking feeling he realized there was only one thing to do.

"Compass, how far is that building?"

After a bit of static, Compass told him the exact distance— the equivalent of one hundred fifty feet. *"Not advisable, Captain,"* Compass added.

"Thanks for the confidence-boost," Aracnus replied dryly.

"No, seriously, Captain. Not advisable."

Aracnus was getting annoyed at Compass. "I didn't ask your advice," he mumbled.

He took several backward steps, judging the distance for a good running start, then he ran—first slowly, then picking up speed as he reached the ledge. With his last step he hurled himself off the roof with the strongest leap he could muster, then once airborne he took aim, jerking both arms towards his destination. Tiny harpoons shot out from each arm of his protective suit, flying on thin wire-like muscle tissue with blazing speed to their target. Once they made contact with the rooftop, they secured themselves and broke Aracnus' fall. Summoning all his strength, he reeled himself to the next building.

Now came the hard part. Using the spike-bones on his body armor, he scaled the building wall three stories to reach the rooftop—

Where Dracus lay in wait. As the space cop pulled himself over the ledge, Dracus slashed at him with laser-claws. Aracnus hooked into one of the smuggler's spindly legs with one his spike-bones and the bastard fell, howling in pain—affording Aracnus just enough time to hoist himself to the rooftop.

"Oh, that had to hurt," he grunted to Dracus as he released the sonic sword from his side. "Consider it payback."

He swiped at Dracus, who deflected the blade with his laser claws, giving him time to get back on his feet. They parried back and forth, Dracus having the advantage since Aracnus was close to the rooftop ledge. That rattled the space cop's concentration a bit; he was already losing his grip on his sword, and Dracus noticed that. With a fierce swipe of his laser-claw, he hooked onto the sonic sword and pulled it upwards and away from him. The pressure forced Aracnus to his knees.

Dracus laughed, a wide grin on his monstrous face. "Oh, I do love this—you on your knees. Now beg for mercy." As he bent over Aracnus, readying to shove him over the ledge, a thin rope of vile drool leaked from his mouth over the space cop's helmet.

"I can take just about anything—" Aracnus roared, shoving back hard against the alien and sending him staggering backwards, "—except freaking alien drool!" He jumped back to his feet on the ledge, then spun around and gave a flying kick to the side of Dracus' head—the sheer force of the kick sending the beast flying into the air, landing atop the rooftop skylight.

Aracnus wiped the disgusting spittle from his helmet and arms, then angrily marched towards the skylight where Dracus lay writhing in agony. There was another sound, too: the glass of the skylight cracking around him. Aracnus took aim with his sword to finish him off. But in the split-second it took for the sonic blast to reach Dracus, the glass shattered completely and Dracus disappeared into the building.

Damn! Aracnus thought.

Standing at the edge of the skylight opening frame, he peered down into the darkened room below, but could find no sign of Dracus—only shards of glass scattered on the floor. Only one thing to do, he thought with a sigh. With his sword poised and ready, he leapt through the jagged edges of the skylight atop the Chariot Hotel and into the new expansion studio of Rapid Action News.

CHAPTER 4
WRONG PLACE AT THE RIGHT TIME

NYGEL HEARD the crashing noise the moment he left the men's room. He hurried to the studio doors.

He knew he was alone in the building, so his first thought was an awful one: the shelf holding the video monitors had collapsed, just as he had feared. He only hoped the damage wasn't too serious.

But when he opened the double doors to the studio illuminated in moonlight, the first thing he saw was shattered glass strewn all over the middle of the floor. The skylight, he thought at once, and looking upwards at what remained of the skylight, he felt mild relief. At least no one could blame *him* for this.

Someone's gonna have a pooch-fit when they see this mess, he thought. Then a strange feeling of foreboding came over him. Someone else was in the room. He either sensed it somehow, or maybe it was just the probability that some crazy burglar had broken through the roof to steal a lot of very expensive equipment.

Nygel knew he should hightail it out of there, but was frozen to the spot. His hand could move, though, and there was the light-switch. Against his better judgment, he moved his shaking hand to the wall switch and turned on the lights.

He blinked, still frozen to the spot. *No, I'm not really seeing this,* he thought, staring at the wall just above the light switch. But he blinked again and it was still there—a person, or something that looked like a person, outfitted in blue and gold body armor, clinging to the wall above his head.

"What the hell—?" he shouted—or rather he meant to shout, but the only thing that left his mouth was a strangled gasp. The

43

man on the wall was frantically saying something at Nygel, not in words but a quick succession of weird tongue-clicking sounds. Nygel opened his mouth to say something (most likely to ask him to quit clucking like a chicken on speed), but was immediately distracted by a ruckus from another part of the room.

From behind the reception desk there arose a . . . *thing*, a creature also outfitted in battle armor, its long black hair streaked with silver, webbed arms and great fanged teeth protruding from its hideous mouth.

"Holy sh—"

The bat-creature was startled by the sudden bright light and Nygel's arrival, but only for a moment. He picked up the reception desk in his hands and hurled it at the man clinging to the wall.

Aracnus jumped. The next thing Nygel knew, he was flat on the floor with two-hundred pounds of alien enforcer on top of him. Unable to scream, hardly able to breath with the weight atop him, his mind ran a thousand miles a minute:

What the— what just happened? Am I dreaming? One minute I'm taking a leak... the next I'm caught between a wall-clinger and a desk-throwing bat-humanoid... it's like something out of a bad episode of Antorian, *most likely a reject from the first season...*

Aracnus shifted a bit, freeing Nygel's head. He looked up at the monstrous bat-creature still standing across the room. Only now he had a strange oval-shaped object in his hand, took aim, then hurled it to the ceiling directly above them. It exploded on contact, bringing a torrent of debris down on them.

This is it, Nygel thought, and closed his eyes to watch his life flash before him. It only took him as far as his third birthday party, though (when Marci Pennington decided <u>she</u> wanted to keep the Lego set she gave him for a present, and actually went home with it).

What happened? he wondered. *Why aren't I dead yet?*

And what the hell was this wall-clinger tongue-clicking about? Trying to tell him something, maybe. Nygel hoped it was "I'll buy you a Porsche when this is all over," because he sure deserved it for going through this ordeal.

Actually, Aracnus had been saying, "For the tenth time, lie down and don't move!" What *was* the matter with this idiot human, he wondered. Didn't he understand Blorch, the interstellar clicking language? Evidently not. There was little else he could do at the moment; he could not avoid the falling debris while trying to protect Nygel. His defense shield would have protected them both, but it would take too much time to activate.

Finally the avalanche of falling debris stopped and Aracnus got up, shaking the bits of ceiling tile, electrical wiring and roofing materials off his back. Nygel got up, too. But once on his feet again and face-to-face with Aracnus, he looked past him and shouted, "Look out!"

Too late—a dull thud, then the space cop doubled over, gasping, his eyes wide in surprise, and a javelin-like weapon piercing his torso.

Nygel couldn't move. He thought it was the shock at first, but then saw he really couldn't move. The javelin, he observed with a strangely detached calm, had pierced his own chest, though not too deeply.

"You're okay, hold still," Aracnus murmured—or rather clicked—then gently but firmly pushed Nygel's body away from his own, slowly extracting the javelin tip from Nygel's chest.

At least Nygel had the presence of mind not to watch. He kept his gaze behind Aracnus, watching as the bat-demon pulled a small tube-shaped instrument from his boot.

"What's he doing now?" he asked in a quiet voice.

"Hang on, almost out . . ." Aracnus tongue-clicked.

As Nygel watched in horror, Dracus smartly flicked the tube, instantly telescoping it into another javelin. "Oh, my God, he's got another—"

At last Aracnus pushed the javelin tip free from Nygel's chest. He roughly shoved him out of the way, then quickly picked up his sonic sword from the rubble. Just as Dracus poised to hurl the javelin, the space cop took aim with his sword and shot a sonic pulse across the room, obliterating the smuggler's left leg.

Dracus, stunned, stood stock-still for a moment, and then looked down at the blood-spurting stump where his leg had once been. His face, once contorted in fury, now took on a pathetic woebegone look. As Nygel would reflect later, it was almost comical in a sick, twisted way, like a cartoon where a character runs off a cliff and doesn't realize it until he looks down at the gaping canyon below—and then he falls.

True to form, Dracus now dropped to the floor, the javelin still clutched in his hand. He screamed in pain and fury, bent over double as he nursed his bleeding stump. Then his little evil eyes rolled upwards till only the yellows showed, and he passed out, his head falling to the floor with a loud clunk.

Aracnus grunted in approval and moved on to more pressing business: giving himself a medical examination. He punched a few buttons on the medical scanner devise on his forearm, then read the prognosis on the scanner face: the javelin had pierced a vital artery near his heart. *Wonderful*, he thought. *A perfect ending to a perfect day.*

Pulling the javelin out, he knew, would only kill him quicker. *Not necessarily a bad thing under the circumstances*, he reflected bitterly, *but I'm not finished here yet. This human is a problem—he witnessed everything and that could be a bit of a problem.*

Nygel, still dazed on the floor, had been babbling the whole time. "You need help. I mean, you're standing there playing with your space gadgets, and in case you haven't noticed, you're *skewered*, man, I'm talkin' shish-kabob here. We gotta get you to a hospital, like right now, you're gonna keel over and—"

I wish this human would shut his yap and take a walk or something, Aracnus thought with a sigh. *There's not a damned thing he can do, and I'd appreciate a little privacy for my final Right of Passage.*

He finally turned to Nygel, motioning him to get up. Nygel complied, feeling he didn't have much choice, and that's when the panic started up again.

"Look," he said in trembling voice, "I really, really need my legs—both of 'em. So if you don't mind not doing to me what you just did to that guy over there—"

Aracnus put his hand to Nygel's mouth to shut him up.

At least he's stopped clucking, Nygel thought. *That's something, anyway.*

Aracnus unbuttoned Nygel's shirt to examine his chest wound, and Nygel suddenly felt both foolish and embarrassed. *Okay, he's the good guy, I forgot. He saved me from flying desks and falling light fixtures and took a friggin' javelin for me, for crying out loud...*

His chest wound now exposed, Nygel didn't have the nerve to look for himself, afraid of what his reaction might be. He was exactly the same way with flu shots. So he kept his eyes on Aracnus the whole time, watching him punch some buttons on his forearm devise again and wondering how anyone could manage to remain so calm and collected with a giant toothpick in him.

After programming the scanner for New Patient Uptake, Aracnus held the devise to Nygel's chest, close to the wound, then read the prognosis.

It was pretty much what he had feared: The human had been infected with his own Spyconian blood when the javelin tip passed through their bodies. Spyconian blood was a multiplier, its yellow and orange cells attacking and replacing the host's blood at an alarming rate, and the scanner reading informed Aracnus that the human's DNA was at that moment being altered—to what extent and to what end, Aracnus did not know.

He turned off the scanner and immediately blacked out, falling to the floor sideways on the javelin. The pain instantly brought him back to screaming consciousness.

"Oh, God," Nygel said, and got down on his knees, feeling alarmed and helpless and slightly insane all at the same time. "What do I do, is there anything—" But Aracnus was lost in his own pain and thoughts.

Okay, focus. What to do with the human? He knows too much. I know what Headquarters would say—kill him. But how does that jibe with "Protect and Serve"? Or my mission? Let me think here…

Finally he decided there was only one thing to do, only one course of action to take. Gasping for air, he motioned to Nygel to come closer. He detached the shield device from the forearm of his space armor, revealing a strange metallic plate underneath. Then he uttered a command in his native tongue (or so Nygel presumed; at least it wasn't tongue-clicking) and the armor suit disappeared in a flash of red light.

Nygel blinked at the sudden transformation. It was too sweeping a change to take in all at once. Aracnus had a much slighter build than his armor suit had led Nygel to believe. He was covered in a light grayish fur, wearing only an alien type of skivvies that covered him from waist to knees. The metallic

47

devise, Nygel observed, was actually implanted into his forearm. And that shield device he pulled off the metallic device was now hovering in circles over their heads. But what really grabbed Nygel's attention was the space cop's face, with four orange eyes set in a V pattern. *Oh, and a tail,* Nygel noticed. *Yep, I'd say he's definitely an alien.*

With a howl of pain, Aracnus yanked the metallic plate off his left forearm. The suddenness of it jolted Nygel, but no more than a hundred other things he had witnessed in the last five minutes. He was both fascinated and repelled by the bloody metallic thing in the space cop's hand. It was as big as a fist and curved at the ends, with fearsome metal spikes on the bottom where it had hooked into his arm.

But why spikes? Nygel wondered critically. *Wouldn't adhesive tape do just as well? Or was medieval torture part of it?*

His mind was idling on these thoughts until Aracnus gestured a very specific instruction to Nygel: to take the spiky metallic devise and lodge into his own forearm.

Nygel simply couldn't believe the suggestion the alien seemed to be making. "You don't mean…" Nygel heard his own voice as if from somewhere far away. "You want me to—what—stick that thing with the *nails* into my arm? Oh, yeah, sure, I'll do that, it'll be a pleasure. Oh, excuse me, I mean *no.* No way, *nein, nyet,* you're outa your freaking mind. Besides—" Nygel looked down at his chest for the first time, barely registering the sight of the bleeding puncture wound. "—I think I've had enough pain and mutilation for one day."

He got up from the floor, dusting himself off. "Look, I'm really sorry about the spear thing. I'll call 911, only I don't know what the hell they can do for you—or your pal over there. Maybe ship you off to Hangar 18 in Roswell. So, if it's okay with you and the freak over there, I'll be off. Thanks for saving my life and all, but don't forget you're the ones who came crashing in here. Take it easy and good luck and all that. Sayonara, Spaceman."

As Nygel ranted, Aracnus had been calmly observing him, taking particular note of the yellowing of the whites of his eyes. He remembered that symptom of Spyconian DNA transference in humans from textbooks, so he knew what would most likely follow: fever, malaise, dehydration, and seizures if the alien blood reached his brain before immunity was established. At the rate this human was multiplying Spyconian blood cells, he might not make it.

So the instant Nygel got up to leave the room, Aracnus tongue-clicked, "Buddy, you're not going anywhere." And taking aim with his tail, he shot out a long, thin string of organic webbing, attaching to Nygel's arm and stopping him cold in his tracks.

"What the—" Nygel pulled at the sticky webbing, but it wouldn't come off. *"What is this crap?!"*

He tried breaking it, but it was stronger than steel. Aracnus pulled his end of the webbing and calmly reeled Nygel in. The room echoed with Nygel's screams, but no matter how hard he tried, he was quickly losing the tug-of-war. He fell on his rump, pulled himself up, fell down again, up and down, butt-bumping across the floor as he tugged with all his might, but it was hopeless. Aracnus gave a final yank and Nygel was suddenly at his side, shouting and begging for mercy until the moment the dying space cop stabbed the spiked devise into his forearm.

"Yow! Damn, that hurts! What the hell did you do that for!"

"I deputize you Seeker," came a voice from the hovering device. Immediately, Aracnus' clicks had converted into English.

Nygel looked at Compass, then back at Aracnus. "Huh? How'd you do that?"

"There's not much time," Aracnus said, "I'm dying." Blood was filling his lungs, making it difficult to speak. "I have sworn an oath to the Space Authority to never reveal alien presence to non-intersteller beings. You must complete what I have started."

Nygel barely heard a word he said. He was freaking out over the weird sensation that overtook his arm. "What's happening to me? Why's my arm tingling?"

Aracnus wisely ignored the question. Were Nygel to learn that the spikes had turned in little worms working their way up his left arm, he'd be difficult to handle.

Just then an unmistakably familiar voice spoke from the other side of the room. It was Dracus. "Aracnus, this simple human will not find them. This whole world will be destroyed and you will take the blame."

"Shut up," Aracnus replied in a raspy but strong voice. "He will find them."

Find what? wondered Nygel.

"Compass, accept commands . . ." Aracnus' breath was shallower now. As he grimaced at the pain that seared his torso, the shield devise hovered lower. ". . . for new host. Go to . . . security mode and protect new host till he is . . . fully developed, then allow full access to your data bank. Do not reveal his assignment until he is ready to accept who and what he will become. Last command: create . . . a site-to-site rift-port two-hundred feet away on ground level."

Compass swung into action. Swooping close to the wall, it dispensed blue particles into the air, then beeped three times. A flash of light, and the particles became a blurry, blue-tinted portal, beyond which Nygel saw a warping mass of cloud-like shapes.

"What is your name?" Aracnus asked.

"Nygel Spinner."

"Well, Seeker Spinner . . . you'd better . . . go. Take my sword. You will . . . need it."

Nygel hesitated a moment, then reached for the space cop's sonic sword. Once he had the hilt in his grip, the three gold claws that created the blade folded inward, and the blade disappeared in a flash.

"What? Where did it—"

"Leave . . . now," Aracnus gurgled, pushing a button on his wrist instrument.

Then Compass spoke: *"Detonation sequence activated. Fifteen seconds before power system overload."*

Nygel's eyes suddenly got very wide. "Did that thing just say 'Detonation sequence'? 'Activated'?"

"Go," Aracnus gasped, and his body went suddenly limp, his head falling to the floor.

"Ten, nine, eight . . ."

Nygel panicked. The remaining seven seconds would barely give him time to dash out the studio doors and make it to the elevator, and that wasn't counting waiting for the damned elevator. And who's to say this "detonation sequence" wouldn't blow up the entire floor—the whole building, for that matter? He looked at the blue portal, the warping clouds within inviting him . . . "What, I'm supposed to walk through that thing? Where does it—"

From the other side of the room came a creepily seductive voice: "Don't leave the party, human," Dracus said, dragging himself with his hands across the room. "Why don't you stay a while, hmm? You, me and Captain Corpse here will have one hell of a party, heh heh."

"Five, four, three . . ."

Nygel thought fast: venture the rift-port thing or be fried? Not a hard decision to make.

As Dracus advanced closer, blood trailed across the floor from his bloody stump. "Come, take my hand, human. Help me through the portal. I am rich; I will reward you handsomely . . ."

Glancing back at Dracus with a final shiver, Nygel stepped into the rift. Compass followed, flying to his arm and attaching itself to the spiky metallic device.

It felt cool inside the portal—but only for a split-second, because the next moment Nygel was standing outside, across the street from the Chariot Hotel.

He didn't know where he was at first. But as he looked around, re-orienting himself to his new surroundings, he happened to look up to see an intense white light in the penthouse of the Chariot Hotel—then a great explosion as the entire top floor disappeared.

Nygel stood immobile for a moment, then ran like hell. He knew he had to beat it before the cops arrived. The streets were deserted except for him, so who else would they suspect? And how the hell could he explain the metallic spiky thing in his arm, the now-bladeless sword, and Compass? What would he say? "An alien gave them to me, Officer"? Oh, *that* would go over big.

Suddenly he stopped, realizing his car was parked in the opposite direction, and ran back the two blocks to his Jetta. When he found it he stopped and gripped the door handle, feeling close to collapse.

He could hear sirens approaching.

Nygel unlocked the car door and hopped inside. His hands shook as he turned on the ignition, and he realized it wasn't just shock that made him tremble; he was coming down with something—a flu or maybe something worse. He felt his forehead. Yep, he was burning up and he was probably delirious, too. He figured he had to be, because just as he pulled into the street, he imagined he had spent the last ten minutes with two space aliens who blew up the new Rapid Action News studio.

Then he saw what was attached to his forearm and was overcome with a terrible sinking feeling. *No use kidding myself,* he thought. *It's real. It really happened.*

CHAPTER 5
POST-MORTEM

AT LEAST some things never change, Nygel thought miserably when he awoke late the next morning. "Damn snooze alarm," he grunted, pushing the bar for the fifth and last time that morning. He yawned and sat up on the edge of his bed in his boxer shorts, rubbing his sleepless eyes.

He wished last night had all been a dream, but evidence to the contrary stared right back at him from his left forearm. He touched the shiny, onyx-black disk again, feeling its strange, alien smoothness. What was it Aracnus had called it? "Compass"— that was it. But what kind of compass was this, with no direction symbols on it, just the strange gold alien symbol on the flat part of the black disk? There were similar symbols on the handle of the bladeless sword he had stashed away in his bedroom closet last night, he remembered.

Last night. It came rushing back at him in a blurry montage: the Chariot Hotel... the explosion . . . driving back home in a delirium . . . then tiptoeing upstairs. His mother always wanted him to at least pop his head inside her door whenever he came home late and her light was on, but last night he had felt too sick and didn't want to worry her. Today, though, he felt much better.

Much better. In fact, he felt like a million bucks. Even his chest wound wasn't hurting any more. Nygel peeled back the bandage he'd put on when he got home and saw with a shock that there was only a small scar there, not even a scab. He was greatly relieved, but also very surprised. How could scar tissue appear so quickly?

The doorbell rang downstairs.

It was eight o'clock in the morning and definitely not the time for company. But as he went downstairs, Nygel began to have a creeping suspicion who the company might be, but he stopped at the bottom of the stairs, spotting a note left by his mother: *I saw on the news there was some kind of explosion at the Chariot Hotel last night. Thank God you weren't there when it happened!! (I heard you come in late last night.) Love, Mom*

He wondered how she knew he was working at the Chariot, then remembered he had called her last night to let her know he would be coming home late.

The doorbell rang again. Nygel put down the note and went to the door, realizing for the first time that he had completely forgotten to put some clothes on. He called through the door, "Who is it?"

"Trenton Police Department. We'd like to speak to Nygel Spinner."

Great, he thought, and me with this damned alien whatchamacallit stuck on my arm. "Give me a second. I have to put some clothes on."

And take something off, he thought as he hustled upstairs again. Back in his bedroom, he pulled at the disc-device, but it was good and stuck. Then he vaguely remembered the alien cop had detached it with a voice command. But what was it?

"Compass, off," Nygel ordered, but nothing happened. "Compass, deactivate," he tried again. Again nothing; the device just stared back at him. "Down, boy." Nope. Then, "Compass, get the hell off my arm!"

Nothing, and the doorbell was ringing again, three insistent buzzes this time. *Those boys really don't like being kept waiting, do they?* he thought. *Well, let 'em.* He tried several more commands but Compass obstinately refused to disengage itself. Nygel felt himself getting more irritated by the second. Finally he said, "Compass, detach," and at once it fell off his arm and to the floor. Great, Nygel thought, but that still left the metallic spiked object underneath, lodged in his arm. "Metal spike-thing, detach," he ordered, but it wouldn't. "Ah, the hell with it," he muttered, then quickly slipped on a pair of pants and a baggy sweatshirt to cover his forearm, and trotted back downstairs to answer the door. The cops probably thought he was flushing his stash, he reflected with mild amusement. He realized then that he wasn't the least bit rattled by the fact that two police officers were standing outside his front door, doubtlessly waiting to question him about the late night party at the Chariot Hotel. Normally he'd be sweating bullets, but he somehow felt more confident, cool and detached.

He unlocked the front door and greeted the two officers with a friendly smile. "Sorry to keep you waiting," he said. "I'm running a little late for school."

"Nygel Spinner?"

"Yes?"

"I'm Lieutenant Sluburski. This is Lieutenant Miller. We'd like to ask you some questions. May we come in?"

Nygel said sure, and gestured for the two cops to enter with a wave of his hand. He sized them up in a flash: they were white, around thirty, thirty-five, Sluburski a hard-ass and Miller scrawny but carrying himself like he was Hercules or something. Neither of them looked stupid.

When they were all seated in the living room, Nygel spoke first. "Now, what can I do for you? Oh wait, I think I know what it is. The explosion at the Chariot Hotel?"

Sluburski exchanged a glance with Miller, then raised an eyebrow. "Then you do know something about this."

Nygel shrugged. "Not really. My mom mentioned it in a note before she went off to work. She's a corrections officer at Trenton State Prison." He added that last part just in case it might score him some brownie points. "She heard it on the news, I guess."

"That is why we're here, yes," Lieutenant Miller said.

Sluburski opened his notebook and flipped open a few pages. "The guard on duty last night stated that you were the last person to leave the building . . ."

"The last person *known* to have left the building, I guess," he told them. "I was working late and he told me to leave out the back exit and make sure the door locked behind me—which I did. It was about eleven-thirty."

"Could anyone else have been there while you were working? Did you hear anything at all—voices, noises—that might indicate the presence of another individual?"

Nygel thought a bit. It would be an easy matter to tell them he *had* heard someone else in the building; that might throw them off his scent. But he hated adding lies to lies and anyway, it wasn't necessary. It was just as likely that someone else had been in the building without him being aware of it. "I can't help you there, sorry. All I know is that I was there doing some late night work and left the hotel as I was instructed by the guard."

Lieutenant Sluburski nodded. "It might have been a faulty gas line or something."

"Maybe," Nygel said.

Thus satisfied, the two officers got up to leave. Lieutenant Sluburski handed Nygel a card and told him to give him a call if he remembered anything else. Nygel said he would and escorted them out the door.

"Thanks for your time," Lieutenant Miller said.

"Sure, no problem," Nygel said, then closed the door. That didn't go too badly, he thought, rather pleased with himself. He went back upstairs to his bedroom to put Compass in his closet next to the bladeless sword, and hurried to get ready for school.

* * *

The city was a wonder, he thought.

The sights and smells, the lights, the strangely-dressed people, but most of all the buildings—simply magnificent! As the resurrected warlord Sage wandered through the streets of Manhattan, craning his neck to gaze upwards at the soaring towers of steel and concrete and glass, he was in awe that people could build such things. He was even more amazed that anyone would *want* to. What kind of fools would choose to walk up (he had actually stopped to count them) eighty-six flights of stairs? And he saw another building in the distance that looked even taller. They certainly didn't look like a race of supermen; on the contrary, they were weak and fat and stupid-faced, he thought. Then the accumulated knowledge he had absorbed from the people he had slain on the freighter gave him the answer. "Ah," he now understood, "elevators." He said the word aloud to himself a few times, enjoying the sound.

As he walked the crowded streets in his ragged, stinking clothing, Sage became aware that he was observing the people with far more curiosity than they were showing to him. But then he saw a man on stilts handing out flyers on 42nd Street, and a homeless man wearing a hat made of aluminum foil on 40th and Broadway, and he understood that perhaps he didn't stand out quite as much as he had thought. These people were not only weak, fat, stupid-faced and useless, he realized; most of them were completely insane. Few of them talked with each other, only into small metal objects they held against their ears. He had actually heard one young man say "I love you," to the metal object, and a crazy woman shout, "I want those papers on my desk by the time I get to my office!"

He laughed to himself, but then the accumulated knowledge imparted the meaning of the metal objects to him, and he understood. "'Cell phone' . . . long-distance communication. Fascinating!"

As the ancient warrior walked on his determined course, he crossed one of the busy intersections without regard for the speeding cars; he simply took it for granted they would stop— and stop they did, though not too happily. Brakes screeched to a halt right in front of him. A cab driver stuck his head out of his window to give the jaywalker a piece of his mind. "Hey, buddy, watch where you're going!"

Who dares show me such disrespect, the warlord Sage wondered. He turned his head to look at the snarling face of the cabbie.

"Get out of the road, you moron!" the cabbie shouted.

Sage's eyes glowed red. Calling forth the power of the demon world, a ball of demonic energy materialized in his outstretched hand. The loudmouth cabby took one look at the glowing red ball, muttered a curse and stuck his head back into his taxi—but it was too late. Sage threw the ball at the cab.

The windshield shattered, a thousand pieces of safety glass flying with tremendous force into the cabby's face and upper body. He screamed, blood dripping from his sightless eyes. A woman in the Mercedes next to the cab started screaming, too, as did passersby on the sidewalks. But Sage remained standing in the middle of Broadway, rather enjoying the spectacle.

A police officer on the scene also witnessed what had happened. He unholstered his gun and shouted, "Stop where you are! Lay on the ground, hands behind your head!"

Sage yawned. All this shouting and screaming, he thought; how dreary these little people are. He mumbled a few words in his ancient tongue.

"I said, lay on the ground! Now!"

Sage pointed a finger to the street and traced a line toward the policeman. As he did, a trail of fire about six inches wide raced along the line, straight towards the officer. Before he realized what was happening, the flames enveloped the cuffs of his uniform trousers, then his trousers and jacket, and then he was engulfed in flames. He ran screaming into the crowd on the sidewalk, everyone backing away in horror from the human torch. He ran in crazy circles, his terrible shrieks of pain echoing in the skyscrapered canyons of Manhattan, until finally he stopped and fell to the sidewalk, drained of his final breath.

There was a silence. Then everyone fled—all at once, a hundred people madly stampeding away from the man who made balls of murderous energy and set people ablaze.

As for Sage, he was thrilled to the depths of his vile soul. Not only had his powers improved considerably since his resurrection, he was tremendously energized by his murders in a way he had never felt before. It gave him—again he paused to extract a word from his accumulated knowledge—an incredible rush.

On he walked.

At Fourteenth Street he observed a young man buying sugared peanuts from a vendor. Well, he thought to himself, he really ought to have money if he was going to live in this city. He would prefer not to just take it from a stranger; that might provoke a fight, a murder, and another policeman or two would come running and—well, he really wasn't in the mood for all that now.

Then he saw the hooker getting out of the cab.

Although he was new to this place and time, Sage could tell she was a prostitute. The garish makeup, the obscenely short skirt and see-through blouse, the walk, the attitude—it was much the same even in his day. This particular example of moral rot and decay (or so he considered any prostitute, conveniently disregarding his own moral shortcomings) was dark-skinned with a red weave in her hair that highlighted its silky blackness, and her full lips were painted with glossy, dark red lipstick.

They locked eyes on each other for a moment.

The prostitute was drawn to Sage, and she didn't quite know why. It could have been his face, the nice athletic build, or the strange, ragged armor he wore; whatever it was, he got her attention, all right. She stood grinning as he approached her and touched her face, but as he leaned forward to kiss her, she put her index finger against his lips.

"Wait, honey, you may look good and all, but I am all about business here."

Sage smiled. "But I would at least like to sample what I may be shopping for. Besides, you will never forget this experience. It is—" Once again he tapped into his reservoir of accumulated knowledge to retrieve an apt contemporary expression. "—to die for."

"Oh, really? Well . . . you *are* cute, so I guess I can bend the rules a little bit," she said as she led him across the street to a construction site. There she led him through a plywood-walled walkway built as a pedestrian detour under the scaffolding. "In here, honey," she cooed, opening the latch to a plywood door, and after closing it behind them, they found themselves in a deserted site where an old building had been gutted.

Now hidden from the world and its prying eyes, she leaned against the door and closed her eyes as she puckered up for a kiss.

Their lips met tenderly, hers parting open to receive his tongue. It tickled her, made her actually quiver as it explored her mouth, moving deeper. She moaned in pleasure, feeling the tingle of his tongue, almost a burning sensation—no, definitely a burning sensation, burning hot, now reaching her throat. Her eyes opened wide in panic as she tried to break away from the kiss, but she could not. She pushed at him as hard as she could, but he would not let her go. She tried screaming but his mouth was locked tight over hers, while the acid he secreted into her mouth from his tongue burned away her mouth, her throat, her esophagus, burning through its delicate lining to reach internal organs, and there melting, sizzling…her body cooking from the inside out.

She was lifeless and limp now, and so Sage released her and she collapsed to the ground in front of him, blood flowing from her mouth, nose and eyes.

"I told you it would be an experience to die for," he giggled. He picked up her handbag, took out a wad of crisp, new bills he found inside, and walked out of the plywood door, still giggling to himself.

On he walked.

When he arrived in Chinatown, he found signs to lead him to his destination. They were graffiti, mostly Chinese characters scrawled on lampposts and sides of buildings. They were signs completely missed by passersby, but clear to those who knew what to look for. It led Sage to the basement entrance of an old and unassuming building on Mott Street. But when he tried to enter, he found the door locked. Indeed, there were no knobs or handles on the door; in the center of the door, however, was a stone puzzle block. The symbols on the blocks, when properly arranged, formed an ancient unlocking spell only a person fluent in the black arts would be able to decipher. Sage slid the blocks into their proper order and the door slid open automatically. He entered, closing the door behind him.

The warlord faced a long corridor lit in the old ways, with torches illuminating the walls, and a delicious, familiar odor wafted into his nostrils: brimstone. As he headed down the corridor, he was confronted by two guards in emerald-green robes embroidered with Chinese characters that read, 'Protector'. The two men brandished axe-style weapons, sleek and deadly-looking.

"Who goes there," the first spoke in the demon tongue.

"I am the warlord Sage. I have come to take my rightful place and bring about the destruction of all mankind. *That's* who goes there."

"Prove yourself to be who you claim," a voice behind them commanded.

Sage peered into the dark corridor to make out the shadowy figure who spoke. "If you insist," he sighed, and calling forth the powers of the demon world, he gathered two glowing balls in his hands. He tossed them into the chests of the two protectors, knocking them to the ground, their axe-weapons flying from their hands. But they were still alive, which both surprised and disappointed Sage; the energy balls should certainly have killed any mortal.

"That's enough, Master Sage," the figureless voice said as it moved toward the fallen protectors. "If you continue, you will kill two loyal subjects."

Sage was puzzled. "Why are these two still living? They should have been dead in an instant."

"The protective spell woven into their robes protected them. But another blast like that would certainly kill them."

The dark shadowy figure then moved into the light to show himself. He was a Caucasian male in his sixties, slender and well-built, and dressed in a white dress shirt and a black silk tie. He had a light grey mustache and a shaved head with a hint of stubble on the sides, and spoke in the pleasantly cultured tones of a posh English accent.

"My name is Talbert Singe, and I am a guide that services the demon world. I am here to provide you with everything you will need to accomplish your task. Kindly follow me." With a smile he ushered Sage down the dark and winding corridor to an ancient staircase. That in turn led to a sub-basement where the heart of the demon cult awaited the arrival of the great warlord Sage.

CHAPTER 6
POWERS

LATE AGAIN.

The story of my life, Nygel thought as he dashed from the school parking lot to his computer science class. He noticed almost in passing that he was running at a faster clip than usual, and even taking the stairs two and a time all the way up three flights didn't seem to faze him as it normally would. But what was occupying his mind (aside from what excuse he would have for Mr. Simon, the instructor) was the annoying itch on both his upper forearms close to his wrists. It had been mild earlier that day, but now it was driving him crazy.

He made his entrance to the usual stares and scolding glare of his teacher.

"Relax, Mr. Spinner," Mr. Simon said. "Your computer is probably running just fine without you."

"Sorry," Nygel said, feigning breathlessness though he was not in the least winded. He then told him the truth for a change: that he had an early-morning visit from the police concerning the explosion at the Chariot Hotel.

"Oh my," Mr. Simon said with a lifted eyebrow. "Blowing up hotels now, are we, Mr. Spinner?"

The class laughed as Nygel went to his computer work station. On the way he passed Carlos Gomez, someone he had known since high school and definitely not a friend. Carlos had been a member of one of the many popular cliques that excluded Nygel, and for some unknown reason he still gave Nygel a hard time.

"Hey, Nygel, lemme guess. They wanted you to put on your lame-ass Antorian suit and solve the crime, right?"

"Oh, you're funny," Nygel muttered as he took his seat.

Carlos' Antorian remark drew a few giggles from the students, and Nygel was glad to see that one of those not laughing was a young woman sitting in the middle of the room, Kira Maru. Nygel had also known Kira since high school. He knew she didn't like teasing, having had enough of it thrown at her when she was younger. She was great-looking now but she wasn't back then, he remembered; she had been a gangly kid with Coke-bottle glasses and burdened with more cruel nicknames than Nygel had ever had: Tin Grin, Metal Mouth, String Bean, Four-Eyes—the list went on and on. But now, after filling out her skinny frame with some nice curves and losing the glasses for laser eye surgery, Kira had grown into a beauty.

Nygel sat down and immersed himself in the class assignment for the day. He was pretty quick on the computer and usually got through his assignments with ease, but for some reason his vision was blurring. Lack of sleep, he figured, and looking away from the monitor to yawn and stretch a bit, he noticed Kira looking back at him. He gave her a smile, feeling a warm glow as she returned the favor. Nygel got back to work, but a few moments later an instant message appeared on his screen. It was from Kira. "Talk to you after class?" it read. Nygel messaged back: "Sure!" Once he sent the message he wondered if the exclamation mark was too much, if it didn't make him appear too eager. This worry consumed him for the rest of the class, to the point that he realized he really must have feelings for this woman to obsess over an insignificant exclamation mark. But obsess he did. Ever since high school Nygel had had a crush on Kira, but never dreamed she would ever have any interest in him. He never had the courage to ask her on a date or anything like that. But today, maybe...

No, he realized with regret, today would definitely not be a good day for that. He didn't need Kira's rejection added to all the other freaky stuff going on in his life.

The bell rang, signaling the end of class. As Kira shyly made her way to Nygel's desk, he pretended not to notice, as if her instant message had somehow slipped his mind. When she appeared at his side, he feigned surprise.

"Oh, yeah, hi!"

"I'm sorry to hear about the hotel incident," she said. "I'm just glad that no one was there when it happened."

How glad, he wanted to ask her; *tell me how glad*. But now, looking into her captivating brown eyes, feeling his heart step up a few more beats a minute, he didn't think he was even capable of speech. "Thanks," he managed to say.

"Nygel, I know this may not be the best time to ask, but I was wondering . . ."

"Yes?"

"If we can, you know . . ."

But just then a loud and annoying and all-too familiar voice cut through the romantic haze. "Ladies and gentlemen, I ask you—what's wrong with this picture? The lovely and talented Kira Maru, engaged in conversation with the definitely *un*lovely and *un*talented Nygel Spinner—"

Giggles broke out in the classroom. Nygel felt himself flush hot with humiliation. He couldn't bear to look at Kira's reaction and turned his eyes away.

"I have to go," she said abruptly, then left the classroom in a flash.

Nygel followed at a safe distance. He didn't want to talk to Kira or Carlos or anyone, plus he was getting a splitting headache. He was glad that class was over, but he still had to go to work—that is, if he still had a job. He was halfway to the exit when he noticed his vision was blurring worse than ever. Maybe that was the reason for his headache, he thought, and wondered it might be his contact lenses—maybe a torn lens.

He popped into the men's room to find out. Standing at the sink, he rolled up his sleeves and washed his hands, then took out his contacts to inspect them. They were fine. But when he reinserted them, his vision was blurry once again. Maybe one or both lenses were turned inside-out, he thought, and he took them out again to check. That was when he noticed something he hadn't noticed before: he could see with absolute clarity.

Impossible, he thought. He had worn corrective lenses since he was eight years old. He was practically blind without them.

But he wondered...

Nygel looked at the spiked metallic thing in his left forearm and wondered if it had somehow improved his eyesight. More likely it had something to do with the nagging itch near his wrists, he thought, then realized that his calves were itching as well. What the hell was going on?

The door opened and Carlos entered. Nygel quickly rolled down his sleeves—just in time, too, because Carlos suddenly appeared behind him at the sink, putting a hand on his shoulder.

"A word of advice," he said.

Nygel looked at Carlos in the mirror. "I'm sorry, did I ask for one?"

Carlos looked hurt. "Hey, man, I just wanted to spare you any future embarrassment." He took his comb out of his back pocket and began combing his hair in the mirror. "You're out of your league, Nygel."

"Meaning—?"

"Meaning, girls like Kira don't go for guys like you. Hey, don't take it personally, buddy. It's evolution, survival of the fittest. Winners attract winners, losers get the losers. It happens in the animal kingdom all the time. You ever see a hot aardvark with an ugly one? You do not."

"Carlos, that is the most retarded thing I ever heard in my life. I can't believe they let you into college."

Carlos frowned as he put the finishing touches on his comb-job. "I'm serious, man. Look, I know I rag you a lot, but when I see a man led astray, I figure it's my duty as a fellow human being to set him straight. Kira's a winner, you're a loser; simple as that."

And he walked out of the restroom, the door closing behind him. Nygel stared at the door in stunned silence. No one had said anything like that to him since high school. Back then he had heard it a lot, but all that was supposed to be behind him. Now all those awful feelings came back at him in a rush: feelings of being stuck—just plain stuck in life, not knowing what to do to have the career he wanted, not knowing if he'd ever find the right girl, never having enough money in his bank account—even after working since he was fourteen years old, for crying out loud. The unfairness of it all, mingled with a deep-rooted, self-hating feeling that it was exactly what he deserved, being a loser and all . . . Well, that *is* what they thought of him, wasn't it, even if they didn't say it to his face like Carlos did . . .

As he turned away from the mirror and headed to the door, the sparks of anger and frustration and hurt ignited into a raging fire, and all he could see was red. Without even thinking of it, his right hand balled into a tight fist, a fist in search of a target—any target—and that happened to be one of the green-painted metal stall dividers.

The punch roared like thunder, echoing throughout the restroom for what seemed an eternity. But Nygel hardly heard it. He was completely absorbed in the fact that his fist had actually gone clean through the metal divider. *How is that possible?* he wondered. Okay, it's probably not steel, only aluminum, but still . . .

He must have broken every bone in his hand. Strangely, though, it didn't hurt. The trauma had probably numbed him, he thought. Slowly he pulled his hand out of the metal divider and looked at it. No cuts, no blood—nothing. He unballed his fist and flexed his hand a bit; wiggling his fingers and moving his wrists about. His hand was definitely not numb and amazingly, he felt absolutely no pain.

He walked out of the restroom and out of the building in a daze. As he went to his car, he stopped and noticed he could easily read the license plates from a good distance, and without his contact lenses. A terrifying but thrilling hypothesis took shape in his mind: the thing in his arm, whatever it was, had given him—there was no other word for it—*powers*.

He got in his car, put on his seat belt, and turned on the ignition. *Or maybe . . .* Maybe, he thought, these "powers" (if they were in fact real, because at this moment he wondered if he was even sane) were somehow transferred to him by the alien cop when the javelin pierced their bodies. Aracnus' blood must have gotten into his chest wound when they both were staked by the alien bat creature . . .

Nygel glanced in his rear-view mirror as he backed out of his parking space.

"I wondered when you'd figure it out," his reflection said.

Nygel ignored the remark, switched from reverse to drive, and left the parking lot, his mind roiling with strange and disturbing thoughts. Maybe the alien's blood on the tip of the javelin-thing had somehow reacted with his own DNA and changed his body chemistry. Maybe that was why he was now, or was becoming, a sort of . . . enhanced human? The idea was thrilling, yet terrifying. So far nothing really horrible had happened as a result; he hadn't sprouted any extra eyes or anything like that.

Nothing except that damned itch.

He drove a few miles on the highway until he approached Brunswick Avenue where Man's World Gym was located. That's when he got the idea. He quickly checked his watch and saw he still had an hour before he had to be at work, so he pulled into the shopping center and found a parking space close to the gym. He wanted to see just how strong he really was.

Once inside the building, Nygel flashed his membership card to the guy behind the front desk and ran upstairs to the second floor weight room. He wasn't dressed for a workout, but he was wearing sneakers, so that was okay. Just as he got to the weight room doors, two hulking bodybuilders were leaving. Nygel knew these guys—two of the most obnoxious members of the gym, they called themselves the Barbarian Brothers, but everyone else called them the Unbearable Brothers. They regarded anyone who wasn't a steroid-pumped freak as an object of derision. One of them gave Nygel a withering glance and said, "Careful in there, junior. No one in there to spot you."

"Thanks," Nygel said, regretting it immediately. He was stronger than the average power lifter and didn't need a spotter, so screw them and their bloated 'roid guts. He went straight to a weight rack in the middle of the room. The rack was stacked with free weights ranging from twenty to eighty pounds. He didn't stop to estimate what the entire rack must weigh; he was feeling kind of cocky, so he just bent down and gripped the horizontal metal support bar at the bottom of the rack with one hand, and lifted.

Or rather, he tried to lift it. It wouldn't budge.

He grimaced and tried again, this time employing a little more effort, but the rack still wouldn't budge. Then he laughed, feeling more than a little foolish. *What did I think*, he wondered, *that I could actually lift this whole gargantuan thing with one hand?* He realized that the stall-bashing incident in the bathroom was probably just a fluke, the result of a momentary adrenaline rush after Carlos had ridiculed him. Nygel started to leave the weight room, but something made him stop.

It was the realization that he did feel stronger, but just how much stronger? He went back to the weight rack to find out. He was about to pick up a dumbbell but something made him change his mind—an idea, perhaps, that if he concentrated enough and focused his energies . . .

Once again he bent low and gripped the metal support bar with one hand, and this time it felt a little different, his grip somehow more substantial. He closed his eyes and let his mind go blank, thinking about nothing else other than lifting the weight rack. Then he felt it rise, actually lifting from the floor, but making a strange crunching sound as it did. Nygel opened his eyes and saw to his astonishment that not only was the weight rack a foot off the floor, but so were the bolts that had secured it through the carpet tiles to the concrete floor—along with a good bit of the concrete floor.

"Oops," he said, cringing a bit, but continued lifting the fully-loaded weight rack higher and higher off the floor, up to the level of his head, then lowered it slowly down to the floor.

"Holy Snap!" he said aloud. He couldn't believe he just did that with one hand. He stood staring at the weight rack as he assessed the situation. *Okay, it's official,* he thought, *I am officially a superhero, right out of a comic book. It's what I always dreamed, to have the power to do what I wanted. Only this is real. Hot damn!*

Then a chill came over him. This was a moment in life like no other, he realized, like when a person commits murder, or wins the lottery, when he realizes his life will never again be the same and everything has changed forever. Then another, more sobering thought occurred to him: he couldn't talk about this, at least not now. He still had to function in the real world, the world where superheroes weren't supposed to exist.

And as he looked again at the weight rack and the concrete debris scattered in the aftermath of his stunt, Nygel wondered, *What the heck am I going to do about this?*

He left the weight room, his grin getting bigger each step of the way. He stopped at the reception desk and said almost in passing to the guy behind it, "You know about the weight rack upstairs, right?"

No, the guy didn't, and when he popped upstairs to check it out, he returned saying, "Jeez, what the hell happened there?!"

Nygel shrugged. "Why don't you ask the Unbearable Brothers?"

"What? Did they do it?"

"Well, I didn't actually see them do it, no," Nygel said truthfully, "but they were the only ones in here before I went in, and I ask you, do I look strong enough to rip a loaded weight rack from a concrete floor?"

The guy gave Nygel a doubtful grin and shook his head. "Thanks for the tip. We've been looking for an excuse to get rid of those two lugs. We know they've been dealing steroids here, we just couldn't prove it."

"Glad to oblige," Nygel said, and as he left the gym he wondered if he should drive to work or just carry his car. He laughed out loud, whistled to himself as he unlocked the door to his Jetta and hopped inside. Looking up, he winked at his reflection in the rear-view mirror.

"I hope you're not going to get a swelled head over this," his reflection sighed.

"Damn right I am," Nygel replied, and started his ignition . . .

CHAPTER 7
THE MAN UPSTAIRS

NYGEL MADE it to work on time, though he was cutting it close. The heavy-set security guard was enjoying his Boston cream donut with his coffee as Nygel breezed past the security desk, calling out a friendly, "Morning, Kevin. Hazelnut, right?"

The security guard nodded with a grin. It was a game they played, Nygel guessing which flavored coffee the guard was drinking that day. Yesterday's was vanilla-mocha, and the day before that was cinnamon Viennese.

"Nygel, wait," the guard called with mouthful of donut. "Almost forgot—there's a message for you. Go to Mr. Payne's office A.S.A.P."

Nygel froze in his tracks. He had expected the cops, and maybe an inquiry from office security, but an audience with the boss himself? This was getting more serious than he had bargained for. "Thanks, Kev. Um, top floor, right?"

The guard nodded and Nygel hurried to catch a waiting elevator. He felt strangely in control of the situation, though that was perhaps by necessity. He couldn't muff this, he told himself; the prospect of being charged and convicted for destroying the new network office at the Chariot Hotel was simply not to be contemplated. So by the time the elevator doors finally opened at the seventh floor, his survival instincts had clicked into gear, everything fully operational.

He had never been up here before, so he stopped to take a gander. The reception area was impressive indeed, lavishly decorated with leather furniture and huge aquarium tanks built into the walls, each with freaky-looking exotic tropical fish swimming lazily about. But what really caught his eye were the

TV monitors, so many he couldn't count them all. They were set in black metal towers that extended from floor to ceiling, six monitors to each tower, a few of them showing the grim aftermath of last night's explosion at the Chariot Hotel.

Three secretaries typed away at three desks. Nygel figured these must be the Drudge Sisters, the near-legendary trio who slaved away for Mike Payne day in and day out. They weren't really sisters, just sixty-something grandmother-types who brought homemade cookies for visitors and fiercely protected their boss.

"May I help you?" the closest Drudge Sister asked him in a pleasant voice.

"Hi, I'm Nygel Spinner. I'm here to see Mr. Payne."

At the mention of his name, the other two secretaries looked up in sympathy, *uh-oh* written on their faces. Nygel stood by as the secretary buzzed Mike Payne's office on the phone and announced, "Nygel Spinner here to see you, Mr. Payne." He couldn't make out the words that answered on the other end, but they were loud and they sounded very angry. "Yes, sir," she replied, and hung up, then got up from behind her desk to escort Nygel to Mike Payne's private office door.

"Good luck to you, honey," another secretary called to Nygel. "I hope he's in a good mood."

"He hasn't been for five years," the third murmured, not looking up from her typing. "Why should today be any different?"

"Well, after last night..." the second replied in a quiet voice.

The first Drudge Sister opened the door for Nygel, quickly closing it behind him—evidently so they would not have to hear the inevitable tongue-lashing that was sure to follow.

Once inside the dimly-lit private office, Nygel stopped to admire the expensively decorated furnishings: the plush grey carpet, the three large plasma TV monitors behind the huge steel and glass desk, and the ominous plaque atop the desk that read, TAKE A FLYING LEAP. A nice, welcoming touch, Nygel thought ironically.

He looked at Mike Payne. Or rather, he looked at the back of the tall black leather chair in which Mike Payne was doubtlessly occupying. But Payne wasn't showing himself yet. A psyche-out,

Nygel thought, suddenly feeling as if he was in a spy movie and at any moment the chair would swivel around and in it would be an evil criminal mastermind, stroking a Persian cat on his lap. But Nygel kept his cool, his attention turning to the three TV monitors behind the desk.

"Nice TVs," he said lightly. "So I guess this is why I didn't get that raise."

The tall black leather chair slowly turned around and Mr. Payne finally revealed himself in all his intimidating glory. He was a big man, neither fat nor muscular, but solidly built and well-proportioned. He was dressed in an expensive black silk suit with a gold pin on the lapel of his jacket, had a full head of just-graying hair and a stare so piercing that it seemed it could bore through steel. Nygel thought all that was missing was the smoke puffing out his nostrils.

Mike Payne had a reputation as a no-nonsense, no-games kind of businessman, but Nygel thought the way he did that dramatic turn-around-in-his-chair peek-a-boo reveal was definitely a game—a ploy meant to intimidate his underlings.

"Well, Mr. Spinner," he said in his low voice, "have you seen the coverage?" His hand gestured to a TV monitor broadcasting a news segment about last night's disaster, with NEWS ALERT in red letters flashing on the screen and below that, CHARIOT HOTEL EXPLOSION. Nygel could hardly recognize the location in the news clip; there was concrete and dust all over the area, and it resembled a war zone more than an office.

"Not until this moment," Nygel said. "I'll say this, though— I'd sure hate to be the one on custodial duty today."

It was a comment meant to break the ice, but Mike Payne didn't appear to find it funny. "I understand you were the last person to leave the building. Correct?"

"I was the last person *known* to have left the building, yes, sir."

Payne nodded slowly. "And you have no idea what could have caused this mess?"

"Not a clue, sir."

"Spinner, I have a disaster on my hands and you are the only known link to what happened last night. If you know anything about this, now's the time to spill it."

Nygel shrugged. "I wish I could help you, sir—"

"*I said, spill it, Spinner!*" Payne shouted, banging his fist onto the glass desk top so hard that his TAKE A FLYING LEAP plaque actually took a flying leap off his desk. "I know that you know what happened! Stop playing coy with me!"

Nygel calmly looked back at the sputtering, red-faced tycoon as he thought to himself: *Okay, this is it, your one chance, so make it good.* So he looked Mike Payne straight in the eye and said in an even voice, "Mr. Payne, I did absolutely nothing to cause that explosion last night. All I did was leave the hotel once I was finished with the installation. As I told the police this morning, there might have been someone else in the building, but I wasn't aware of it."

He paused a moment, then went on, "I might add, sir, that I stayed till eleven-thirty doing equipment installations—with no overtime pay, because I'm just an intern. The guard on duty last night can confirm that I was actually doing something constructive, not destructive, so I ask you, why would I bother to do all that set-up work, just to blow it all to smithereens? You have to admit, sir, it doesn't make any sense."

Mike Payne, in addition to being a brilliant media magnate, considered himself to be a master interrogator as well. He had kept his eyes locked on Nygel eyes the whole time, perhaps to see if he'd flinch, but no such luck. Now he nodded slowly at Nygel and sat back in his soft leather chair. "I was all set to have Security work you over, see what they could get out of you," he said, "but I called Human Resources first. They informed me that your supervisor has consistently given you good reports."

Thank you, Q! thought Nygel in relief.

"So I called James Booker myself—as much as I try to avoid the acrimonious jerk, he is your supervisor and I wanted to hear what he had to say. You know what he told me? He said you were the most honest and hard-working individual that has ever been his privilege to work with. You know what clinched it for me, Spinner? The story of the coffee carafe."

Nygel had no idea what he was talking about. "The uh, coffee carafe, sir?"

"Yes, you know, the time you accidentally broke a coffee carafe in one of the office kitchenettes, and felt so responsible that you went out and bought *two* replacements out of your own pocket."

It was all Nygel could do to maintain a straight face. "Well, sir, I felt I was responsible, accident or not."

"Booker also told me you once broke a pencil and actually wrote him a letter of apology, begging him to dock your pay."

Q really went overboard, didn't he? thought Nygel.

Mike Payne leaned forward and looked incredulously at Nygel. "For a *pencil*, Spinner? I never heard such a thing."

"Well, sir," Nygel said, his eyes downcast modestly, "it *was* company property."

"Luckily our insurance will cover the damage to the new studio," Payne said, then sighed as he eased back into his seat. "You can breathe now, Spinner. You're in the clear. I just had to check you out for myself."

"Thank you, Mr. Payne, I'm just sorry that—"

"But don't expect that raise you asked for."

"No, sir, you probably need a few more monitors here, right?" *Easy, Nyge*, he told himself, *don't push it.*

Mike Payne ignored the dig. "But I think anyone as hard-working and relentlessly honest as you deserves something. So I've decided to make you a P.A. and put you on the road with the live camera crews to do tech support."

"What?"

"A P.A., Spinner, a production assistant."

"Yes, sir, I know what a P.A. is, I just—"

"Go downstairs to dispatch and see what they got for you," Payne said, standing up and extending his hand across the desk. "And keep up the good work, son."

"Yes sir," Nygel said, pumping Payne's hand vigorously. "Thank you, sir!"

"Whoa, easy, that's some grip you've got there, Spinner."

"Yes, sir. Sorry, sir." Nygel left Payne's office feeling an incredible rush of relief and shock at this unexpected outcome. It was quite a move-up from intern to P.A., though the salary probably wouldn't be much different. He flashed the Drudge Sisters a big okay signal as he passed their desks.

"Have a cookie, honey," the first secretary said, holding up a plate of macaroons. "You look like you survived the Blitz."

"I did, thanks," Nygel said, taking two macaroons.

"Take care, honey," the third secretary called out.

"Don't be a stranger," the second one chimed in.

Nygel grinned back with a mouthful of macaroons and pushed the down button on the elevator bank. When the doors finally opened and he stepped inside, he waited until the doors closed before shouting out a celebratory *"Yeeeeeeeow!!"*

The Drudge Sisters laughed behind the elevator doors.

The dispatch office downstairs was buzzing with activity when he got there, with several crew people shouting and grabbing camera and sound equipment as they rushed off to their assignments. At the main desk sat a very wired, very hyper Indian man with an unlit cigarette in one hand and a cup of espresso in the other.

"I'm Talex Bachi," he told Nygel. "The 'Bachi' is shortened because my last name is apparently too hard for most Americans to pronounce correctly."

Nygel nodded, thinking 'Talex Bachi' was going to be hard enough to remember.

"So you're the one creating so much havoc to my schedule," Talex said with an accusatory glare.

Nygel blinked. "Excuse me?"

"Take a look around, kid. The equipment, the crews, the vans—all this chaos is my orchestra and I am the maestro trying to keep the symphony playing from first movement to the finale. A lesser man would crumble under the pressure, and I've got so much going on in my head, I'm surprised if I can think straight half the time. Then I get a call just a minute ago from Mr. Payne's office, telling me to stick you with one of the news crews, and what is the result? My nerves are shot and my performance suffers; the orchestra rebels, the audience is booing and getting up from their seats, and the critics are writing devastating reviews. If it were up to me, I'd toss you out on your butt till next week when things settle down a little, because I simply can't handle another variable in this exquisitely controlled madness I call my job. So . . . you have anything to ask or say before I send you out with the news crew who are doubtlessly waiting to tear you to pieces?"

Talk about divas, thought Nygel. And judging by the way this guy was fidgeting with that unlit cigarette in his hand, he was probably having a nic-fit. "Um, when do I start?"

Talex sighed as he ruffled through papers on his desk. "You can go out with van number three. The loading area is down the hall, first right and out the door. You'll be riding with Sandy Castle."

"Yes, sir, I just want to say—"

But Talex didn't need a thank you; he needed a cigarette, and he was already hurrying to the nearest exit for his hourly smoke. Nygel went off in the other direction to find the van loading area. He was feeling psyched to work with Sandy Castle, who was known as the premiere news-chaser of the network. People said she went after scoops like a bloodhound goes after a fox. Nygel was surprised that he got a chance to tag along with the network's best-known reporter.

By the time he walked outside to the van parking area, two men were already beginning to load the white van. It was an unimpressive-looking vehicle, but Nygel knew it came equipped with an advanced satellite system for direct transmission to the Rapid Action News station. The two guys at the van gave Nygel a friendly greeting. He had seen Max, the producer, and Andrew, the cameraman, running around the news building before, but this was the first time they had actually met. When Nygel told them his name, they both did an unmistakable double-take. It was clear they knew he was the lone suspect in the hotel incident, and the way gossip traveled in the office, he wouldn't have been surprised if they had him already convicted and sentenced in their minds. But before another word could be spoken, Sandy Castle came flying out the rear exit door. She was talking on her hands-free cell phone, the tell-tale microphone clipped to her red silk blouse.

"Thanks for getting me a new P.A., Talex," she was saying. "I know I go through them like Kleenex, but the way the last one ran out in the middle of that hostage negotiation—well, you know I can't work with wimps."

Nygel hung onto her every word. He knew Sandy Castle's crew was always in the thick of the action, covering the high-risk news events: murder scenes, bank robberies and shoot-outs, floods and hurricanes, drug busts and other assorted SWAT team raids. One of her cameramen was even shot in the arm by a crazed gunman while covering a live broadcast of a domestic violence scene gone amuck. That guy was replaced by Andrew, and Max had been Sandy's producer since she started working for the network two years ago. He also had had a few scrapes here and there, but still hung in there with the strikingly attractive blonde reporter because he was as fearless as she was.

Sandy Castle momentarily raised her head to acknowledge Max, Andrew and the guy she didn't know standing by the waiting van. "So who's the next victim?" she asked Talex on her cell phone, and as she paused to listen, Nygel couldn't miss seeing her expression turn suddenly sour. "Who?" She turned around and lowered her voice, though not low enough for Nygel to miss a word. He felt suddenly like a criminal again. "Wait a minute, isn't he the guy who was at the hotel last night? Look, I don't care if Payne okayed it or not, I don't even care if he didn't have anything to do with it. He sounds like trouble and I don't need a jinx on my crew. You know better than that."

Max cleared his throat; Andrew pretended to busy himself with a loop of cable. But Nygel kept still, hanging onto every word and feeling himself flush with embarrassment. Nice way to start a new assignment, he thought.

"Okay, okay," Sandy Castle sighed, "I'll take him along but I don't want to be held accountable if something goes wrong, you got that? Bye."

She disconnected the call and now stood with her hands on her hips, sizing up Nygel with a doubtful look. Nygel looked back with a weak smile.

"Okay, Nygel is it? Looks like we're pretty full here in the van, so take your car and follow us."

Nygel nodded, knowing damned well the van wasn't full. This woman was just punishing him for being thrown at her so unexpectedly. As Sandy got into the van with Andrew and Max he said, "Okay, just give me a few minutes to meet you at the garage door."

"What're you waiting for, then?" she barked at him. "Chop-chop!"

Nygel ran off, feeling royally pissed for being treated so brusquely. He had survived Mike Payne, but this hurt. Okay, he told himself, he should be used to being left out of things—he was the all-time champ at being left out, ever since grade school—but even with his new-found powers he was still exquisitely sensitive to rejection.

As he got to his car in the station parking lot, he wished that annoying itch in his wrists and calves would stop. It had been bugging him off and on all day, and added to his major put-down from her Royal Highness, Sandy Castle, Queen of the Airwaves—well, it was just another day with problems, he thought glumly.

* * *

"As you can see, Master," the stooped old jeweler said with an obsequious bow, "everything has been prepared for your arrival. I saved these gloves for last..."

It was an exoskeleton for the hands, an exquisitely-designed, diamond-studded glove of malleable steel, with razor-sharp claws on the left hand. The warlord Sage tried it on and admired the craftsmanship of the glove, its surprisingly lightweight feel. It fit perfectly.

"Not only stylish," the old jeweler cooed, "but perfect for hand-to-hand combat."

Sage thought he might test them out now by swiping at the stupid old ass-kisser's face, slashing it to ribbons, but the old codger had done his job well and besides, he might require his services again. "They will do," he said, dismissing the jeweler with a bored wave of his hand. The head servant standing at the temple entrance clapped his hands once to dismiss the old man, as Sage reached lazily for a ripe, juicy cherry from the silver tray at his side.

The underground temple was quite lovely, he thought. He liked the robes he was given, spun of the finest silk and dyed the deepest blood-red. He admired the demonic imagery in the stained-glass doors and faux windows lit from behind, and he chuckled in amusement at the ancient prints on the walls depicting various scenes of torture. There was food aplenty, all deliciously prepared and beautifully presented on dishes of beaten gold and silver. And there was lovely music issuing from behind an enclosed chamber where ancient Chinese instruments played to the accompaniment of live screams of torment. They thought of everything, Sage thought as he popped the cherry into his mouth. He smiled at the comely female servants attending his every whim; he especially delighted in the fear that flashed in their eyes.

Now the head servant clapped his hands twice and three handsome men entered the room in succession, each modeling differently-styled leather trench coats. Disco music blared from hidden speakers as they turned and posed for the warlord on a makeshift runway.

Sage yawned. He was not particularly impressed by what he saw, especially after having glimpsed—though his accumulated knowledge of his slain victims—the fashion styles in the old blaxploitation films of the 70s and the 80s. He admired the more flamboyant pimp-style of dress, the over-the-top and in-your-face manner and style. A dozen or so trench coats were modeled before Sage saw the one he knew was just right. It was black leather, but striped with different-colored leather patterns across the chest.

"Now <u>that</u>," he said, pointing a long finger at the model, "that one is—" He paused to retrieve the right phrase from his brain bank of accumulated knowledge. "—a keeper. Set it aside."

He was then shown dozens of different black leather shoes and chose a pair with platform heels and a high shine. Then he smiled at the twins massaging his feet and murmured, "That will do, my lovelies."

The head servant clapped his hands once and the twins rose to their feet and bowed, backing out of the temple. The warlord chose a ripe plum from the fruit tray, handing it to a waiting servant to peel for him. He sighed with contentment. Never, he reflected, did he imagine the future could have such comforts. He enjoyed every minute of it.

Talbert Singe entered the temple. "I trust your servants are making you comfortable, Master Sage," he said as he stepped down the marble steps into the sunken chamber.

"They serve me well, Mr. Singe, much to my delight," Sage said, taking the peeled plum from the hand of the servant, not before kissing her trembling hand. She moaned in a semblance of pleasure, just as she had been instructed.

"Are you prepared to take your rightful place in Chinatown?" asked Singe.

"Yes, of course I am. But tell me, Singe," he said, suspicion clouding his face, "what exactly do you get out of all this? And how did you know of my coming?"

Talbert Singe smiled as he took a seat on the couch that Sage was occupying. "The answer to your first question is simple: the prestige, the honor. I am a man driven to serve a higher power that will dominate this world. I would rather be on the side of the victor. Master, I feel the dark forces building up each day on Earth, and I have a vested interest in helping in the destruction of mankind. Our master, Satan himself, has promised me immortality when the dark forces conquer this world. So you see, we both have a role to play. You want power, and I desire to live forever throughout time itself."

Sage grunted his understanding as he nibbled on the servant's trembling hand.

"Now, to answer the question of your how I knew of your coming," Talbert Singe went on. "I was one of those who funded the expedition that led to the discovery of your grave site. Your remains were to be sent to the Museum of Natural History, but I paid mercenaries to board the freighter and steal your sword. Our plan was to resurrect your body once the sword was in our hands, but as it happened, the mercenaries saved us the trouble of bringing you back into the world of the living."

Not only that, Talbert Singe reflected, the War Pack had saved him the trouble of paying for their services, since they were all dead. Well, almost all; only the one called Mayhem had managed to escape.

Sage bit into the servant's hand, drawing blood, and then dismissed her with a wave. "I can see that you are indeed a valuable person to assist me in this new world, Singe," he said, a satisfied smile on his face. "So what is my next step?"

"One I'm sure you will enjoy, my Lord. It is time for you to meet the crime boss of Chinatown, Mister Lee Fang."

"Ah," said Sage, a huge smile spreading across his face.

An hour later, there was a buzz on Lee Fang's telephone. He was luxuriating in his hot tub after the five minutes he called his "morning workout," sipping from a steaming mug of green tea as the jets of warm water soothed his corpulent body. Lee Fang weighed two hundred sixty pounds and stood five feet, seven inches tall. Mr. Fang liked his pork dumplings—he liked them all day long, as a matter of fact, and was anticipating his next one when the phone rang. He angrily reached for the telephone on the edge of the hot tub and greeted the caller with a typically curt hello: "This had better be important, whoever this is."

"Hello, Mr. Fang," the familiar voice on the other end said. "I do apologize for having caught you at an inopportune moment."

"Ah, Mr. Singe, so how is the art business going for you? I presume you have some artifacts to show me?" Lee Fang collected items of the Ming Dynasty and Talbert Singe was his favorite art dealer.

"You could say that," Singe said with a mild chuckle.

"Fine, fine. I will expect you in ten minutes, then." Mr. Fang hung up the phone, reached over and grabbed two steamed dumplings in a bowl next to the phone and shoved them down his throat with barely a chew in between. Never a moment's peace, he thought with a contented gulp, but he did want to see what treasures Singe might have for him that day.

Lee Fang stepped out of the hot tub, wrapping a plush robe over his dripping wet, obese body. He went off to his dressing room to dress in a freshly-pressed pair of pants and a white shirt, selecting a dark blue tie from the tie rack inside his walk-in closet. He selected a dark grey suit jacket to match the pants, and then modeled the results in the full-length mirror. This is as good as it gets, he thought with a gloomy sigh. He ran a comb through his hair as he surveyed the pot-belly spilling over his belt loop. Perhaps liposuction, he mused. But then his mind went back to Talbert Singe's fine artifacts and he considered how much he should spend on them.

Mr. Fang walked into his office. It was a large room with a teakwood conference table in the center, his custom-made desk (again teakwood, the edges inlaid with gold trim) and fine impressionist paintings on the walls. The room was not empty;

sitting in a chair next to his desk was his bodyguard and henchman, Dragon Eye, a grim-faced and athletically-built Chinese man in his thirties, neatly attired in dress shirt and loose navy blue pants. A casual observer might think Dragon Eye was practically dozing as he sat motionless in the chair, but Lee Fang knew him to be as alert as a cobra, ready to pounce if needed. Mr. Fang often required that of his bodyguard.

Dragon Eye looked up at his boss as he entered the office.

"We will be expecting guests," Lee Fang told him as he sank into the leather seat behind his desk. The bodyguard nodded in acknowledgment.

Within a moment of sitting down, the phone rang and Lee Fang answered it with a weary hello. It was the security guard on the ground floor announcing the arrival of his expected guest. Fang told the guard to allow Mr. Singe upstairs, and then hung up the phone.

Dragon Eye got up from his seat to await the arrival. He stood straight and tall and still, his eyes riveting on the office door.

A minute later there was a knock. Lee Fang stood up from behind his desk and called out pleasantly, "Please, do come in, Mr. Singe."

The door opened and Talbert Singe entered, accompanied by an unfamiliar person wearing a leather trench coat and a strange, diamond-studded clawed glove on his left hand. Lee Fang was immediately uncomfortable. Dragon Eye remained still but ready at his side.

"I see you have brought a…friend," Lee Fang said, looking warily at the stranger. He then noticed that Talbert Singe's hands were strangely empty. "But where is your case of goodies, the artifacts you were to show me?"

"Oh, yes," Singe said, permitting himself a small chuckle. "Well, one particular artifact stands right here before you."

Lee Fang didn't like surprises; he liked jokes even less. "I am in no mood for games," he said, sighing with impatience. "What the hell are you talking about?"

"My dear Mr. Fang, this man *is* the artifact. This is the warlord Sage, resurrected from the dead. You do remember the tale of a sorcerer on the verge of conquering China? Now here he is, in the flesh—in the *living* flesh, once again." Singe proudly turned to Sage, who was now engaged in something of a stare-down with Dragon Eye.

The crime boss of Chinatown laughed, but it was a hollow, mirthless laugh that betrayed more fear than pleasure. "Surely you're joking. The warlord Sage? I remember that silly tale from my childhood, but it's only a story—a myth!"

"This is no myth," Talbert Singe said with dead seriousness.

"Oh? And for what purpose have you brought this 'Warlord Sage' to my office? Do you propose I hire him as a servant? He looks rather thuggish to me, and as you can see, I already have a bodyguard."

"No, Mr. Fang, he is here to claim his seat of power, and you are to kindly step down."

"I see," Mr. Fang said, though he didn't see at all. He was becoming increasingly tired of this bad joke. "Did you expect me to step down just like that?"

"That's the idea," Singe replied, nodding.

With one quick movement Lee Fang pulled the silver Smith and Wesson revolver from under his desk and aimed it at his visitors. "Dragon Eye, get these two out of here before I kill them on the spot and soil my expensive Aubusson carpet."

"Hmm, I don't advise it, Mr. Fang," Singe said, his eyebrows arching in warning.

The warlord Sage looked away from Dragon Eye and now focused his attention on the gun in Mr. Fang's hand. As he did, his eyes took on a different color—a glowing red that burned across the room to the weapon in the crime lord's hand.

Before Lee Fang knew it, the gun was glowing red-hot in his hand. "Ahhh! Damn it!" he shouted, dropping it on his desk. "Kill them!" he shouted to Dragon Eye, "Kill them both!"

Dragon Eye did not move a muscle. He appeared to be frozen to the spot where he stood.

"What's wrong with you?" Lee Fang shouted at him. "I said kill them, you idiot! Are you deaf or something?"

Sage spoke for the first time: "He is under my power now, Mr. Fang. Dragon Eye, kill your master. I want you to take his head off for his insolence."

Lee Fang's eyes widened in horror as he watched his trusted bodyguard take the clip model switchblade from his pocket and spring the catch. Dragon Eye moved without hesitation, the two-inch high-carbon steel blade flashing before Lee Fang's unbelieving eyes as it tore into his throat, hacking away at flesh and cartilage and arteries as his screams became mere grunts and gurgles, and his priceless Eighteenth Century Aubusson carpet was soiled indeed, his blood drenching a good-sized patch of it until he fell to his knees and could scream no more. As his head dropped and rolled across the wet carpet, Lee Fang wondered why the room was spinning before his eyes, but then the spinning stopped as his head knocked against a leg of the conference table. Mr. Fang looked quizzically at the approving faces of his favorite art dealer and the warlord Sage, and at the strangely blank face of Dragon Eye, and then the former crime boss of Chinatown saw no more, only a wall of blackness.

"Now, Master Sage," Talbert Singe said, "my task is done. You have Chinatown and the power that occupies that seat. I shall leave you to fulfill your destiny and open the gates of hell. Serve our master well, my friend, and we both shall be rewarded."

And with a happy smile, Talbert Singe turned and walked out of Lee Fang's office, leaving behind the warlord Sage and his new servant, Dragon Eye.

CHAPTER 8
A TWISTED RIDE

"REPEATING OUR top story: a severe thunderstorm warning in Mercer County and surrounding areas is in effect. And if you're wondering how the temperature managed to drop fifteen degrees from a record high for this month of eighty-six, you can thank our Canadian neighbors for the fast-moving cold front they've sent us."

The deejay played "Blame Canada," and from the back of the Rapid Action News Network van, Sandy Castle announced that she had a splitting headache and would they *please* take an axe to the radio?

Andrew turned it off and Max slipped Sandy an evil grin over his shoulder. "Cheer up, Sandy, the shoot's over."

"Only in reality," she groaned. "The memory still lingers."

"Oh, come off it. They were a nice bunch of folks, and they were thrilled to meet you."

"Thrilled?" she shrieked in disbelief, taking the pack of cigarettes from her pack. "Half of them weren't even breathing. What did I do to deserve this second-string puff-piece assignment from hell?"

Neither Max nor Andrew dared to answer, but Sandy already knew the reason: she had turned down an interview with the governor at the State House. It was only an interview about the new state budget, so she let one of the other reporters take it, never dreaming that her only other option would be covering the New Brunswick Senior Center Art Show.

"My two year-old nephew can paint better than those geezers," she went on, lighting her cigarette. "And this right on top of missing that Chinese freighter scoop. I could *kill* Mike Payne for not sending me on that assignment."

"That was no assignment," Max told her. "It was strictly undercover—strictly *illegal*—there's no way someone with your high profile could get past that barricade on the pier."

"I could've done it," she said, blowing a huge cloud of smoke. "A wig, a pair of specs, a black medical bag—what's the big deal? I could've pulled it off . . ."

Max shook his head. "Nope, what Mike Payne needed was a cameraman, and Marty was the only one desperate enough to do it."

"Stupid enough, you mean," Andrew muttered.

"Stupid got him a nice bonus," Max shot back.

Which probably explained why Andrew had been so quiet all day, Sandy thought; no doubt he was mentally kicking himself for turning down Mike Payne's offer. Yes, right there—she just saw it—Andrew's jaw muscles were working overtime. He was definitely pissed off.

But Andrew was irritated for a completely different reason. "Uh, Sandy," he said, turning around to face her with a forced smile, "you mind cracking that window a bit and letting us non-smokers breathe?"

She puffed out another cloud of smoke. "Would love to, hon, but it just started raining. Hey, how's he doing back there, Max? The new guy, I mean."

"Nygel? He's keeping up. Why, you want me to lose him?"

Sandy snickered. "Yeah, maybe fire-bombing the hotel wasn't enough for him. Maybe he'll graduate to tossing Molotov cocktails into vans."

"C'mon, he did okay today," Andrew said.

"'Okay' doesn't cut it. Did you notice, he nearly dropped the boom mike on my head."

Max laughed. "How could I not notice? You made a big enough stink about it. Besides, it wasn't close to hitting you. It wasn't even in the shot."

"And he apologized," Andrew added. "It slipped his grip—he said his wrists were itching him like crazy."

Sandy didn't say anything for a while. "I had a boyfriend who had that—itchy wrists, I mean. Turned out to be scabies." She took another huge drag and leaned back in her seat. "I don't know. He seems preoccupied, and I need someone completely focused."

As they lapsed into silence, Sandy stared at the passing vistas out her window. What had been a brilliantly clear and unseasonably warm spring day was only a memory now; the dark convergence of storm clouds that gathered in the distance represented to her what she feared was the trajectory of her television career.

"Check out that sky," Andrew said, pointing out the window.

"And we're heading right into it," Max said, frowning. He flicked on the radio.

The latest report was that the cold front had moved southward quickly, spawning multiple and severe thunderstorms. But of course they already knew that: it was raining buckets. Traffic slowed to a crawl and any pedestrians foolish enough to still be outside were scrambling for shelter. Then came the news that the severe thunderstorm warning was upgraded to a tornado watch, and whatever little conversation they had in the van came to a complete stop. Now it was just three pairs of eyes warily watching the road; three overworked newspeople anxious to get home.

* * *

"This is a local weather alert from the Emergency Alert System. This is not a test. The severe thunderstorm has been upgraded from a tornado watch to a tornado warning. Repeat, a tornado warning. All pedestrians are strongly urged to seek immediate shelter . . ."

But Nygel could barely hear the announcement. The pelting of BB-sized hailstones that rained down on his car made far too much racket. He was already thinking about the five hundred dollar deductible he might have to pay to get the dents out of his car roof.

"Don't worry about it," his reflection said. *"You're using your own car on the job, so they're liable. They should spring for the gas, too."*

"Don't count on it," Nygel muttered. "The network cuts corners like . . . like . . ."

"Like what?"

"I don't know, there's gotta be an expression."

"Cuts corners like a blue-tag sale at K-Mart? Like a Lamborghini doing a right-hand turn? What?"

"Nothing! Would you kindly shut up?"

"Whoa, testy, are we? That Sandy Castle really got to you, didn't she?"

"Damn right she did. Making me take my own car—'Looks like we're pretty full here in the van', she says . . ."

"I know what she said. I'm you, dim-wit."

"And now they're trying to lose me in traffic. And these damn hailstones are gonna shatter the windshield and—"

"Uh-huh, just get a grip, okay? You're making me nervous."

But soon the hailstorm started to let up, as did the rain, then it was just the angry storm clouds above—a sick-looking greenish hue that filtered into dark grey. And there was something else that made him sit up straight: an unmistakable funnel shape in the clouds. It was not huge, but big enough to get Nygel's attention. He switched the radio on again.

"A tornado just touched ground in the southern part of Trenton. Early reports describe the twister snapping tree limbs and tearing off rooftops. The tornado is headed in a northerly direction now..."

Great way to start a new job, Nygel thought to himself. Through the madly slapping windshield wipers, he saw the left signal lights on the Rapid Action News van blink as the van pulled over to the side. "Are they crazy?" he wondered aloud.

He pulled over right behind them, just as Andrew and Max started hauling out equipment from the van. With Sandy barking orders, they were soon rolling tape as they broadcast on live satellite feed from the side of the road.

"And right on the cross-street behind me, about an eighth-mile back—can you get that shot, Andrew—yeah, there! A blue Pontiac just stopped—the driver jumping out, running into the field out of the path of the twister, and just in time— *Oh my God, it's tossing that car like it's a freaking toy!* Look at that! Only on Rapid Action News, folks—live, on-the-spot coverage of the New Jersey twister—"

Nygel held the boom steady against the wind, but kept his eyes peeled on what loomed ahead: the twister took an unexpected turn in a westerly direction, heading straight towards them.

"Wrap it up, Sandy," Max murmured, "We gotta move—"

"And my producer is telling me to pack it in, so I'll defer to his judgment. This is Sandy Castle, Rapid Action News."

"And we're off," Max said.

"Damned babies," she muttered as they all jumped back into their vehicles and sped away from the tornado.

Nygel followed the van, the twister hot on their tails as it headed straight up the road towards the Trenton Bridge. Nygel turned off the first exit, already jammed to the beginning of the exit ramp with cars waiting out the spinning devil.

Stopping, he braced himself as he watched it spin right past him, rattling his car as it skirted the edge of highway. But it was the noise that was most unnerving; it sounded strangely like a freight train speeding down railroad tracks.

It passed and he was safe, but he wasn't breathing yet; the tornado was heading straight for the news van. "Get off the road!" he screamed, and to his immense relief the van swerved off the next exit— the last turn-off before the bridge.

Now sighing with relief, he watched the twister continue up the road towards the Trenton Bridge—affectionately known to the locals as the "Trenton Makes Bridge." This historic landmark connecting New Jersey and Pennsylvania bears the legend "TRENTON MAKES – THE WORLD TAKES" in giant letters across the width of the Delaware River. The gigantic letters light up at night in a brilliant red neon.

From his vantage point he could see the tornado moving across the bridge; about halfway across it veered off into the Delaware River. Already he could see it beginning to fizzle out.

Luckily, no one was behind him, so he put his car into reverse and backed out into the highway, then drove ahead towards the bridge. There was a traffic jam ahead, and he couldn't see the van. It might have been there, but some twelve-wheelers and other trucks obscured his sightlines from where he was in the right-hand lane.

He'd just have to wait it out.

But as he did, he wondered if the twister had wreaked damage on the bridge. He stepped out of his car for a moment— as did many of the other drivers around him—but he still couldn't see anything through the traffic.

It was not on the radio news, either; not yet, anyway. So he listened to snatches of conversations from the cars around him, hoping to hear some news of what was happening on the bridge ahead, but everyone was clueless. He listened closer, focusing on hearing anything pertinent, and suddenly he *could* hear—voices reaching him from the Trenton Makes Bridge a quarter-mile away, seemingly dozens of voices, all yelling and jabbering at once. He could make no sense of anything except one recurring word shouting through the racket: *"Help!"* Nygel tried focusing on just one voice, and like a radio dial turning from static to a clear signal, it suddenly came in loud and clear: *"My God, it's going to fall!"*

Not the bridge! he thought in panic. The babel of voices continued again, and he focused on isolating them from one another to make sense of what was being said.

"Emergency 911, may I help you?"

"Yes! There's a camper on the edge of the Trenton Bridge! The tornado picked it up and dropped it on the rails. It's going to fall! Omigod…"

"A camper on the bridge? Is anyone inside?"

"Yes! A family. Please hurry!"

Nygel sat in shock at discovering yet another power that seemed to activate on impulse. He might have given this newly enhanced power of hearing more thought, might even have played with it a bit, but he knew he had to act fast.

But he was paralyzed with fear and indecision. He was strong, he knew—tearing a bolted weight rack from the gym floor told him that—but was he strong enough to take on a *camper?*

That wasn't his only concern.

It's not like I have a costume or mask I can put on, he thought, *and I sure don't want my face plastered all over the five o' clock news.* He hadn't planned for something like this. All that rah-rah, chest-beating, ego-trip he was having at the gym being a superhero—it didn't mean squat unless he actually *did* something super-heroic, and now he was—what, too damned camera-shy to jump to the rescue? *That totally bites,* he thought. *If I'm a superhero, where're my super-balls?*

Take it easy, he told himself. *You can't just expose yourself in front of the whole world like that; it's the first rule of being a superhero—don't let 'em know who you are, 'cause you've gotta live in this world. Man, if I had something to protect my identity . . . like that bitchin' armor suit that alien cop had on—that'd do it.*

As Nygel envisioned that armor suit, he heard a faint hissing sound that seemed to be coming from his forearm under his shirt, the spot where the alien implant had been spiked into his forearm. He cautiously rolled up his shirt sleeve and saw, to his utter horror, a clear, thick liquid seeping out from under the edges of the implant.

"Holy—"

It didn't pour off him, not a drop; rather, it spread quickly across his arm as if it were on a flat surface, covering his wrists and hands, while also oozing up his arms and over his shirt, covering all his clothing as it spread upwards to his shoulders and down his waist. As the implant hissed and leaked the clear substance that was wrapping his entire body, pants, shoes and socks and all, Nygel panicked and tried taking it off—peeling, tearing at it with his fingers and nails—but it was as shell-hard, even as it oozed out from under the implant and moved over his body.

Is anyone seeing this? he thought in panic. *How could they not?* But a quick glance around him told him that no one was looking his way. Everyone—whether inside or standing outside their cars—was staring straight ahead at the traffic that didn't move.

Still, he was seized with panic and began to hyperventilate, thinking the implant was drowning or suffocating him with the seeping substance. He shut his eyes and took deep, slow breaths, trying to calm himself. But even with his mouth closed he couldn't help screaming—a high-pitched whimper accompanying the higher-pitched hissing of the implant as the liquid seeped out and covered every inch of his body.

Then the hissing stopped, there was a *clickety-click* from the implant, and then all was silent. His eyes still closed, he saw a bright light peering through his eyelids.

When Nygel opened his eyes, he was looking through some kind of gold casing but could still see true colors around him. When he looked up at the rear view mirror, he nearly jumped out of his seat. This face looking back was not his at all. It was alien.

"Nope, it's you," his reflection said. *"I mean, it's me."*

"Shut up, I'm mildly freaking out here," Nygel said, touching his face. It was rock-hard; even his hands were a navy-blue colored armor, leathery in texture, with a high-gloss shine. He looked about his entire body, which was now shelled in a blue-and-gold suit—the same type of suit that the alien officer wore, just a bit bulky but form-fitting, accenting his musculature. Nygel felt as if he was dreaming again, but if this is a dream, it was the best damned dream he'd ever had.

"Anytime you're ready, champ," his reflection said.

Nygel looked to his right. He was in the right lane, so no one could see him from that side. *It's now or never*, he thought, and took a deep breath. He unbuckled his seat belt and crawled out the right-side front door, slamming it shut behind him, then rushed ahead towards the bridge as he bent low to the ground. Once ahead a few cars, he ran. Ran like the wind.

* * *

"The twister just fizzled out over the Delaware River, but it's not over yet," Sandy Castle shouted over the noise of the crowd behind her. "I'm speaking to you live from the Trenton Makes Bridge, where a heart-stopping drama is unfolding. A camper is teetering like a see-saw on the edge of the bridge. Can you get a shot of that behind me, Andrew—there it is, about a hundred feet behind me—the twister somehow caused the beige-colored mobile home to go between the metal supports and hang dangerously on the bridge railings—"

There was shouting and crying in the background, as people got out of their cars, some with scrapes and bruises.

"There were also a few pile-ups here on the bridge, but no serious injuries—not yet, that is. You can't see it from here, because the cops and a crowd are gathered around the vehicle, but yes, there are people inside the camper. The cops told the driver to try putting the vehicle into reverse, but he's just spinning his wheels. There's a woman in the passenger side, presumably his wife, because we can also hear children screaming in the back. Folks, *please* cross your fingers and say your prayers, and I mean it, because this could possibly end very badly if help doesn't arrive soon. I don't know how far a drop it is over the river, but—wait a minute . . ."

Sandy squinted into the distance, a confused look crossing her face.

"There's someone approaching the bridge, running like a track star. But he's dressed like a…I don't know how else to describe it, like a comic book superhero! This is too weird. Andrew, get that shot of that guy, right behind you…"

Andrew turned the video camera around and focused his shot on the strange man in navy-blue-and-gold armored plating, running towards them across the bridge.

"He's coming this way, let's see if we can— Sir, can you tell me— Okay, he wouldn't stop, he's running off to the camper, I guess. Some people just don't want to be on TV. Sorry, folks, but a little levity is just what we need sometimes to break the tension. Let's see if we can get any closer and see what that dude's up to. Keep up with me, boys . . ."

The camera followed Sandy as she pushed her way through the crowd of spectators on the bridge. The tilt of the camper was now so extreme that the cops held the crowd back, for fear that they might upset the camper over the edge in their eagerness to help. Inside the camper, the driver was frozen in his seat, too afraid to move, his wife sobbing as her hand reached behind her to comfort her children.

A jolt—a shout—and the camper pitched further off the bridge.

* * *

He wouldn't make it.

There wasn't time, he knew. The camper was leaning too far over the bridge, about to tip right over into the river, and he would never get there in time. If he hadn't wasted all that time in his car freaking out over the possibility of other people merely seeing him, if he had gotten here only seconds earlier, he might have made it. But now the camper pitched forward even more, making a horrible grinding noise along with the screams of bystanders—and what happened after that would be something he'd have to live with for the rest of his life.

"No!" he screamed, reaching his arms out in desperation.

Then he felt it—a shooting pain in his forearms. His hands had involuntarily thrust forward into balled fists, and before his unbelieving eyes two harpoon-like projectiles shot out from his forearms from a string of red organic tissue, piercing the rear of the camper. He felt himself being yanked forward with the camper.

But just as he became aware that he was going to be pulled off the bridge along with the camper, he was seized with another shooting pain, this time from the back of his legs. He glanced down and saw a pair of harpoon-like claws shoot out from the bottom of his calves and anchor him to the bridge pavement. Without thinking, he pulled back hard, and the organic tissue lines immediately retracted back into his forearms, pulling the camper back, inch by inch, the crowd screaming and gasping all the while, until the rear wheels solidly hit the bridge pavement— and the danger was over.

He had done it. He heard a roar in his ears as blood rushed to his head, but there was another louder roar, too—the whoops and hollers of the crowd, who simply could not believe what they had just witnessed.

* * *

"Would you listen to that crowd! They can't believe it, and neither can I, frankly. The cops are just standing there, scratching their heads...

"It's unbelievable, but you saw it here, folks, live, on-the-spot coverage only on Rapid Action News! If you just tuned in, a quick recap: that weirdly costumed man in blue and gold just yanked a camper back onto the bridge, using some kind of wire. I can't figure out that blue and gold outfit, though. Maybe he was on his way to a combination costume-ball-and-tractor-pull and jumped in to save some lives—I don't know.

"It looks like he's got some gadgets attached to his arms and feet—there, you can see it—he just unlatched some bizarre hook-thing from his feet that seemed to brace him to the bridge pavement, and now—whoa!—these harpoon-things that he threw to the back of the camper just reeled right back into him!

Look at that crowd—not a closed mouth among them—no one can believe what they just saw. I don't know how he did it, though my best guess is it's some kind of grappling tools he had attached to his wrist and legs, that's all I can figure..."

A bystander who just left the site in a daze suddenly appeared at Sandy's side and started jabbering: "They weren't tools! Those things came out of his skin! They were *part* of him! I saw it, I was that close! Whoever he is, he's not human!"

"Whoa," Sandy said to the man, "steady, fella, you're shaking like a leaf . . ."

"I never saw anything like that. That guy—he saved that family . . ." The man collapsed into tears, overcome by the miracle he had witnessed.

"Understandably, a very emotional reaction from an eyewitness," Sandy said in dramatic tones to the camera. "The crowd has gathered around the hero, applauding and shouting at him, though it looks like he's trying to get away. Let's see if we can get a word with this amazing man..."

The camera followed Sandy as she pushed past the crowd on the bridge. When she was within microphone distance of the crusader, she grabbed his arm, stopping him.

"Excuse me, sir. Sandy Castle, Rapid Action News. A word, if you can, for our viewers. What just happened there, and who the heck *are* you?"

She thrust her microphone toward the strangely-dressed hero, but he looked stunned, as if he wasn't at all sure what had just happened. "I was . . . just trying to help, that's all. I'm just a regular citizen lending a helping hand."

"That's the understatement of the century," Sandy Castle said.

"I . . . I have to be going now," he said, then bolted from the scene just as the emergency rescue crews arrived, blaring their sirens.

"Wait!" she shouted after him. "Sir, what's your name?"

But the costumed stranger was gone.

* * *

Now what?

He had to get out of this costume before he got back to his car, that was for damned sure. Or else he'd have everyone nearby—including Sandy Castle—following him home. God, that had been a close call, talking to Sandy—though she couldn't tell it was him underneath that suit, and he did try disguising his voice, speaking in a lower register than usual. So at least that part of the ordeal went okay…

Just when he despaired of finding a place to get out of his costume, he spotted a porta-potty ten feet below, at the base of the bridge. Evidently they were doing some repair work on the bridge, though all the workers were gone. Probably on the bridge watching the show, he figured.

He ran down the steep embankment and popped inside the porta-potty, closing the door behind him. Standing there, he looked for buttons or zippers that just weren't there. The armored suit was seamless, zipperless, buttonless, and molded to his body. So how the hell…?

One thing was for sure: he couldn't stay in this get-up forever. He had to pee sometime, right? *Okay, don't panic . . .* Nygel closed his eyes and thought about how he first caused the protective armor to encase his body. He came to the conclusion that the metal implant in his forearm must be controlled by his thoughts, unlike Compass, which was controlled by voice command.

Nygel cleared his mind of all thoughts and envisioned the suit coming off. Almost at once, a red light started *consuming* the suit, just gobbling it up, like the old Pac-Man game he played when he was a kid. Before he knew it, the costume dematerialized in front of his astonished eyes, leaving only the clothes he had been wearing.

He patted himself all over his body to make sure all trace of the uniform was completely gone, and then checked his forearms to make sure that the harpoon-type bones that protruded from them didn't cause any bleeding. He unrolled his left sleeve to cover up the alien implant in his forearm. Even completely covered, it created a slightly obvious bulge.

"All set," he murmured to himself, then opened the door.

A beefy construction worker was standing right outside. "What'ya think this is, a public restroom? Beat it."

"Er, sorry," Nygel mumbled, then ran back up the embankment to the highway. He was just thinking about what he'd say to Sandy Castle and the crew when he saw them, ransacking his brain for one of his better late-for-class excuses.

Then there she was, Andrew and Max tagging behind her. "Where the hell have you been?" she shouted at him.

"I, uh, took cover till the tornado passed through," he said.

She looked down the embankment from where he had just climbed. When her eyes landed on the porta-potty she laughed. "You were hiding out in the stoop 'n' poop? That's hilarious. What makes you think a tornado could lift a freaking car and not a porta-potty?"

Nygel felt himself flushing with embarrassment. "Well, I had to go, too—"

"Uh-huh. Well, if you hadn't ducked for cover like a scared rabbit, you would've seen the scoop of the century. A camper nearly went off the bridge, and some crazy guy in a Halloween costume pulled it back to safety."

"Crazy guy"? he thought with resentment. *"Halloween costume"??*

"Good thing *some* guys had the guts to brave the storm . . ." She walked off and let Andrew and Max fill him in on what he'd missed—as if he needed filling in, he thought.

"Man, you don't want to piss off Sandy, not on your first assignment," Andrew told him.

"It was a tornado!" Nygel pleaded. "And I had to go to the toilet!"

"Yeah, well," Max said, "what if that super-freak had to go to the toilet—where would that camper be now, huh? In the Delaware River, that's where."

"Super-freak"?? Nygel didn't know if he could keep himself from telling them the truth. But he had to. *Just keep it zipped,* he told himself, *take it like a man . . .*

He cleared his throat again and apologized for not being there to assist with the live report. Max sighed and nodded, then wandered off with Andrew back to the van. It nearly killed Nygel not to tell them what he actually did. In fact, it was a lot harder than rescuing the camper.

CHAPTER 9
CELINE

THE WHOLE drive home was an exercise in self-control. Nygel knew if he allowed himself to unwind before he was safely back home, he'd be unwinding himself into a major anxiety attack. He kept his eyes on the road, and when the news radio announcer came on with the latest report about the blue-and-gold crusader who saved a family of four from tipping into the Delaware River, he quickly changed the station.

He made himself think of other things—other, non-superhero things relating to his life outside of, and prior to, his encounter with aliens in the Chariot Hotel. He thought of Kira Maru and her dazzling smile. He thought of Antorian and his—

Nope, don't think of Antorian, he told himself; and he changed his train of thought to his art history class and deciding to buy another alarm clock to guarantee he'd never oversleep again.

When he pulled into the driveway and got out, he ran with his house keys to the front door as fast as he could. Only he didn't have to take a trip to the john, he just needed to hit the couch.

Once he was inside and had the door locked behind him, he made a swan-dive for the couch and then, and only then, did he really let go. An incredible wave of exhaustion overtook him, mingled with relief that he was finally home. He then started thinking about the events of the day in a relaxed position.

Try as he might, he simply could not figure out how the "spike-bones" (as he had come to think of the harpoon-like spikes) just *happened* to zip out of his forearms and calves exactly at the moment he needed them. But maybe that was the wrong question, he thought. He remembered how his arms shot up in balled fists right before the spike-bones shot out. So shouldn't the question be: *why* did he thrust out his balled fists at the very moment he needed to activate his spike-bones? How did he know spike-bones would come out?

The answer was, of course, he didn't. But some part of him—the new, improved him—did, if only by instinct. The most frightening thing was experiencing these new powers and physical changes before he knew they were going to happen—like when those spike-bones shot out of his wrists and calves without the least warning. And he hadn't yet learned how to control these new powers (though that would come with practice, he assured himself). But it almost paralyzed him with fear to contemplate the possibility that before he mastered his new powers, he might mistakenly hurt someone.

As he contemplated all these things, he heard his mother's SUV pulling into the driveway. He would have loved to tell her about what happened on the bridge, would love to see the look on her face when he announced that her son was a genuine superhero, but he knew he couldn't. There were a million reasons why not, but the main one was that it would completely change their relationship—or challenge it, at any rate. They already had a great mother-son relationship, and if she knew he had changed so totally overnight—well, that might ruin everything. Besides, he didn't have the energy to field the million different questions she'd lob at him, and he was way too drained to do some super-stunts when she said, "Super-hero, huh? Okay, prove it, smart-aleck." And when he did prove it, she'd get all weird about their personal safety and the risks he was taking...

He heard her coming through the basement door from the driveway at the rear of the house, and quickly sat up straight. "Hey," he called to her, his usual greeting.

"Hey, yourself," she said. Celine Spinner always managed to greet Nygel with a great smile, even when she was worn to a frazzle. He remembered how crisp and clean she looked that morning in her corrections officer uniform with the dark blue shirt and black slacks with a solid blue stripes on the outer seams; now it looked just as she did—a bit rumpled and worse for wear.

"Hope you didn't get caught in the storm," she said. "I was worried about you."

"Not only was I out in the storm," he told her, "I was with the camera crew covering the story on the bridge. You heard about that?"

Her eyes widened in surprise. "Omigod, you were really there? Did you see him?"

Nygel hesitated. "See who?"

"The guy! The guy who kept the truck from going over the bridge. I heard all about it on the radio."

"It wasn't a truck, Mom, it was a camper, and yeah, I saw him," he said casually, glancing at his fingernails.

"Turn on the TV. It's time for local news. It's probably the top story."

Nygel then turned on the big screen, high-definition TV and there he was, talking to Sandy Castle: *"I was . . . just trying to help, that's all. I'm just a regular citizen lending a helping hand."* He could not believe that was him in that get-up. But more than that, he could not believe that was his voice. He had disguised it by speaking in a deeper register, but didn't realize it sounded quite so . . .nerdy. *Gotta work on that,* he told himself.

They cut to a shot of him shooting the spike-bones from his wrists and stopping the camper from tipping over the bridge. Nygel wanted to do a victory dance right there in the living room, and it killed him that he couldn't. When the news story was over, he looked at his mother, half-expecting her to ooh and ahh over the blue-and-gold crusader, but instead she yawned.

"Pretty cool, huh?" Nygel said.

"Yeah, I guess," Celine said, a bored look on her face. "Pretty cheesy effects, though, don't you think?"

"'Pretty cheesy effects'? What's that supposed to mean?"

"Well, honey, he's obviously got some gadgets up his sleeves shooting out grappling hooks. What else can it be?"

"Those aren't grappling hooks!"

"How do you know?"

"Because . . . because it doesn't make sense, Mom. He didn't know the camper was going over the bridge. You think he just walks around town with a grappling-hook contraption on his wrists, just in case he has to pull a camper off a bridge?"

She smiled knowingly. "Honey, they were making a movie."

"What? No, they weren't! That's the craziest—"

"How do you know they weren't?"

"For starters, who'd make a movie in weather like that?"

"Nygel, don't be silly. Of course they didn't *know* there'd be a tornado. Sure, it made the scene more difficult, but with a low-budget movie like that, they can't afford to cancel the shoot. They've got actors on salary, they've already got the city permits—"

Keep cool, Nygel told himself, *don't blow your cover.* "Okay," he said in a quieter voice, "if it was a movie, it definitely wasn't low-budget. What makes you think it was a low-budget movie?"

She held up her fingers as she enumerated: "A, no recognizable stars. A big budget movie would have a big star in the lead. B, the cheap costume on the guy. I could whip up a better outfit in my sewing room in fifteen minutes."

"'Cheap'? Did you say 'cheap'? Mom, you know that *I* know something about superhero costumes from my Antorian days, and I can assure you that is not a 'cheap' costume! It's an incredible, top-notch, million-dollar costume—"

A puzzled look crossed her face. "Wow, why are you taking it personally? You'd think it was *your* movie."

"It's not a movie," he said through gritted teeth.

"I say it is, and when it opens in probably six months or so, I'll take you to the opening and say, 'I told you so' all through the damned thing from the opening titles to the final credits."

He grinned. "Okay, suit yourself."

"I usually do," she said, looking pleased with herself. "I gotta start dinner before I collapse. Fried chicken okay?"

"Of course it's okay. It's more than okay. When is fried chicken *not* okay?"

She giggled and disappeared into the kitchen. He came in a bit later and offered to help with the dinner preparations, which she always appreciated. While she prepared the chicken parts for frying, first flouring, then seasoning the pieces, he set the table and got the mixed veggies in the pan.

"So I guess you were questioned about the explosion at the hotel last night," she said, out of the blue.

Nygel was caught off-guard, but told her that he was, that two policemen came by the house early this morning.

"Yes, I know," she said with a smile. "That's why I asked."

"Uh, how'd you know they were here?"

"Oh, Mr. Meys told me. You know how he is, into everyone's business. He ran up to tell me as I was parking the SUV in the driveway." She placed the chicken parts into the hot cooking oil and watched them sizzle.

Nygel rolled his eyes. "I'll bet he was looking out his window for the last few hours, just waiting for you to come home so he'd be the first to tell you. That man needs a hobby."

She laughed. "He needs something, all right. So, you in for the night?"

"Yeah. I'm just going to surf the 'net a bit, maybe do some research for school."

What he had really planned to do was search online to see if he could find out anything about the alien devices he had hidden away in his bedroom closet. But he was in no rush to go upstairs. After the crazy day he had just had, he needed this time with his mom to settle down. He was also wary of discovering any new surprises that day, and didn't know what secrets he might discover about the implant or Compass—or how dangerous they might be.

Soon they sat down at the table, said grace and began to eat. Celine asked him how work was going, especially in light of the hotel incident, and he told her the news he had completely forgotten. "I got a promotion," he said.

"What!" She almost dropped her fork.

"Yeah, Mike Payne made me a P.A. A production assistant."

She stared at him in disbelief. "Mike Payne—*the* Mike Payne—*personally* gave you the promotion?"

"Yep," he said, grinning as he wiped his mouth with his napkin.

"Let me get this straight," she said. "We've been talking for the last hour I've been home and just *now* you're giving me this news? First of all, what's the matter with you? And second of all…congratulations, honey!" She reached over and gave him a bear hug and slap on the back. "Okay, now I want to hear all about the new job."

He told her about working with Sandy Castle and her producer and cameraman, and she asked if she was nice to work with. "Not particularly," he said. "She's a bit of a diva."

"Well, you can tell that just by looking at her," Celine said. "She gave you a hard time, then. You know, sometimes that just means she really likes you."

Here it comes, Nygel thought with a sinking feeling, *The Talk*. This was just the set-up; within two sentences, she would come right out and ask him The Question.

"No, I really don't think she likes me, Mom. But once she gets to know me—"

"That's all it takes," she said. "To know you is to love you— that goes for anybody. So, anybody special you're seeing?"

Bingo, he thought. "Nope."

"So, no girlfriend. Not trying, or just no luck?"

He shrugged. "Maybe a little of both. Things could be better in that department, I guess."

"I'll say," she murmured.

He played with his food a bit, moving his peas into a circle of carrots with his fork. "There *is* somebody…"

Celine looked up hopefully from her plate.

"I mean, not yet, just one girl that I'd kind of like to go out with."

"So? What's stopping you?"

"I don't know," Nygel shrugged as he picked up a chicken leg. "Maybe the fact that she'd never go for me."

"Oh, really? So who is this high-and-mighty so-and-so? I want names."

"Her name is Kira."

"I said *names*, plural. I assume she has a last one?"

"Kira Maru."

"Kira Maru," she said thoughtfully, rolling the name on her tongue. "Pretty name. Kira Spinner would sound a lot better, though. So tell me, why wouldn't she go out with you? She married? Engaged? Or only has two weeks to live?"

"Mom, I am way, way too weird for any girl to take seriously."

"Honey," she sighed, "she doesn't have to take you seriously—not at first. That'll come later, once she gets to know you. It's like I always say, to know you—"

"—is to love me, yeah, yeah. Well, I say, once she'll get to know me, she'll like me a whole lot less."

She put down her fork. "Okay, I'll play this game. Why? Because you're not the usual, run-of-the-mill guy you think a girl likes? Because you like science fiction and dressing up in a superhero costume to movie openings? Nygel, you've got something that *all* girls like. You're *interesting*."

"No, I'm not."

"Yes, you are! I've known you all of, what, twenty-four years, and I still find you totally fascinating. If I didn't, I'd be talking to my friends on my cell right now, instead of talking to you." She reached across the table and touched his hand. "Now, I don't know if this Kira is the girl for you, but even if she isn't, you'll find a girl that suits you."

"Never," he said, half-smiling.

"Never say never. Now, give me one good reason why you won't find that special girl."

"I don't know," he said. "My life has gotten more...complicated lately."

"What's that supposed to mean? Your new job?"

"Yeah, and school and stuff..."

Celine was about to say something, but stopped. By the way Nygel was hurrying to finish his dinner, keeping his head lowered over his plate, she understood that he really didn't want to continue the discussion. So when he excused himself to go upstairs, she ended it with a light comment. "To be continued," she said with a sly smile.

He laughed and turned to look back at her. "I'm sure," he said. "Great dinner, Mom, thanks."

She just smiled back from the table and gave a quiet "uh-huh." But it was the way she did it—with sincerity and warmth and reassurance—that told him that no matter how bad things got, it would all work out in the end. It made him feel good to know that.

CHAPTER 10
TOOLS OF THE TRADE

WHEN HE got to his bedroom, Nygel closed the door and locked it. Not that his mother was likely to burst into his room without knocking, but better to be safe than sorry. He then closed the blinds on the single window in his room, just in case there was a neighborhood peeping tom he didn't know about. *Mr. Meys?* he suddenly thought, realizing that it wouldn't surprise him a bit.

Now assured of absolute privacy, he sat down on his bed and took a few deep breaths to prepare himself for what lay inside his clothes closet.

The sliding closet doors were decorated with posters from some of his favorite sci-fi movies. Nygel reflected that he was now *living* a sci-fi movie, with all the props hidden inside that closet.

He slid the closet door open slowly, then took a quick peek inside just to be prepared in case anything might jump out at him. But everything checked out pretty much the way he had left it last night, so he looked where he had stashed the two alien objects that he covered with his old racing jacket.

He cautiously lifted the jacket, and below it he saw Compass glowing a brilliant blue, as if it somehow sensed his presence. The sword, on the other hand, remained the same—still just a hilt with no blade.

It was at that moment that Nygel realized that he had been drawn to this closet—not out of simple curiosity, but because of some indefinable need. He knew he didn't *want* to explore Compass and divine its mysteries; he was frankly afraid of the thing and what harm it might cause. He didn't know what force was driving him, but something inside him compelled him to hook up with Compass again. For all he knew, it might have been the spiked metal device in his left forearm. Nygel rolled up his sleeve and got another jolt: the device was almost completely covered up by his skin, leaving just a small bulge.

He stared at it a bit, then shrugged. Just one more weird thing, and God knows there'd probably be a lot more coming. But with his skin now almost completely covering the spiked metal device, how was he supposed to attach Compass to it?

"We'll find out," he muttered to himself, and bent over the closet and picked it up from its hiding place. It seemed to have hardly any weight to it—two pounds at the most, but it looked like it would be heavier. Clearly not of this Earth, Nygel thought. He touched it to his arm where the spiked metal devise was buried, and for the life of him couldn't figure out how he'd attach it.

"Come on, *stick*, you little bastard," he said, getting more frustrated by the second. He now wished he hadn't taken it off that morning. Then he remembered how he *had* taken it off, the exact command he had given—"Compass, detach"—and now the solution to his present dilemma was clear as day.

"Compass, attach," he commanded. Immediately Compass reattached to his left forearm without any assistance by Nygel's hand.

Now Nygel asked Compass what was happening to his body. He had expected a reply on the read-out display, but not this message: *Accessing visual cortex...*

Whatever the hell that means, Nygel thought, hardly noticing that his right eye was twitching. But after he blinked three or four times, his vision through his right eye suddenly blurred, then refocused, then to his astonishment, a grid-like computer template came into view. It was translucent, so he was able to see both the computer display and his room at the same time, but it still weirded him out.

If this had happened, say, last night or this morning, he wouldn't have known what to do. But he somehow felt more confident, maybe just more trusting of Compass' abilities. So he closed his eyes and gave another command.

"Compass, allow me to see this through both eyes." He felt his left eye twitch, he blinked, and the display was now three dimensional, both eyes envisioning the translucent computer grid. Nygel was tickled with this new ability. It was odd but fun at the same time, and it was just that kind of day, so he just rolled along with it.

Some weird green-colored symbols appeared at the bottom of his visual display. They looked like Egyptian hieroglyphics, and he wondered if the stories he had heard about extraterrestrials visiting the ancient Egyptians were actually true. But whatever the symbols stood for, he couldn't make head or tails of it.

"Compass, I don't understand those symbols. Can you translate into English?"

The visual computer screen went blank, then a blinking green square, like a computer prompt sign, suddenly appeared. Nygel waited for something to happen, but the little square prompt just kept blinking.

"Well, I am officially stumped," he said aloud. He wondered if he could maybe translate the hieroglyphics by finding a hieroglyphics dictionary online—assuming there was such a thing. So he sat down at his desk and turned on his computer. Within a few minutes he did a search for "hieroglyphics," but too many items showed up and there was nothing that looked like a hieroglyphics-to-English dictionary. Just when he was about to give up, he saw something else on his visual computer.

It was a diagram of Compass itself, revealing a stem that evidently could come out and connect to the cable modem. "Weird," Nygel whispered. Apparently Compass saw the cable modem as an access device that it could use to download the information it needed. So Nygel tried it. He positioned his left forearm next to the cable modem, and at once a probe-type needle emerged from Compass. It punctured the modem wire and within a few minutes, Nygel saw very quick flashes of ones and zeros. Once Compass gathered all the data it needed, the computer grid reappeared but with English text replacing the hieroglyphics.

But after all that work and anticipation, Compass' response was a single English word that did not please him at all: *Classified.*

"Classified? That is all you can tell me? Okay, then what about these spike-bones that came out of my forearms and calves," Nygel asked, hoping to get at least that answered.

Maddeningly, he got the same reply: *Classified.*

Nygel put his hands on his head and tapped his skull with his fingers. "Think, think," he said aloud. He had to think of *something* that was not classified information. He felt a little outraged that anything should be "classified" and off-limits to him. Didn't he have a right to know what was going on with him? Then he thought to ask something besides a biological question.

"Compass," he sighed, "can you tell me about the device in my left forearm that you are attached to?"

The *Classified* text in Nygel's visual cortex suddenly vanished and three new words appeared: *Neural Interface Implant.*

"Okay," he murmured. "Compass, are you saying that this device in my forearm is hooked up to my brain, allowing me to interface with you and you interface with me?"

Correct. The Neural Interface Implant extracts plasma from the user's body and synthesizes the plasma into a protective bio-armor.

That sounded familiar. Nygel vividly recalled what happened in his car at the bridge earlier this afternoon, when that oozing substances covered his body. It was his new alien plasma that was extracted and synthesized into the bitchin' dark blue and gold armored suit.

"Okay, now, can Compass tell me about its own capabilities?"

Access Granted, level 3, basic functions of Compass unit. Artificial intelligence super computer, with the ability to open a spatial phenomenon called a rift-port, causing a dimensional break to allow instant transport. This unit is also able to provide tactical functions on a field of battle or track, and produces a protective electron shield.

"That sounds simple enough," he replied sarcastically. "What about the sword?"

Sonic Sword. A weapon with very destructive capabilities. The weapon is designed to send out sonic waves of energy to stun, paralyze, or decimate a target. Effective range: two-hundred feet, adjustable settings of power output by the user only. The blade of the weapon will appear when the sword is commanded to activate by the user. The weapon will not operate for others besides this unit and the Seeker, Nygel.

"Well, that's a relief," Nygel said. God forbid the sword should ever fell into the wrong hands and allow some alien psycho access to operate the weapon.

"By the way Compass, what is a Seeker?"

Classified.

"That bites," Nygel said, but he knew that sooner or later he would get all his questions answered. He just didn't know why he couldn't have the information now.

Was it possible, he wondered, that Compass somehow knew that he was still too new at this game to handle all of its capabilities? Maybe.

"All in good time, I guess," he sighed. But for now, he could use some sleep. It had been a long day, and he felt that he had more than enough information to digest for now. He commanded Compass to detach and then put it back into his closet, next to the sonic sword.

"Sleep tight," he said, not feeling at all silly wishing Compass a good night. He felt they were already becoming best buds.

CHAPTER 11
WHAT DID I GET MYSELF INTO?

A FEW days passed without incident. At nine o'clock on Sunday morning, Nygel was still in bed, in that strange grey zone between sleep and consciousness, when the phone rang. He didn't want to talk to anyone; it was his day off and he just wanted to get up when he felt like it, maybe spend the day lounging around the house and browsing the internet. But the ringing telephone already changed those plans.

"Hello," he said, his voice still groggy.

"Hey, Nygel, you going to church this morning?"

It was his best friend, James.

"Well, Q, since you got me up—"

"Good man. So I'll see you at Shining Light in about an hour," James said, then hung up the phone.

"Okay, time to get my praise on," Nygel groaned, and dragged himself out of bed. So much for his Sunday plans to do absolutely nothing. Unlike James, he wasn't much of a churchgoer and considered himself less the religious type and more the spiritual type—a type which had the distinct advantage of not requiring a person to haul his butt out of bed on a Sunday morning. His mother was a churchgoer (in the evenings, due to her work schedule), but she never pushed Nygel into it; she would just drop hints that he should go when he felt like it.

"Compass, detach," he commanded before stepping into the shower. He knew by now that the alien device was waterproof; he just preferred a little more privacy. But before Compass detached from his forearm, it informed him of his status:

Host Nygel, body transformation sequence is complete. Host Nygel can now perform Space Officer duties.

"'Space Officer'? Oh, please," Nygel groaned, "I hardly know the laws of my own country, much less the galaxy! Compass, just detach. I'll deal with this later."

Compass detached, then whirred mid-air as it flew into Nygel's bedroom and deposited itself in the closet, sliding the closet door shut behind it.

As Nygel showered, he looked at the small bulge of skin on his left forearm, feeling a bit resentful. He did not like this heightened responsibility, the idea that his life would never be the same again. No, he was the kind of guy who liked going through life being fancy-free, and now Compass tells him he's all set to be some sort of intergalactic space cop? Forget the space angle—he couldn't feature himself being *any* kind of cop, being in a position where people depended on him for their very lives. And the idea of putting himself in dangerous situations where people could get hurt or even die . . .

Although, he reflected with pride, he did do okay with that camper, didn't he?

Besides, he was still just discovering his powers. It would take him a while to learn to control them. But that in itself made him a danger to others, didn't it?

Easy, Nygel, he told himself. *This is new and you're just going to have to learn to deal with it.*

But the more he thought about it, the more he wondered how he would manage to keep his new identity a secret. Look at what the other superheroes in the comic book world went through, balancing lives of duty and privacy. Look at Antorian...

* * *

James was prompt as usual, waiting to greet Nygel when he arrived outside Shining Light Baptist Church. Standing alongside him was his fiancé, Tasha. She was very cute, had a nice figure, a little junk in the trunk, and luscious lips that displayed an awesome smile that complemented her lovely dimples. For church, though, she dressed a bit more conservatively in a red blouse and black suit. Before going inside, Nygel stopped to marvel at the exterior of the five year-old church—all glass and white cross-beams with a soaring dome.

It was already packed inside; the only seats left were the ones up front in what Nygel referred to as "the nosebleed section." He didn't like sitting up this close at the movies, let alone a church, and he felt like turning tail and heading out. That, and the fact he just didn't feel like being face-to-face with the gospel today—he just was not in the mood. But since he was already here with James and Tasha, it would have been too weird and downright rude to leave all of a sudden, so he decided to tough it out.

It was the usual Sunday morning service: a little prayer, some music, followed by a little bible reading along with some preaching by Reverend Squire. The grey-haired minister was an old-style southern preacher, a popular fixture in the community, and beloved by the congregation. He returned to the podium after some hymns were sung to get a little more preaching time. He moistened his lips a little, and then spoke in a deep voice honeyed with a southern accent:

"I would like to send my blessings to all the families that may have lost their homes or property during the tornado last Monday afternoon. Thank God no one was hurt or killed. That in itself is a blessing. I pray that all those families and individuals will have peace and comfort wherever they are.

"Even I was a little shaken up by the storm. I went down to my basement along with my wife, just as we always did in North Carolina at times like this. God knows those storms can kill in an instant, without warning.

"Thank God someone showed up to save that family in the mobile-camper before it went over the side of the bridge and into the Delaware River. The person that rescued that family was not an ordinary man, but someone gifted with special abilities. That was a blessing. Can the church say Amen?"

"Amen!"

There was a shadow of a smile on Nygel's face. Not for the first time he was dying, dying to take credit for the bridge incident. He wanted to stand up before the congregation and take a bow. Sure, it was just his ego talking, but he just couldn't help feeling that way. Of course, he could not tell a soul—not even the people closest to him—that it was he who saved that family. He knew that would be one of the hardest things to deal with.

"Once all the events of the memorable day were over," Reverend Squire continued, "we stop and reflect, but some of us have the nerve to complain. I don't know why; I am guilty of that at times myself. Just think about some of the people in this world, in your very city, that don't have a roof over their heads tonight."

Reverend Squire cued the church band, and if anyone had dozed off during the service, they were fully awakened by now. Nygel thought the music had a really nice beat to it, like most black gospel songs, and it really got the church members into the swing of things. The reverend began talking to the beat of the music playing softly in the background:

"Look down, how many of you walked in here this morning?
Look at your feet and point to them, and say, thank you, Lord,
That you got feet to walk,
You got a voice to talk.
How many of you,
How many of you had a place to sleep last night?
Aren't you blessed?
Aren't you blessed?
And yet there are some people who are always complaining.
I don't care, mamma used to say that we would be crying
With a loaf of bread under our arm.

"I heard a story the other day, that there were some people,
Folks just like us, out there on their way to church.
All dressed up,
Bible under their arms,
Looking all saintamonial,
But they were complaining.

"Here's old wino, hehehehe
Wasn't dressed up,
Didn't have no bible,
Wasn't on his way to church.
But I heard him say, I'm blessed. Wooo!

"And it's just good to wake up in the morning
And know that you're blessed!"

Reverend Squire then began to sing the song which Nygel figured must have been called "I'm Blessed." Without realizing it, the song resonated someplace deep within him, made him feel a little less put-upon than he had felt earlier that day when he was moping in the shower. The old guy's right, he told himself; some people can't walk—I have super-powers and I'm feeling sorry for myself? He had no right to complain about the new responsibilities that had been given to him.

"Praise the Lord!" the congregation sang in the refrain, and Nygel joined in, shouting with the rest of them.

When the service was over, Nygel felt that a special warm glow he hadn't felt in a long while. For the first time he thought that what had happened to him was either God's will or some divine plan. And if he had ever felt victimized by having been, well, *chosen*—then wasn't he a likely candidate? God knows he knew all about superheroes, being a comic book nut and even dressing as a superhero! Maybe it had been preordained; maybe, without realizing it, it had all been a preparation for actually having super abilities.

He just hoped that he could still have some kind of normal existence, without causing too much havoc in his own life. That would take some work, he knew, but it was absolutely necessary.

CHAPTER 12
FIRST KNIGHT ON THE JOB

THERE WERE only two weeks of classes left before the semester was over. Nygel attended all his classes, but felt a little distant from Kira Maru. He just didn't know how to approach her, and especially now he worried that merely being associated with him might put her life in danger. This didn't keep them from glancing at each other during computer class, though.

One day she walked over to Nygel's desk during class and tapped his computer to get his attention. As if she didn't already have it, Nygel thought.

"Guess what? I got a new job."

"Yeah?" Nygel said. "That's great. Something you'll like, I hope."

"I hope so, too. It's just for the summer, though. I'll be assistant computer programmer at Marble World Corporation."

The very mention of Marble World gave Nygel pangs of regret, remembering how hard he had tried to get hired as an Antorian actor for personal appearances. But he managed to hide his feelings and beamed a huge smile at her. "That's terrific," he said. "Congratulations. I hope it's everything you're hoping for."

"Thanks," she said, looking kind of coy with her head lowered shyly. "Nygel, I was wondering…what're your weekends like?"

"Boring," he said with a smile. "Why?"

She still didn't look him straight in the eye, and he found this shyness a turn-on. "I don't know. I was thinking maybe we could hang out…"

Nygel was shocked and thrilled at the same time. But before he could answer, Carlos appeared at their side.

"You don't want to go out with Nygel. I don't think he could handle a real date, since he's probably never been on one before. Now, if you're looking for a great time with a guy who knows how to treat a lady, Carlos is your man."

Nygel had an incredible feeling of déjà vu. The same exact thing happened the last time Kira was about to ask him out.

"I didn't say a date, Carlos, I said to just hang out. You need to mind your own business. So how about it Nygel?" she asked, more aggressively this time, obviously meant to spite Carlos.

And Nygel was happy to rub Carlos' nose in it, too. "Sure, Kira, that would be great!"

They made plans to meet outside the Marble World offices on the Saturday after the first day of her new job. They'd go to Dexter's, only a few short blocks away. Carlos actually turned red with rage that Kira didn't ask him, and stormed back to his computer as if he had been personally insulted.

Now officially committed to a date (no matter what she told Carlos, a girl asking a guy to "hang out" with her was virtually the same as a date), Nygel felt an additional burden added to the already heavy load he was carrying on his shoulders. He liked Kira—liked her a lot. And the fear that the date would turn out badly was almost the same pressure he had felt before rescuing the camper.

It was clear that Kira like him, too, and he had no idea why. He rarely asked girls out himself, and this was the first time in his life that a girl actually asked him out. He greatly admired her taking the initiative and asking him. She was definitely a different type of girl.

It was late afternoon as the sun was starting to set and Nygel watched *Star Questers* on his big screen TV in the living room. It was the final episode of the season, but was suddenly interrupted by a live breaking story.

"Damn!" he shouted, angry that he'd miss who killed the two-dimensional troglodyte and he'd have to wait till the summer repeats to find out.

He was about to switch channels when Sandy Castle appeared on camera. No big wonder she was on the scene of a breaking news story; she was always showing up in the wrong place at the right time, sort of like Nygel.

"Just about a half hour ago, police officials were informed that there is a hostage situation in the downtown Newark branch of the New Jersey National Bank. The reports are early, but so far we know that a security guard who activated the bank alarm was shot and killed. As the robbers were about to make their escape in a getaway van, a police patrol car pulled up next to them. What happened next is still a bit sketchy, but it seems a large man then left the van with a large bag and fired at the police with a hand gun, and then made his way inside the bank.

"There are also reports that six customers and seven employees of the bank being held at gun-point. The five bank robbers have automatic weapons and have blown out all the surveillance cameras inside the bank, so the authorities can't see what's happening inside.

"Oh wait, there seems to be some movement inside. Someone just screamed 'rocket-launcher', it sounded like . . ."

Suddenly a missile came screaming out of the bank window, hitting one of the squad cars and exploding it on impact. All the officers standing near the vehicle fled or fell to the ground.

"Oh my God, we'd better keep some distance here. The perps seem to be very hostile," Sandy said as she ducked for cover, the camera following her. *"We'll keep you informed on any developments on this late-breaking story. Sandy Castle, Rapid Action News."* Then the station returned to *Star Questers*, but sure enough, it was the final credits.

Nygel stared at the closing picture as he nodded to himself. "I guess it's time to go to work," he sighed, and then hurried up to his room. He swung back his closet door and grabbed Compass.

"Compass, lock onto that transmission bandwidth of the Rapid Action News Channel and set up a rift-port about fifty feet away on rooftop level from where the reporter is."

Nygel looked at the read-out, confirming that Compass did as commanded: *Transmitting tachyan-pulse to Rapid Action News satellite system . . .*

Compass then dispensed tiny blue ion particles toward an empty space in his bedroom, outlining the shape of a circular doorway, then beeped three times in rapid succession. Nygel had witnessed this phenomenon before in the penthouse of the Chariot Hotel, and the memory of that awful night made him weak in the knees. There was a flashing light, and a portal appeared where Compass had outlined it, inside of which a flurry of cloud-shapes warped and weaved.

Nygel then mentally commanded the Neural Interface Implant to activate the protective suit. Within seconds his clear plasma oozed out from the spot, wrapping around his body. Then a blue glow enveloped him as it changed the clear plasma into his bio-protective armor. Nygel looked at himself in the mirror. He had to admit, he liked the intimidating appearance the suit gave him. He looked tough as hell.

He retrieved the sonic sword hilt from the closet and placed the hilt at his side, just as he had seen Aracnus carry it—attached to the gold magnetic strip on his right leg. Now fully-suited, Nygel looked at himself again in the mirror. For the first time he really felt he *was* this awesome person he saw in the mirror. It wasn't just a disguise, a custom-made costume worn for a movie premiere—it was the real McCoy. He was still a little nervous, sure, but it all felt natural in a way it hadn't before. And he knew it wasn't just because of confidence borne of his new and limited experience; the extraordinary courage he felt came from something else: from his ever-evolving alien self. It came from the transformation of his DNA, as well as his acceptance of his destiny. He was now, and was becoming more and more, this new fighter that emerged from within himself.

. What happened tonight would most likely put him in the public eye again. One thing was for sure: he no longer thought of himself as Nygel Spinner—at least, not when outfitted and ready for action like this. He felt like a completely different person, a hero without a name. It was just "Seeker" for now. But it seemed to be missing something.

"Oh well," he sighed, "I guess I'll have to play this by ear."

With a quick look back at the mirror in his bedroom, he walked toward the rift-port to face this new challenge.

Once again, he felt the refreshing blast of cool air for the brief moment inside the rift-port. The next thing he knew, he was balancing dangerously on the ledge high atop a fifty-story building.

"Whoa!"

He pushed himself back, and just in time. One inch closer to the ledge and he'd have stepped right over. "Compass, make a note: when I say set up a rift-port on rooftop level, make sure I get some leeway, all right?"

Through the visual computer he read the message from Compass: *Leeway, noted.*

The Seeker looked down at the street below. He had always been terrified of heights, but strangely, he wasn't now. He wanted to get closer to the scene of the robbery but didn't want anyone to notice him. He had a crazy urge to scale down the side of the building to get a better view. He had a strong feeling that he could do it just on instinct, but he stopped himself for a moment and asked himself if maybe he wasn't confusing himself with another comic book character, because he definitely did not have sticky palms. But still the feeling persisted that he really could scale down the wall. Then he remembered his spike-bones. "Well, why not?" he said to himself.

He concentrated for a moment, and the spikes on his forearms and the back of his calves emerged instantly. Without any hesitation whatsoever, with no fear that he had never attempted such a stunt before, the Seeker stood on the edge of the building, jumped into the air and spun himself around, then grabbed hold of the ledge with his spikes. Then he began scaling down the wall using his spikes, as if it were the most natural thing in the world.

"Now this is tight," the Seeker said in excitement. Just another great surprise he did not expect. He continued his downward journey, scaling quickly and quietly, unobserved in the dark as he dug his spike-bones into the side of the building.

The police were keeping some distance from the old one-story landmark building that housed the branch of the New Jersey National Bank. An unmarked armored van had come on the scene, and the SWAT team it transported to the site had already dismounted.

The bank thieves, still waiting for a negotiator, got a little impatient. They aimed a rocket at the gas tank of the SWAT van, knocking it over to its side as it exploded into flames.

"Oh, man," the Seeker groaned as he scaled down the building, "these guys ain't kiddin' around." In the darkness he could feel the searing heat of the flames shooting four stories into the air.

The police took out the power to the bank, which left the criminals in the dark. The thieves were none too happy and demanded that power be restored immediately. The police captain told the robbers that the negotiator would be there in two minutes, and they will see what has to be worked out to insure the safety of the hostages inside.

Apparently the bank robbers were not too thrilled to hear that bit of news. They took the liberty of firing another rocket out of the broken window, which struck an empty squad car and flipped it into the air and landed on its rooftop. Anyone nearby had managed to get out of the way of the missile, but that in itself was no cause of rejoicing among the ever-growing ranks of police onsite.

"I've got to stop this trigger-happy lunatic," the Seeker said. He was only ten stories above ground level, and no one had noticed him yet—mainly because he was just behind the police defense line. The searchlights were all focused on the bank building and no one paid the least interest to the figure clinging to the building right behind them.

The Seeker studied the large windows on the front of the bank, each one on the sides of the main entrance. Other smaller windows were off to the sides, and further above street level than anyone could reach without a ladder.

The Seeker was suddenly seized with a curious compulsion to do something with those windows—what, exactly, he wasn't yet sure—but as the strange sensation grew it became more specific action in his mind: he felt the urge to thrust his arms out towards the two windows. Luckily, the spike-bones at his calves allowed him to stand perpendicular to the wall. Fully supported, he discovered he was able to climb or descend the wall with only the use of his calves' spike-bones. Nygel had no idea what he was doing, but he was doing it anyway. Standing perpendicular to the wall and facing the heavens, the Seeker thrust out his arms towards the bank windows as a targeting display appeared on his visual computer. On the bottom it read: *Plasma net launcher activated . . . Targeting . . .*

Well, this is something new, the Seeker thought with mild amusement. He remembered the weird webbing Aracnus had used to rope him in; this must be the same sort of thing. "Well, here goes nothing."

He aimed both his forearms at the bank's two front windows, and the targets locked into place. The gold metal gauntlets created sounds of an engine revving up followed by a hissing sound, and suddenly a pair of gold strips resembling gun barrels arose from both gauntlets. They shot out two streams of different liquids that collided mid-air, forming cloudy white plasma nets that stuck to the bank windows. Within seconds, both windows were completely covered with webbing material.

The Seeker's gold gauntlets lowered back to their normal position until they were needed again, and then he took off. Already the police were looking in his direction to see where the plasma nets had come from, and got only a fleeting glimpse of the shadowy figure jumping away from the building. They quickly turned their search lights to find him, but he was already halfway down an alley.

He had figured the police would take over and move in on the bank now. But then he thought of the hostages and stopped. "I'd better rethink this," he said aloud. If the SWAT team charged into the bank, the hostages might be killed by either friendly or unfriendly fire. Either way, they were still in jeopardy, and rescuing them required a little more subtlety than a SWAT team. It would be a serious mistake.

He would have to attempt a rescue. But how?

Use the sonic sword? No—it would be the same as if the SWAT team charged into the bank with guns blazing.

Another possibility was from underground. He stared at a manhole cover a moment, then bent down and lifted it. He ignored the cars and pedestrians watching him; what were they going to do—perform a citizen's arrest?

He jumped into the manhole and dropped into a stinking pit.

"Yuck," he said, sidestepping the sewage as best he could to the raised concrete walkway. He tread carefully along the tunnel, until he realized he wasn't sure he was headed in the right direction. "Compass, can you illuminate my path somehow?"

A message blinked on his visual computer screen: *Engaging thermal detection mode . . .* The Seeker's visual cortex was suddenly able to pick up heat signatures, enabling him to find his way in the pitch-blackness of the tunnel.

"You're full of surprises tonight, Compass," he commented, but another one was in the making: a map overlay showing where he was standing in relation to the street above suddenly illuminated. He walked toward the place directly beneath the New Jersey National Bank.

"Okay, focus," he murmured to himself, knowing he's damned well better focus and not dwell on the stench in the sewer—or on the huge rat that just crossed his path. "How am I going to get the hostages out of the bank safely . . ." Another more irritating thought crossed his mind: *Why do I have to be stuck with this job? Why couldn't the SWAT team take these guys? But no . . . Man, I've been had.*

Outside the bank, Sandy Castle was on the air.

"Another startling development in the New Jersey National Bank robbery in downtown Newark. Just a minute ago, the front windows of the bank were somehow covered with a . . ." She paused to search for the right words. ". . . a sticky, web-type substance that's preventing the bank robbers from firing heavy artillery at the police outside the building. We have no information at this time as to who it was who shot this substance—presumably from some long-range firing mechanism, since that person has not been found. But a police spokesperson just told me that this may just antagonize the bank thieves further, since they have repeatedly demanded that no one interfere or attempt a rescue, 'or else the hostages will pay dearly'. That's a direct quote from one of the bank robbers—I just got that from the police spokesperson. Obviously, this situation is extremely volatile."

Sandy paused to listen on her headset. "Yes . . . Yes, I've just gotten word that the hostage negotiator has finally arrived on the scene and is trying to talk to the armed men inside the bank to calm them down until they can come up with a solution to save the hostages. More to come, we will keep you informed. This is Sandy Castle signing off for now, stay tuned to Rapid Action News for further updates on this late-breaking story."

Back in the sewers, the Seeker had reached the underbelly of the bank.

"Compass, activate the sonic sword."

Activating...

Almost immediately, three gold claws opened and an energy spike shot from the claws, turning the shaft of pure energy into metal. *Very cool*, the Seeker thought. But was not entirely comfortable with firing off a weapon he had never used before. In fact, he had never fired *any* kind of weapon in his life.

"Er, Compass, can you control the power output of the sword? I need enough power to break through the floor, but I want to be sure that no one is near where I will be firing."

Setting requested energy level . . .

At the same time, a circular window appeared on his visual cortex. It had five blips on it, all of which were moving, and they were all at different corners. "Compass, what are you showing me?"

Motion Detection Mode.

He nodded. He paused to consider his next move very carefully. He decided to blast two holes—the first to distract the robbers, the second for his entrance. "Compass, show me where I am in relation to the bank interior."

Another overlay appeared on his visual computer screen: a detailed map of the bank floor, and standing near the entrance of the bank, a blinking stick-figure, representing his present position. He chose the first spot directly below the lobby entrance, close to where the bank robbers were standing, and chose the second spot at a safe distance away from them. He'd have to blast through the second spot very quickly after the first, or else he might be seen making his entrance.

"Compass, show me Motion Detection Mode."

Good—the bank robbers' positions hadn't changed. Now he stepped to the spot under the lobby entrance, raised the sonic sword, and shot out a sonic blast. As the ceiling above him exploded and showered concrete, he dashed to the second, more remote spot, and blasted his entryway with the sword, jumping back momentarily to dodge the falling debris. Then he deactivated the sword, placed it quickly on the magnetic sheath strip, and jumped up, grabbing hold of the edges of the hole with his spike-bones and hoisted himself up into the bank.

The first explosion had given him the cover he needed. As he climbed into the bank he saw the bank robbers and hostage all temporarily blinded and disoriented by the billowing clouds of dust and debris. Now he scurried with lightning speed up the walls with his spike-bones, then upside down over the ceiling where he stopped.

Looking down, he quickly studied the layout of the bank. It was darker than usual; the emergency generator lighting was spare—safety lighting, really. But he was able to scope out all the desks, the checkered black and white tile floor, and the red carpet at the entrance.

The dust was settling below; the robbers were wiping tears from their eyes. But before they could turn their weapons back on their captives, the Seeker acted quickly.

"Compass," he whispered very softly, "I need your help."

He didn't have to say anything more. Compass sprang into action, spinning down and around the masked men and snatching their guns with its magnetic hyper-drive. Before the bandits could even say "Huh?" the whirring disk crashed through an upper window and hovered near the chief of police, who only had one thing to say:

"What in God's name—"

With a click, Compass de-activated its magnetic hyper-drive and the weapons dropped at the police chief's feet with a clatter of metal on concrete. Then it rose to the height of the shattered window and zoomed back inside to join the Seeker.

The bandits followed its flight path to the ceiling, and now for the first time they saw the Seeker, still poised with his spike-claws dug into the ceiling.

"Hey Jack, what the hell is that?" one of the robbers said aloud.

"Damned if I know, but just in case he's got some ideas . . ." The masked bandit called Jack grabbed one of the female hostages, a young, attractive Latina woman who worked as a teller at the bank. She screamed her head off as she sobbed, "Please don't hurt me!"

"Shut your trap or I'll break your neck," he shouted.

The Seeker looked down at the security officer who had sounded the alarm—lying dead in a pool of blood. He was able to tell which of the seven hostages were bank employees by the name tags they wore, so he assumed the remaining six were bank customers. But he could not find the fifth bank robber. Whoever and wherever he was, he was the guy with the heavy artillery. Just then the Seeker's curiosity was answered.

"Hey Lew, you back there? We got a pest problem—some fly on the wall—I mean, on the ceiling. Get your Raid out and bring this joker down!"

From the back of the bank the fifth robber now revealed himself, crawling out from under one of the customer service tables. "You got it, Jack."

The Seeker glimpsed a flash of steel-grey as the heavy-set masked man pulled a gun from his waist. He heard the click of the trigger, and then jumped away from the ceiling as it was riddled with bullets. When the hero jumped over to one of the bank walls, he was amazed to see this guy was firing a G.E. XM214 automatic gun, also known as the Minigun, a six-barreled killer capable of firing 166 shots per second. After blasted the hell out of the ceiling, Lew got another beat on the annoying intruder, and fired again.

The Seeker knew he couldn't dodge a weapon like that; not for long, anyway. The way this idiot was firing, odds were he'd hit a hostage or two. It was time to change tactics. "Compass, activate plasma net launcher."

Outside of the bank, the police chief was getting worried. "I hope those are just warning shots," he said, but he felt sure the shots were emptied on the hostages. He was about to order the SWAT team to go into action, but then everything fell silent.

Sandy Castle was also curious. Thrusting her microphone into the police chief's face, she inquired, "Chief Higgins, those rapid-fire gunshots and the silence are very ominous. Your thoughts for our viewers?"

"Get that damned microphone out of my face," he growled, pushing her aside.

But the chief was thinking the worst had happened. Maybe the masked bandits saw no way of getting out of this. The threat of their lives or a life sentence could have pushed them to kill the hostages and maybe even themselves. It was time for action.

"Lieutenant, send a team in there now. I hope to God we're not too late,"

The SWAT team took up their riot shields and charged for the doors. But the doors flew open before they got there, and a large bundle came flying out of the front doors, landing on the sidewalk.

"What the hell is that?" the police chief shouted.

His lieutenant examined the strange bundle and answered in a trembling voice, "Sir, it appears to be one of the bank robbers . . . encased in a . . . thick web substance."

The police chief came over for a closer look. "Holy cow, it's Lew Langford. The brains of the operation."

The lieutenant scratched his head. "Chief, I would guess that whoever did this probably has the situation under control."

But the Seeker was by no means finished. Yes, he had dispatched Lew—wrapping him up in organic webbing, then snatching his Minigun with his spike-bones and tossing him out of the bank like a sack of potatoes. But there were four more masked men to go.

And one of them—the bandit called Jack—now roughly yanked the Latina bank teller's hair and shouted to the Seeker, "If you or anyone moves, Brown Eyes here gets sliced from ear to ear."

"Idiot," the Seeker laughed. "You're forgetting my friend here"—he pointed to Compass—"snatched your guns and knives. You have no weapons."

For a long moment Jack didn't reply. Then he said in a quiet voice, "That's where you're wrong, my friend." With one hand wrapping around the bank teller's throat, he used the other to unsheathe his hunting knife from a belt-loop.

Whoa, the Seeker thought. Evidently Compass was only able to magnetize and snatch away the weapons it actually touched.

Jack savagely yanked the woman's hair back, exposing her long, delicate throat, his lethal knife poised to slash. The woman screamed. And Jack laughed.

CHAPTER 13
STAND-OFF

"YOU DON'T want to do that," the Seeker said.

Mad Jack laughed again. "Oh, man, you don't know how *much* I want to do it!"

He tightened his grip on the woman's neck with one hand and with the other, ran the sharpened tip of his knife lightly across the side of the bank teller's throat. A thin red line appeared where he sliced. Mrs. Perez (as her employee's name tag identified her) whimpered in fear, her eyes wide with terror. What worried the Seeker was not only that the maniac did it efficiently, but with real enjoyment.

"No listen up," Mad Jack said in a calm, cold voice. "Me and the boys are leaving the same way you came in, down these holes you thoughtfully blasted for us. And to make sure we're not followed, web up the front door with that gunk you wrapped my buddy Lew in."

The Seeker paused for a moment to think. The SWAT team was probably getting ready to storm into the bank at any moment, and if he webbed up the door, that would surely prevent them from coming in—not a bad thing, actually. He didn't need an army of cops crashing this party right now; there would probably be a bloodbath.

"Do it now, or she dies," Mad Jack said, a dangerous edge in his voice.

"Okay, okay," the Seeker said. He did not want to see anyone else die at the hands of these murderous lowlifes. "Compass, plasma-net, wide dispersal pattern," he commanded, and the gun barrel-shaped gold strips on the gauntlets arose once again.

127

Taking aim, he fired off a volley of netting that completely gummed up the double doors.

When the police and SWAT teams charged into the bank's vestibule where the after-hours ATMs were located, they found themselves faced with a slight obstacle: the double doors opening onto the main bank floor were at that moment being clogged with a strange, web-like substance.

"What the hell—?" the commander said. "What is this junk—sticky foam nets? Tanglers? Manetti, what is this?"

"Some kind of foam," the SWAT cop suggested, examining it closer. "Spaghetti rounds, maybe?" He tried breaking through it with the butt of his Beretta M12 sub-gun, but the weapon immediately stuck to the gluey substance so completely that it was hopeless irretrievable.

"Let me try," a SWAT team probie grunted, aiming his pulse-high-powered HP microwave interpersonal weapon at the cross-hatched mass of webbing.

The commander barked at him, "What're you trying to do, numbskull, give it a heart attack?"

The probie put down his weapon sheepishly as the SWAT commander reviewed the situation, taking a quick mental inventory of his team's weaponry: shotguns equipped with TKO, 12- and 37/40-mm gauge gas rounds, low-frequency infrasound and buckshot rounds; Sig Sauer, Glocks and H&K handguns; Ruger mini 14 and Colt 177 submachine guns; HK 53/42 assault rifles, air Tasers, tear gas canisters, flash-bang and stinger grenades, dazzler guns, isotropic radiators . . . He took a long-hard look at these eye-popping killer toys and sighed; a million bucks of cutting-edge weaponry, and they might as well have pea-shooters and slingshots.

"Get a blow-torch in here," he sighed. But the man he addressed didn't move. "Well? Why are you still here, Manetti?"

"Er, Captain, we don't . . . have a blow-torch."

"What do you mean we don't have a blow-torch? We got enough fire power to blow the Great Wall of China to kingdom come! Isn't it part of the arsenal?"

"Er, no, Captain," another cop answered quietly.

"Then find one, damn it! And a bullhorn!" he roared, and Manetti was out the door in a flash. The Captain turned and looked again at the sticky wall of webbing blocking their entry. Just another element of the situation that was slipping out of control, he thought. "This stuff's thick. You can't even see through this mess..."

Which had been precisely the Seeker's intention. He didn't want anyone even looking inside the bank, so that he could handle this situation himself. Were the SWAT team commander able to observe what he was doing, he might give him an order—and the Seeker didn't have time for that. If it turned out badly, then only he would be blamed and the SWAT team and police could plead plausible deniability. That was as it should be, the Seeker reflected; he needed to take responsibility for his own actions.

"Hey, I'm talkin' to you, clown," Mad Jack shouted to him.

The Seeker broke away from his thoughts. "Yeah, what?"

"I said, give Einstein that sword-thing you got on your leg."

The Seeker turned to see another member of the criminal crew standing next to him with his hand outstretched. He started to reach for his sword hilt, but stopped and asked the bandit next to him, "They call you Einstein? How come?"

The man shrugged. "I dunno."

"Because you're smart?"

The other bandits snickered. Einstein turned to look at them, and though the Seeker couldn't see his face, he had no doubt Einstein was confused. "I'm not smart," he said to the Seeker. "Why?"

"Because Einstein was a genius. They call you Einstein as a joke, that's what kind of pals you're hangin' with. Guys who don't respect you . . ."

Einstein turned to Mad Jack and said in a hurt voice, "You said Einstein meant 'good buddy'!"

The other crooks renewed their giggles, even louder now. "It does!" Mad Jack shouted. "He's lyin'!"

"No, *he's* lying," the Seeker said in a low voice to the very confused Einstein.

"Shut up!" shouted Mad Jack. "Give him the sword!"

The Seeker did as told, but was at least content to have sown the seeds of discontent among the criminals. With luck, maybe they'd shoot themselves before anyone else got hurt. "Need anything else, Mad Jack? A gin and tonic? A lap dance?"

"Since you asked," Mad Jack replied, "I'll take that doohickey on your forearm."

"What, this?" the Seeker said, indicating Compass. "This is just a mole, though I call it a beauty mark. It doesn't come off." As if demonstrating, he tugged at Compass to show them it was permanently affixed.

"Cut the comedy. Hey, Einstein, yank it off him"

"But Mad Jack," Einstein said, "he just said he don't come off. It's a mole. Watchoo want with a mole, anyway, Mad Jack?"

"It's not a mole, you complete and utter moron from the Planet Dimwit! I said, yank it off him!"

The Seeker offered no resistance as Einstein tugged on Compass as hard as he could, but the device would not budge.

"Ouch, that hurts, man," the Seeker said, lying through his teeth. "Take it easy, you're gonna pull my doggone arm off."

"It won't come off Mad Jack," Einstein said.

Mad Jack roared, "I saw it come off! That's the gadget that snatched our pieces, remember?" It flew off his friggin' arm and flew back! Don't you remember?"

"I don't . . . remember things so good, Mad Jack, not since I was little and my mom—"

The Seeker would have been glad to hear the story, but there was another welcome distraction—an amplified voice blaring from behind the massive web-net obstructing the bank doors: *"This is Captain Higgins of the Newark Police Department. Whoever you are who gift-wrapped Lew Langford and put this glue-webbing-crap over the doors—stop interfering with police business. We can handle the situation from here!"*

The Seeker was a bit peeved by the message. *Talk about gratitude*, he thought. Most of the hostages and probably a few of Higgins' police force would have been hurt or killed if it hadn't been for him.

"Okay," Mad Jack shouted. "Everybody line up single-file, march to the vault. Move!"

One of the bank employees led the line of hostages through a door in the back of the bank that led to the walk-in vault. The heavy steel vault door was still wide open after the robbers cleaned out of substantial amounts of cash, money bonds and gems.

"Everyone get in," Mad Jack ordered.

The hostages did as they were told. "You, too, Tinkerbell," he said, pushing the Seeker into the vault. "By the time the cops blast through that crap you squirted on the door, we'll be long gone."

"But, Mad Jack," Einstein said. "It won't do you any good puttin' him in the vault. He's a superhero!"

All the other bandits roared with laughter. "You tellin' me you actually think this clown's got super-powers?" laughed Mad Jack incredulously.

"Well, yeah! He climbs walls and ceilings..."

"Yeah, with *tools*, you moron. Tools and high-tech gadgets. You've been reading too many comic books, Einstein. He's just a stupid jock who likes to dress up." He glared at the Seeker, who insolently had his back to him. "I'll show you what kind of superhero he is," he added under his breath, and in one quick movement he picked up a nearby steel folding chair and smashed it across the Seeker's back. The hostages shrieked as he fell to the floor of the vault, moaning in pain.

Mad Jack now looked with disgust at the sword hilt in his hand. "Even his toys are crap. Some sword—a sword without a blade. A half-assed sword for a half-assed superhero."

Pleased with his joke, he roared with laughter as he tossed the sword into the vault on top of the fallen Seeker. Their raucous voices were immediately silenced by the clanging of the vault door as it locked shut.

Everyone had expected the lights to go off once the vault door was closed. But as another bank employee informed them, these were the emergency lights operated by a generator. As she was saying this, the Seeker quickly got back on his feet, looking pretty chipper. Everyone else was surprised, considering the nasty blow Mad Jack had given him.

"Are you okay, sir?" Mrs. Perez asked in concern.

"Right as rain," he said. "But now it's time to get busy. Compass, rift-port to the second underground opening I made."

The people stared in fascination as Compass dispensed tiny blue particles from its ion port on the sides. But they gasped outright when the blue, warping portal appeared before their eyes.

"Hang tight, folks, I'll be back," the Seeker said to his astonished vault-mates, then jumped into the shifting cloud-like shapes in the portal.

But he wasn't the only one busy at the moment.

"All right, guys," Mad Jack said, "Me and Dino are gonna grab the last two bags outside the vault. Einstein, Tim—check and make sure the holes in the floor are clear. I don't want any surprises."

As he went off, Einstein got down on his knees and lowered his head into the dark hole as he shined the flashlight to see down the tunnel. Tim stood nearby, waiting for the all-clear signal. But before his lying eyes he watched as Einstein suddenly disappeared—head-first, whisked off his hands and knees through the hole.

Tim stood blinking a moment, then shouted, "Hey, Mad Jack! C'mere!"

By the time Mad Jack and Dino reappeared with two heavy bags of cash and gems, Einstein came flying up from out of the hole, landing on the floor with a crashing thud. He was mummified in organic webbing—and struggling to get free. Then the Seeker emerged from the hole.

"Isn't this where we started, boys?" he asked, getting up to his feet. "Now the gloves are off."

Mad Jack got a panicked look on his face. "Tim, Dino—take care of Houdini here."

"Let's see," the Seeker said, "three against little ol' me, hmm. I think I'm going to kick your butt first, Tim, then yours, Dino, and I'll save you for last, Mad Jack. Everyone happy with that order, or do you want to change the rotation?"

The big bruiser named Tim slipped on a pair of brass knuckles. "I think it's time for you to taste the floor," he said as he rushed towards the hero. The Seeker grabbed his brass-knuckled fist with one hand, and unmasked the goon with the other.

"Now I'll have to kill you," Tim said in a quiet voice.

But the Seeker shouted with the shock of recognition. The young black man standing unmasked before him was a once-famous Golden Gloves boxer. "Tim *Roberts*? No way! What the heck are you doing wrapped up with this crew?"

"None of your damn business," he muttered.

"You were the undefeated champion in the boxing ring. I watched all your fights on TV. And now you're nothing but a damn *crook?*"

Tim Roberts glared at him, then shoved his face one inch from the Seeker. "Who are you to talk? You know what its like to lose everything you got? I had a home, money in the bank, and a girl I was going to marry, and then all of it was gone in one stroke."

"Oh, yeah," the Seeker said, remembering the stories he'd heard. "The steroid thing, right? You flunked one too many tests . . ."

"You think I forgot that? I need this money, and no one will hire me because of that incident. I need this score, so get out of my way or so help me you will surely go down." He put up his hands and started jogging around him, waiting for the Seeker to take the opening punch. He had never once been beaten in a fight, and there was no doubt in his mind he could take this guy, whoever the hell he was.

"No, you first, be my guest," the Seeker said as he put up his dukes, "but you're still going to jail for trying to pull a stunt like this."

"The hell I am!" the ex-boxer shouted, and came in blasting at him with his fists. The Seeker's reflexes were lightning fast: he blocked and batted away the fast-moving hands with his palms, and Tim Roberts felt as though he was in a practice session with his old coach wearing a pair of punch mitts. The other bandits could not believe what they were witnessing. The two opponents' hands were moving in a blur, and the Seeker gave no ground at all to Tim as every brass-knuckled punch was deflected or dodged.

The ex-boxer was getting exhausted, but he still had one trick up his sleeve, though it would hurt—though not nearly as badly as it would hurt his opponent. He slowed down his punches, tricking the Seeker into thinking he was about to collapse, and just when the Seeker's defenses were down, he rammed his head into his face mask. He had braced himself for the head-butt, but the head mask felt soft, like foam padding.

"Okay, I'll give you that one," the Seeker said. "My turn."

Another barrage of punches came from the boxer and another head-butt, but the Seeker tossed his head back, caught both fists in his hands, and shoved Tim back into the wall with such force that he was knocked unconscious.

The hero shook his head in disappointment. "Way too easy. Next!"

"Here, Dino," Mad Jack shouted, tossing the hunting knife to his accomplice, "cut this guy down to size."

Dino tossed the knife menacingly from hand to hand, his eyes locked on his target as he walked towards him in a low, almost crouching position.

"Hey, Dino," the Seeker said pleasantly, "didn't your mom teach you never to play with sharp, pointy objects?"

As Dino swung at him with the deadly knife, the Seeker jumped back. Dino lunged forward again with a stabbing motion, but his opponent stepped aside quickly and connected an uppercut to Dino's chin, lifting him off the floor and sending him flying three feet into the air, landing on the floor with a crash. There he stayed, semi-conscious and dripping blood from his open mouth.

"Two down," the Seeker said, then went looking for his next and last victim. "Oh, Jaaaaaack, where are you?" He peeked under desks and looked in trash cans, pretending as though he might find him there. "C'mon, Mad Jack. I don't want you to feel left out and forfeit your turn on a much-deserved butt-whoopin'."

"Right here, pal," Mad Jack muttered as he popped up from behind a desk with the rocket launcher Lew had used on the police blockade. Once targeted, he launched the small missile.

"Oh, snap," the Seeker said as he jumped clear across to the other side of the bank to avoid the missile. It exploded against the far wall, sending bricks, plaster and dust in a whirling mini-tornado in the air. The hostages screamed for their lives, but no one was injured in the blast.

The Seeker knew it would take mere seconds to reload the rocket launcher, and Mad Jack was hustling to do just that. But the very next instant the Seeker was at his side, yanking the launcher out of his hands with a flick of his spike-bone.

"I'm getting a little tired of this, Jack," the Seeker sighed. "And there's a movie on cable I want to see tonight. So you want to end this real quick and you can catch the next bus to the county lock-up, or should I just drop-kick you where you stand?" As he ambled toward his prey, he casually flipped over a heavy wood desk out of his way with the flip of a finger.

Mad Jack backed up towards the teller line. "Okay, I was wrong—you do have super-powers, but I'm still gonna make sure you remember this day." He quickly unhooked the velour-covered ropes from one of the crowd control posts. It was a brass stanchion with a weighted dome base, somewhere between forty to fifty pounds, the Seeker estimated. He may have enhanced strength, but he didn't yet know if he had enhanced vulnerability; either way, a swing to his head with that mother could do some serious damage.

"Compass, shield!"

He held up his left forearm to receive it, and in seconds a diamond-shaped blue translucent shield appeared there.

Mad Jack swung, but the warrior blocked the attack with his pulsating electron shield. It was an unfair fight, but he didn't mind. His shield deflected the brass stanchion like it was swatting a gnat, and he polished the goon off with a stupefying love tap to the jaw. Mad Jack dropped the pole and fell to his knees.

"Shield off," the Seeker said, and the blue-tinted shield disappeared without a trace. He then picked Jack up by the scruff of his neck and whipped his mask off. "Gee, you're ugly, too. Who'd have guessed?"

He left the incapacitated hoodlums to free the hostages from the vault. "Compass, open the vault."

The disc detached itself from his forearm and latched onto the locking panel on the steel vault door. Very quickly it cracked the locking code and the door opened, revealing the stunned hostages inside the vault. The Seeker retrieved his sonic sword where it had been thrown into the vault, and he led the speechless hostages out the steel door and back to the main floor of the bank.

He stepped up to the prostrate figure of Mad Jack, giving him a little kick to get his attention. "Now, Jack, I think you owe an apology to these fine people, especially Mrs. Perez," he suggested.

"What? You're kidding, right?" Mad Jack said, coming to. He had never apologized to anyone for anything in his life, and he sure wasn't going to start now.

"Do it," the warrior said, raising his voice slightly while lifting Jack off the ground by his shirt. "Pretty please."

"You're off your blue-and-gold rocker," Mad Jack muttered, already suffocating as the Seeker tightened his grip on his shirt.

"Now, Jack, you remember how I gift-wrapped your buddy Lew a short while ago?"

Fear flashed in the crooks bloodshot eyes. "Okay, okay. I'm . . . I'm . . . I'm . . . *sorry.*"

"And Ms. Perez . . ." the hero reminded him.

"Oh, you gotta be kiddin' me," Mad Jack protested.

The warrior gripped his sonic sword hilt and the blade appeared a millimeter within Mad Jack's neck. "My toys don't work, huh? Believe me, you don't want to see what I can do with this," he whispered into his ear.

Mad Jack's eyes rolled at the sight of the blade appearing out of thin air. He turned white as he looked toward the bank teller. "Sorry," he gasped.

"Oh, come on, you really put her out, you know. I think a *nicer* apology is in order—what do you think, folks?"

The other hostages cheered and shouted, "Do it! Do it!" as the hapless thug twisted in the Seeker's mighty grip.

"Mrs. Perez," he gasped, "I am truly sorry for my rude and murderous intentions towards you . . ."

"And you promise never to do it again . . ." she added.

"Yes," he groaned.

"And turn your life around?" another hostage prompted. "And turn state's witness against your partners-in-crime and change your name to Nice Jack?"

"Oh, come on!" he shouted.

The Seeker shrugged. "Well, we can't fairly expect miracles. But I'll hold you to that promise to never hurt anyone again. Do I make myself clear?"

Jack nodded his head in compliance.

"Good," the Seeker said, then commanded the blade to vanish from the sword. He holstered the hilt back on the magnetic sheath. Mad Jack breathed a sigh of relief—but only for a moment, because the next thing he knew, the Seeker tossed him back to the floor and began wrapping him in a plasma net.

"What—wait a minute!" Mad Jack protested. "You said you wouldn't do to me what you did to Lew!"

The Seeker shrugged. "No, I just meant I won't throw you through the plate-glass window. That's something, isn't it?" He looked at his handiwork, brushed his hands, and then turned to the hostages. "I'll let the authorities take it from here," he said as he started off to make his exit through one of the holes. "Sorry to run, folks—"

"Wait a minute," Mrs. Perez said. "We don't even know your name!"

He stopped in his tracks. "Er, it's just . . . Seeker."

She beamed in appreciation. "Well, Seeker, you saved my life. You're my knight in shining armor."

He smiled at the charming compliment. He thought the name fit him; he *did* look knight-like with his sword and shield and shining armor. In fact, he thought, if he wasn't already named Seeker, he'd probably choose Knight.

"Thank you, ma'am," he said, "I—" The hero stopped cold. His next thought came to him like a blot out of the blue. "Knight Seeker," he said softly to himself.

"Excuse me?" Mrs. Perez asked.

"My full name, Lady Perez, is Knight Seeker," the newly-named hero said as he bowed his head. But now something else was vying for his attention. He turned to look at the double doors, where a blow-torch was quickly burning a small hole . . . then a larger hole . . . and now an entryway clear through the organic webbing.

"That's my cue," he said, and with a wink to the cheering hostages, he slipped down the second hole—just as the SWAT team burst in, weapons poised to fire.

"Everybody, hands up!" the SWAT commander shouted.

"You're just a teensy bit late," Mrs. Perez giggled with a sly smile.

The commander and his team were stunned into silence. Then Captain Higgins jumped through the newly-created entryway and shouted, "What's going on, Jenkins?"

The SWAT commander suddenly snapped back to life, ordering his men to cover the perps and retrieve the stolen loot. He mumbled to the captain, "The hostages appear to be fine, Captain. We got here just in time."

"Oh, brother," Mrs. Perez said, rolling her eyes.

Captain Higgins sized up the situation with a sweeping glance, but the man he wanted most of all wasn't anywhere in sight. "Okay where is he? I want that bozo right here, right now!" he screamed.

"Bozo?" a hostage said. "While you guys were eating doughnuts, that man saved our lives!"

Captain Higgins was speechless with rage. He was overly sensitive about cop-doughnut jokes, even though he had a Platinum Club membership at his local Donut Delite. "Is someone going to tell me where that damned vigilante—"

"If you mean Knight Seeker," Mrs. Perez interrupted, "you just missed him."

The captain gave her a blank look. "Knight *what?*"

"Knight Seeker," Mrs. Perez said, still tingling at the memory of her hero.

"A superhero," another hostage said.

"And a gentleman," Mrs. Perez added. "Unlike some law enforcement individuals I could name."

The Captain was outraged that the self-appointed crime-fighter could have slipped through his fingers like that. But how? Where?

Then he observed one of the hostages looking towards a blasted hole in the bank floor and figured it out. "You—and you!" he shouted, pointing to two SWAT team troops, "Get in there and get him!"

They slipped into the hole to capture the blue-and-gold vigilante. But Knight Seeker was long gone. Once he had entered the underground tunnel, he rift-ported back to the rooftop across the street to watch the drama play out to the end. It was worth the effort, just seeing the police scratching their heads as they tried to figure out the what, where and how of the amazing hostage rescue and capture of the bank robbers.

Knight Seeker looked down at all the TV news vans, ambulances, police cars, and crowd of onlookers crowding the street below. And there was Sandy Castle giving her live report on the sidewalk, getting fresh, first-hand accounts from a few of the exiting hostages. Knight Seeker used his enhanced power of hearing to overhear part of the interview:

"Wait a minute. Did you say he wore a costume of blue and gold armor? And did he give his name?"

"Knight Seeker," he heard the hostage reply. *"That's K-N-I-G-H-T."*

"Okay, folks, it's official. The same man who rescued the camper on the Trenton Makes Bridge was back in action tonight, rescuing the six bank hostages. And I suspect we'll be hearing his name again and again: Knight Seeker."

High atop the building across the street, the hero nodded. "Yeah, I like it," he said, repeating his new name to himself. And now satisfied that everything was under control, he commanded Compass to create a rift-port that would take him back home. There was still time to catch that sci-fi movie on TV.

CHAPTER 14
RUMBLE IN ATLANTIC CITY

TO HIS enormous relief, Nygel had been cleared of all suspicion pertaining to the incident at the Chariot Hotel. The only disturbing thing was the occasional awareness that he was being followed—by special government agents, he supposed—but he tried not to worry too much about that. Besides, even if he had been followed, it seemed to be happening with less frequency now, which meant they were probably losing interest in him. He just wanted to put that night far behind him.

Work was the best remedy for that, and now he was back on the road with Sandy Castle's team on an undercover assignment. According to some reliable sources, an illegal extreme fight ring was operating in the sub-basement of the Coliseum Hotel and Resorts Casino in Atlantic City. Mike Payne had instructed Sandy to infiltrate the ring, but with a warning to proceed with caution, intimating that it would be a risky assignment.

"I think he's snowing me," Sandy said to the guys in the van. "He just wants me to get pumped over something else besides Knight Seeker. He hates that dude."

"Hates him? Actually *hates* him? Why?"

Sandy turned around in her seat and looked at Nygel, his mouth agape in astonishment. He was shocked that anyone could actually *hate* him.

"*Why?*" she repeated, an amused look on her face. "Oh, right off the top of my head . . . a threat to his massive ego? Maybe he's pissed *he's* not Knight Seeker."

Nygel nodded and went back to inspecting the surveillance equipment, and Sandy went back to unloading the latest newsroom gossip.

Mike Payne's plan was elaborate, even by his standards. Max and Andrew were to pose as high rollers at the Coliseum Hotel and Resorts Casino, equipped with thirty thousand dollars of company money to spend at the tables—the mere thought of which made them giddy with delight.

"I think that'll buy a few lap dances," Max said with a lascivious grin.

"Easy, boys," Sandy murmured. "Payne will want to see receipts."

"Killjoy," Max replied.

Sandy chuckled and returned to applying her makeup in a compact mirror. "Tarty but tasteful," she said approvingly. She was to pose as a lady escort, complete with skin-tight dress and wig. As for Nygel, he was to stay in the van to monitor surveillance. Max had a tiny video camera built into his fashion frames, Sandy had one in her fake cameo brooch, and all three were wired for sound. There was one significant drawback: since an ear receiver would be easily noticed by the security guards of the casino, Nygel had no way of communicating directly with them.

The rest of the trip was taken up by newsroom gossip—a specialty of Sandy's, and greedily consumed by Max and Andrew. As much as Nygel was intrigued hearing the latest office dirt, he couldn't help wondering what Sandy Castle would be saying about him behind his back.

When they finally arrived at the casino, they parked in the multi-level parking lot across the street. Nygel stayed in the van as the others got out all psyched for the assignment.

"Bring me a nice platter from the buffet," Nygel said. "Crab cakes, shrimp cocktail, prime rib—you know, the usual."

"I don't think they allow doggie bags," Sandy replied wryly.

They waved goodbye to Nygel, now barely visible through the tinted back window of the van, then proceeded across the street to the casino.

The hotel was huge, sprawling, and tacky. The façade resembled the Coliseum in Rome, crumbling walls and all. Inside was a different story—vast acres of open space in the lobby, the smell of stale cigarette smoke in the air, and the slots playing bright musical noises as their handles were pulled. And that was just the hotel; the casino was even more sprawling and hopping with activity. In the middle of the floor were the gaming tables: black jack, roulette, Kino . . . Max, Alex and Sandy all stood dazed and befuddled in the middle of it all, wondering where they should start blowing their company dough.

Then, from right behind them, an old lady pushed them aside.

"Hey, get out of the way. You're blocking my way to the slots."

They obediently scooted out of old lady's way, marveling at her frantic walk to the dollar slots.

"These old ladies are a trip," Alex said. "They act like they own the place."

Sandy nodded. "And if she hadn't pushed through so quickly, I would've snatched that cheap wig off her head."

But then she remembered she was wearing a wig herself, and her hand instinctively went to it for a second to make sure that it was staying in place properly.

"Anyone for roulette?" Max asked.

"Sure," Sandy said as she gently grabbed both the guys' arms and led them over to the action.

They breezed past the poker tables as they looked for Mr. Melborne, the casino owner and manager. Mike Payne told Sandy that Melborne made an appearance on the casino floor around 7 p.m. while scouting for high-rollers. It was now 7:15 p.m., and Sandy scanned the playing area until her eyes finally landed on an executive-looking floor walker skulking around the craps tables. It figured; craps was always the liveliest game in the casinos, and it was a game for high-rollers, drunks, or fools. This man looked like more of a pit boss, looking over the dealers and the players, so they came in for a closer look.

Sandy was the first to spot the name tag the man was wearing on his blazer, and gave Max and Andrew a jab in the ribs for confirmation. Their timing couldn't have been more perfect; there was an opening at the table for new players to come into the game. There were already some moneyed-looking players at this particular table—judging by their attire as well as their blasé reaction to losing their stacks of chips on a single roll of dice.

Alex took a wad of one-hundred dollar bills out of his pocket and put them on the table. With a pang of regret he watched the dealer rake in the bills; he knew he'd never see money like that in his hands again. Max was thinking the same thing as he felt the bulge of greenbacks in his pocket.

Mr. Melborne looked at the new players and their lady escort with evident interest. From the corner of his eye Max noticed the casino owner's eyebrows lift when Alex laid his wad of dough on the table. Now Melborne gave a barely perceptible nod to the dealer, who in response assembled a stack of black chips worth one hundred dollars apiece.

"Five thousand dollars to you, gentlemen," he said as he pushed the chips toward Alex. "Good luck. The maximum bet on this table is one thousand dollars."

"Thank you," Alex replied as he gave half of the chips to Max.

Alex had the first roll. Luck was with him from the start; he was hitting good numbers and all the players were winning money. This went on for a few minutes.

"Very good, Mr.—" Melborne said, pausing to allow Alex to give his name.

"Robert Williams," Alex said. "This is my partner, Charles Mason, and our financial secretary and babysitter, Ms. Tara Davis."

Max and Sandy gave smiles in turn.

"Delighted," the casino boss said, flashing his pearly whites. "I'm Kevin Melborne, the owner of the hotel and casino."

"Pleased to meet you, Mr. Melborne," Sandy said with a cutely coy smile.

"The pleasure is all mine," he replied, smoothly taking her hand and giving it a continental kiss. Sandy reacted as if it were something that happened to her eight times a day.

Now it was Alex's turn to roll again, but he passed off the dice to Max.

"So what is it that you two gentlemen do? Business-wise, I mean," Melborne asked in a light, settled tone.

"Charles and I are national distributors of J.A.A.," Alex said.

Mr. Melborne looked puzzled. "J.A.A.? I don't believe I've heard—"

"Just About Anything," Max explained with a smile. "For, shall I say, various private concerns."

Melborne raised his left eyebrow in curiosity. Alex's occupation sounded, as Alex had intended, vaguely illicit. "Ah, I see. Very interesting, indeed."

"We heard through the grapevine that you are the go-to man for high-risk games and...the like," Max chimed in after he had crapped out and lost his turn.

While Melborne was pondering what to say next, Max reached into his pocket and pulled out another wad of one-hundred dollar bills. He placed the new bundle of money on the table and looked directly into Melborne's eyes.

"Well, I think I can handle some personal requests. Meet me in my office in about half an hour. In the meantime, Mr. Williams, Mr. Mason, Ms. Davis, please enjoy yourselves."

And with a courtly bow, Melborne turned on his heel and left the casino floor.

Meanwhile, Nygel was keeping track of what was going on inside the casino. He was frankly astonished by Max's hot streak and wished he could play with that kind of money.

After twenty-five minutes, Sandy, Max, and Alex left the craps table after having almost doubled the money they started out with. "I don't suppose Mike Payne will let us keep the winnings?"

Sandy laughed. "You don't suppose right. Besides, everything is on tape, so he'll know exactly how much was coming back to him."

When they got to the main lobby of the hotel, they went to the front desk. There they gave their names to the desk clerk and asked where Melborne's office was located. The desk clerk, an older gentleman with a short silver goatee, had already been informed about Mr. Melborne's invited guests. He instructed the three to ride the elevator to the top floor where the office was located. They thanked him and headed to the elevators.

Nygel listened closely in the van as the three chatted on their way to the top floor. They sounded a little too confident, he thought. If he were in their shoes, he'd been a nervous wreck worrying whether he could pull off such a scheme. It seemed to him that it wouldn't be an easy matter to convince a casino owner that they were high-rollers. Melborne could even do a background check on them. This whole scheme had been so hastily thrown together that Nygel just hoped it would go off without a hitch.

The elevator bell dinged when it reached the top level. Sandy, Max and Alex got out and started to walk down a hallway carpeted in plush dark green, with half-columns of marble artfully spaced along the walls.

"Usually these casino interiors are butt-ugly," Sandy said. "But this guy Melborne has some taste."

Alex and Max agreed with her observation.

As they approached the solid mahogany double doors at the end of the corridor, a tall, large-built gentleman emerged. Sandy supposed he was an American Indian, judging by the high cheekbones and skin tone. But then his clothing gave it away. Besides his navy blue suit and black dress shirt, this goliath had a large hoop earring in his left ear with a white feather that hung in the middle.

"This way, please," he told them, welcoming them inside with a bow. "Mr. Melborne is expecting you."

Nygel felt his heart thumping as he listened to his cohorts entering Melborne's private office. "Be cool," he urged them.

"Ah, welcome, friends," Melborne boomed from behind his emerald-green-topped desk. "Please have a seat." He turned to the giant at the door and said, "Thank you, Mr. Stroke."

The trio sank down in an ivory white leather couch set in the middle of the office as Mr. Stroke—a bodyguard, Sandy presumed—closed the door behind them. He walked to the right side of Melborne's desk and stood there at ease, though one had the impression that he would be ready at a nanosecond's notice to—what? Spring into action, pull a gun, a knife, or disarm a gang of crooks—anything required of him. The icy, guarded look in the giant's eyes told them that so far he had not made up his mind about them.

Now Mr. Melborne sat forward on his stylish black leather seat and propped his elbows on the desktop. "So tell me, friends," he said in his best, silky-smooth voice, "what kind of games were you looking to play?" When no one answered at first, he looked directly at Max. "Mr. Williams?"

Max cleared his throat. "The word around town says that you have an invitation-only extreme fighting ring. We were wondering if we might qualify as one of your, um, invitees."

Max capped off his remark by making a subtle rubbing motion with his fingers: the universal sign for money, and plenty of it.

"Hmm, well, that depends," Melborne said. One of his shoulders dipped as he seemed to reach under his desk. Sandy caught it and her eyes flashed in alarm. "Relax," he chuckled, "I've just activated the electronic jamming system in the office. You won't mind if I have Mr. Stroke frisk you? In my line of work, I have to keep my guard up around new visitors, you understand."

Sandy realized that things had suddenly taken an ominous turn. They were all locked and loaded with ten thousand dollars' worth of surveillance equipment, and it wouldn't take Mr. Stroke more than a few seconds of frisking to find that out. Ever the smooth professional, her exit strategy was to appear to be offended. She stood up and glared at Melborne and spat out, "Frisk us? What is this, Homeland Security?"

"We seem to have misjudged Mr. Melborne," Alex said to Max in an aggrieved tone.

"Indeed," Max said stiffly, rising from the couch. "I suggest we take our business elsewhere."

"Sit down. You're not going anywhere," Melborne said darkly as he pushed another button under his desk. The couch tilted toward the floor, the floor opened beneath their feet, and the hapless trio dropped eight feet onto a cushioned floor below the office.

They sat stunned for a moment, blinking at the darkness around them.

"You've got to be kidding me," Sandy finally said. "This is like something out of a comic book. What's next, alligators?"

In a moment a light switched on in the confinement room and Melborne appeared at the opening above, leering down at his captives.

"No alligators, I'm afraid, Ms. Castle. But I can oblige you with slow suffocation."

Sandy's eyes widened in surprise. "How did you know it was me?"

"Elementary, my dear. Our security cameras take pictures of everyone entering the casino. Then our computer technology does a facial scan—mainly to keep out banned gamblers. But in your case, I recognized you on the spot. I watch your news reports all the time! I'm a big fan."

"With fans like that . . ." Max murmured to Sandy.

Sandy barked up to Melborne. "This is not going to look good for you, Mr. Melborne—holding members of the media. If we don't return to the studio unharmed, the police will be all over this place like white on rice."

"Oh, I am well aware of that, Ms. Castle. Now, I have some business to attend to. I will be back for you three later. Enjoy your little holding cell till I return. Mr. Stroke, watch them."

Melborne glanced at his watch and left the office, leaving Mr. Stroke standing over the open confinement cell, his arms folded in a posture that let them know he was not nearly as good-humored as his boss.

Back in the news van, Nygel was getting worried. Only a minute after Sandy, Max, and Alex had walked into Melborne's office, the reception was suddenly cut off. He did a diagnostics check on the equipment, but it all checked out fine; even the monitoring equipment was in good shape. Something had to be jamming the signals.

This wasn't a good sign.

Five minutes had passed, and Nygel decided that it was time for Knight Seeker to swing into action. He reached into his book bag and shuffled his books around to locate Compass and the sonic sword hilt. Once he found the alien devices, he activated his bio-armor, which quickly wrapped around his body.

He stepped out of the van and looked around the parking garage. Completely deserted—good. "Compass, create a rift-port to the rooftop of the Coliseum Hotel."

He stepped through it, and there he was atop the hotel, looking around very cautiously. The rooftop was flat with pillars encircling the ledges. Directly behind him was the glass-walled structure that he knew had to be Melborne's penthouse office.

147

Night was approaching, so the interior of the office was brightly lit. Better for him—he would not so easily be spotted from inside the office.

He noticed a large-framed man standing in the middle of the office, looking down at something on the floor. Or at a hole in the floor, Knight Seeker realized as he crept closer. *What the heck—?*

Now he heard the seven-foot giant calling down the hole: "I will be back. Don't move from where you are."

"No problem there, big boy," came a voice from the hole. *"Where are we gonna go?"*

That's Sandy, Knight Seeker thought. Trapped with the others, no doubt. Figures they'd get themselves in a spot like this...

The giant turned around and left the office, unaware of the blue and gold figure outside the glass walls.

Well, Knight Seeker thought to himself, this is my cue.

"Compass, set up a rift-port inside the office, but avoid motion detectors, if there are any."

The portal frame sketched itself into view, the cloud-like warping shapes moving inside, and he walked straight through, into the office.

He cased the room first to make sure it was clear. All was pretty quiet; perhaps a little too quiet. If Sandy, Alex, and Max had been talking prior to Knight Seeker's appearance, they had stopped now. Yes, there were their whispered voices below. There wasn't much time. He walked to the trapdoor and looked down.

Sandy gasped, startled to see the hero standing over them.

"Knight Seeker? How did you—?"

He put his finger to his masked lips to signal her to be quiet. Then he whispered, "I'm here to get you out this hole you dug yourselves into."

He was just about to jump down the trap door and work his way down the walls with his spike bones, when he heard footsteps outside the office door.

"Hang on," he whispered down to the crew. "I got to take care of some bad habits real quick." But before he could make another move, the door opened and he found himself facing eight casino guards armed with electronic batons.

"Well, isn't this nice!" he said. "I'm glad you girls made the cheerleading squad."

One guard snorted and pressed the trigger on his baton as a warning. It sent an electric charge zigzagging out a half-foot. Knight Seeker yawned, angering the guards even further. He took his stance, lowering his body to the floor, his arms angled in striking position. The guards tensed their grips on their weapons. Then it began. As one guard to the right side of the warrior came in swinging his baton, Knight Seeker neatly stepped aside and punched the guard in the abdomen, then delivered a blow to his jaw. The guard was out for the count.

Another guard came into the circle from behind, swinging his baton in a backhanded motion intended to target the hero's mid-section. But Knight Seeker caught it in his right hand, mid-swing, then yanked it from his attacker and elbowed him with his opposite arm in the gut.

Next, another guard boldly lurched forward, but Knight Seeker zapped him with his pilfered baton before his opponent could press the trigger. The guard shook, rattled and rolled with the electric current surging through him, until Knight Seeker back-fisted him, sending him crashing into a nearby glass shelf.

"What the hell is going on up there?" yelled Max from below.

"Don't know," Sandy sighed, "but I've got a feeling the Knight is holding his own."

Two more guards moved in with their batons at the ready. Knight Seeker saw the pair coming in, turned, and delivered a roundhouse kick to their chins, knocking them both out cold.

Another guard stood ready, and seemed a little more skilled than the others with his baton; he was just waiting for the right moment to act. Then he came in kicking with the electro-stick swinging. The Knight moved back a few paces, the guard following his movements, then lurching forward with the electro-tips to stab at the hero. Knight Seeker quickly reacted—he bent his back down to the floor, supporting his upper body with his hands, then kicked away the shock-stick and planted the same foot into the guard's stomach. The kick was so hard and sudden that the guard started to vomit.

"Oh, man, that is nasty," Knight Seeker said as he got back on his feet. "You better hope Mr. Melborne can get that spot out."

The last two guards charged at him from the front and rear. Quick as a flash, the hero jumped into the air and landed, planting his right foot in the face of the guard charging him from the front, his left foot on the face of the one behind him.

Now all the guards were on the floor. Some looked at him but had enough after seeing such a display. The blue and gold hero looked around, waiting to see if the big Native American was lurking around. Clapping rang from the doorway of the office.

"Well, well," said Melborne heartily, "I guess I have the honor of meeting Mr., um, Knight Seeker, is it? I must say, you put on quite a show."

"I'm glad that you found some entertainment in all of this. Now if you don't mind, I have to get Sandy and her two co-workers out of this hole in the floor," the hero said flatly.

Melborne was smiling despite the fact that his office now looked like a war zone.

"Oh, that," he said, gesturing to the trap door with a fake grin. "That's just part of our in-room entertainment. It was just a practical joke. As you can see, they were not harmed in the least."

Knight Seeker ignored him as he went to the trapdoor, pushing the other guards out of his way. He fired the spike-bone from his left forearm to the ceiling, securing it, then lowered himself into the confinement room and carried up the news crew one by one. Once the captives and Knight Seeker were on floor level, Sandy stormed over to where Melborne was standing.

"Mr. Melborne, you got a hell of a nerve."

"Who, me? Ms. Castle, it wasn't me who came in with spy cameras and raising accusations about my business. And you are not an officer of the law, so kindly get out of here before I call my lawyers. As for you, Knight Seeker, I suggest that you also leave before I press charges for trespassing."

The hero glared at the hotel magnate for a long moment. "All right, but I'll be keeping an eye on you."

"And I shall keep an eye on you," Melborne countered as Knight Seeker and the news crew brushed past them and headed out the office door.

Melborne immediately went to his phone and ordered security to make sure that Knight Seeker and Sandy's crew were escorted out of the casino. He then walked back to his desk and looked with disgust at the battered and bruised security guards.

"A lot of help you guys were. Get out of my sight, now!"

Melborne looked around his office as his security team shuffled out in humiliation. He took account of all the shattered remains of priceless antiques and felt his blood pressure rising. Then he turned to his bodyguard.

"Death Stroke, the next time you see Knight Seeker on my premises, I expect you to deal with him personally."

Mr. Stroke nodded solemnly. "Understood, sir."

On the way down to the lobby floor, Sandy and the others stayed absolutely quiet as they stared openly at the hero. The elevator stopped halfway down to admit two security officers, who locked eyes on their prey as they stepped inside. Once they arrived on lobby floor, the security guards hustled them out of the building.

"What I want to know is, how did you know we were here?" Sandy asked, very intrigued to hear his response.

He had his cover story ready. "Well, I've been watching Mr. Melborne's activities for a while," the hero replied, keeping it short and sweet.

They walked briskly through the lobby, gawked at by hotel and casino guests, most of whom figured Knight Seeker was part of the stage show. Once they neared the doors of the casino, Knight Seeker saluted this trio, saying, "Here's where I get off," and started dashing out the doors.

"Wait a minute!"

Knight Seeker turned around to face Sandy Castle. The look she was giving him was something quite different from any look she had ever given Nygel Spinner.

"Thanks for helping us out there," she said. "No telling what Melborne would've done to us if you hadn't shown up."

Max and Andrew nodded in agreement. "Yeah, thanks, man," Max said, seconded by Alex.

"No thanks needed. I'm just doing my thing and looking out for others. Take care of each other and the guy with you in the van."

"Who, Nygel?" said Sandy, her hot-and-bothered expression suddenly cooling several degrees. "Oh, he's okay. We keep him out of the trouble spots. We don't want him to get bruised or anything."

"How very thoughtful of you," Knight Seeker said sarcastically. After giving another brisk salute, he dashed off around the corner, shed his bio-armor, and rift-ported back to the parking garage.

By the time Sandy and the guys arrived, Nygel managed to look both worried and busily occupied with the surveillance equipment.

"What happened?" he said in a panicky voice, "I lost contact. Something went wrong with the equipment—"

"No, it was jammed," Max sighed.

Sandy thought it best not to report anything about the incident; Melborne could easily press charges, since they had nothing that could incriminate him. Once they all piled into the van, they left Atlantic City and headed back to Trenton.

"All is not lost," Max said, "at least we won at the craps tables."

"You mean Mike Payne won," Alex reminded him with a groan.

CHAPTER 15
FIGHT NIGHT

KEVIN MELBORNE sank back into his leather chair and cast a weary eye over the shambles in his office. He never should have invited Sandy Castle and her crew in here, he realized; but he wanted to find out exactly what she knew about his more . . . exclusive entertainments. And thanks to the unexpected arrival of that super-nuisance, Knight Seeker, now he was left with no answers and several thousand dollars in damaged goods. He stared mournfully at what had once been a priceless porcelain figurine of a nude holding a vase, now reduced to a hundred shattered fragments and chips on his carpeted floor. *Heads will roll*, he thought.

"Get those bumbling idiot security guards back in here to get this place cleaned up," he ordered.

Death Stroke nodded. "Yes, Mr. Melborne, it shall be taken care of right away."

Melborne got up from behind his desk and left his office, heading for the elevator. Granted, he reflected, Knight Seeker was not the run-of-the-mill nuisance guest his security detail usually dealt with, but they had still performed abysmally. Above all else, Kevin Melborne was a man who prided himself on running a smooth organization.

When the elevator arrived he stepped inside and punched a coded sequence of floor buttons on the panel. The elevator made its descent towards a sub-basement level inaccessible to most guests and hotel staff.

Well, he thought with a sigh, at least he had recognized Sandy Castle before he got himself into any more serious trouble, so he supposed he could count himself lucky this time. Melborne

153

smiled to himself. Lucky. It might as well have been his middle name.

Not that he had always been lucky. Born and raised in Las Vegas, Kevin Melborne had had a tumultuous upbringing with a father who gambled and a mother who dealt with it by drinking herself into oblivion. His father's uncontrollable gambling addiction was a constant source of screaming fights between his parents, and their eventual divorce came as a great relief to the young boy.

He vowed he would never succumb to his father's addiction and once he graduated from high school he threw himself into hard work—catering jobs by night, cooking classes by day, eventually becoming an accomplished chef at the age of twenty. But one does not live in Las Vegas without succumbing to the lure of the casinos at least once. So at the age of thirty-two Kevin Melborne threw caution to the wind and tried his hand at some low-stakes gambling. When he noticed that he won most of the time, he started to make a habit out of visiting the casinos once in a while. Unlike his father, he was a smart gambler, never risking more than he could afford to lose. But he proved to be a natural, winning ninety per cent of the time, and somehow knew how to balance the adrenaline rush over winning with a remarkable self-discipline and savvy. Soon he was living on his winnings at the casinos, and was emboldened enough to quit his work as a chef to become a full-time gambler.

Most casinos banned Kevin from playing—he was that good—so he decided to start betting on sports games through a handful of select bookies. He quickly amassed enough money to open his own casino. And why not? After working for years in them, he felt that he could do it as well as anyone else in the business. Melborne put his plans in motion three years ago when he decided to open his own casino in Atlantic City. The plans were drafted quickly, and the construction of the Coliseum Hotel and Casino took two years to complete. It opened to great fanfare in a city usually unimpressed with the lavish hotel-casinos that sprouted like crabgrass along the Boardwalk. Melborne's Coliseum was different. Its requisite flashiness was confined to its exterior; inside it was something this jaded town had never before seen: a model of unparalleled taste and lavish restraint. It appealed to the more cultured class of gamblers, but Melborne had a darker, more exclusive entertainment in store for his high-rollers: an extreme-fighting arena built in the bowels of the hotel.

The elevator doors now opened and Kevin Melborne stepped out onto the concrete floor. It looked like a typical basement with overhead pipes, circuit breaker boxes, and metal doors leading to boiler rooms and storage facilities. His footsteps echoed down the long corridor until he reached an entranceway protected by two clean-cut, black-suited security guards with transceivers in their ears. They looked more like Secret Service men than hotel security, but that was exactly the professional touch Melborne had intended.

"Good evening, Mr. Melborne."

He returned their greeting as he passed through the entrance to the stairs that led down to the arena. When he reached the bottom of the carpeted stairway he could hear the muffled cries of the crowd awaiting the special event. Melborne, greeted by another pair of guards, was escorted to his private booth.

The audience in attendance (two hundred-plus, he estimated) was well-dressed and doubtless had a great amount of cash to blow. They were a motley assortment—well-heeled businessmen, corrupt government officials (some on Melborne's payroll), and a few well-known sports figures. They were drawn here by the lure of a game where anything could happen.

Intermingled with the crowd were a select number of drug dealers—though not the usual variety. These were well-spoken, professionally attired men who might be mistaken for corporate lawyers, though their attaché cases held more exotic wares than legal briefs and contracts. They conducted their business openly here, greeted their regular customers with handshakes and chummy jokes. It was all civilized and a very, very lucrative business.

When Melborne reached his private booth he took his seat and gazed through the window, protected from curious eyes on the other side with a silver mirror coating over polycarbonate glass. It was a fairly large arena, circular in shape, and enclosed within a ten-foot-high brick wall. Four gated archways led into the arena, each controlled by the uniformed arena handlers. The spectators were seated above the ten-foot wall on leather upholstered bleachers in stadium seating fashion. At the highest point of the arena, seated in a black chair, was the ringmaster. He wore a long dark brown robe with a hood that drooped over his head, giving him a spectral-like appearance. Next to him was a globe-shaped machine that resembled a bingo ball cage, filled with balls bearing each fighter's name.

It was time to begin. Melborne signaled the ringmaster on his call button, and the spectral figure arose from his chair. The house lights dimmed, and a spotlight shone on the ringmaster as he made his opening announcement. A hush fell over the arena as all conversations ceased and the spectators listened attentively.

"Ladies and gentleman, welcome. Tonight you shall bear witness to the most exciting and bloodiest battles you will ever see, events not for the faint of heart. This is no-holds-barred, hand-to-hand combat where anything can happen."

The ringmaster explained the rules. A round ended only with a knock-out, and the winner of each round would move up and any fighter who killed his opponent would be immediately disqualified.

The fighters numbered twenty that night. Each time a fighter won his fight, his ball was put back into the cage to be spun again. If all the events went as planned there would be an entertaining eighteen rounds of fighting.

The fighters, assembled deep within the tunnels within the four archways, were busy warming up. They were of many different nationalities, each schooled in various fighting techniques that made them very dangerous in the arena. Many of them were capable of killing their opponents with a single blow, but that would immediately disqualify them from the subsequent rounds and chance for final victory. The reason for this was not humanitarian; rather, Melborne had decided, a killing in the arena would be difficult to conceal from the authorities.

The ringmaster spun the cage and read the balls that rolled down the chute. He called out the names in pairs, which determined which fighters would be squaring off in the upcoming ten rounds.

Then the black steel gates of two archways opened, and two fighters emerged to the cheers of the spectators.

One fighter was bare-chested, with black leather pants. He was Hollywood-handsome with a swimmer's build, though his no-nonsense demeanor suggested that he played no games when it came to fighting.

His opponent was a short and stocky, wearing a red singlet that showed his hugely muscular arms to full advantage. The calm look on his face belied his lethal abilities as a black-belt karate expert.

When the gong sounded, the two combatants faced each other. They circled each other and studied each other's eyes with grim determination. The shirtless man, an Asian by the name of Swift Kick, attacked first with a fast-moving kick towards the face of Mad Bull, the fighting name of his stocky, muscular opponent. Mad Bull blocked the kick with his huge arms, then countered with a forceful punch to the head that might have taken Swift Kick's head off if he hadn't dodged the blow, bending his back downwards like a limbo dancer. Swift Kick suddenly lurched his body back into an upright position and delivered a punch at Mad Bull's stone-cold face. But Mad Bull jerked just slightly and smiled, as if he had received only a glancing blow to his jaw.

Then he charged at Swift Kick. Using his head as a battering ram, he plowed into his chest, knocking the wind out of him. Mad Bull followed with a merciless volley of punches to his opponent's head that brought him down to the arena floor, coughing up blood. The ringmaster counted to ten, and Swift Kick was out for the count.

A gong sounded, signaling the end of the fight, and the crowd got to their feet and applauded Mad Bull's performance. He raised his arms in victory and left the arena to wild cheers from the crowd.

Then the arena was cleared and the ring handlers helped Swift Kick to his feet and dragged him through the archway for medical attention.

The matches raged on for ten bloody rounds. The fighting was intense, the snap and crunch of breaking bones filling the arena. Money flashed in the bleachers as the spectators placed their bets for the next five rounds, which pitted the remaining ten combatants against their new opponents.

In the prep area deep within the archways, a cat-like fighter and his protégé were meditating before the next round. The cat-like warrior wore a face mask with his mouth area exposed. His tan-colored singlet was striped with orange cat-like stripes, with a lion's head emblazoned on the chest. His name was Irtizza Raffidia, but he went by the fighting name of Lion Fist. He was a twenty-nine year-old Pakistani who employed a unique style—a hybrid of Kung Fu mixed with Aikido. He had just acquitted himself well in his match against a six-hundred and twenty-five pound sumo wrestler named Mitzu, an arena favorite who had won most of his fights in the past several months. But not tonight. When the sumo had grabbed Lion Fist to bear-hug the life out of him, the Pakistani fighter downed him with a well-aimed head-butt. Once he fell to the sand-covered floor of the arena pit, Lion Fist finished him off with a chop to the liver. The ring handlers had to get a band of assistants to carry the mountain of a wrestler out of the arena.

Now as Lion Fist meditated, his eyes shut and body perfectly still in full-lotus position, allowed himself a slight smile of appreciation at the memory of this night's victory.

The younger man meditating at his side was his eighteen year-old cousin, Syre. He had been sent to America by his parents to live with Irtizza. They had no choice, because they knew that if he stayed in Pakistan he would become a weapon for the Pakistani military. Syre was an "altered," a mutant capable of harnessing the natural bio-electrical forces in his body and discharging them through his hands, delivering a powerful shock to anything he touched.

Irtizza had been teaching Syre to control his mutant abilities through meditation and ancient fighting techniques, and both teacher and student had done very well. Syre had learned to restrain his powers and only used them when training. This was to insure that he would not be detected by organizations that may be tracking mutant activity. Irtizza gave him the fighting name of Tygron.

Syre was dressed in black leather pants, a black spandex short-sleeved T-shirt, black boots, and sporty sunglasses with orange mirror-coated lenses. It perfectly matched his orange-tipped black hair, spiked in a stylish cut. As they quietly meditated in a quiet corner, they served as a marked contrast to the other fighters who did their far more strenuous warm-ups.

CHAPTER 16
BLOODY ARENA

KEVIN MELBORNE was enjoying himself over an expensive Merlot, a cute brunette dressed in a form-fitting sequined evening dress at his side. She whispered into his left ear about the things they would do to end the night properly upstairs in his state room.

Seated next to Melborne was an Asian man in a multi-colored leather trench coat, with an excessive amount of jewelry on his body, neck, and ears. The most distinctive feature, however, was the shiny metallic glove that covered his left hand. It was sleek in design, with claws at the fingertips. He wore it as if it was jewelry, but it looked unnervingly like a weapon.

The young, small-figured Chinese woman at his side fed him slices of apple that she carefully cut to serve him. But the silver-gloved gentleman kept his attention on the fighting arena.

Melborne leaned over and said to him, "Well, Mr. Sage, I see that your fighter has done well for his first match."

The Warlord Sage merely nodded his agreement. "Ah, yes, Dragon Eye is one of the best fighters in Chinatown—and an excellent personal bodyguard. There is nothing he cannot handle." Truth be known, Sage thought Dragon Eye had dispatched his opponent rather too quickly. Surely the audience would have appreciated a more drawn-out competition. He would tell him that afterwards, and the hulking fighter would nod stupidly like a puppet. He would have no choice; his mind had been enslaved by the Warlord Sage.

When he had first arrived in Chinatown, Sage thought he would have to enslave the minds of the demon cult to gain his power. But they served him willingly. The only ones who had resisted were the crime boss Lee Fang and his bodyguard, Dragon Eye. Of course, he had to enslave Dragon Eye when the bodyguard tried to prevent Sage from killing his master.

"Enough of that, my sweet," he said to the beauty at his side, dismissing her freshly sliced apple. "Bring me a drink from the bar—a glass of Merlot, the same as Mr. Melborne is having, I believe."

The comely attendant bowed her head and slinked off to the bar to do his bidding.

Melborne watched the sensual sway of her hips with approval. "Your taste in women is impeccable," he told his guest.

Sage nodded in agreement. When the lovely young lady returned with the drink, he motioned with his silver gloved finger to come closer, and then whispered into her ear as he took hold of the drink from her hand. She nodded and went over to Melborne.

Melborne smiled at the young lady, completely forgetting the sequin-gowned female escort sitting next to him.

Sage's servant then went down to her knees and slowly started to remove Melborne's shoes. She then began to massage his feet, soon peeling off his socks, and the foot massage went to another level.

"That's . . . nice," Melborne fairly moaned as he luxuriated in the sensual foot massage.

"Consider it a professional courtesy," Sage said.

The rounds that followed were bloodier still, the crowd thrilled by the thundering clatter of flying bodies. After the brutal five matches concluded, there were five combatants left, each as hopeful as the next. But there could be only one victor that night.

The next to last series of matches consisted of two rounds. The first round would be fought with two opponents, and the second round will be fought with three opponents as a wild card match. The fighter that stood after the wild card match received an automatic twenty thousand dollars. The overall winner of the night received two hundred thousand dollars.

The combatants that were left included Dragon Eye, who left his opponent with a serious concussion after he slammed his fist into his temple; Black Wolf, an African fighter who used an unorthodox combination of fighting and tribal dancing techniques that left his opponents dazed and flattened; and Mad Bull, who broke the collarbone of his adversary and then savagely kicked him until the fight was ordered over. Mad Bull was being merciful this night. At any other time his opponent would not have lived to see the sun rise. The fourth to make it to the next series of matches was a Hispanic Tai-boxing fighter by the name of Flash Fire. He wore a head band with a fire design and trunks spattered with the blood of his opponents. The fifth and final remaining combatant was Lion Fist, who had won his last match with a sleeper hold that knocked out his opponent.

The referee spun the balls in the cage and called out, in order, the combatants' names. The two fighters who would square off against each other in the first round were Flash Fire and Dragon Eye. The wild card fighters for the second round were Black Wolf, Lion Fist, and Mad Bull.

The round rang, and Dragon Eye and Flash Fire emerged from their archways, locking eyes on each other with cold, hard stares. As they approached the middle of the arena pit, Dragon Eye allowed himself a wry smile as his opponent spit off to his side.

"Let's see what you got, hombre," Flash Fire grunted as he assumed a fighting stance.

Dragon Eye remained motionless, keeping a fixed eye on his opponent as he watched him shadow-box and dance around him. Then the Hispanic Tai-boxer made his move with a quick kick from behind Dragon Eye's head. Dragon Eye ducked the kick quickly, as Flash Fire's right foot swung harmlessly over his opponent's head. Flash Fire tried a few more times to kick Dragon Eye's head from different angles, but kept missing as the Chinese man dodged his attacks, moving with such lightning-quick reflexes that the crowd blinked in disbelief.

Flash Fire soon became impatient and went in with his fists. That was exactly what Dragon Eye had been waiting for. He jumped up and aimed to kick his opponent in his chest. Flash Fire managed to block the kick, hopping backwards a step, then throwing a quick barrage of punches that were skillfully blocked by Dragon Eye.

The applause gasped in surprise and delight, many screaming their approval.

Dragon Eye heard none of it. His focus was on his opponent as his eyes locked onto his throat. The moment Flash Fire stepped into range, he punched him in the Adam's apple with enough force to have him lose his breath, but not enough to make him go down. Dragon Eye wanted to finish the job as he seen the combatant try to get back into his defensive posture. Flash Fire was still gasping as he tried to get oxygen into his lungs, but the impact of the hit to his throat made him cough in hellish pain. Then Dragon Eye made his move. With a twisted smile he lunged at the right knee of his opponent, breaking the femur in two. Flash Fire screamed in agony as he fell to the sandy arena pit, clutching his crooked leg and the splintered bone that broke through the skin. Dragon Eye smiled at his handiwork, then turned his back and walked out of the arena.

The spectators were on their feet, shouting and clapping deliriously.

"Your fighter is vicious," Melborne said. "I am surprised he has not killed anyone yet."

Sage glanced over to Melborne. "The night is still young," he murmured in a seductively devilish tone.

After Flash Fire was dragged out of the arena, the next match was underway.

None of the three men in this match was on any side but their own. Nor did any of them know what to expect as they circled each other in the arena. The most aggressive of the three was Mad Bull, so he went into action first by attacking Lion Fist, aiming to chop at his legs to bring him down. But Lion Fist countered by flipping backwards and catching Mad Bull in his chin with his right foot before Mad Bull was able to touch a hair of his cat-like body. Mad Bull stumbled backwards and Black Wolf took his advantage with a frenzy of dance-style moves mixed with brutal kicking attacks.

Mad Bull noticed the advance of Black Wolf and began blocking the African Fighter's kicking attacks. Not all the kicks were blocked, but the hits that got through hardly fazed him. Mad Bull was still annoyed by getting caught off-guard by Lion Fist. He still felt the pain to his chin. So he decided he'd make no time for games with Black Wolf. He reached out and grabbed the fighter's leg, then punched him soundly in the groin. The agony was plain on Black Wolf's face, but he was not out of the picture until Mad Bull pounded his face with his forearm until his eyes rolled into the back of his head. Grunting approval, Mad Bull let him fall to the arena floor, where he went out for the count.

Then he set his sights and all rage on Lion Fist.

Lion Fist seemed amused, taunting Mad Bull with "come're" gestures.

Mad Bull accepted the invitation, rushing his opponent head-first, with as much speed as he could muster.

Lion Fist quickly dropped into a crouching position. Mad Bull expected him to then leap over his head, but surprised him by rolling out of his path at the last possible second. Mad Bull stopped in his tracks as the clever cat sprang to his feet and followed with a spinning kick that connected to Mad Bull's chin.

Mad Bull was dazed again, but Lion Fist took no chances. He used the palm of his hand to finish Mad Bull off by giving his chin a final punch, sending him flying to the blood-drenched, sandy floor.

The crowd went hoarse shouting their approval of the masked cat fighter. As he lurched out of the arena, he knew in his gut that the final round would not be this easy. Even his protégé, Tygron, felt the same as he handed him his water bottle.

A ten minute intermission followed, during which more money changed hands as the final bets were placed. This was the part Melborne liked best, watching his audience go berserk as they nearly trampled one another, vying for the arena attendants' attention. The names of Dragon Eye and Lion Fist were screamed as they forked their wads of cash to the frazzled attendants.

Sage and Melborne wanted this to be a sporting challenge, so they excused everyone else from the private booth. Melborne was a little reluctant to see Sage's lovely assistant leave after such a magnificent foot rub, but this was business.

Melborne bet Sage one million dollars that Lion Fist would win the final bout against Dragon Eye. Sage readily agreed to the wager, as he had full confidence in his own fighter.

The gong sounded and the spectators settled back down in their places for the main event to begin. The arena lights faded to black and the referee stood up to make an announcement.

"And now, ladies and gentleman, the main event. These two warriors have fought bravely, but only one can be victorious. Re-entering the arena, From New York City's Chinatown…the menacing and stupendous Dragon Eye!"

The spotlight flicked on the opening gate as Dragon Eye appeared. He entered the arena pit stiffly, his face devoid of any emotion. Sage smiled at the ice-cold indifference on his bodyguard's face, admired the calm way he stood in the middle of the arena as he awaited his opponent.

"And his opponent . . . from places unknown, the fighter with nine lives, feline grace and poise: the masked big cat—Lion Fist!"

As Lion Fist was about to emerge from behind the steel gate, his assistant and grateful cousin Syre wished him luck. Irtizza told his cousin not to worry; the worse that could happen was that he would wind up with twenty thousand dollars in his pocket from the wild card round.

"And if I go down," he added, "I'll live to fight another day." He grinned and gave Tygron an affectionate slap on his face. He then turned and walked into the arena, leaving behind a worried protégé.

Lion Fist walked into the arena pit looking around at the crowd and then to his determined opposition who stood waiting as if to square off to the death, which, with Dragon Eye's reputation, was not too far from the truth.

The referee rang the gong, and the spectators were on the edge of their seats. The arena lights fully illuminated, and the final round of the night began.

Both fighters circled around each other as they both looked for targets of attack. Dragon Eye stood in a defensive posture, on his guard because he could not see the eyes through the silver mirrored lenses that covered Lion Fist's eyes. He depended on the minute fluctuations of pupil size of his opponent in sizing up his moves, and in this fight he was at a disadvantage.

Lion Fist threw a jab towards his face. Dragon Eye dodged, barely avoiding the punch, and countered with a roundhouse kick that was blocked by the forearm of his adversary. A series of foot sweeps followed, but each was blocked. Both opponents were well-matched. Dragon Eye looked up to the private booth in wait for a command from his master.

Melborne felt a little cocky. He grunted approval when Lion Fist threw some combination punches that caught Dragon Eye by surprise.

"Seems your fighter is outclassed," he told Sage.

Sage had no emotion on his face as he kept his eyes on the fight. "Luck can turn bad," he said.

"Well, my luck's holding out so far," Melborne countered as Lion Fist landed another hit to Dragon Eye's midsection.

"This fight is not over yet," Sage said coldly. "Watch and learn."

He got up from his seat and left Melborne's private box.

Dragon Eye looked up and knew it was the signal to make his move. And just in time, he thought; he was starting to lose his composure and possibly the final match. Sage stood outside the door to the private box, staring at his fighter and using his dark powers to put him into a deep trance. Suddenly Dragon Eye stopped for a brief moment, letting his guard down. Lion Fist looked bewildered, not knowing if his opponent was surrendering or thinking of another line of attack.

In this deep trance, Dragon Eye mentally disconnected the area of the brain that registers pain. His eyes gleamed red—only for an instant, but it threw Lion Fist's concentration for a moment. He wondered if his own eyes were playing tricks on him. He snapped back to attention and began pummeling Dragon Eye with his fists.

He and the spectators were astonished that the blows did not faze Dragon Eye. From his position at the doorway, Sage smirked at the sight of his fighter moving in for the kill, oblivious to everything else.

Lion Fist backed up, swung some roundhouse kicks, but it only slowed down his opponent's advance. *Why doesn't he go down?* he thought in panic.

Dragon Eye had a sinister smile now, his mouth so full of blood that it dripped from his teeth. He now had Lion Fist exactly where he wanted him. One punch to his stomach doubled him over, and the following punch to the chin brought him to his knees. Dragon Eye picked up the fighter by the back of his singlet and tossed him across the arena on to the sandy floor.

From behind the steel gates Tygron cried, "Get Up! Get up, Irtizza!"

Lion Fist struggled to his feet.

"Get up now!" Tygron shouted.

When Dragon Eye reached his fallen adversary to engage him again, the Pakistani fighter threw a punch to his face. Dragon Eye caught his arm in mid-flight and pulled his opponent toward him. The unstoppable Asian fighter then grabbed hold of Lion Fist's head, ripped the mask off of his head and revealed the face of Irtizza. A well-planted knee-hit Lion Fist in his mid-section, sending him sprawling to the arena floor once again.

Tygron shouted, "Stop the fight! Stop the fight! He's killing him!"

Irtizza struggled to his knees, signaling his frantic cousin to stay in the archway and not get involved. He feared Tygron might forget himself and reveal his mutant powers. Summoning what little strength he had left, he roundhouse-kicked Dragon Eye in his face. Dragon Eye staggered just a bit, more blood pouring from his mouth and drenching the arena floor. He decided that was the last attack he would allow from his opponent. He hit him in the face with a sharp jab, then quickly came from behind his unmasked opponent, grabbing his head with both hands. Dragon Eye looked at his opponent's protégé in the archway and then, turning Lion Fist into position so that his last glimpse on earth would be the frantic figure of his eighteen year-old cousin, he snapped Irtizza's neck—a sickening sound that resounded throughout the arena—then let him fall lifeless to the sandy floor like a rag doll.

The crowd was stunned. No one made a sound. No one ever expected such a thing to occur.

The only one clapping was Sage himself.

When Syre looked at his cousin motionless on the arena floor, he became enraged. The handlers holding him back noticed that his eyes began to glow behind his sunglasses, and his hair was spiking up even more as his bio-electrical field built up inside him. The handlers were almost cut by the two fine elbow blades that emerged from the middle of his arms.

Then popping sounds of muscle and bone could be heard. To the guards' astonishment, the slender young mutant was growing a more muscular physique, stretching the black spandex shirt he was wearing. Tygron's handsome features changed before their eyes into the face of a man-beast, while black fur-like hair with orange stripes sprouted rapidly over his whole body.

Then his hands glowed electric-blue. The two ring handlers holding him back felt the surging electrical current go through their bodies. They screamed in pain, all backing away quickly, though one had the presence of mind to disable the controls to the gates so that Tygron could not enter the arena.

"He's an altered!" one of the ring handlers cried as he let go of Tygron.

Tygron extended his fingers as his fingernails grew at an astonishing rate. They turned into claws—the strong, retractable claws of a wolf.

"Get out of here and call security!" another ring handler shouted as they all ran out of the mutant's way.

Tygron ran back toward the steel gate and sliced through it easily with his claws, making an opening for himself.

Dragon Eye watched Tygron coming for him. He had only one thing in mind: to rip the boy's head off to keep as a trophy. That thought alone made it very satisfying to face this unexpected opponent.

Melborne shouted, "Your fighter is barbaric! You have outstayed your welcome, my friend!"

Sage re-entered the private box as he waved his silver gloved finger back and forth. "Mr. Melborne, you do not dictate when I can come and go. I am in control here."

"Like hell you are!" countered Melborne, "This is my arena, my hotel!" Furiously, he reached for the red security button near the back wall.

Sage pointed his silver-clawed finger towards the box, and a red beam shot out in a flash, incinerating it.

Melborne gasped at the sight of the control box blowing up in front of his eyes. There was only one thing to do, he realized. He raised his left arm, as if checking the time, but the watch on his wrist served another function. Pressing the stem at the bottom of the time piece, a tiny stun dart fired from the wristwatch. It met its target—piercing through Sage's leather trench coat and into his right shoulder. Sage looked down at the small needle and chuckled.

"Is that all you've got, Mr. Melborne?" he asked with a broad smile.

Melborne was baffled why Sage was not affected by the tranquilizing dart. He should have been reduced to a heap on the floor, but there wasn't even the slightest indication of wooziness.

Sage pulled the dart from his shoulder and flung it back at Melborne. It hit him in his chest, the tranquilizing effects working before he could pull it out. The next second Melborne was out cold on the floor, and Sage turned his attention back to the arena. Kevin could count himself lucky that Sage liked the entertainment served that night in the arena. Otherwise the casino owner might never have awakened from his tranquilized slumber.

CHAPTER 17
TYGRON'S REVENGE

WHEN THE gate that he cut away with his mutant claws fell into the arena, Tygron stopped and stared at the body of his cousin lying lifeless in the bloody pit. "Irtizza, I will avenge you! I swear," he whispered, and then looked up to see Dragon Eye waiting for him to advance.

Tygron took a bounding leap into the arena. When he pounced within eight feet of Dragon Eye, he crouched to the ground, ready to tear him apart with his razor sharp claws. He sprang towards him, but the Asian hit man quickly moved out of the way. With his long claws slashing in a criss-cross motion, Tygron came in swinging. Dragon Eye avoided the long claws with grace and cunning, knowing that if Tygron kept fighting him with such naked, raw hatred, he would eventually find his mark.

The Asian bodyguard saw his opening: the exposed rib area of his young adversary. With one well-planted kick, Tygron jumped back in pain, nursing his aching ribs. Good, he thought; not broken—at least not yet. He knew that he was not as skilled as his opponent, so he got sneaky. He allowed Dragon Eye to get in some glancing blows as he backed himself up to one of the gates. Tygron could easily have dodged the attacks, but he wanted to keep up the illusion that he was fully outclassed by the Chinese hit-man. It worked; Dragon Eye was smiling with his teeth still stained with blood, enjoying every minute of punishment he was inflicting on the young fighter. Tygron was then backed up to where he had entered the arena.

He jumped on top of the section of the metal gate that he had sliced away with his claws to gain entry to the arena, and looked down as Dragon Eye approached. He went in towards

Dragon Eye one more time to stab at him with his claws and got one of his claws to slice Dragon Eye across his right arm. The Asian fighter looked at his wound and frowned. The more experienced opponent then floored his young adversary with a kick to his face, knocking off his sporty sunglasses and exposing his intense blue eyes.

"You're mine now," Dragon Eye said.

Tygron got to his knees as the hit man approached. "That's what you think," he said, a hint of a smile on his face. Then came the electrical charge. It began with his hair spiking up once again, and his eyes glowing an electric blue; his hands also turned blue as the current of bio-electricity charged through them.

Dragon Eye didn't see the starbursts of blue light that suddenly filled his own eyes, yet the moment he stepped onto the piece of metal gate where Tygron was kneeling, he knew he had made a serious mistake. He didn't know there was enough bio-electrical energy coursing through Tygron's hands to power the entire Coliseum establishment; all he knew was pain—searing, shocking pain as his internal organs fried with unbelievable heat. He didn't move, only vibrated on the metal gate as his eyes sparked and sizzled, as black smoke arose from his scorching skin and his melting costume. A sickening stink filled the arena as his entire body turned to charcoal with only its skeletal structure remaining; flakes of dead, burnt skin dropped like tiny black leaves onto the sandy arena floor. The skeletal remains soon followed.

Half of the spectators had already left, and the security detail did not want to tangle with this mutant. They had already dealt with one super-being that night, and since Melborne gave no order to confront Tygron, why make more trouble for themselves?

The ringmaster also had been wondering what was going on with Melborne, and the absence of his boss's squawking voice over his two-way began to gnaw at him. Something was up, he realized. He quickly roused the few remaining spectators out of their stunned stupor, ordering them to evacuate the arena, then hustled over to Melborne's private booth.

But when he got to the door his way was blocked by Sage. He instinctively reached for the nine-millimeter pistol he was carrying at his side.

When the first silver glint of the gun appeared, Sage quickly kicked it away. The shot went off, the bullet piercing into an adjacent wall and making a deep hole the size of a quarter.

As the ringmaster turned to look, Sage lifted his clawed, gloved hand and drove it into his head, breaking open his cranium like a cocoanut. As he looked in confusion at the chunk of brain matter that spilled to the polished marble floor, the ringmaster thought to himself, Mr. Melborne won't like this, no sir . . . better call the custodial staff . . .

The next moment he fell dead to the floor.

Sage now turned his attention to the arena, where Tygron was weeping uncontrollably over the body of his dead cousin. The warlord was truly intrigued by Tygron. It was obvious the young man was a mutant—he had watched him transform into a wolf-like creature behind the metal gate, right before his mutant claws tore a passageway through the gate–and he had never met one before. A being that appeared to have power and magic without sorcery... marvelous! Sage walked down to the arena pit to examine Tygron more closely.

Tygron noticed his approach and felt nothing but hatred for this stranger in the stylish, long leather trench coat. He knew Sage had been responsible for Dragon Eye's actions. "Who are you, and what do you want?" he demanded.

Sage shrugged his shoulders. "Who I am is not important. As to what I want, you killed one of my most valued servants, and I need a replacement. You are young, but you possess great power." He looked the young man-beast over, nodding at his youth and splendid physical condition. "You shall now be in my service and under my will," he said as he stopped at the last step over the arena pit.

"I serve no one!" Tygron yelled out in rage, then leaped to his feet with his claws ready to strike.

Sage calmly spoke an ancient chant and raised his left hand. As he leapt into the arena, a ball of red light flew from his hand and knocked Tygron to the sandy floor. Before the young mutant had a chance to get up, Sage reached into his coat pocket and grasped a handful of a white powdery substance, then cast a spell that made it change into yellow sleep dust. Sage threw it at Tygron. He did not want to take a chance on injuring the young fighter any further; Tygron was too valuable a subject to permanently damage.

The mutant barely made it to his feet before the yellow sleep dust he inhaled took its effect with startling speed. His strength was completely sapped, grogginess overtook him, and he fell back down to the sandy arena floor.

Sage smiled with satisfaction. All in all, he thought, it had been an enormously enjoyable night. He'd have to come back and pay the presently tranquilized Kevin Melborne another visit—maybe even stay there for a little rest and relaxation—but sadly, it was time to leave.

Using his metallic gloved fingers, he drew a large pentagram on the blood-drenched sandy floor of the arena. He then walked over to the defeated Tygron, limp and groaning on the edge of the arena pit, and picked him up in his arms.

"What . . . ?" the mutant moaned in confusion.

"Patience, my boy," Sage chuckled, then roughly tossed the semi-conscious mutant over his shoulder like a safari trophy. He stepped into the center of his pentagram, making sure not to disturb the outlines with his feet.

He uttered seven ancient words—words forgotten to all mankind and remembered only by him—and a thousand filaments of red lightning filled the lines of the pentagram. Sage smiled; the transportation spell still worked! Within seconds, Sage, along with the defeated Tygron, left the stench and gore of the arena of death and disappeared without a trace.

CHAPTER 18
BIG DATE

TWO WEEKS is a long time to get worked up over a date, Nygel thought. If he had to wait one day more, it might have killed him.

But somehow he made it so far. It helped that school was over for the semester and he passed all his classes, including Mr. Zimmer's Art History course. It also helped that it was a beautifully clear day, the air cool and clean, and everywhere he looked, he saw visions of Kira Maru dancing in his head.

The train ride on the local to Newark calmed him; he liked watching the scenery pass by out his window, and the mellow music playing over his portable CD was carefully chosen for the trip. Nothing too rambunctious to get the blood boiling and the juices flowing—not yet, anyway. There'd be plenty of time to work up a nervous breakdown once he arrived at Newark.

When the train finally pulled into the station, the butterflies started. It was only a mild flutter, but he mentally commanded them to chill and take a nap, and strangely enough, it worked. The power of suggestion, he reflected; it was almost as powerful as his Knight Seeker powers.

He grabbed a shuttle bus to downtown Newark outside the train station, happy to find row after row of empty seats. Good— he required a bit of solitude to completely decompress. To say Nygel had been nervous about his first date with Kira was the understatement of the century. She was a very special, different kind of girl (not that he was an expert in that department, he had to admit—not by a long shot), and he did not want to blow his chances at a shot at a good relationship with her.

Nygel's attention was diverted by a newspaper one of the commuters was reading. The headline told him that two new drug gangs were waging a brutal turf war in New York City. He just hoped they stayed out of New Jersey; he didn't need to go up against them—not as Nygel Spinner or as Knight Seeker.

When the bus dropped him off at the corner of the fifty-story high Marble World Corporation building, the butterflies started up again. Nygel still had bad memories of that part of his life. But at least the restaurant where they had planned their date, Dexter's Bar & Grill, was conveniently located only two blocks away— which had made him decide to take the train to Newark. Driving would have made him even more nervous about their date.

When he entered the huge building, the first thing he noticed was the lavish black and white décor, all done in a stunning retro space-age design. In the center of the lobby was a bigger-than-life statue of Antorian holding up a globe of the world—exactly like the famous Atlas statue. He marveled at the statue but at the same time it made him sick to his stomach. He felt an almost irresistible impulse to take out his sonic sword and obliterate the damned thing. But fortunately or not, the sword lay peacefully in his closet back at home, along with Compass.

Nygel walked to the security desk and told the guard that he was there to meet Kira. The guard called upstairs for confirmation, then hung up and directed Nygel to take the elevator to the twenty-seventh floor. When the elevator doors closed, Nygel checked himself out in the mirrored back wall, and he approved at what looked back at him: a good-looking (If I do say so myself, he thought) young man in khakis and a nice Jamaican-style long-sleeved shirt. He would rather have worn a short-sleeved shirt in such balmy weather, but the small circular bulge from the neural implant in his left forearm would have looked very odd.

Finally the elevator door opened onto a wide hallway with an ominously impressive set of black double doors some feet away. There was an array of tinted grey glass panels that covered and concealed the offices, and Nygel felt for a moment like he was in some secret service government building—not exactly conducive for settling the rampant butterflies in his stomach. But he steadied himself and took a deep breath and rang the door bell, and in a moment Kira's melodious voice rang out over the small speaker.

"Be out in one second, Nygel!"

He smiled at the sound of her voice, relieved to hear it cheerful and optimistic. He quickly straightened himself up and in a few moments the door swung opened and she stepped out, looking like a million bucks in her dressed-down professional attire. She wore a black skirt that went down to her knees; comfortable, black, mid-heel shoes; and a bright blue blouse that highlighted her beautiful face. Her skin was so clear, it was almost translucent. Was it possible, he wondered, that she wore no makeup? If she did, it was so little that you couldn't tell. And the way her long, black hair was done up in a bun, it made her look like an exotic beauty. . .

"Well, what're you gawking at?" she laughed.

Nygel came back to earth quickly and regained his composure. Then he looked into her eyes and felt himself melting all over again. "Nothing," he mumbled. "I mean, you…"

She laughed again, her smile wide and friendly. "Hey, Nygel, how are you?"

He forced himself to calm down and returned the smile. "I'm doing great, thanks. How'd your first day on the job go?"

"Omigod," she laughed again, "it was a nightmare! So unbelievably hard learning everything new and people's names, but everyone's been so nice to me . . ."

Then, from behind Kira, a young and handsome Italian-looking teenager came out the door. He wore black slacks and a short-sleeved blue dress shirt.

"Hey, Kira," he asked with a friendly grin. "Who's your friend?"

Kira made the introductions. "Nygel Spinner—Paul Sole. Nygel's a friend of mine from college, Paul. He came to take me out to dinner."

"Oh," the teenager said, his smile diminishing slightly. "That's . . . nice."

Nygel knew enough about Marble Corp. to recognize Paul's last name. "Sole . . . Any relation to the owner?"

Paul raised an eyebrow, both impressed and surprised. "Yeah, my dad."

As they shook hands, Nygel got another surprise. Even in his pre-Knight Seeker days, Nygel had a firm handshake, but Paul

Sole's grip was something else. *Works out*, Nygel thought. *A lot.* And it wasn't a normal handshake in one other regard; Paul's grip actually tightened as he applied more pressure to the shake. *What is this*, Nygel wondered; *male domination, or just old-fashioned jealousy?*

"Nice grip there, Paul," he managed to say.

There was the merest hint of a smirk in Paul's smile. "Yeah? You think?"

Nygel reflected with some satisfaction that he could easily break every bone in this dude's hand with his Spycon hybrid strength, but held back and kept his pleasant smile.

"Nygel . . ." Paul murmured under his breath, as if trying to place the name. "What did you say your last name was again?"

"Spinner."

A light of recognition fell on Paul's face. "Nygel Spinner. You dress up as Antorian, right?"

Nygel was embarrassed and nodded shyly. "Uh, yeah. How'd you know that?"

"My dad's got me working in the legal department, so I hear a lot of things," he said, then turned to Kira. "Man, this guy's a legend! He's the one who goes around making unauthorized personal appearances in his own Antorian suit!"

Nygel nearly dropped to the floor in shock. "No, I don't, not anymore," he interrupted, but Paul kept talking right past him.

"Then he calls Legal and says, 'Well, authorize me, then,'" and you know we've got a strict policy against anyone—"

This was Nygel's worst nightmare come true, and it was happening right in front of Kira—who, bless her heart, actually managed to look bored with Paul's trash talk. Nygel could only wish he'd wake up any second, but this jerk just wouldn't shut the hell up.

It was Kira who finally saved the day. "Sorry, Paul," she said, holding up her hand in a halting gesture, "but if I want to hear tired old gossip, I'll call my grandmother. C'mon, Nygel, let's eat."

Paul's dropped jaw as Kira led Nygel down the corridor to the elevators.

They laughed all the way down to the lobby. Just a minute earlier, Nygel had been mortified by Paul's embarrassing exposé of his Antorian past, but Kira had managed to make it seem like nothing more than a mild annoyance, like a pesky fly she swatted.

As they walked outside and down the two short blocks to Dexter's, Nygel shook his head and said, "What a jerk that guy is. Figures the boss's son would be like that."

"Oh, Paul's all right—nothing like Carlos. I think he's just—"

Nygel finished her sentence. "Jealous that I'm taking you out to dinner?"

"Bingo," she said, laughing again. "Yeah, I think so. And by the way, I had no idea you applied to the personal appearance department! I mean, I knew you had the suit and all, but I figured it was just for Halloween and few conventions here and there."

Nygel felt his face flush as the subject of Antorian reared its ugly head again. "Yeah, it's true, but that's just old baggage. I have other things going on in my life now. And top of the list is showing you a good time tonight!"

She beamed a lovely smile at him, took his hand, and they crossed the street to Dexter's Bar and Grill. It was that precise late afternoon moment when the neon sign outside the restaurant lit up. Nygel took it as a happy omen.

They entered Dexter's to the sounds of Miss Elliot belting out "Get Your Freak On" from the jukebox. Kira started bopping her head in rhythm to the beat of the song, and her upbeat mood was infectious. Nygel felt confident in a way he hadn't before—at least in the company of a lovely lady. Battling twisters and bank robbers was a cakewalk for Knight Seeker, but as Nygel Spinner he often felt woefully inexperienced with women. But as they waited to be seated at a table, Nygel felt he could handle the task at hand with all the aplomb of Knight Seeker.

The restaurant was an old Newark institution, long admired for its architectural splendor as well as its ambience. The ceiling was three stories high, on which enormous chandeliers hung from gold cables. Restaurants and businesses come and go in Newark, but Dexter's had remained like a steadfast friend.

After a short wait, the restaurant greeter seated them in a booth. Nygel approved; he loved the high-backed walls that afforded them privacy, the comfortable, worn leather seats, and the art deco wall-lamps that cast a warm glow.

"We're lucky to get a booth so quickly," Kira shouted over the booming music. "This place fills up quickly after work."

Nygel nodded as he looked around. It was a good mix of a young crowd here with a few older couples who still knew how to have fun. The bar ran down the middle of the restaurant and was packed with the after-five crowd enjoying their well-deserved happy hour. As if someone had read his mind, the booming music lowered in volume as a romantic ballad played over the speakers.

To Nygel's surprise, he noticed that Professor Zimmer and his wife were sitting a few tables away. He wondered what they were doing in Newark, and then he remembered Zimmer mentioning his wife commuted here to work. He wondered if his favorite teacher did this every Saturday—took a train to Newark to meet his wife for dinner after a long work week. The idea touched him. It was the sort of thing he hoped he would do when he was settled down and married.

"Somebody you know?" asked Kira.

"Huh? Yeah, Professor Zimmer, my art history teacher."

"Oh! You want to go over and say hi?"

Nygel thought about it for just about a second, but then shook his head. The old couple was holding hands over the table; he couldn't interrupt a sweet moment like that, and besides, he just wanted to have Kira on his mind and nothing else. The next moment, a waiter appeared at their table to take their drinks order.

Kira greeted him with a pleasant smile. "I'll have a Virgin Mary."

"And a Virgin Harvey for me," Nygel said.

Both Kira's and the waiter's faces clouded in confusion. "Now, I'm rarely stumped, but that's a new one on me," the waiter admitted.

"It's a Harvey Wallbanger without the vodka and Galliano," Nygel explained.

"So in other words," the waiter said slowly, "you just want a plain glass of orange juice…"

"Right," Nygel nodded, "but a Virgin Harvey sounds more sophisticated."

They all laughed at that one, and watched as the waiter left and passed the joke on to the bartender.

"You don't have to tee-total just because I am," Kira said.

"I'm not, really! I only drink once in a blue moon. Just health-conscious, I guess."

Kira flashed him a dazzling smile. "See how much we have in common?"

Nygel felt himself melting in the reflection of her smile. "May I say something, Kira? First, you look great tonight—but that's no surprise because you always look great. And second, I'm still surprised you wanted to hang out with a guy like me."

She smiled with her head tilted slightly, as if she was slightly confused. "A guy like you? Now, why would you say that, Nygel? I've always thought you were a cool person. A little weird at times. . ."

She stopped to laugh, and he couldn't help joining in. Their waiter appeared with their drinks and asked if they were ready to order dinner. Kira told him that they had barely looked at their menus, and asked for his recommendations. The waiter replied with his memorized list of specials and his own personal favorites. Nygel ordered the chicken fettuccini Alfredo, and Kira chose the broiled sea bass. Once the waiter went off with their orders, Kira smiled sweetly as she leaned over the table and cooed, "Now, where were we?"

"My pathetically low self-esteem," Nygel reminded her, and she laughed. "Okay, I was saying, I'm not a typical guy. I like to think for myself and tend not to follow the crowd. I like to be creative and keep an open mind to things. And I try to become a better person each day of my life. But I guess I still feel so different in my own ways that I'm not sure people understand that."

"Maybe not, but they're intrigued," she countered. "And no, they don't like cookie-cutter coolness and that jazz—maybe in high school, okay, but we're grown-ups now."

Nygel laughed. "Sometimes I forget."

She was looking intently into his eyes and he looked away, embarrassed by her scrutiny. He felt he had said too much, exposed too many of his deepest fears and insecurities, and it would reduce him to an object of pity. But Kira's eyes were not scornful; no, they radiated a warm understanding and approval of what he had said.

"Nygel, for some reason I knew you were going to say something like that, and I'm glad that you did."

Nygel raised his eyebrows. "Something like what?"

"Something honest and real. Guys like you don't grow on trees, in case you didn't know. You're openly genuine, have a great smile, and . . ." She stopped, reached over and touched his face gently with her hand. Nygel stopped breathing. He had not anticipated a moment as intimate as this on their first night out. As she stroked his cheek he picked up the scent of the perfume she had dabbed on her slender wrists, and he nearly swooned under the power of his heightened sense of smell. He had another heightened sense, he realized with a mixture of dread and delight; at any other time he might have been thrilled about it, but not here, not now, not so close to Kira on their first date! Simply put, Nygel realized he had—no other way to put it, he realized— a heightened urge for sex.

Yes, he could feel his body temperature rising higher and higher...

"Nygel? Are you okay?"

He couldn't speak; he could only feel his body temperature rising, his heartbeat accelerating, and he felt all his muscles (all of them, he thought in horror) stiffen alarmingly. If he stayed here one second longer, he knew the inner seam of his pants would split under the pressure of his ever-growing—

"Nygel! What's the matter?" she asked—almost shouting, really—and heads turned to see what was going on at their table.

"I'm sorry," he gasped, "I gotta— I gotta go to the bathroom."

Without thinking, he grabbed the white linen napkin from under his knife and spoon, and used it to cover the mammoth tent that formed in his khakis as he trotted to the men's room in the back of the restaurant.

It was vacant—good, he thought with vast relief—and once inside the tiny restroom, he locked the door, unzipped and dropped his pants, and finally rolled up his shirt sleeve. Nygel glanced at the mirror; once he wiped the sweat off his face, he saw the irises of his eyes were changing from brown to brilliant orange.

"Compass, activate! What's goin' on with me? I've had major wood before, but this is ridiculous!"

Compass activated in an instant. *Diagnostic medical scan complete. Hormone levels rising from pheromone release from the opposite sex.*

"Compass, can you stop the hormonal reaction," Nygel asked as his spike bones started to appear out of his forearms and calves.

Negative, this unit can not control the hormonal reaction. Subject must regain control of hormone production.

Okay, okay," Nygel muttered, then sat down on the closed toilet seat to regain control of himself. He closed his eyes and began to meditate, trying to calm down as quickly as possible, before his whole night was ruined by this mutated sexual impulse.

It took a minute or so for Nygel to center himself and begin to feel his spike bones submerge back under his skin, and his irises return to their normal brown color. It took another few minutes for his muscles to loosen up—all of them, thankfully!

Nygel put his pants back on and looked at the mirror above the sink. He noticed a sheen of perspiration on his face, but at least he wasn't sweating bullets anymore. He went to the sink to splash cold water on his face. The water pipes banged when he turned on the faucet, but as he leaned over the sink and cupped his hands full of the ice-cold water, he realized it wasn't the pipes making the racket.

It sounded like gunfire, and it was coming from the heating vent in the far wall of the restroom. Nygel turned off the faucet and listened. Some yelling followed, and then there was a sudden silence. He stepped closer to the vent to see if he could hear anything else. More gunfire erupted. He did not like this at all. It seemed to be coming from upstairs, then he heard the sounds of heavy footsteps running right behind the wall—there were stairs there, he realized, leading to the restaurant offices.

Suddenly more gunshots rang out and there was screaming on the floor of the restaurant.

"Compass, rift-port to my location and bring the sonic sword in transport," Nygel commanded. Compass locked onto the neural implant interface device as it magnetized the sonic hilt to itself. It then opened a spatial fissure in Nygel's bedroom clothes closet.

Nygel hated this, and Kira would hate him for blowing their date, but . . .

Nygel cursed and gave the next order. "Bio-armor."

The neural metal implant activated, causing Nygel's clear plasma to flow out and encase him in his own fluid. As it spread over his body, it hardened into a glowing blue body-shell that was Knight Seeker's protective suit.

A circular blue field appeared before him and from inside it, Compass emerged with the sonic sword in tow. The warrior grabbed the sword and attached it to the magnetic strip on his leg, while Compass assumed its place on top of the neural implant interface device. Then he fled the restroom, not giving a thought nor care to who might see him exit from where Nygel Spinner had entered. Lives were at stake here.

Everything had changed in the restaurant from when he had left it. The music had stopped, replaced by the roar of gunfire and shattering glass and screaming people. With all the chaos, Knight Seeker could easily have made his way to the center of action without being noticed. However, a better form of stealth was needed, so using his spike bones, he scaled the wall and was up to the ceiling in no time.

Once he had a full view of the restaurant floor from three stories above, the Seeker saw who was in the gunfight: rival gangs of Hispanics and Asians. The diners had taken cover under the tables and booths while bullets were flying about. With enormous relief, he saw the tip of Kira's shoe hiding under their booth table, so she was all right for now.

Then his eyes fell on a tall and slender Hispanic male hiding behind a metal pillar, a large shotgun in his hands. "Hey, Chen, you and your people started this drug war, and I'll be damned if I give up my turf to you!"

A voice behind the bar laughed. "*Your* turf, Papi?"

"Yes, *our* turf," Papi shot back. "We rule this area, and there's no way you and your boys are going to roll in here and take it over!"

He fired at the bar behind which the Asian gang (six in that gang, the Seeker observed) had taken cover. The Asian gang returned fire, hitting the pillars with bullets sprayed in every direction by their Uzis. It was a bloodbath. Within seconds, Papi's gang had dwindled down to four men including himself.

"Papi, you should have taken the offer, now we're gonna have to kill you," Chen shouted, then opened fire once again.

Knight Seeker knew he had to stop the melee before innocent people were hurt. But how? He looked over the width and length of the restaurant below, until he got an idea. "Compass, patch me into the stereo speakers."

Compass instantly established a remote transmission link with the microphone receiver of the sound system, and signaled an okay when it was ready.

The next moment, a voice boomed over the restaurant's speakers, startling the diners and thugs alike: *"Uninvited guests, leave now or you all shall pay."*

Everyone looked around to see where the dark and ominous voice came from. Most looked to the glass-walled sound booth, but it appeared to be empty.

From behind one of the bar's cash registers, Chen shouted, "Who dares to interfere in the business affairs of Lord Sage!"

There was a moment of silence. Then one of the thugs looked up and spotted a muscular figure that actually seemed to be clinging to the ceiling. The dark blue-and-gold figure looked down at him and pressed his index finger to the mouth of his mask to silence him.

"Hey, Papi, lets get out of—" the thug yelled, but he was suddenly silenced by plasma webbing that shot down from the ceiling and tied him to the pillar he had been standing beside, covered his mouth and upper body in the sticky, powerfully strong substance.

Papi shouted frantically, "Caesar, Caesar! What's up, bro?" When he looked over to his accomplice, now wrapped from head to toe in the plasma netting, he shouted, "What the hell? Caesar, what happened to you, dawg?"

Then he followed Caesar's terrified eyes upwards to the ceiling and for the first time saw the blue-and-gold crusader, waving in a wicked parody of a greeting. He watched the warrior shoot something from his forearm that appeared to be a spike, and then whoosh to the opposite wall of the restaurant so fast that it was only a blur.

When Knight Seeker was on the other side of the room, he dispensed another plasma net that covered one of the Asian thugs, spinning him around until he dropped to the floor, stuck.

"What the—" Chen said as he watched his own men being immobilized left and right.

"I see that you're having the same problem I'm having, Chen," Papi said.

A shouted conference between the two gang leaders came up with a joint decision: to beat it out of Dexter's quick. "Apparently we have a common enemy here," Chen shouted. "I think it would be wise for us to combine our efforts to get out of this in one piece."

"But how do I know you can be trusted, Chen?" Papi said as he shot his gun at the ceiling. He missed the blue and gold warrior, who swooped past him in a flash.

Then, without warning, another one of Papi's goons was picked off by Knight Seeker. The hero used his calf spike-bones in bungee-fashion to lower his body to floor level, then quickly grabbed his prey, picked him up and batted his gun away. While the goon was up off the floor, the hero threw him against the wall, knocking him out cold.

"Trust is irrelevant at this time," Chen shouted to Papi as he peeked out from behind the bar counter to take aim at the swiftly moving hero.

But Knight Seeker moved too quickly to be an easy target, bolting from corner to corner of the restaurant until he was only a blur of blue and gold streaking across the vast room.

One of Chen's three remaining men looked up to the ceiling and saw the hero, but the vigilante already had a lock on the thug. The plasma net launched at the same moment the thug opened fire. Some of the bullets made it through the webbing, and two of them impacted the hero's armor. Luckily, the bullets only dented the armor on his chest area, which did hurt a little, but it wasn't anything as dangerous as being hit with heavy artillery, which would definitely hurt—possibly even kill him.

The Seeker's instincts kicked into high gear as he quickly moved down to the floor, scooped up the plasma-netted thug, and heaved him easily out the storefront window of the restaurant. The shattering glass could be heard all over the place, and the hero quickly scuttled back up to the ceiling. He took no special pleasure in throwing criminals out windows; it just seemed the most efficient way of clearing out the debris and saving some lives.

"He's picking us off one at a time!" Chen said as he cautiously stepped out from behind the bar with his Uzi in hand. "We don't have a choice!"

"You're right, I'm coming out," Papi said as he and his partner came from behind the pillar.

They both aimed at each other, and the rest of Chen's men emerged, taking aim at Papi and his partner. Papi wanted to blow Chen's head off, but he knew now was not the time to let feelings get in the way of business.

"Let's whack this super-weirdo before we all wind up in jail tonight," Papi said. "Five-O will be in here before you know it."

Both drug-dealing gangs stood back to back with their fingers on the triggers, ready to shoot at anything that remotely came into range. But outside the restaurant, a more compelling drama was beginning to unfold.

CHAPTER 19
WHEN CHOICES ARE MADE

IN THE graveled parking lot next to Dexter's Bar and Grill, a man stepped out of a black limousine. He walked in the early evening twilight to the sidewalk where Chen's goon lay in a heap of broken glass. The goon struggled to break through the plasma netting that bound his arms and legs like a cocoon, as he remembered only dimly being thrown through the restaurant window. But he stopped cold at the sight of the high-polished black leather shoes that stood inches from his face.

Sage looked down at the man on the sidewalk, and from the deep reservoir of his accumulated knowledge, he extracted an apt expression: "Baby faw down, go boom?"

The goon's blood froze. The streets were eerily quiet, and for the first time in his life he wished he could hear the sound of a police siren rushing to the scene.

"Lord Sage, many apologies," he croaked. "Knight Seeker did this to me. He's inside the restaurant right now."

Sage heaved a great, weary sigh and squatted down to his henchman's side. He shook his head sadly and grabbed the webbed-wrapped goon by the throat with his clawed hand.

The goon started choking as he felt his whole body being lifted off the sidewalk. He had the presence of mind to fire the Uzi still in his hands, but the clip was out of bullets.

"Your apology is accepted," Sage said in a quiet voice, "but sadly, you have failed me. And you know the penalty for failure."

Sage squeezed his henchman's neck slowly, so he could enjoy the mounting fear and pain that wracked his victim's face. He was most amused by the wheezing, strangled sounds that left the goon's open mouth.

"*G-g-gack!*"

"Hmm, what's that?" Sage inquired in polite tones. "'Gack'? I'm afraid I don't know that word, but then there's so much about this world and time that's still new to me."

He chuckled as the goon fought for life, his webbed body shaking convulsively in the light of the shattered restaurant window. Sage enjoyed it so much that he was almost reluctant to deliver the *coup de grace* by crushing the little worm's Adam's apple. But crush it he did, then threw the goon by his twisted neck into the windshield of a parked Buick LeSabre.

It's the little things in life like this, he thought, *that make me truly happy*.

* * *

"You guys ready to kick some ass?"

The shouts of "Yeah!" filled Dexter's as the drug dealers cocked their weapons and aimed in a dozen different directions.

Knight Seeker knew if he made one false move, a stray bullet might hurt an innocent customer or member of the restaurant staff. He couldn't risk that.

"Compass, reestablish link with the sound system," he commanded.

Connection reestablished.

Once again the crime fighter's voice boomed over the restaurant's speakers: "*It's about time you guys put aside your differences. Makes me kickin' yah butts a lot more enjoyable.*"

The hoods looked and cursed in a dozen directions, their brows creased in frustration as they tried to locate the crusader.

Then, before they could see where he had come from, the warrior stood at the main door in a straddled stance, smirking as he asked, "Looking for someone?"

"Kill him now!" cried Chen.

"Diamond Shield," the hero commanded, and immediately four pieces of the blue translucent electron shield merged together to form the protective barrier.

Good timing, he thought as the shield appeared, a mere second before the bullets started flying towards him. They smashed into the shield, shimmering for an instant as they absorbed the impact, then fell to the ground harmlessly.

"Guys, quit tickling me," he said.

The drug gang exhausted their ammunition and frantically started to reload their weapons.

"You finished? Now it's my turn," the warrior said as he deactivated the electron shield. With the help of Compass, he aimed at one of Chen's goons with the gold gauntlet on his right arm, raising the barrel-shaped gold rods and shooting a plasma net that wrapped his target in a tightly packaged cocoon. The goon fell to the floor and screamed, "I can't move!"

But the hoods were still busy reloading their weapons. They fired again at Knight Seeker, but he took a flying leap over them all in a full somersault, landing on top of the bar smack in the middle of the restaurant, then quickly reactivated his shield. The thugs fired again, breaking bottles and glasses in the hanging shelves over the bar but not so much as making a crease on the Seeker's costume.

"Help me," a voice below croaked. It was the bartender hiding behind the bar.

"Lay low," Knight Seeker ordered, then picked up a full bottle of rum. He flung the bottle at the four remaining thugs, hitting one of Papi's men square in the forehead.

One down, three to go.

He deactivated his shield again and leaped off the bar, twisted in the air, and landed behind the three remaining goons. Chen was one of them and tore out of the bar while the Knight took on the other two—Papi and one of Chen's goons—in hand-to-hand combat.

Chen's goon tried to blast him point-blank with his Uzi, but Knight Seeker grabbed the weapon and crushed the barrel of it, rendering it useless. Panicked, the goon tried to kick him in his walnut sack, but was blocked by the Seeker's hand.

"You don't even want to go there," he muttered, then bitch-slapped the thug, sending him flying backwards into the bar head-first, knocking him out.

Now it was Papi's turn to panic. Seeing his comrade-in-crime getting his lights punched out put the fear of God in him. He tried to bash the Seeker with the butt-end of his shotgun, but it was blocked by the hero's gold gauntlet. A solid uppercut to Papi's belly sent him doubled over, coughing so hard he thought he was going to hack a lung.

"Take a seat, Papi," the hero said as he pushed the goon backwards into a chair. "You've done enough for one night."

"What're you gonna do to me?" he shouted.

"Watch," Knight Seeker said, and webbed him to the chair.

He scoped out the restaurant and saw movement as the customers cautiously began to get up from under their tables.

"Everyone stay where you are," he ordered. "This isn't over yet."

He caught a glimpse of Kira as she looked up from their booth, her faced etched with fear. At that moment he wanted more than anything to whisk her out of this place, but he wasn't finished here just yet.

"Where are you, Chen?" he shouted, turning quickly away from Kira. "Don't make me play hide and seek. You'll just tick me off even more than you already have."

As he scanned the restaurant, a low voice bellowed from the front of the restaurant, "If I were you, I wouldn't worry about him when you have me to contend with."

Knight Seeker wheeled around and blinked at the stranger standing at the open doorway. Just another hood, he thought, only this one looked more stylish than the others. He liked the dude's black leather trench coat with the patchwork of dark colors on the chest, but he didn't like the eyes that met his. They were cold as ice. Still, he shouldn't have any problem dispatching this troublemaker.

"So I see someone else has joined the party," he said in a mocking tone.

The stranger smirked and stepped into the restaurant. "Well, I wasn't invited, so I decided to crash it anyway. I see you've been busy with my servants."

"'Servants'?" Knight Seeker laughed as the stranger looked about the restaurant at the hero's handiwork, nodding appreciatively at the thug cocooned in plasma netting in the chair. Then he remembered something that Chen had shouted a bit earlier: *"Who dares to interfere in the business affairs of Lord Sage!"*

"I think," the stranger said, "you will learn the price for interfering."

"You must be Sage," Knight Seeker said. "So where's Parsley, Rosemary and Thyme?"

The stranger's smirk disappeared, his face now flashing with undisguised anger. "I see you need a lesson in manners," he said, and reached inside his leather jacket, pulling a sword from its concealed sheath. The blade of the sword, Knight Seeker observed, had an opening in the middle that was occupied with a large, clear crystal that looked like a flat diamond. But seconds after it was unleashed, the crystal began to glow with a brilliant white light.

"Well, you've got my attention," Knight Seeker said. "But if you're gonna step up to me, you'd better have some skills." He unholstered the sonic sword hilt from the magnetic strip on his hip. "Blade," he murmured, and a ball of energy—no bigger than a quarter—appeared at the clawed handle and spiked downwards to form the silver blade of the sonic sword.

"And I'm impressed," Sage admitted, stepping closer to Knight Seeker. "Another producer of magic. You will make a fine addition to my new empire. And you can start by calling me Master."

Knight Seeker laughed in his face as he met Sage in the center of the restaurant floor. "You've got another thing coming if you think I'll join your crew."

Both of them had just about had enough playing around. Sage sized up the situation: he wanted control of the drug traffic in the metropolitan areas of New Jersey and New York, to consolidate his power and enrich himself; this strangely costumed crusader who stood before him, however, seemed determined to stop him at all costs.

Actually, Knight Seeker had another goal in mind: to get back to Kira and finish the date he had planned for two weeks. This leather-coated freak who stood before him with a jeweled sword poised at the ready was ruining his plans. The fact that Kira was cowering under the table just pissed him off even more.

"Join my empire, Knight Seeker," Sage said in a low voice, "and I will make you my avenging warrior. You can have power, money, and as many women as your heart desires. I will only make this offer once. If you do not accept it, I will destroy you where you stand."

Knight Seeker yawned. "Blah, blah, blah. Okay, here's my offer: you'll be my lap dog and bring me the paper and my slippers every morning. Just bring it on, Oregano, I don't have all night."

Lord Sage clenched his teeth in fury. "So be it," he said, taking aim with the mighty demonic sword in his hand.

He was poised to slash in a diagonal stroke, but Knight Seeker took a quick step back to avoid the flashing blade. He countered with a slashing attack of his own, but Sage was a skilled warlord and blocked the sonic blade, locking both weapons in place.

Knight Seeker tried to bully his strength on the blocked blade, but it was not so easy. Sage could not believe how much strength his opponent had in one hand; he immediately realized this would require magical help. He murmured a chant—ancient words that gathered a ball of kinetic energy in his other, silver-gloved hand, then threw it with mighty force at the Knight's belly. The force of the kinetic blast sent Knight Seeker flying backwards fifteen feet with sledge-hammer force, landing flat on the floor and wondering what the hell just knocked the wind out of his lungs.

"Man, what the heck was that!" he groaned in confusion.

Unknown power, Compass replied.

Sage gaped at the sprawled superhero getting up from the floor, surprised that anyone could shake off the effects of the kinetic blast so quickly. Most men would have died from such a force of energy! *Then he'll get another one,* Sage thought with a shrug, and sent another blast of energy at his still-stunned adversary. But before the destructive k-ball left his hand, Knight Seeker made a fist with his left hand and pushed his thumb into his forefinger and took aim at a pillar nearest him, launching the spike-bone. It instantly bolted and yanked him to safety six feet up the pillar, and not a nanosecond too soon: the k-ball shot past him and blew up a video driving game right behind him. Screams went up under the tables and booths of the restaurant as exploding debris from the video game flew to all corners of Dexter's Bar & Grill.

"Everyone stay down!" the Seeker shouted, and the screams dissolved to sobs and whimpers. Now the hero took aim with his sonic blade.

"Sonic Shock," he commanded. The gold claws cupped the blade like a sonar dish, and then a wave of blue energy leapt from the sword at lightning speed toward its target. Sage was just as quick; he back-flipped out of the shock wave's path as the floor tiles on which he was standing instantly shattered and crumbled on impact. Now it was Knight Seeker's turn to gape. *No way!* he thought, but he had seen it with his own eyes—a man outrun the shock wave of the sonic sword. Then again, he reminded himself, he had only used fifteen percent power. He didn't dare go over that power level with so many innocent civilians around; he was still unsure how much destructive power a high-powered sonic shock could have when unleashed.

Sage looked up in disbelief at his nemesis clinging to the pillar. He taunted him with a gesture to come down, as one might signal to a dog.

"Glad to oblige," the Seeker muttered as he jumped down, his sonic sword aimed to slice down the middle of the trench-coated goon. But Sage was just as quick, blocking sonic sword with his own sword—the Soul Taker. It was more of a struggle than he had expected, and had to use both his hands on his weapon to force back the advancing Knight.

Both swords were about to meet again, and Sage noticed his servant Chen behind the hero with his gun ready to pump holes into the warrior's head.

The crusader heard the gun trigger as Chen pulled back on it and saw Sage's diverted attention.

"Behind you!" Kira Maru's voice rang out.

The crime fighter quickly moved out of the way of the bullets which hit Sage in the chest and head. Sage fell to the ground. In only seconds, Sage's human appearance changed to an almost reptilian appearance.

"What the—" the hero said as he knelt close to Sage. "You aren't so pretty, are you, pal?"

Since the drug lord was evidently dead, he thought it was now time to take care of Chen, which should be a piece of cake after battling this freak. But just that moment he heard police sirens getting closer to the restaurant—maybe only a few blocks away.

Knight Seeker turned to Chen and said with a smile, "Guess you're next, huh?"

Chen backed up in a panic as the hero got up and made his way towards him. He had nowhere to go, and the cops sounded like they were just about there. There was also the fact that his employer and master was on the floor apparently dead. Chen quickly grabbed the person nearest him—the woman who had called a warning to Knight Seeker and prevented Chen from killing him.

Kira struggled for a moment. The hero was about to run over to assist, but he stopped instantly in his tracks as he noticed Chen grabbing the back of her hair and pointing the gun at her.

"Get off me," she yelled as she tried to elbow Chen in his face. He blocked her arm with the hand with which he held the Uzi.

"Stop it! Unless you want a hole in your head," Chen threatened as he held the barrel of the gun to her temple. She stopped struggling, knowing she had no more control in the situation, knowing that fighting this goon might cost her own life.

"Let her go now Chen, or so help me—" the hero threatened as he aimed the sonic sword at the thug.

"Put down the sword hero, or risk killing the both of us," Chen said.

Knight Seeker knew he was right; Chen had a wild-eyed look that didn't bode well for Kira's safety. No telling what this desperate nut-job would do, and besides, Knight Seeker knew he hadn't yet mastered the sonic sword. Better not take any chances, he told himself.

"You win," he said, deactivated the sword and putting the hilt back on its magnetic strip. "For now."

"Good answer," Chen said. "Now, me and bright-eyes here are gonna back outa this place nice and easy…"

"You're not leaving here, Chen, get that through your head right now. Let her go, or I promise you this: if you harm her in any way you will pay."

Chen laughed crazily, the barrel of his Uzi poking into Kira's cheek. "Such big talk, Mr. Seeker. Why do you care about this lady, huh?" He licked her right cheek while keeping one eye steady on the Knight standing only ten feet from him.

Kira looked like she wanted to spit in Chen's face, but she was at his mercy and turned her face away from him.

As for Knight Seeker, his steady resolve had broken the instant he watched the slimeball lick Kira's face. Some primal protective instincts kicked into gear and without realizing it, his hand shot out in front of him and made a fist. The spike-bone protruded out of his right forearm, pointing in Chen's direction.

"Let her go now! Don't force me to act. I'm begging you," the hero said.

"Oh, so you beg to him and not to me?" a voice from behind him spoke. "My word, where do you place your loyalties?"

Momentarily startled, Knight Seeker jerked his head around and could not believe what he was seeing. It was the supposedly dead drug lord, Sage, no longer reptilian but back to his formerly vital-looking self. As he got back onto his feet, brushing the dust from his legs, the hero pivoted slightly to his side to keep his attention on both his adversaries. "My loyalties are with the people I have to protect from the likes of you two," he said.

"So be it," Sage said plainly.

"Let her go now," the Knight repeated, his voice deepening in anger.

Then both Sage and Chen started speaking in Mandarin. Nygel had no idea what they were saying.

But Compass translated the speech and displayed it in the Knight's visual cortex: *"Kill her now,"* Sage said.

"Yes Master, I shall follow your will," Chen replied.

Once he understood that, the warrior cried out, "No!"

Chen smiled as he took aim with the Uzi, and Knight Seeker reacted with lightning-fast speed: the spike-bone launched with extreme velocity and embedded itself into Chen's head, making a small crunching sound as it broke through his skull.

"Omigod!" Kira screamed.

Chen's crazy grin disappeared and in its place was the frozen look of the brain-dead. Kira kept screaming, no longer words but keening wails of horror. Knight Seeker quickly removed the spike-bone from Chen's head. Anxiety hit him full-force: his breath grew shallower and his heart pounding inside him and he commanded himself, *Keep it in control!*

Kira cringed as she looked at Chen's motionless body. Scared out of her wits, she looked as if she thought her time on earth was over.

Chen started to fall backwards, the gun still in hand with his finger on the trigger. The Uzi hit the ground first, firing a single bullet on impact.

The stray bullet found a target.

People screamed in horror, and among the shriek's one man's voice shouted over them in anguish, "No, no! My God, no! She's dead!"

That voice struck terror in the Knight's heart because it was familiar. He took his attention off Sage and Kira for a second, turning to locate the voice coming from under a table on the far side of the restaurant. There was his Art History teacher, Mr. Zimmer, cradling his murdered wife in his arms.

"Oh no, that can't be," the Knight said as he sunk down to the floor on his knees, his head downcast in utter shame. It was bad enough that he had to kill Chen, but now an innocent bystander was killed in the process.

Appreciative clapping could be heard coming from one person on the other side of the restaurant. "So much for the people you 'protect'," Sage laughed. "Looks to me like you are the predator. Face it, Knight Seeker, you are like me—a beast and a killing machine. Serve me by my side and nothing on this earth shall stand in the way of what we may accomplish."

But he heard no words, only a droning noise coming from trench-coated drug lord—so profound was his grief. The Knight looked up at Kira Maru and read the shock, confusion and fear on her face. She looked on the verge of tears, not understanding anything that had happened, so she backed away from the blue and gold crusader.

Now he turned back to gaze at Mr. Zimmer weeping over the lifeless body of his beloved wife. As he looked at the blood spreading across the professor's shirt from the open wound in his wife's head, he, too, felt a blood-red rage clouding over all his thoughts, his only desire cold, swift vengeance. Still, he gathered what little self-control he had left and got up from the floor to face Warlord Sage.

"I am nothing like you," he said. "I don't kill to gain power or for the sheer pleasure of it."

"No? I must say it was fun, more fun than—" He paused momentarily to extract some appropriate expressions from his brain bank of stolen memories. "—a barrel of monkeys, and on the whole, I'd say it was a pretty good floor show. And thank you for killing Chen for me. You saved me the trouble and a possible prison sentence—not that any prison could hold the likes of *me*. Until next time we meet, Knight Seeker . . ." With a wave of his hand over his face, he disappeared in a cloud of smoke.

"Sage, get back here!" the hero shouted.

But the only reply was a collective shudder of fear from under the restaurant tables.   Knight Seeker retracted the spike bones into his forearms and went to Mr. Zimmer's side. Kira followed closely behind to offer support to the professor.

As they approached, Mr. Zimmer looked up and said, "I don't think she felt anything. But now she is at peace . . . and cold . . ." He looked directly at Knight Seeker, his face full of sorrow. "Why did this happen?"

"I . . . I don't know," the warrior said in a quiet voice.

The professor's expression changed from sorrow to bitter anger as he placed his wife's body to the floor and stood up to face Knight Seeker.

"You don't know? That's your answer? That's all you have to say to me and our children? All this happened because you got involved, and now that you are involved, you damned well better take care of your business! You hunt this bastard Sage down and you destroy him! You go and finish what you started. Don't let anything stand in your way. You finish what you started! You finish what you started," the professor said, beating his fists on the Seeker's chest plate. Finally he collapsed, sobbing with grief into his dead wife's hair, as little by little other patrons of the restaurant crawled out from under their tables and gathered at his side to offer comfort

"I . . . I," the hero stuttered. He simply didn't know what to say to a man in such pain and anguish. And Mr. Zimmer's words—"You finish what you started"—echoed in his ears.

Something similar was said to him by Aracnus, the alien cop who aided him in becoming Knight Seeker. But what did Aracnus mean, exactly? He had died before he was able to explain.

Knight Seeker turned to leave as he heard the Newark Police with Captain Higgins arriving on the scene.

"Wait—" Kira shouted.

Knight Seeker looked back to see her running to his side. "I have to leave now," he told her. "This whole thing is out of my control now."

"I just wanted to thank you for saving me from that guy. He would have killed me if you hadn't come to my rescue. I'll tell the police what happened. And if you need a friend to talk to . . ." She suddenly flashed that smile he loved so much. "I'll be here for you."

He grinned back at her. "You know you're playing with fire, and I don't want you to get burned."

"So I'll wear my asbestos suit," she replied.

He smiled back, touched her face gently with his bio-armored hands, then instructed Compass to form a rift-port. Before everyone's disbelieving eyes, a doorway of shifting clouds appeared and Knight Seeker stepped into the rift-port—and was gone.

When Captain Higgins arrived with his police force, he grilled everyone who witnessed the acts of the so-called superhero. Even Kira gave her own rapturous account of the amazing and brave Knight Seeker and how he had saved her life. But there were mixed views on that score; Mr. Zimmer did not want to press charges against Knight Seeker at that time, but it was obvious he didn't view the hero in such glowing terms. Still, he knew that only Knight Seeker could avenge his wife's death, not the police. As Kira went in the back of Dexter's Bar & Grill to search for Nygel, Captain Higgins ordered his deputy to post a state-wide alert for the vigilante to be brought in for questioning.

"Captain," the deputy interjected, "shouldn't our top priority be finding this Sage guy?"

"I want them both," the captain shot back.

CHAPTER 20
REVELATIONS

WHEN COMPASS folded dimension, the rift-port opened at the top of a warehouse roof. From it emerged Knight Seeker, first checking to make sure no one else was around, then ordering the bio-armor to dematerialize. In a flash of red light, the bio-armor broke down to energy practicals that lightly blew across the rooftop like fine, sparkling ash and scattered to the four winds.

Nygel kept seeing the deaths of the drug dealer, Chen, and Mr. Zimmer weeping over the lifeless body of his wife. He tried to imagine other scenarios that could have prevented the deaths from happening. Other questions plagued him: why was he Knight Seeker? Why did he feel so compelled to kill Chen? True, Chen would have killed him, but still—

Suddenly he slumped to his knees and cried out, "Why me? Why did I kill! I am not supposed to kill! Oh God, I'm a monster. What the hell is happening to me?"

Tears streamed down his face and onto the powerful sword still in his hands. He threw it down and the blade disappeared in a flash of light. He wished he was never at the Hotel Chariot when the two aliens were fighting. If he hadn't stayed late to work that night, none of this would have happened.

"Seeker Spinner, you are fulfilling your purpose," a deep male voice with a British inflection spoke.

Nygel looked around quickly but saw no one.

"Who's there?" he called.

"This is the voice of the unit called Compass. This unit has not communicated with you verbally, because you were not ready to accept the facts of whom and what you have become. This unit will now explain these things to you…"

The alien computer hovered in the air by using its anti-gravity generator. Nygel stared at the onyx-colored device with the gold alien markings on its top surface and said, "You can talk? Why the hell didn't you tell me I'd lose control at Dexter's like that? Now two people are dead because of me!"

"There was no need for this unit to interfere in that situation. This unit only assisted with the targeting. Your instincts guided you on your decision. Your reflexes are attuned to your emotions and at that time your instincts were telling you to decimate your opponent."

"So in other words, a Seeker is a killer or some kind of bounty hunter?" Nygel asked with anger. "In that case, I quit."

"Your assumptions are incorrect. A Seeker is a Space Authority Officer. Their purpose is to hunt down criminals who cause chaos and destruction in this galaxy. The deceased Officer Aracnus, who was of the species known as the Spycon, was a captain of the Seeker Command Task Force in this quadrant of the galaxy—their best Crime Seeker, in fact. Aracnus' DNA combined with your human DNA at the subatomic level, which caused a mutation in your internal structure. Although your outward appearance remains the same, your internal structure has been altered to that of a hybrid type of humanoid."

Nygel stood up and began to pace the roof as he processed all this. "So I posses all his abilities . . . even the hunting instincts? My God, what has he done to me?"

"Since your human DNA is simpler to mutate than Spycon DNA, it gave you greater enhancements than any Seeker that has ever existed. Your muscle structure is stronger, and you have a better bone density. Your hearing, vision, and sense of smell have been enhanced as well. In essence, you have become the ultimate crime hunter or Seeker."

"Oh, please," Nygel sighed. "Aracnus definitely made a big mistake in choosing me. I bet before this night is over the police will have a bounty on my head."

Compass said nothing in reply, which didn't thrill Nygel too much; he wanted reassurances that everything would work out okay. If the see-all-know-all Compass couldn't tell him that, then he really was in trouble.

He got up and picked the sword hilt off of the rooftop and stuffed it inside his pants pocket. Then he looked up to the hovering alien computer and told it to establish a rift-port back to his home town.

"Location?"

"I don't know, someplace where I can have some time to think. Someplace quiet, like the capitol building complex. No one is around there at this time of night."

When the dimensional rift was created, Nygel hesitated for just a moment, realizing how quickly he had come to accept these new marvels as now a normal part of life. But he had still not accepted the role he was given to play. Would he ever?

He sighed deeply and shook his head, then walked through the clouded rift-port, which closed behind him.

CHAPTER 21
IS THERE A HIGHER PURPOSE?

IT WAS exactly where he wanted to be that serene night. The stars were dim in the city lights, but there was a half-moon shining brightly. The dome of the capitol building reflected the moon's glow, giving it a very tranquil appearance.

Everything was so different at night, Nygel reflected.

As he walked past the capitol complex, he realized he was only about fifteen minutes walking distance from his home. It wasn't nearly enough time to sort out in his head everything that had happened that night—or shake it out of his mind. He turned off at West State Street and headed north on Calhoun Street. It was just a typical, rundown city street badly in need of repairs. The housing developments he passed were not all that desirable, but there were a few homes that looked okay.

There were people hanging out on the street, or taking in the evening breeze as they sat on their porches. Nygel ran a thought across his mind as to what would happen if people saw Knight Seeker walking down the street. He wondered if they would run in fear of his alter ego. The thought had never crossed his mind before tonight, before he actually killed a man...

A police cruiser came down the street. Nygel felt a bit nervous at first, but realized that it wasn't him they would be looking for, it was Knight Seeker. He wondered if he could, if only for a little while, forget he was Knight Seeker, pretend he was just the same old Nygel Spinner. It worked for a brief moment, even put a smile on his face, but then he passed an open window through which he could hear a news report. He heard the gist of it: Knight Seeker was wanted for questioning in connection to a drug shootout at Dexter's Bar & Grill and (this part hurt Nygel most of all) in connection with the death of Mrs. Zimmer.

A black cloud seemed to fall heavily over him at that moment. Nygel was more than haunted by what had happened that night; he felt he had reached a crisis point that he might not be able to overcome.

As if in answer to an unspoken prayer, he looked up and saw he was nearing Shining Light Baptist Church. The lights were on, so there must be a night service taking place, he figured. More than anything he wanted to go inside, rather than wander the streets feeling he was on the run.

But as he walked up the concrete steps to the church, he realized the service was just about over. He decided to go up to the choir loft since most of the worshipers were down on the main floor.

To his relief, there was no one in the choir loft. He just wanted to be alone while he looked at the night sky through the glass dome of the church. Taking careful steps so as not to make the floorboards creak, he found a comfortable seat in the rear and sat down just as the bible reading seemed to be ending. Nygel just wanted to hear some singing to lift his spirits that night.

But Reverend Squire was not finished preaching for the night. He motioned the band to give him a nice little beat to work with, then began speaking. He was famous for telling a story before he launched into one of his songs. This style of ministry made him unique and his services very popular in the city.

"I, I, I, want to,
To share with you a little story that I heard.
And I'm sure that many of us can identify with it. Hehehehe.
A young man who went swimming the other day,
Went on out there into deep water.
His father and uncles were standing there
On the bank.
When they looked up,
This young man was about to drown.
Something had happened while out there trying to swim,
And they saw him going down.
No, this can't happen, not to his family!

The father got excited,
Got nervous,
But the father couldn't swim.
And you know how it is standing by,
Wanting to do something for a child and you can't—
You are helpless!
So the father reached around and it just so happened
There was a rope there.
And he took that rope
and threw it
Hallelujah!
And said, 'son, catch hold of the rope!'
The young man caught the rope,
The father start pulling him in,
but he looked up, and saw that the rope was breaking—
Can I get a witness?
And he cried to his father:
'Father, father,
my rope is breaking!'
The father replied to the son by saying,
'Reach beyond the break, and hold on!'
Look at somebody out there and say,
'Reach beyond the break.'
Come out there and tell somebody,
'Reach beyond the break and hold on!'
And that's all I want to tell somebody:
If your rope of hope is almost broke,
If your rope of faith is almost broke,
If your rope of patience is almost broke,
Just reach,
I want you to tell somebody,
'Reach beyond the break and hold on, hold on, hold on!'"

And the choir sang out, *"Hold on and don't let go of your faith!"*
After that, the night service was finished. Nygel started making his way down the choir loft, feeling a little better. Yet again he had heard something that he needed to hear. It was something that came at the right time in his life. The only thing he had to decide is whether everything that was happening to him

was destiny. Then the other thing he had to think about was his faith in God and his faith in being a Seeker. When he reached the vestibule of the church, he was surprised to see his mother Celine leaving at the same time he was. They almost bumped into each other.

"Nygel! What are you doing here? What happened to your date with Kira?"

"There was some trouble at the restaurant. I got sick anyway and had to leave," Nygel said, telling her only half the truth.

Celine detected a little bit of uneasiness in his face, but said nothing.

"I just needed some time to myself, I don't know. A lot is going on in my life right now and I'm just trying to figure things out," he said to her while people were filing out of the church.

Celine nodded. "Well, you know I am always here for you no matter what."

"Spoken like a true mom," Nygel said with a grin.

She laughed the whole way out the doors of the church, stopping to say goodbye to her friends. When they were outside and alone again, she said, "Continue."

Nygel sighed deeply. "I don't know. It's just things that I have to work out on my own. I'll be okay in time."

"Mr. Independent, as usual. Well, you take care of whatever you need to do. I know you'll always follow your heart and do what is right. You'll just have to trust your instincts and your decisions. They are a part of you, you know."

Nygel stopped on the street, looking very surprised. "You know what? Something else told me the same thing tonight."

"Well, good advice bears repeating," she said. "Come on, I'm parked down here. I'll give you a ride home."

They drove home in silence, but it was an easy silence that two close people can share without feeling uncomfortable. In the space of only one minute, Nygel felt his worries and anxiety settle down to an almost unrecognizable calm. How long had he felt this calm? Not for days, not since—

Since he asked Kira out for a date, two weeks ago.

He realized two things then: how much energy he had expended in worrying over this date going off without a hitch, and the most upsetting thing—how much he screwed it up. What could he tell Kira? That he got scared when he heard the gunshots and climbed out a back window—leaving her to fend for herself? She might buy that, but she sure wouldn't like it. And who could blame her?

What could he tell her?

"Home again, home again, jiggity jig," Celine said, putting the car in park.

When they got inside the house, Celine went straight to bed and Nygel went into the shower to wash away the whole miserable day. Usually he grabbed a snack late at night, but tonight he didn't, so he knew he must be tired. When he stepped out of the shower, he could hear his mother snoring. He didn't need his heightened alien senses to hear Celine's log-sawing, not even in a thunder storm. When Nygel returned to his room, he slipped on his boxers and plopped down on his bed to go to sleep. He didn't know how long he slept—maybe an hour—but he awakened from dreams so vivid and haunting that he awoke in a sweat. The murders of Chen and Mrs. Zimmer again. He couldn't escape it, even in his dreams. He just could not go back to sleep. He had to do something about it, right this moment. Even if it was only to make a plan. He sat on the edge of his bed in the darkness for a moment longer, then switched on his bedside lamp and went to the closet to pull out Compass.

"Compass," he said, "I've decided to take on the responsibility of a Seeker. I will hunt down Sage and take down his drug empire."

"Understood, Seeker Spinner."

"Also, I ask that you keep me in check from killing anyone else. I don't have the right to take a life."

"You are a Seeker. You have the right to take life when it is necessary."

"I don't like the sound of that, Compass, not at all. Well, like you said, I am the higher form of a Seeker. And since I am the user, that means you will have to follow whatever I say, and I order you to restrain me from killing my opponents. Only when I deem it absolutely necessary will I take a life. Understood?"

There was the briefest of pauses before Compass replied. *"This unit shall comply with Seeker Spinner's commands."*

"Good, I'm glad we understand each other."

Nygel put Compass back in the closet and went back to bed and turned out the light. Taking care of that piece of business was a load off his mind, but apparently there was another load he hadn't yet dealt with.

Was it his imagination, or didn't she seem kind of—how to say it—*hot* for Knight Seeker? And this, while she was out on a first date with his alter ego, Nygel Spinner? How do you like that!

Nygel wasn't sure what he thought of it. He felt slightly nuts for being jealous of himself, but the fact was, Kira didn't know he was Knight Seeker. The timbre of his voice was different when he was transformed into the Knight—deeper, more testosterone in it or something—so she wouldn't have recognized his voice. And yet she practically threw herself at that blue-and-gold show-off—

Wait a minute, he reminded himself again, *that's me I'm talking about.*

One the other hand, he reflected, it *was* him she was responding to, whether she realized it or not. It was just another persona, but the same flesh and blood. Maybe she felt a bit guilty for finding herself flirting a bit with Knight Seeker, but after all, he did save her life. *Face it*, Nygel sighed to himself, *Knight Seeker is a stud.*

And maybe she was ticked off at him for ditching her in Dexter's, so she had no qualms about cozying up to the Knight...

Nygel groaned. Now he was definitely wide awake and there'd be no sleeping as long as this matter was unresolved. He reached over to turn on his bedside lamp again, then shuffled back to the closet to retrieve his trusty Compass.

"Sorry to bother you again," he started to say.

"'Sorry'? You need not apologize to the unit, Seeker Spinner."

"Yeah, whatever. Listen, I still need to know what I'm gonna to do about Kira. I know right now she's maybe fuming at me, but maybe, hmm, maybe the Knight may have a chance."

Nygel told Compass to display the city database on his visual cortex, and then accessed Kira's address from that.

"Got it. Now create a rift-port outside Kira Maru's house..."

In a few seconds, the alien computer created the rift-port while Nygel changed into his alter ego. After stepping through the blue-clouded phenomenon, he found himself standing on the sidewalk outside Kira's house in Hamilton Township, New Jersey. With no street lights, the neighborhood was fairly dark, and at this hour most homes had their porch lights off. The half-moon still shone in the night sky, and away from the city lights he could clearly see the stars. As he stood there in the quiet darkness, he wondered if one of those twinkling beauties was the sun of Spycon, Aracnus' home planet. In a way, it was Nygel's home planet as well, since Aracnus' blood flowed in his veins.

The portal closed behind him, and he now looked at Kira's house. It was a nice two-story dwelling, like many on this street, but it was the only house with a light glowing in a corner upstairs window. He somehow knew that was Kira's bedroom; at this late hour she would also have been too restless to sleep, the chaotic events at Dexter's still spinning in her head.

At the corner of the house there was a tree that went right up past the bedroom window. Knight Seeker didn't hesitate; he climbed gracefully up the tree, careful not to make any noise to awaken Kira's parents. He tried to block out the nagging suspicion that he was behaving exactly like a stalker—a fact that became abundantly clear when he reached the second story and watched Kira combing her long, black silky hair. That was when he asked himself, *What the hell am I doing?*

Still, he didn't leave the window. He stayed rooted to the spot, clinging to the tree with his spike-bones as he took in the delectable sight of Kira in an exquisitely embroidered Japanese robe, sitting at her vanity table as she brushed her lustrous hair.

Finally she got up and turned off the light and strolled over to the window. Perhaps she went there because she had heard a noise, or perhaps because she wanted a last, lingering look at the half-moon illuminating the heavens before retiring for the night; Nygel never would find out for sure what drew her to the window just then. But as she opened the window and poked her head outside, she froze as if startled, then quickly stepped back from the window. Knight Seeker didn't move, didn't breathe for the duration. When she returned to the window to look out once more, it never occurred to him that she had seen him; or rather she had caught a glimpse of gold in the tree—a gold that reflected brightly off the moonbeams. But it was the visor she saw most clearly, and she recognized its wearer at once.

"Are you some sort of stalker or something?" she called out.

The Knight stayed perfectly still; he thought maybe she hadn't seen him, only heard a noise and was trying to scare away a suspected voyeur.

"Yo, I'm talking to you," she said, a hint of teasing in her voice.

"Nah, I'm not a stalker. That's not my deal at all. I am a good hunter, though. I just wanted to make sure you were okay after everything that happened tonight."

"I'm not sure if I should be flattered or creeped out," she said. "But I'll play along. Sure, I'm getting along okay, what about you?"

"I'm feeling kinda itchy," the Knight replied. "This tree wouldn't be poison ivy, would it?"

"If poison ivy were a tree, then I'd say maybe. But since it's not, I'd say you're just feeling as jumpy as I am. A definite possibility, considering what we've both been through tonight. Come on in, before one of us catches a cold. It's chilly out now."

"Yeah, okay," he said, and in one quick movement he leapt through her window and landing inside her room.

"Whoa," she said. "That's a nice bit of choreography."

"Thanks," he said, grinning shyly. He suddenly felt very flushed, very excited and very awkward all at once. Would she recognize him now, he wondered?

Her face turned serious for a moment as she looked him over, studying every curvature she could see in the moonlight. "So tell me, any particular reason you came here tonight?"

He hesitated, not knowing what he was about to say. "Like I said, I just wanted to make sure you're all right."

"Uh-huh," she said, looking skeptically at him. "You're a hard man to read with that mask on, you know that? You mind taking it off?"

"I . . . can't," he said, feeling foolish as the words stumbled out of his mouth.

Kira sat down on the edge of her bed and looked thoughtful a moment. "Since you asked how I'm doing, I'll tell you the truth.

What happened at Dexter's scared the bejeezus out of me, but now that I'm safely home, I'm starting to get royally ticked off."

"Ticked off?"

She nodded. "I had a date at Dexter's with this guy tonight. Started out okay, but he takes a potty break and never comes back. I figure he heard the gunfire and hid out in the back of the restaurant or sneaked out a back exit. But does he bother to wait for me outside to see how I am or anything like that? No."

"Maybe he, I don't know, maybe he had an anxiety attack or a bathroom accident—maybe he was embarrassed he didn't come back to save you—"

"And he doesn't call me to explain? I'm not stupid. I can pretty much figure this one out. I think he had second thoughts about the date and ditched me before the gunfire even started."

"He wouldn't do that!"

She gave him a curious look. "How would you know that? You don't know the guy."

"Er, no, but—there's got to be an explanation. Did you try calling him?"

"Why should I call him? He ditched me!"

He knew she was right. But he couldn't tell her *why* he had ditched her and it was killing him. It had been a complete mistake to come here, he realized. He should have just called her the moment he got home and made up some story.

"It's too bad," she went on, "'cause he was one of the good ones—or so I thought. He's kind of goofy—into comic books and superhero stuff, but he's a genuine guy, has a gentle manner, not like most of the guys I meet. He's kind of old-fashioned in a way, it's really sweet. Easy to talk to . . ." Her voice trailed off a bit, and the next moment a curious look came over her face. She looked up at Knight Seeker and said, "Kind of like you."

His heart started pounding in his chest. Had she put two and two together?

"What?" he asked, afraid of what was to follow.

"You're easy to talk to, obviously. I can't believe I've been unburdening myself like this to a, a—what are you anyway? Are you a man or a machine?"

He shrugged, mostly with relief. "A little of both, I guess. I'm a hunter and my instincts are to kill. I don't know yet how much I can control that impulse."

She smiled and touched the bio armor suit, which was smooth to the touch. "I want to meet the man behind the machine, because I know he is no killing machine," she purred.

He was shocked. Was she throwing herself at him, a near-total stranger? This didn't seem at all like the Kira he knew. He stood stock-still as her fingers slid up his left arm, stopping at the metal implant. "Here's the machine part, I guess," she said with a giggle.

He felt beads of sweat forming on his forehead beneath the mask. "Yes, it's called a—"

"Shut up," she said, and glided up to his side, nuzzling his neck, her fingers tracing the outline of his mask as she pressed her lips on his. The moment their lips locked he felt his alien hormones starting to kick into gear. He broke away before the spike-bones emerged as they did before. His breathing started to become heavy, and his temperature started to rise.

When Nygel pushed Kira back gently, she looked at him with a puzzled expression, trying to figure out why he stopped.

"Er, did I do something wrong?" she asked gently.

"No, I just can't. You don't understand. I gotta leave now, I'm sorry. I will carry out my quest and put a stop to this drug war. That is my word to you as a knight."

He commanded Compass to form a rift-port to return home and Kira gaped as she watched the portal form in her bedroom. Before Nygel stepped through it, he looked back at Kira and said, "I will always be around when you need me. You can count on it."

He smiled and stepped through the circular spatial rift. The next moment he was in his bedroom. When the rest of the suit dematerialized, he thought of nothing more than taking down a drug empire the next day. With his heavy heart feeling somewhat lighter, and with a smile on his face, Nygel then went to sleep.

His dreams were mercifully sweet, unsullied by murder or bloodthirsty criminals; they were the dreams Nygel Spinner had before the time he became Knight Seeker, and for that, his unconscious mind was deeply grateful. In one way it was a blessing that he didn't know of the drama being played out that very moment on a quiet block in New York City's East Village. He did not know of the man dressed in black with black hair and orange stripes scaling the side of a high-rise apartment building. He climbed without the benefit of a harness or grappling hooks, only two sets of immense claws that dug into solid bricks as he scaled the forty-six stories to the top.

CHAPTER 22
THE SLAUGHTER

THE BEAUTIFUL woman only pretended to sleep. In a moment she would hear the god-awful snores of the fat man lying next to her, and then she would quietly slip out of bed, get dressed, and tiptoe out of the room—not before picking up the envelope fat with cash on the bedside table, of course. It was the way she always did it and the way the fat man preferred it—to wake up and not see her still there, not having to say, "Beat it, babe." Many of her clients used her like that and she didn't mind; God knows they paid her well enough.

She opened her eyes and looked at the grossly obese man lying next to her, his mountainous belly heaving as he drifted off to sleep. Tony Lucci controlled most of the drug trade in Manhattan, she knew. Once she had foolishly asked him if he spent all his drug profits on the meatball sandwiches he shoved down his throat, and for that wisecrack he took the cigar out of his mouth and ground its burning tip onto her bare breast. A new Porsche made it all better—kind of, anyway—and now in the dark, moonlit room she looked down at the scar from his handiwork. *Bastard*, she thought.

Still, she thought she was still luckier than most girls in The Life, as they called it. Another girl from the same escort agency had been killed just a few weeks ago, found in an abandoned construction site on Fourteenth Street off Union Square. She didn't really understand the newspaper item she had read about it; it said Clarissa had her insides cooked. What did that mean? Like she'd been stuck inside a giant microwave? Or maybe she had been made to drink some awful corrosive liquid like drain cleaner...

She shuddered and slipped out of bed. A girl had to be careful, all right. And she was luckier than most. So far.

In the upstairs living room of the duplex apartment, Tony Lucci's bodyguards and drug dealing cronies were playing poker and drinking beer, as usual. One of them had just lost his shirt, and now he was wondering how the hell he'd ever be able to pay back the thirty grand the other players had stood him for. He was already in debt to three loan sharks for much more than that. He realized that nothing short of every man at the table dropping dead before sunrise would solve his current problem.

He would get his wish.

The crashing sound over their heads stopped the game cold. They all looked up at the skylight, then quickly jumped out of their chairs to avoid the broken glass that showered over the card table. Five pleasantly intoxicated thugs and one miserably drunk one suddenly became stone-cold sober.

"What the—"

"Holy—"

They immediately drew their weapons. One of them ran out the room to get Tony Lucci's security team in the other upstairs room. It seemed an unnecessary precaution; the high-tech security system had instantly activated when the intruder broke through the skylight. Two large metal grates slid into place below the skylight to keep out whoever was trying to get in.

Tony Lucci awoke from the shouts and scuffling noises coming from upstairs. He was just as startled as the naked woman standing frozen as she reached for her panties.

Tony shouted towards the closed bedroom door. "Hey, Joey! Joey!"

"What's happening?" the prostitute gasped. "Tony!"

"How the hell should I know!" he barked at her.

Muffled footsteps outside, then the door to Tony's bedroom suddenly opened. His personal bodyguard appeared in silhouette in the hallway, his automatic pistol at the ready. "Boss, stay here," he said. "We'll handle this."

Upstairs, Tony Lucci's security detail had already assembled in the living room, and the head of security dispatched his men to cover all windows and exit doors. There was a big enough arsenal in the duplex to take down a S.W.A.T. team if necessary, and sixteen men ready to fire. One thing they didn't expect was an intrusion through the already locked and impenetrable skylight security shield. But a terrible metal-on-metal crunching sound overhead told them that they had made a serious miscalculation. As they looked up, the security shield's steel plates were torn apart by what they thought must be a machine—until he saw the massive claws ripping a hole through solid steel. That was the moment when Tony Lucci's crack security team realized they were dealing with something way beyond their job description.

With a streaming flash of black and orange stripes, Tygron dropped to the floor and landed without a sound. He was outfitted differently this time, courtesy of the same jeweler who had designed Sage's gauntlet. On his face was a metal mask with a fearsome cat-like image, with orange mirrored lenses affixed to the eyes holes.

"He's in! He's in!"

He crouched cat-like on the floor before them, his mirrored eyes glowing orange, then shooting sparks. He had the look of a hungry alien predator—a predator who was just waiting for the first bullet to be shot.

One of the gunmen obliged him, firing from behind, but at the first sound of the trigger click, Tygron managed a superb back-flip that put him within two feet of his assailant. Before the gunman could blink, Tygron grabbed his fat throat in his clawed hand and electrocuted him with a blast of his bio-electrical energy. At the same time, he used the firing hand of his would-be assassin to shoot two other bodyguards in the room. Then with a high-pitched howl, Tygron picked up the body of his electrocuted victim and threw him at the other would-be attackers.

They scattered out of the path of the flying corpse, and then opened fire on the intruder. Bullets ripped across the apartment ripping through walls, paintings, and antique furniture— everywhere except at Tygron, who dodged the gunfire as he counted his targets. He opened his hands, outfitted with metal gloves that consolidated his mutant electrical power. The gloves glowed blue, and then, like bolts of lightning, lethal jolts of bio-electrical energy shot from the fingertips. Two gunmen fell dead, their chests blackened from the blasts.

One of the gunmen foolishly squatted next to a fallen comrade. "Andy— no! He killed Andy! Waste that bastard right now!"

As he took aim at the intruder, Tygron fired another lethal finger-bolt at the gunman's chest, killing him instantly. It went on like this, armed men screaming and dying their horrible deaths in quick succession, and after less than a minute of chaotic gunfire, there was no one left to scream.

Downstairs was a different matter.

The naked blonde prostitute was hysterical. "You didn't pay me enough for this! Let me outa here, Tony! Or I swear I'll—"

"Shut up!" he screamed at her, then turned to shout to the door, "Joey! What the hell's goin' on up there?"

"I . . . don't know, Tony. Just stay put . . ."

"You don't know? My whole security detail can't take care of this? What the hell kind of operation am I running anyway!"

"Honest to God, Tony, I don't know what's—"

Joey suddenly stopped. The door at the top of the stairs behind him exploded off its hinges.

"What the hell was that!" Tony Lucci shouted.

"I— I'll . . . check it out," Joey said, then cautiously tiptoed up the stairs. Through the haze of clearing smoke he gazed at what was left of the upstairs. It was difficult to comprehend what exactly he was looking at. What had been a designer showcase living room now looked like a slaughterhouse a day before cleanup. Bodies lay strewn about the floor in pools of blood, many with their organs spilling out of gaping wounds.

"Jesus . . ." he gasped. He felt his gorge rise, but swallowed hard when the intruder suddenly appeared in the demolished doorway. Joey fumbled for his pistol. "What— who the hell are you?" he shouted, trying to target Tygron through the haze.

Tygron didn't answer. He jumped to the top of the door frame, scaled down the wall, and sent a wide high-voltage wave of energy down the stairs, hurling Joey down to the foot of Tony's bedroom door in a twisted heap. Scorched from the blast of bio-electrical current, his face already blistering from the burns, he could barely open his eyes to see Tygron slowly coming toward him.

"What the hell's happening out there! Joey!" Tony shouted from behind the door.

Joey blindly aimed his gun at the approaching intruder. "Don't come any closer or I'll . . ."

"All shall die this night," the dark servant of Warlord Sage said in a strangely lilting, hollow-sounding voice. Then Tygron aimed his finger at the gun in Joey's hand and shot a small charge of electricity at it, making Joey scream and drop his weapon. With one quick movement, the mutant intruder jumped to the bodyguard's side, picked him up off the floor by the back of his shirt, and kicked in Tony Lucci's bedroom door.

Tony had a shotgun ready and fired at the figure swinging at the doorway. Joey yelped in a new agony as the bullet tore into his chest.

"Joey, no!" Tony screamed.

Tygron calmly stepped into the bedroom with the mortally wounded bodyguard in his grip, and disarmed Tony with an electrical pulse that made him drop the shotgun instantly. The naked prostitute was at the window, tearing at the curtains as she desperately tried to find an exit. Tony stepped backwards into his bed and impulsively and uselessly grabbed a pillow for protection. "What do you want? I can pay you anything... just don't hurt me. I'll give you...*her*," he said, pointing at the woman at the window behind him.

"You bastard!" she screamed back at him.

"Take her—she's yours. Kill her, for all I care—"

Tygron did not reply. He took aim with his gloved finger and set fire to the goose down pillow Tony was clutching. Tony screamed and tried to drop it, but the pillow slip was nylon and it melted to his hands in a flaming mass of satin, nylon and goose feathers. Tygron stood impassively watching, the moaning bodyguard still clutched in his clawed grip. As Tony screams became high-pitched howl of torment, he fired another bio-electric pulse that set the silver satin bed sheets ablaze all around the drug lord's corpulent body.

While Tony shrieked in agony, the prostitute sobbed as she frantically unlocked the window and pushed it open. Just as her bare feet fumbled to reach the windowsill, a searing pain paralyzed her to the spot: her hair was on fire.

"Help me!" she screamed, "God help me!" She beat her head against the curtains to put out the flames, but now they too were on fire. The stench of burning hair mingled sickeningly with the smell of Tony Lucci's melting body fat as the hungry flames licked his flabby folds of flesh.

Joey, still alive in Tygron's grip, twisted his neck to sneer at his tormentor, "You will . . . burn in hell for this."

Tygron shrugged. "All shall die this night," he said for the second time that night, then tossed Joey atop Tony Lucci on the flame-engulfed bed. A new howl of agony came from across the room as the prostitute, her body now wreathed in twisted, flaming curtains, hurled herself out the window, pulling the curtains with her. Her screams continued for the entire sixty-three story drop to the pavement below.

Now nothing could be heard in the room but the dry, rattling gasps from the bed as the conflagration consumed Tony Lucci and his bodyguard. Tygron turned and left the room, closing the door behind him. He nodded to himself as he left the apartment, satisfied with a job well done. His master Sage will be pleased.

* * *

Captain Higgins was just wrapping things up at Dexter's Bar & Grill when he got the call about the Lucci gang murders. It was an interstate investigation, since Lucci's business dealings and criminal activity also extended to New Jersey. "Great," he mumbled to his deputy after he finished the call, "Just when I was developing a thirst for an ice-cold beer."

"Hanging around bars will do that," his deputy said. "I can take it from here, Captain."

Higgins headed off to Manhattan and by the time he arrived at Tony Lucci's address on Lafayette Street, police, fire, EMS and news crews were swarming the outside of the building. Two paramedics were lifting a sheet-covered body from the sidewalk to the ambulance—a jumper, Higgins supposed. As he entered the lobby, he overheard nervous residents giving their accounts of what had happened. The accounts were vague at best, since no one actually saw what had happened. The only evidence was gunfire and the screaming heard from the duplex apartment on the top floors. And, of course, there was the fire that set off the alarms and sent a hundred bathrobed or hastily-dressed residents out into the street.

Upstairs was crawling with more police personnel—forensics, and homicide detectives mostly. Captain Martin Brooks of the New York Police Department approached Captain Higgins. They were both dressed in street clothes since neither was usually working this time of night.

"Rich, we got to stop meeting like this," Captain Brooks said. "My wife's getting suspicious."

Captain Richard Higgins nodded solemnly, ignoring the same tired joke Brooks used every time they met at a crime scene. "Yeah. So get me up to speed here, Marty."

"Seventeen bodies. Most of 'em crispy critters."

Higgins stiffened slightly. He never liked that slag term for burn victims, and neither did the fire department personnel, two of whom shot Captain Brooks a dirty look. Some cops used gallows humor to release the tension of a grisly crime scene, but Higgins demanded dignity from his own cops. This time, though, he was on Captain Brooks' turf.

"Seventeen *armed* men, if you can believe," Captain Brooks went on. "Tony Lucci and his goons. Amazing that one person could create so much chaos."

"One person? No way in hell!"

"Rich, the blood trail has only one defined track. The blood on his boots—see that? Even on the walls."

"Whoa. What're we dealing with here?"

"Something very crazy," Captain Brooks said. "Get this: the perp slashed most of their necks using very sharp instruments which the coroner swears look like claws. Even if he was wearing an armored vest, I don't think that anyone could have done this hit job solo."

"Remind you of anything?"

"Damn straight. The Dragon Feather case. Evidence showed one man killed everyone aboard that freighter, then left without a trace."

Captain Higgins nodded. "I'm beginning to get a hunch who did this, and he's been a busy boy tonight."

Brooks waited for clarification, and when none was forthcoming he asked, "Who? You're not thinking Knight Seeker did this?"

"Marty, you're damned near psychic tonight. Let's just say I'm not ruling him out. You know any other vigilantes with the capabilities to do this?"

As Captain Higgins looked over the breadth of Tony Lucci's living room, he thought that he had never before seen such a display of mutilation. The stink of the burned apartment and burned bodies would stay with him for days, he knew, if only in his sense memory. "Where's Tony Lucci?" he asked.

"Big Boy? Still in his bed, charred to cinders. They found him after the fire was put out."

Captain Higgins' jaw muscles clenched as he considered his next move. Only one man he knew could bring in Knight Seeker—maybe. And that was a big maybe.

"I'm going to take a walk around, Marty, check out the rest."

"Enjoy," Captain Brooks said with a smile.

Captain Higgins walked down the long hallway to an empty room untouched by the bloodbath, and closed the door behind him. He needed absolute privacy for this call. He found the number saved in his cell phone directory and hesitated before punching its code key. He hated making this call, but all his other options seemed to have run out.

After three rings, a groggy voice answered on the other end, "Uh, do you have any idea what time it is?"

"Just add it to the bill for services rendered."

"Higgins," the voice said, more awake and more amiable now, "it's been a while."

"Yeah, listen, I need you to bring in someone for me, and I want to keep this quiet, meaning out of the papers." He paused, listening closely to make sure no one was lurking outside the closed door. "I want you to bring in Knight Seeker."

"Now, that's a challenge. A dangerous, possibly life-threatening, *expensive* challenge, I'd say. So what kind of pocket change are we talking about?"

Captain Higgins began pacing the room as he mulled over the question. "Let's just say I can take care of a few, um, 'parking tickets'."

The voice on the other end chuckled softly. Any parking tickets the man had, he could take care of himself. But there were other, more serious charges he was facing—armed assault and kidnapping heading the list—and it was obviously these the captain was alluding to. "Yeah, okay. You want any, uh, special treatment?"

"Just bring him in, Mayhem—alive, please," the captain said, then hung up.

Mayhem lit a cigarette and went to his bedroom window overlooking Fort Dix. Good, he thought; now he had something to focus on, something to get his mind off the crazy dreams that had been haunting his sleep for weeks—dreams of the resurrected warlord who butchered all the other mercenaries as the Dragon Feather made its final approach into New York Harbor. Whenever Mayhem closed his eyes, that was the first thing he saw: Warlord Sage resurrected from the dead in the cargo hold of the Dragon Feather. The scenes played in his mind like a movie montage from hell: the stinking, rotting heap of flesh and bones in the ancient coffin, the skeletal hands gripping a magnificent sword with a crystal set in its blade . . . Malice swinging the sword, lopping off Captain Lu-Wan's head . . . the neon-blue light drifting eerily from the severed head to the red-glowing sword . . . the screams and gunfire echoing inside the freighter as he, Mayhem, the only survivor of the massacre, pulled away from the death ship on a speedboat . . . and finally, the bone-chilling sight of the revitalized corpse standing at the deck of the Dragon Feather, commanding Mayhem with eyes glowing blue: *"Don't go away, Mayhem . . . Take witness of my wonders!"*

Mayhem realized his body was drenched in sweat. The cigarette trembled in his hands as he took another drag. He had no idea who or what Sage was, but he knew evil when he saw it, and he had never before encountered such a dark, evil power.

He put out his cigarette and went back to bed. Maybe he'd manage to get a couple hours of sleep before going to New York City to track down Knight Seeker.

CHAPTER 23
SEEKER ON THE MOVE

WHEN NYGEL awoke the next morning, he checked his answering machine in his room and saw that Kira had left a message. Her voice was mercifully pleasant and leavened with a touch of dry humor.

"Hey, Nygel, it's me, Kira. I figure you were chloroformed and kidnapped in the men's room at Dexter's last night, so when the bad guys release you, please call and let me know how things are . . ."

She went on to tell him in brief detail what had happened at the restaurant that night, including how Knight Seeker had kept her from being harmed. The last thing she told him was about the death of Professor Zimmer's wife.

"I'm sorry, I know you really liked the guy. I'm still in shock over the whole thing. So...let me know where I send the ransom money and I'll talk to you later, okay? Bye."

Nygel smiled. He was glad he talked with her last night—or rather, he was glad Knight Seeker did. It gave her time to consider the possibility that maybe he *did* have a valid reason for ditching her at the restaurant. Of course, he did; he just couldn't tell her the truth, that's all.

As he stared at the message machine, Professor Zimmer's words to Knight Seeker echoed in his head: *"Finish what you started."*

He looked down at the circular bulge in his left forearm that housed the Neural Implant Interface—or N.I.I., as he had come to think of it. He knew that the duty and responsibility of an officer was to protect the innocent and uphold the law for the good of the many. He also knew he didn't have a law degree, let alone space law, but he did have a good conscience and knew the difference between right and wrong. It wasn't rocket science. If he wasn't qualified to fight for right against wrong, then he didn't know who was. And the time to do what was right, was right now.

He picked up the phone and called Rapid Action News to say he was taking a sick day. The dispatcher who answered the phone, Talex Bashi, wasn't at all happy.

"Nygel, no way can you call in sick today. Too much stuff is going on with the murders last night in Manhattan. I need you here. You're booked to go out with Sandy's crew—" He broke away to bark orders to someone to get a van rolling to another story.

"Murders—what murders?" Nygel asked. The only news-worthy murders he knew of were the ones at Dexter's Bar & Grill last night, and that was in New Jersey.

"That drug lord, Tony Lucci and his gang," Talex said impatiently. "Be here in thirty minutes, Nygel."

"All right," Nygel grunted, then hung up the phone and turned on his bedroom TV. Rapid Action News was broadcasting a live report, giving the grisly details of the Lucci gang massacre. As he listened, Nygel started getting dressed and stuffed Compass and the sonic sword in his backpack. He left a hurried note for his mother on the kitchen table, telling her he would be home late tonight, then hustled off to work.

No rest for the weary, he said to himself as he started the ignition.

"You've got that right," his rear-view mirror replied.

Nygel grinned at his reflection. "I haven't heard from you in a while."

"Yeah, I know. But we need to chat."

"I'll say," Nygel sighed as he pulled out of the driveway.

* * *

It took a lot of string-pulling to get Rapid Action News approval to shoot inside Tony Lucci's blood-soaked duplex, but station owner Mike Payne had connections second to none. He also wasn't opposed to greasing city officials' palms to get what he wanted. That didn't mean the various police and fire department personnel were thrilled to see Sandy Castle barge into their crime scene like she owned the place.

"Okay, Max," she told her producer, "see if you can find me a nice blood-spattered wall to stand in front of for this shoot."

"Jeez, Sandy," Max said, abundantly shocked.

"Jeez, yourself. Would you prefer I stand in front of the refrigerator? This is a crime scene, boys, let's show 'em some crime!"

As Nygel was setting up the camera equipment, he discovered that his Spycon blood had given him another unique ability: an enhanced intuition that told him he was being watched. With a conviction of absolute certainty, he turned around and looked out the window and saw a man in the apartment window directly across Lafayette Street looking into the building. Usually, there would be no reason to be suspicious of a man staring at a crime scene—particularly one as notorious as this one. People do it all the time. But this man quickly backed away from the window once he realized he had been observed by Nygel. People don't usually do that unless they don't want to be caught, he thought.

He wondered . . .

Then he told the crew he was going to head back to the van to get set up for the transmission back to the station.

"We got a half-hour," Sandy said, then added with a teasing smile, "What's the matter, Spinner, can't take a little blood?"

"Not if I can help it," he said truthfully.

Max gave him the station cell phone to call him when they were ready, and Nygel headed out the duplex. Once outside, he crossed the street to the building directly opposite and used Compass to gain entry by having the alien device use an override code to open the computerized locking system. Nygel had figured out which floor and most likely which apartment belonged to the mystery voyeur, so he took the elevator to the top floor. Once the elevator door let him out, he told Compass to perform a motion detection scan, figuring that most people were probably at work at this time of day. A movement blip was detected in the apartment that happened to be exactly where Nygel had already determined was most likely the voyeur's apartment.

Bingo.

He knocked on the door and in a moment could hear someone softly creep to the door. He didn't need his enhanced intuition to know that he was being observed through the door's spyhole. Anyone who tiptoed to their door always did that, too.

"Good morning, sir," Nygel began, but the man inside cut him off.

"We don't want any, whoever you are," he said.

A lifetime of living had taught Nygel that the best way to get what you want was to ask for it as nicely as possible. "I'm sorry to disturb you, sir, but I wanted to ask you a few questions about last night."

There was a moment of silence with no answer.

"Look sir, I don't know who you are, and I promise it can stay that way. I will not have reporters or police bother you. I thought you might want to do a civic service by answering a few questions, that's all."

Another long silence, during which Nygel wondered if he had the nerve to command Compass to unlock this door, too. But then he heard the welcoming sounds of the bolt lock unlocking and the chain lock being removed, and the door solely opened to reveal a man in his late fifties. He let Nygel into the apartment. It was cluttered but not messy, just crammed with a lifetime of books, antique furniture, knick-knacks and framed photographs. The furniture was worn but comfortable-looking.

The man closed the door behind Nygel and started talking. He told Nygel that he was sitting at his window last night, as he normally did, and happened to see a man in a black and orange-striped costume climbing the apartment building across the street.

"All the way to the roof. I know this will sound strange, but he appeared to be using long claws. Once he got to the rooftop, he disappeared. All hell broke loose after that, and the intruder started running south, leaping across rooftops. I couldn't believe it."

"And then just disappeared," Nygel finished for him.

"Not just yet," the man said, surprising Nygel a bit. "I'm agoraphobic. Do you know what that means?"

"You, uh, prefer to stay at home?"

The gentleman smiled. "A very diplomatic answer. I have a neurotic fear of open spaces, particularly public places. But it gets so lonely living alone, and it was late, so I figured no one else would be around, so I went up to the rooftop of this building."

Nygel was impressed. "Yeah?" he asked, his eyebrow lifting in interest.

"It's quite a view up there. And as it happens, one of our residents is an amateur astronomer and has quite a nice telescope up there. It's mounted on the ledge and he keeps it under a heavy tarp, but he allows the other residents to use it—respectfully, of course."

Nygel smiled. "Sounds a little foolish to keep an expensive instrument like that up on the roof."

The gentleman shrugged the suggestion away. "It's an old residential building. All the tenants know each other, and the front entrance is well-locked. How did you manage to get inside, may I ask?"

Nygel dropped his jaw in surprise. He wasn't at all prepared for that question.

"Never mind," the gentleman smiled. "You don't look the sort who'd usually break into buildings. Anyway, I managed to find the intruder in the telescope's view finder, and followed his progress all the way downtown."

"How far downtown, do you happen to know?" Nygel asked.

"Chinatown."

"You can see all the way down to Chinatown from here? Even with a telescope?"

"Sure," the gentleman said "From here at the north end of Lafayette Street, the blocks run straight all the way down to Canal Street. That's the main hub of Chinatown, and that's where he took a left turn."

Nygel nodded. Whoever this orange-and-black building-climber may be, he evidently escaped the fire, as well as the Lucci gang's considerable arsenal of weapons.

"You didn't call the police?"

"No, I'm ashamed to say. I was afraid that . . . well, I was concerned that they'd want me to come in for questioning, and for someone with my particular phobia . . ."

"Sure, I understand," Nygel said.

The cell phone in Nygel's pocket rang. It was Max, telling him they were ready to start broadcasting in five minutes. Nygel got off the phone thanked the kind gentleman for his time, again promising not to reveal his source.

The gentleman sighed with visible relief. "I appreciate that very much, thank you."

Back on the elevator, Nygel had a feeling that everything was leading him to Chinatown. Even Chen, one of Sage's dealers, was reportedly operating out of a dumpling shop a few blocks off Canal Street. As for the infamous orange-and-black building-climber, Nygel was amazed that one person could create so much carnage and leave unharmed, and still have enough energy to jump from rooftop to rooftop all the way to Chinatown.

Nygel monitored Sandy's broadcast from the van. It was more or less what he had expected, opening with her grim tour of Tony Lucci's lavish duplex: *"Here's what ten thousand dollars a month will buy you in the East Village, folks—twelve bedrooms and ten baths, all designer-decorated and liberally splashed with blood and gore . . ."*

"Crazy," Nygel muttered, shaking his head.

Towards the end of the broadcast, Sandy roused Nygel out of his mounting boredom with a jaw-dropping scoop: *"There are unconfirmed reports that Captains Martin Brooks of the N.Y.P.D. and Richard Higgins of the Newark P.D. have one suspect at the top of their list—the local phenomenon known as Knight Seeker . . ."*

"Whoa!" Nygel shouted.

"Anonymous sources have told Rapid Action News that similar killing sprees in the tri-state area—most recently, last night's massacre at Dexter's Bar & Grill in downtown Newark—placed Knight Seeker in the middle of the action. Could the same man who saved a trailer from going off the Trenton Makes Bridge have switched his allegiance from good . . . to evil?"

Nygel felt he was going to puke. The broadcast then returned to the Rapid Action News studio for a remote interview with a "prominent psychologist" who advanced the opinion that "the archetypal hero may become so drunk with hubris and power that he may turn to 'bigger kicks' like murder . . ."

Nygel sat still in the van, feeling like he had been hit over the head with a mallet. *Okay, focus,* he told himself. He knew he had to go to Chinatown to try to put an end to Sage's drug ring. But he also had to clear Knight Seeker's name before the officials started pointing the finger at him for any more murders they couldn't find answers to.

But the more he thought about the injustice of it all, after everything he'd done and sacrificed for good, not evil, he wanted to smash his fist through the TV monitor. The idea that he was suspected of having a connection to this horrible event and was being sought for questioning—it more than infuriated him, it made him want to—

Nygel blinked. He saw two things at the same time, and they filled him with horror. The first thing was his spike-bones ripping through the sleeves of his shirt. The second was Sandy, Max and Andrew leaving the apartment building and heading toward the van.

"Oh, man," he whispered hoarsely. "Compass, you got to help me here! I'm sprouting spike-bones!"

Compass replied from inside Nygel's backpack. *"Duly noted. Seeker Spinner, may I suggest you do what Seeker Aracnus did in similar situations?"*

"Yeah, yeah, what is it!"

"Think of something joyful and inspirational. That should take care of it."

"Something—yeah, okay . . ."

Nygel wracked his brain, but the hardest to do when a million horrible thoughts are flying around in your head is to think of something joyful and inspirational. Just when he thought his head would explode from panic, Compass spoke again:

"May I suggest the song Reverend Squire sang last night?"

Nygel didn't need any prompting after that. He closed his eyes tight and mentally transported himself back to the choir loft in Shining Light Baptist Church. The deep bass voice of Reverend Squire echoed in his ears:

> *"If your rope of hope is almost broke,*
> *If your rope of faith is almost broke,*
> *If your rope of patience is almost broke,*
> *Just reach,*
> *I want you to tell somebody,*
> *'Reach beyond the break and hold on, hold on, hold on!'"*

Suddenly the back door of the van opened and Sandy's voice broke the spell.

"Hey, Spinner, what the hell did you do to your shirt?"

Nygel opened his eyes and looked down at his arms. There were gaping holes in the sleeves, but the spike bones had mercifully retracted out of sight.

"Must've been that pack of pit bulls I just fought off," he said with a smile.

CHAPTER 24
SHAKEDOWN IN CHINATOWN

THERE *WAS* good news: Andrew told Nygel that Mike Payne was happy with the live news report and gave them the rest of the day off. So Nygel made a quick goodbye and found a deserted spot a few blocks away on the corner of Third Avenue and West Fourteenth Street—a gutted store just perfect for a quick-change artist. He slipped inside and found a private spot behind an old beat-up display case. There, to the curious stares of two rats, Nygel retrieved the sonic sword and Compass from his backpack, stashed the backpack on a shelf behind the display case, and then called forth the bio-armor.

"Compass, create a rift-port to the center of Chinatown, rooftop level," Knight Seeker ordered.

Compass gravitated in midair and dispensed ion particles into the familiar circular formation, forming the spatial rift in front of him. Nygel—or rather, Knight Seeker as he was now—stepped through the gateway that folded space and the next moment he found himself on the rooftop of a four-story commercial building on Canal Street. He immediately started to scout the area for any drug dealers who might lead him to Sage.

He hopped building to building, swinging and pulling his body with his spike-bones as they lodged into the sides and ledges of buildings. The muscle tissue strands attached to the spike bones pulled him as slowly or quickly as he needed them to as he worked his way down to street level. He had gotten to be pretty adept with this technique, and he loved it even more than his climbing prowess. It was probably the most thrilling part of being a superhero.

He landed in an alley and walked out onto Canal Street. "Okay, let's find us some drug dealers," he told Compass.

"Request received, Seeker Spinner," Compass said, and whirred ahead of him, leading the way.

"Whoa, fella. Where're you going?"

"Looking for drug dealers," Compass replied, *"with the aid of this unit's artificial olfactory sense interpreter."*

"The what?"

"This unit's nose, so to speak. Now, what type of drugs are we seeking?"

Nygel stopped in his tracks, impressed once again with Compass' seemingly unlimited abilities. "Cocaine, I guess."

Compass came to a grinding halt. *"Cocaine, cocaine . . . Oh, you are referring to $C_{17}H_{21}NO_4$. Search commencing. Please follow."*

They traveled five blocks west on Canal Street. Knight Seeker had to jog to keep up as Compass spun and whirred ahead of him, sometimes zigzagging close to a shop door or going after a moving car as it sensed trace amounts of cocaine. Knight Seeker had to keep it in line with a specific instruction that they were going after dealers on the street, not individual users.

Occasionally passersby stopped and pointed, whispering as they passed, and it was not long before the Knight realized it wasn't because they were thrilled to be treated to a celebrity sighting: Knight Seeker was wanted by the police, he now remembered, and if he didn't play it cool, this A.P.B. might interfere with what he needed to do.

Compass stopped at an intersection. *"Objective located, Seeker Spinner. In the black vehicle parked across the street. There you'll find benzoylmethylecgonine."*

The Knight sighed. "Do me a favor, Compass. Just say cocaine and spare me the chemistry lesson." He was beginning to suspect that Compass was having a few laughs at his expense. There was just no telling. "Let's go."

As they crossed the street and approached the black Jeep Cherokee, Knight Seeker also wondered if Compass was sending him on a wild goose chase. The van looked like it belonged to a suburban soccer mom; the obnoxiously smug bumper sticker read "My Child is an Honor Student at Ridgecrest Elementary School." But in the next moment, a well-dressed man jaywalked across the street to the van and knocked on the tinted rear window. Then it happened—the window lowered a crack, the well-dressed man leaned in to whisper something, and then money and drugs changed hands. Then the well-dressed man hurried back the way he came, across the street and out of sight.

"Well, thanks," the Knight said to Compass, then paused to consider his approach. Being direct was always a good bet, but he also knew whoever was in that van was probably well-armed. Knight Seeker ran to the Jeep at a nice clip, and then pounced atop the Jeep. When his feet met the metal roof, the cries broke out at once:

"What the hell is that?" the voice in the passenger side shouted. Before they knew it, the young Asian driver was yanked out of his seat through the open driver-side window. He screamed bloody murder as he struggled to free himself from the hand that gripped his designer shirt, during which the Knight gave him a quick frisking.

Well, he thought, *this one doesn't appear to have a gun. That means . . .*

Sure enough, the passenger door flung open and a tough-looking hood jumped out with his semi-automatic pistol ready to do damage. But before he was able to get his licks in, a plasma net shot out of the Knight's right forearm gauntlet, and the thug found himself immobilized and flat on the street, encased in the sticky net.

That left at least one other person—whoever was dispensing the drugs from the back of the Jeep. He was already climbing to the front seat to take charge of the wheel in order to shake the hero off the Jeep and make his getaway. The Knight was one step ahead of him: he jumped in front of the vehicle with the driver still hanging in his grip, and before the new driver could put the van in reverse to make his escape, the warrior took hold of the front bumper with his right arm and inquired politely, "Going somewhere? I don't think so."

With one quick movement, he picked up the entire front of the Jeep and flipped it over backwards, until it came down crashing down on its roof. The moans that issued from the front seat gave the Knight a good indication the new driver had not buckled up.

"Don't forget, kids: seat belts save lives," he offered helpfully.

"Punk-ass!" came a muffled shout from the driver's seat.

The Knight now considered the punk still had in his grip, his small black eyes flashing with fear. "What do you want from me," he cried out.

"Do you work for Sage?" the hero demanded as he lifted the punk higher off the ground. "Well? Do you?"

"No, I can't tell you anything! He'd kill me if I— Damn it!"

Knight Seeker brought him close to his face. "I suggest you tell me what I want to know, or so help me . . ." He popped a spike-bone from his right forearm as a demonstration. The Asian punk really started sweating now, but he still wasn't talking. So the Seeker slammed the uncooperative punk by the back of his designer shirt against the brick wall, using his spike-bone to hold him there.

* * *

Five minutes earlier, a man in a black Hummer was cruising the city, looking for trouble—literally. Since dawn he had been driving all over Manhattan, from the Battery to Washington Heights, hoping to find a jumper on the Brooklyn Bridge or a sniper laying siege on an elementary school—something, *anything* that might drag that damned Knight Seeker dude out of his hidey hole. He was counting on Captain Higgins taking care of those "parking tickets," but it wasn't looking so good.

He had figured Knight Seeker was maybe hanging out in New York City, since he was the chief suspect in last night's Lucci gang massacre. But so far all the police, fire department and transit channels he had been monitoring on his trusty Bearcat scanner had yielded nothing. And it wasn't as if Knight Seeker had a web site where he posted his daily itinerary. So Mayhem decided to pack it in and head back to Jersey; maybe he'd have better luck there.

He was driving on Broome Street, headed towards the Holland Tunnel, when he switched the scanner off and turned on the car radio. It was amazingly good timing, too.

"And Chinatown is abuzz with the appearance of crime fighter Knight Seeker running like hell down Canal Street in broad daylight—as we speak!

Hey, does someone wanna tell this guy that the cops are looking for him? In sports today..."

Mayhem did a quick U-turn on Watts Street, avoiding the tunnel to New Jersey, and drove back the way he came.

"Thank you, news radio," he murmured to himself.

* * *

"All right, all right!" the Asian punk screamed. "We get our supplies from the Jade Tower building on Maiden Lane, near Wall Street. Our old boss, Lui Fang, owned the top four floors, and this dude Sage killed him and took over the whole downtown drug trade. That's all I know, I swear to God! I'm just doing what they pay me for. It's just a job, okay? So don't kill me."

Knight Seeker nodded, then retracted the spike-bone that had pinned the punk to the brick wall. The punk fell to the sidewalk, still frightened out of his wits.

"Oh, man, he's gonna kill me..."

"Like I care," the Knight said. "You and your pals better make a quick career change if you don't want to see me again." He then webbed the drug-dealing punk to the wall as a nice package for the police.

"Hey!" the punk yelled. "What're you doing? I told you everything you want to know!"

"And I appreciate it," the Knight said, bowing. "Thanks!"

Just as he was about to turn and make his departure, a large U-shaped device came flying at him. He heard the whizzing noise, but had no time to act. Once the device made contact with him, it closed like a clamp.

"You're not going anywhere until the cops get here," Mayhem said, tossing his launcher on the ground. "And I collect my reward."

Knight Seeker looked up at the man in combat uniform and a wide belt loaded with accessories. His eyes were hidden behind large sunglasses.

"I don't know who you are or what your issue is with me," Knight Seeker said as he was about to snap the titanium bonding clamp, "but I gotta tell you something: I don't go down that easily."

Mayhem had heard the blue and gold vigilante was strong, but he never imagined he'd be able to break the trap that could hold a grizzly bear. Already the titanium clamp was starting to crack from the astonishing pressure the hero was applying to it.

"Oh no, you don't," Mayhem said as he pushed a button on a remote control on his belt. Once the button was pushed, a pulse of high-voltage taser energy zapped through the Knight's body.

Knight Seeker screamed; he had never before felt such pain. His alien devices and weapons were immune to electrical shocks like this, but he was not. Mayhem smirked and gave him another jolt, bringing the Knight down to his knees.

He snapped open his cell phone and speed-dialed Captain Higgins' personal number as he kept an eye on his captive. "This is Mayhem. Come pick up your package. Yeah, I got him."

Knight Seeker knew that he was better than this. He knew that he had to keep fighting despite the pain that racked his body. He then staggered up to his feet.

Mayhem frowned. "I told you to stay down," he said as he pressed his remote control, sending another jolt of Taser energy to the restrictor clamp.

The Knight wailed in agony, but then gritted his teeth and bore the pain as he broke the titanium bond with one concentrated move. The capture device fell to the ground, and he was loose.

"Like I told you, I don't go down easy," he said to Mayhem. "Now, if you're finished, I'd like to get back to work. If you get in my way, you're gonna have a serious problem with me."

"Oh, I already have a serious problem with you," Mayhem said as he reached into his pocket. He took out a handful of little metal balls and tossed them lightly in his captive's direction. The velocity-activated balls burst in the air, making a quick smokescreen. Knight Seeker couldn't see anything.

"Compass, switch to heat-detection vision mode."

Compass did as commanded and at once the Knight could make out the clear form of Mayhem running towards him, then taking a mid-air kick at his helmet. He grabbed his foot and threw Mayhem to the ground.

The bounty hunter felt a little dazed but still wanted to fight. As the smokescreen cleared, he quickly got back up to his feet.

235

"You're beginning to work my nerves," the warrior huffed, putting his hands on his hips. "You're a little out of your league, you know."

"Nah, I can handle myself," Mayhem said, reaching for something that looked like a night-stick from his belt.

For a fleeting moment Knight Seeker considered pulling out his sonic sword, but that would hardly be a fair fight against a billy club. "Drop the nightstick, Mayhem, before I stick it where the sun don't shine."

The bounty hunter just grinned, then swung the stick. The Knight caught it in his armored hand, but to his surprise, it emitted an electrical charge far greater than that of the restrictor clamp. The hero released his grip once he saw that the protective armor on his right hand was actually singed by the super-charged nightstick. The nerves in his right hand were half-numb, half-tingling, and he reflexively cradled his injured hand with the other.

Mayhem pressed his advantage by immediately driving the charged nightstick into Knight Seeker's mask. The hero was overcome with the shock and fell to the ground once again.

The police were around the corner now; sirens blaring, and news choppers were closing in on the area. A special unit of police was also on its way, outfitted with special weapons and vehicles that could take down full platoons with only a dozen men. This special unit, called the Sovereigns, was the last line of defense when it came to police and military control.

Knight Seeker shook the cobwebs out of his head and got back up. When he saw his opponent approaching quickly with his electric nightstick, he bolted up from the ground with his hands and landed directly behind him. He tagged a punch right into Mayhem's gut when he turned around to face the Seeker, and the bounty hunter gasped and doubled over, the wind knocked out of him.

Mayhem tried to jab the Seeker with the shock-club, but he saw it coming. He grabbed the bounty hunter's wrist and squeezed it tightly, forcing him to drop the weapon. Then he applied a sharp uppercut to Mayhem's chin with a force that knocked him against the brick wall, where he slid down as limp as a rag doll to the sidewalk.

"Just something to remember me by," the Knight said, then bolted from the area, using his spike-bones in bungee-style as he disappeared out of sight.

Mayhem lay on the ground bleeding at the mouth, checking his jaw to make sure it wasn't fractured. It wasn't, but hurt like hell. He picked up his nightstick and staggered to his feet as one Sovereign vehicle arrived. One of its officers, dressed in a crisp grey uniform with a blue pyramid insignia on the left breast pocket, dashed out of the vehicle and ran up to Mayhem. "What happened?" he shouted. "We were told you had Knight Seeker in the bag."

"He got away," Mayhem said as he spat a mouthful of blood onto the sidewalk.

The Sovereign officer stared at him in disbelief. "He 'got away'? Do you have any idea the number of units dispatched to this area? Where'd he go?"

"I didn't ask him," Mayhem replied, shuffling over to the drug dealer webbed to the brick wall. "Hey, what'd you tell him?" he asked the cocooned thug.

"I can't," the drug dealer pleaded as looked into the enraged bounty hunter's eyes. Mayhem pressed the thumb-trigger on the taser club, releasing a mini-shower of shooting sparks, and the drug dealer wisely gave in. "Okay, okay, turn that thing off. I told him where we get our merchandise—"

"Where?" Mayhem demanded.

"From the Jade Building off Wall Street. But you don't want to go there—Sage'll kill you right after he kills that blue-and-gold dude."

Mayhem's eyes lit up. "Sage? What do you know about Sage?"

"Nothin', he's just our boss. We run drugs for him, that's all. But he's scary, man. I mean, crazy-psycho scary."

Mayhem nodded. "Okay, thanks."

As he walked back to his Hummer, Mayhem thought a bit. If Knight Seeker was going after Sage, then he was most likely one of the good guys, not the blood-thirsty killer Higgins had thought—especially since he had harmlessly wrapped up this dealer in sticky webbing for the cops to pick up. But that didn't matter to him now; Higgins' promised reward did, and he needed to cash in those chips.

Tailing the vigilante would lead him to Sage, which was something he had never intended to do. But now he felt a chill of apprehension wash over him. He never thought he would see Sage again—not in the flesh, anyway. But now he felt emboldened with a new purpose. He wanted to kill this monster who had murdered Malice and the others that night and now plagued his dreams; he wanted that torment to end. *And* collect his reward.

"Where are you going, Mayhem?" the Sovereign officer called after him.

"To settle an old score," he shouted back as he drove away from Chinatown.

CHAPTER 25
BRINGING DOWN AN EMPIRE

TALBERT SINGE was not a man who liked to be kept waiting. Yet every time he had come to see Sage at his office, the warlord kept him cooling his heels in the reception area without apology or explanation, and each time the wait had been longer and longer.

The dapper Englishman, dressed in a white Italian suit with a dark red dress shirt, checked the time on his gold Piaget wristwatch. An hour late this time.

He sighed heavily, prompting the glassy-eyed reception to flash him an artificial smile and say, "He'll be right with you, Mr. Singe, as soon as he's finished his meeting."

Talbert nodded curtly in reply. They all had that glassy-eyed look, he thought; all Sage's office workers and minions and—well, *slaves* were what they were, the whole brainwashed bunch. And as for the warlord's "meeting" she had mentioned, the nature of that "meeting" had been made abundantly clear every few seconds, when a piercing female cry (of ecstasy or pain, it was sometimes hard to tell which) echoed through the door of Sage's inner office. The fact that he had been kept waiting so that the ego-bloated warlord could sate his carnal appetites infuriated him. He would have to bring *that* matter up, as well. It was unseemly that an emissary of the evil one would be so self-absorbed at the expense of—

His thoughts broke away as the inner office door opened and Sage stepped out, wearing a black silk robe with a train that dragged on the floor like a shadow that followed him. The robe was open at the chest and showed off his well-defined pectoral muscles, now slick with sweat from his recent physical exertions. Following him was a young Asian woman who looked disheveled and shaken, clutching her tattered robe close to her emaciated body. He starves them, too, Talbert thought with revulsion as the young woman fled the reception room. Still, he smiled genially as he stood up.

"Ah, Master Sage," he began, but the warlord ignored him, crossing the reception room to roughly bang on a door and shout, "Tygron!" Then he returned to his inner office, signaling Talbert Singe to follow with a careless backward wave of his hand.

Talbert flushed red with anger, but followed Sage as he had been commanded. In a moment the brainwashed slave, Tygron, entered the room as well, taking his position at the side of the desk, behind which Sage now seated himself.

"Sit," he commanded Talbert, who did as told, though perhaps taking slightly more time than he might have, just to show that he was not to be regarded as one of the warlord's slaves.

"Master, I—"

Sage cut him off as if he hadn't uttered a sound. "So, Talbert, you requested an audience with me. What is so damned important that you had to interrupt a critically urgent business meeting?"

Talbert pursed his lips and weighed his words carefully. "Master, thank you for agreeing to see me—"

"Get on with it," Sage mumbled impatiently. His eyes scanned his desktop for something—anything, it looked like, to occupy his attention, since nothing Talbert Singe had to say could possibly interest him. He finally picked up a nail file and began filing his nails.

"Very well," Talbert said. "I came to confirm your commitment to our mission. You have the power you sought, so now it is time to open the gates of hell and gain control of all mankind."

Talbert awaited a reply but Sage seemed preoccupied with his own fingernails. The warlord finished one nail, blew on it to dispel the nail dust, admired the result, then moved on to the next fingernail. Talbert contained his annoyance and went on.

"I am concerned that you are losing focus on what is important. I wanted reassurance from you that together we honor the will of our master. We are losing time, and time is of the essence."

Sage put down the nail file and sighed. "I will choose the time that is right, not you. And as for 'our master' . . . let him stew in his own juices—in hell where he happily sits. I am your master here on earth."

Talbert Singe jerked in disbelief. Such words, coming from a high servant of the Evil One, were heresy.

"Listen to me, you simpering fool," Sage went on, now looking at Talbert for the first time. "I was trapped in damnation and limbo for nearly nine hundred years. I was tortured by his minions for failing those many years ago. Now that I have the power I wanted in my life back then, I will establish it here. I will not give up this power I fought and suffered for, and I'll be damned if I give it up to live like some kind of dog under his feet. You can if you wish, but not me."

"My Lord," Talbert interrupted gently, "I ask you to reconsider—"

"And if you dare to talk about this again, you won't live to regret it, Mr. Singe. It will be as quick as this—" He waved a signal to Tygron, who aimed his right gloved hand in Talbert's direction, letting loose a bio-electrical bolt that scorched the thick-pile carpeting under his feet. Talbert jumped back, his eyes looked down at the smoking carpet fibers. He thought it best to leave before Sage decided to kill him.

"Very well, my lord. I shall keep to my own counsel as you wish," Talbert said as he looked back at Tygron with a boldly unimpressed frown.

"Good," Sage said in a pleasant voice, "and I'll send you the bill for the new carpet."

Talbert stopped in his tracks. He was a breath away from giving Sage a sharp reply, but just then the receptionist appeared in the doorway.

"Master," she said, "the guards report that Knight Seeker is on the rooftop across the street. They thought you should know."

Sage looked out his window and met Knight Seeker's gaze from the rooftop across the street. "Oh, dear," he said. "I wasn't expecting company, and the house is such a mess." A faintly bemused smile curled on the warlord's face as he picked up his phone and punched a button on his speed-dial.

As he left the office, Talbert overheard Sage order his guards to evacuate the building immediately and to prepare for an attack from Knight Seeker. This cheered up Talbert a bit. Perhaps, he thought, Knight Seeker would help in his desire to remove Sage from his seat of power and send him back to hell where he belonged.

* * *

"Compass, create a rift-port to the top floor of that building."

"May this unit make another suggestion, Seeker Spinner?"

"Sure, but you can stop saying 'this unit.' From what you've told me, you're an artificial-intelligent computer and self-aware, so refer to yourself as 'I' once in a while. Plus, you're my partner and a part of me—quite literally."

"This uni— I understand. My olfactory sense detects benzoylmethylecgonine moving in a perambulatory pattern throughout that building."

"Damn it, can't you speak English, Compass?"

"Sorry, Seeker Spinner. I detect several drug couriers stocking up their supplies in that building. If you take out Sage first, you will not be able to stop the dealers from escaping back onto the streets."

That may be, Knight Seeker thought, but working his way up the Jade Building—and fighting off hordes of Sage's security guards—would be a far more dangerous undertaking than simply rift-porting to Sage's office floor. As he thought it over, the hideous gargoyles on the upper ledges of the Jade Building seemed to mock him, dare him to accept the challenge. He looked up at the sky, now darkening with ominous storm clouds. It was, he thought, as if the Almighty had set the stage for battle.

"You're right, Compass," he finally said. "I think a more direct approach is in order."

* * *

Once he received the call from Sage, the head of building security made an announcement over the public address system that all office workers, building tenants and visitors—in a word, everybody—were to evacuate immediately. The announcement never reached the top four floors, and that was also at Sage's command; he needed all his personnel on hand to battle against the interloper, Knight Seeker.

Guards were dispatched to all the other floors to make sure the order was taken seriously. As the various tenants and office workers unhappily left the building lobby, they demanded to know why the building's owner, Mr. Sage, had ordered an evacuation.

"A gas main broke," the guards lied as they had been instructed, and that was all they needed to say. The panicked reactions this provoked guaranteed everyone would be far, far away when the showdown with Knight Seeker began.

The building now vacated, the security team, along with Sage's cadre of drug dealers, cordoned off the narrow street at both ends of the block, and then returned to position themselves outside in the main doors of the Jade Building. There they stood, armed and ready for what they had been told would be one hell of a troublemaker. As each minute passed, the deserted street seemed to grow quieter. None of the men awaiting Knight Seeker had any idea what they might expect. They only had their orders: to kill on sight.

Suddenly a low rumbling sound from above caught everyone's attention. All day long the skies had promised a thunderstorm, and here it was—the opening chords of a hell-raiser of a storm, just what the guards needed to set their nerves and teeth on edge. As the rolling thunder subsided, a more explosive sound followed. It was a sonic shockwave that shattered the plate-glass windows in the front of the Jade Building, then moved inward and flattened every man guarding the lobby under a hail of plaster and debris.

"Jesus!" more than one man cried. *"What the hell was that?"*

They had expected trouble, but not one of them had expected heavy artillery. Coughing in the clouds of plaster and dust, they got up from the floor and repositioned themselves, taking aim this time. And then, as the haze of dust settled, they caught their first glimpse of their expected guest, walking toward them with the determination of an unstoppable force—and worse, a smile. His bio-armor glistened from the rain that started to pour, giving him the glowing aura of an apparition.

The men blinked, unable to believe that this was the troublemaker they had to take out. "Hey," one of them shouted, "nobody told us it was gonna be that Knight Seeker guy!"

One of the guards had the presence of mind to give the order. *"Fire!"*

"Compass, shield," the Knight commanded.

It materialized just as the bullets came flying at him. He ducked, leapt, swerved and turned to catch the fire, each projectile dropping harmlessly off the mysteriously absorbent shield. The hero reattached his sonic sword to its magnetic holder, so that he would not be tempted to kill someone with it.

The guards fired until their ammunition began petering out, and that was when the Knight saw his opportunity to take action. He targeted two guards who were reloading their firearms, and then, moving his shield to protect himself from the gunfire coming from his left, he raised the pair of pistol-like barrels on the gold gauntlet on his right forearm and shot a plasma net at the two targeted thugs. They smashed against the building façade, frantically tearing at the sticky netting to free themselves.

Another guard shouted, "Fire!"

"It's a waste of time—" another answered.

"I said fire, you idiots!"

Gritting their teeth, the thugs fired their weapons with as much intensity as they could muster. But once again, their ammo was useless against the Knight's shield; it shimmered with every bullet that hit it, then dropped harmlessly to the sidewalk outside the Jade Building's entrance. The Knight then targeted the guard who gave the order, encasing him in a plasma-net cocoon before he hit the pavement.

It was too much for the others. After seeing this, and realizing that their weapons were useless against the Knight, the guards backed away in fear—straight into the lobby of the Jade Building. Inside it looked like a stage for battle; its former owner, the drug lord Lui Fang, had decorated the walls of the cavernous lobby with still-serviceable antique weapons from the Orient, and the security team had been trained to use them.

As the Seeker stepped out of the rain and into the building, leading with the shield as he moved toward Sage's army like an unstoppable machine, the guards all looked seriously worried. There were only six of them left; their firearms were useless against this man. One of them had an idea.

"If you truly are an honorable warrior, fight us in the traditional ways of combat," he said, reaching for one of the antique weapons mounted on the lobby walls.

The Seeker shrugged. "Fine by me. But after I get done, all of you will know who's your daddy." He released the sword hilt and deactivated his electron shield. He did not want to kill these hoodlums; he just wanted them to have their day in court. It was up to the justice system to decide their fate, not him.

But Compass could foresee trouble for the Seeker. *"I understand that you do not wish to kill these men,"* it said, *"but you are risking your life without the shield. I have another option for you."*

"Surprise me," the Knight said.

"Engaging battle-staff mode," the alien device said. Immediately two energy-spikes leapt from both ends of the sword's hilt, taking the shape of blunt metal rods. The gold claws of the hilt folded inwards towards the rods to give it a smoother symmetry.

"Hey now, that'll work," the surprised Knight said. "Man, I love this sword!"

* * *

The dark warlord felt uneasy. As he watched the security monitors in his office, Sage marveled that a man could possess such abilities not of a supernatural nature. He knew that if worse came to worse and he had to face Knight Seeker alone, he would need all the power at his disposal to kill him.

He went straight to the closet and pressed a button hidden behind the clothing rack. The wall at the back of the closet slid open, revealing a more private closet deep inside. Sage retrieved a garment that hung on a gold hanger. It was stinking, worm-eaten and tattered beyond recognition, its once rich colors faded to ash-gray and thickly encrusted with ancient fungus and rot. It was the battle armor he had been buried in, and he would wear it again to fight Knight Seeker to his death.

245

He put it on with reverence, dimly recalling the glory days when he battled Mongol hordes in the Asian plains. Ah, the joys of spilling the blood of his enemies, the wailing of the women, the crackling sound of burning villages and bodies!

Sage reached again into the secret closet and took the Soul Taker from its hook. The moment he lifted it, he was shocked and dismayed at its insufficient weight; at its peak condition, it had a certain heft, a thrilling charge of energy and power, and now it felt not unlike an ordinary weapon. As he unsheathed it and examined the crystal set into the blade, Sage knew at once that his suspicion was correct: the Soul Taker had been weakened from overuse. There was only one remedy for that.

He quickly called Tygron. "Summon my followers," he told him, and when the brainwashed slave nodded and left the room, Sage looked again grimly at the security monitors. That damned pest Knight Seeker was taunting his guards with the battle-staff that materialized in his hands.

"Who wants some of this?" the Knight shouted. *"Come 'n' get it!"*

Sage frowned as he watched. Yes, he would need the blood of his followers, just in case.

* * *

Few of the guards were eager to take on a man who could forge a weapon out of thin air; it was obviously not of this Earth. They were armed with mere swords, sais, staffs, axes, and a huge hammer—nothing like the battle-staff that had magically appeared in Knight Seeker's hand.

At least one of the guards had a kill-or-be-killed attitude. Bellowing a war cry, he came running as he swung two ivory-handled swords meant to slice the interloper into stir-fry-sized pieces.

Knight Seeker crouched into a battle stance with his battle-staff in front of him. It felt surprisingly natural in his hands, almost as if it was a part of him. He lowered his head and batted the two swords with his weapon, then twisted his body around to execute a roundhouse kick that sent the guard crashing to the floor.

Another enforcer found his nerve and rushed into the fray with a pair of sais in his hands. He furiously jabbed at the Knight, trying to find an opening for his point blades.

Knight Seeker blocked and countered but failed to get in his own hit. Then the sai-wielding enforcer swung back to kick, but the Knight caught his foot and spun him around. Quickly connecting the battle-staff to the attacker's jaw, he put him to the floor in an instant.

A loud roar came from behind, and the Seeker whipped around to see a hugely-built guard swinging a silver combat-hammer. The Knight ducked, dropped his battle-staff in an upright position on the floor and, still gripping it, swung his body in a wide arc to clear the combat-hammer before it came crashing on his head. Instead, it smashed the floor where the warrior had stood, reducing the marble tiles to tiny marble chips and fine powder. With his body still being supported by the battle-staff, Knight Seeker swung back full-circle to deliver a powerhouse kick to the hulking guard's head. It sent him staggering backwards like a drunken ox, but he somehow still managed to keep the combat-hammer in his hands.

"Cho, leave him to me," another guard shouted. He walked towards the Knight lightly swinging his Chinese bow-staff, its dagger-edged blades shaped like crab claws. As he came closer, Knight Seeker surprised him by holding up his hand in a halting gesture, and then drawing an imaginary line with his battle-staff on the floor. Then he stood back, crossing his arms as if daring the guard to cross the line. The guard shrugged, took a bold step over the line—and they were off.

Their staffs twirled like batons, each managing to block the other's attack with the click of metal echoing in the cavernous lobby. Suddenly the guard reversed direction of his spinning bow-staff—a maneuver that made Knight Seeker lose his focus for just an instant. An instant was all it took. Finding his opening, the guard pushed through the Knight's defense and slashed through the blue plasma armor on his right arm. It was not a deep wound, but it stung like hell; the Knight winced in pain as blood oozed from the thinly sliced armor sleeve. The guard grinned, relieved to see that his opponent was neither a machine nor invulnerable.

But the Knight did not drop a beat. As they resumed spinning their staffs and blocking each other's attacks at top-speed, he remarked, "Nice moves."

The guard smirked. "Thanks."

"Try this one," the Knight said, swinging back his battle-staff to swipe low at his opponent's legs. The guard jumped in the air, avoiding the whooshing weapon as it sliced through the air under his feet. Back and forth it went, the guard adroitly leaping over the Knight's swinging battle-staff, not even breaking a sweat.

"That's pretty good jump-roping," the Knight said. "I didn't think you had any balls." He stopped the swinging battle-staff halfway through its full range of motion, and then thrust it upwards between the guard's legs. The hapless guard let out a yelp of agony as he fell to the lobby floor, clutching his family jewels.

"My mistake," the Knight said. "I guess you *do* have a pair."

Then the hero heard the pitter-pat of quick footsteps coming from behind him. He whipped his head around to see a pair of axes coming at his head. He bent backwards, barely avoiding the whizzing blades, then stood back up to the axe-wielding lumberjack and punched him square in the jaw. Stunned, the guard swung at the warrior again, missing by inches. Knight Seeker replied with a swift, single-footed one-two combination kick in the ribs, and then at his head. The attacker met the floor as he dropped the axes in his hands.

CHAPTER 26
THE FINAL CONFRONTATION

QUICKLY, BECAUSE there was not much time left, Sage told the sixteen devoted followers the story. When he was finished, they uttered cries of protest and despair. "No, Master! It cannot be!"

"It's true," the warlord said, "The man coming upstairs this moment intends to kill me. And if I am dead, what will become of you, lowly worms who only live to serve me?"

But not for one second did the tearful group of sixteen think of themselves; in fact, they were incapable of it. Even Tygron, who stood behind his liege, was sobbing at the thought of life without his beloved master.

"Then you will defend me?"

All of them swore they would defend his life with their very own.

"Good," the warlord said, "because my sword, the Soul Taker, it's—" He paused to retrieve a modern-day phrase from his bank of stolen memories. "Well, let's just say the batteries have run low and I need to recharge it with fresh souls. Now, who'd like to die for the warlord Sage?"

All sixteen followers thrust their hands into the air and waved them frantically. "Me, Master!" they cried, "Pick me! Please, Master!"

Sage chuckled to himself. It did his black heart proud to see these brainwashed idiots begging to be murdered, each of them eager to throw their once-productive lives away, forever forsaking the families who had so feverishly prayed for them to come to their senses and leave the dangerous and bizarre cult of the madman Sage.

"All right, settle down . . ." the warlord said, enjoying the outlandish spectacle enormously. "Honestly, I don't know whom to pick. I guess I'll just have to kill . . . *all of you!*"

The followers squealed with excitement, jumping up and down and clapping their hands in delight.

"Excellent! If you all will defend me with your lives, then your lives are what I shall have. Come, my angels, my precious fools, gather in a circle around your master. Except you, Tygron. I will need you for other things."

Tygron's face fell, but only momentarily. He stood watching enviously as the other followers encircled their master as he said, "Now kindly bend your necks back so that I may cut your throats more quickly."

They did so gladly, gazing upwards to the ceiling as Sage went around the circle and positioned the blade of his sword at their throats and gracefully sliced them open. And as he went about this murderous business, he whistled a song he picked up from his mental bank of stolen memories. It happened to be, curiously enough, "Whistle While You Work." He whistled as his servants' blood splattered over the walls. It certainly wasn't pleasant for them; they coughed and vomited and their blood spurt out of their necks in wide arcs, splattering the walls and each other with gallons of thick, sticky fluid that reeked of death. But they did it joyfully—that is, until the last moments of their lives, as each heart pumped its last labored beats, when they unmercifully came to their senses and the full impact of what they had done came crashing down on them. It was that look of dawning horror and anguished regret that Sage liked the best.

Once he was finished and the room fairly glowed red with the blood of the innocents, the Soul Taker also glowed red as the victims' souls were swept from their bodies and sucked into the crystal. Sage held the sword aloft and felt his power growing as each soul passed into the enchanted blade. He was ready, should he need to battle Knight Seeker. One way to find out, he thought, and turned on the monitor to see how his guards had fared against his nemesis.

When the screen came to life, Sage was greatly disappointed to see the blue and gold superhero still standing. There was only one remaining guard—Cho, his best fighter, a two hundred-eighty pound beast wielding a mighty combat-hammer.

"Just looks like it's you and me now, Slim," the Seeker said, then uttered a command to disassemble his battle-staff. The blades disappeared into the sword hilt, and with a smile the Knight slapped it onto his leg attachment. "Hand-to-hand?"

Sage was impressed—and worried. As he watched, Cho tossed his combat-hammer to the floor. "Idiot," Sage murmured. It was one thing for the Knight Seeker to play dare-devil, but he didn't like to see his own men being that foolish.

Cho cracked his knuckles and growled, "I am going to enjoy this."

"Not for long," Knight Seeker replied with a smile.

Sage turned off the monitor and frowned. "Come with me," he said to Tygron. "I shall put an end to this Knight Seeker once and for all. Then no one will dare oppose my power."

* * *

The Knight had underestimated the abilities of the last remaining guard.

Cho proved to be a powerhouse boxer, surprisingly quick and nimble for his massive size. He started with a relentless flurry of punches, all of which the Knight managed to avoid, though he did sustain a painful hit on his injured right arm.

The Knight cried out in pain, emboldening Cho to take him in a killer bear hug. The other guards, trapped in their plasma-netting, shouted encouragement to the last remaining fighter, but Cho didn't need it. This was his specialty, the lethal move that got him banned from professional wrestling many years ago. As he began to squeeze the life out of his opponent, his massive torso and arms tightening his prey to the crushing point, Cho cooed into his ear, "C'mon, sweetheart, let's hear ya crack."

There was a crack—the sound of a rib breaking. The Knight determined that this would be the first and last bone he'd break that day. Summoning all his strength, he thrust his arms out, snapping free from Cho's crushing grip. The other guards shouted in dismay as Knight Seeker grabbed Cho's left arm and swung him towards the others. The walls shook with the crash of

Cho's massive body against his cocooned associates, the crunch of broken bones echoing throughout the cavernous lobby.

"Done," the Knight murmured to himself. The first stage of the battle won, anyway, he reminded himself. There was still Sage to deal with.

It was a moment's work to quick-wrap Cho in sticky webbing against the wall along with the others, all gift-wrapped for the police when they finally arrived. With a nod and a wave to the angry bunch of plasma-netted goons, Knight Seeker started for the elevator.

He pressed the button for the twenty-fifth floor, where the drug-dealing punk in Chinatown had told him he'd find Sage. He closed his eyes, ignoring the insipidly cheerful elevator music as he mentally geared up for his greatest challenge.

"Seeker Spinner, you have sustained various cuts and bruises and two broken ribs. Would you like the complete medical read-out on your visual cortex?"

"Later," the Knight told Compass. "I'll save it for my bedtime reading."

The elevator doors opened and he stepped out, ignoring the shooting pain in his ribs as he readied himself for anything that Sage had to throw at him. But it was strangely silent on the top floor. Only the rumbling of thunder outside disturbed the absolute quiet. And the strong scent of blood in the air; the Knight didn't need his heightened olfactory sense to notice that; the entire floor reeked of death.

He crept around to see if anyone was about, but the floor seemed to be completely deserted. Following the scent, he stepped into an office and was assaulted by the obscene sight of Sage's butchery. It made Knight Seeker sick to his stomach.

"Oh man, oh man . . ." he whispered to himself. "This is one sick guy. I gotta stop this nut-job . . ."

The last thing he expected was the phone to start ringing. He waited two rings, then picked it up. He did not say a word. The long silence was broken by the person on the other end.

"I take it that this is Knight Seeker?" a man with an English accent said.

"And who wants to know?" the Seeker asked bluntly.

"My name is not important, but I have some information for you," the voice said.

"I'm listening."

"Good. Now listen. To defeat your adversary, you must take his head with his own sword. That is all you have to know. Oh, and also be cautious of his bodyguard, Tygron. He will also be a bit of a nuisance to deal with."

"Why are you telling me this?"

"Mmm, let's just say that Sage was a business partner of mine and I want to dispose of the partnership—" The man chuckled a bit. "—if you know what I mean."

Talbert Singe didn't wait for a reply; he hung up the phone and breathed a sigh of relief. He was glad to do Knight Seeker this favor; he certainly didn't want this souped-up superhero gunning for him after he disposed of Sage. His one regret was that he would miss seeing the ensuing fight.

As for Knight Seeker, he didn't want to spend one more second in that sickening slaughterhouse of an office. He hung up the phone and left the room, following the bloody footprints that led out the door to a stairwell. As he climbed the three flights of stairs to the roof of the Jade Building, he felt absolutely sure that he was walking into a trap. He might have felt a twinge of nervousness about knowing this and confronting Sage, if it wasn't for the bloodbath this monster had left behind him. The sight of such a brutal, senseless violence enraged him—but it was a tightly controlled rage that took the form of a sharply focused, icy calm.

When he opened the door at the top of the stairs and looked out onto the roof, the first thing he saw a bloody puddle being washed away by the driving rain. Then as he stepped out onto the roof, he saw something that reminded him of something straight out of an old kung-fu movie from the Seventies.

He might have missed it, if a bolt of lightning had not flashed just that moment, illuminating the grotesque scene: there was Sage upon a throne, a scalding stare on his face, his body hunched forward. Behind him stood Tygron.

They were surrounded by rows of marble pillars, blood-red and veined with streaks of black. Strange vines grew wild from the tops of the pillars, giving the whole rooftop the atmosphere of a bizarre courtyard—a garden in hell.

"So you have come to die, Knight Seeker," the warlord said in his booming voice. "Let me help by sending you on your way." He raised the Soul Taker, aiming its blade at the sky, then lowered the sword to point in Knight Seeker's direction.

A sizzling streak of lightning shot from the stormy sky. The Seeker jumped out of the way, but still his leg armor burned from the proximity of the intense heat. In one swift movement he rolled to the ground, got back onto his feet, and then activated his electron shield.

Sage sent another bolt racing towards his enemy, and two other bolts after that, but the Seeker deflected them all with his shield. The diamond-shaped electron barrier worked, but the shield that was generated would not stand up to this much punishment for long. Compass informed him through his visual cortex that the shield's integrity had been diminished to fifty-eight percent. He knew he had to take action. Quickly he unleashed the hilt of his sword, which sprang to life in his hand, just as Sage was about to command another lightning strike from the storm-tossed heavens to demolish his nemesis. A sonic wave leapt from the Knight's sword and struck Sage in the chest, leaving a smoking hole the size of a shotgun wound.

To the Knight's amazement, the warlord's real appearance was revealed once his body was damaged. Sage's eyes glowed an icy blue, and from his mouth dripped something green—blood or bile, Knight Seeker did not know which. He watched spellbound as the ancient warlord's face and hands turned reptilian—scaly and mottled green and brown.

But it was a momentary metamorphosis. Sage quickly regenerated his body, the hole in his chest healing as it sucked energy from the Soul Taker still in his hand.

"Your feeble attempts at stopping me are useless. Tygron, kill him," Sage ordered, then sat back in his throne to see how his slave would do pitted against the Seeker.

Tygron, his face unreadable under his metal mask, obediently leapt into the air and came down in the middle of the rain-spattered court yard. Once on the ground, he crouched in a pouncing position and was ready to fight.

"Another lackey to take care of your dirty work, I see," the Knight said as he stepped across the court yard. "I had fun dealing with the last one you sent, so I'm sure I'll enjoy this."

Sage grinned. "You mean Chen? He was a stooge. Tygron, however, is a work of art. Pounce, dear boy," Sage commanded, and Tygron obediently lunged for the warrior, his mutant claws extended to their full eight-inch length. But Knight Seeker did a back-flip to avoid Tygron. But Tygron was soon fully engaging Knight Seeker, ripping his claws at the hero's still-functioning shield. The Seeker jabbed his shield at Tygron, forcing him backwards a few steps.

Sage got bored and decided he wanted to play, too, so he raised his sword and took aim. A white energy beam leapt from the Soul Taker and flew towards Knight Seeker, grabbing hold of his legs and lifting him off the ground, finally slamming him back-first against one of the marble pillars.

Even with his bio-armor, he felt the searing pain that shot through his body as he hit the ground. The shield, because it was controlled mentally, deactivated at once. The Seeker forced himself back to his feet; there was no time to rest while Tygron was on the prowl. He hid behind a pillar and noticed that Sage had disappeared from his throne.

Suddenly a fiery red ball of kinetic energy came streaking towards him. He rolled out of the way quickly and the ball struck the pillar, shattering it into thousands of pieces. He got up from the asphalt roof, unaware of what was coming from behind: a blue bolt of energy roared into him and smashed him back to the ground. He then felt an intense wave of pain as the blast ate through his armor, burning his back.

Knight Seeker screamed in agony, then gritted his teeth to hold it in. Footsteps behind him—he rolled away quickly, and sharp claws, meant for his head, went through the roof instead. Knight Seeker kicked Tygron in his masked face, then jumped to his feet and picked up the sonic sword that had fallen a few yards away. As he straightened up, he glimpsed the fiery ball rushing towards him.

Quickly he reactivated his shield to take the brunt of the blast, but the force of the attack sent him flying backwards into another pillar. He yelped in pain, and for the first time he felt he was losing this fight; both Sage and Tygron emerged in front of him, powering up for another assault. *Seems like everyone wants to kick my ass today*, he thought. In his agony, he could only manage the strength to concentrate on keeping his newly-formed electron shield up.

The faces of Tygron and Sage seemed to grow as they came closer. A twisted smile curled on the warlord's face as he reared the Soul Taker and swung towards Knight Seeker.

Knight Seeker could do nothing. He closed his eyes.

He heard a loud *crack!*—and then a whizzing sound as bullets streaked across the rooftop. He opened his eyes to see the bullets flying into the warlord's head and arms, jerking his body into a quick spastic dance, and then Sage fell to the ground.

And instantly began to regenerate, all thanks to the power of souls trapped in his weapon. The warlord got back to his feet, and stared across the rooftop towards the door. The man standing there dropped his jaw but not his smoking revolver. Then Sage roared with laughter.

"Ah, the infamous Mayhem! I see you made it to the party after all. It's been a while. Not since the bon voyage party I threw aboard the Dragon Feather. Tygron, kill him quickly."

Tygron let loose a bio-electrical bolt of energy that totally obliterated the small housing that opened to the stairway. Mayhem dodged the bolt by a few inches, then leapt down the stairs two, three, four at a time, and pushed the stairwell door open and closed it, locking it shut.

He leaned against the steel stairwell door, exhausted but giddy with relief that he was safe from that Tygron freak. But what was strange, he thought, was the rain that was pouring into the office area.

"What the hell—?" he said aloud, then looked up to the ceiling.

There was Tygron, peering through the hole he had ripped through the rooftop, and ready to fire another energy-bolt at the bounty hunter. Mayhem quickly ran out of the way, letting the stairwell door he was standing against sustain all the damage.

And then Tygron leapt down the hole in the roof.

* * *

"Now where were we?" Sage asked with a leering grin. "Oh, yes…" His eyes gleamed a glossy blue as another fireball materialized in his clawed glove.

Knight Seeker jumped out of the way as the kinetic ball of energy streaked towards him. The blast ended up destroying a good chunk of the roof. It was the biggest fireball yet, he noticed; despite all the hits Sage had taken, his power only seemed to build up.

"You can't stop me. Why do you keep trying?" the warlord asked in a lazy drawl as he turned around to track the Seeker's movements. He created another fireball and threw it at the pillar Knight Seeker was hiding behind.

The force of the blast sent him stumbling to the asphalt. He quickly rolled over to get a clear shot with his sword, but Sage jumped out of the path of the sonic wave.

"Pathetic," the warlord said. "Mere props. A child could do better with that sword." He traced a circle in the air with the Soul Taker, levitating one of the pillars and moving it directly over the Knight's body. Knight Seeker moved out of the way, but Sage guided his sword, making the pillar follow each step he took. The Knight stepped back, the pillar followed; he leapt sideways, so did the pillar. On and on it went like this, Knight Seeker trying to out-step the pillar, while Sage made it follow him from above. And when a certain rhythm had been established—when it seemed Knight Seeker had fallen into a panicky pattern of side-stepping, backwards-leaping, forward-jumping and so forth—the warlord tricked him with an unanticipated move and let his sword fall. As he did, so did the pillar fall. Knight Seeker tried to catch it, but it was too much for him and he toppled to the asphalt roof, the marble column pinning him down.

There was no movement from the limbs underneath the pillar. Sage was pleased. He returned to his throne and sat down in exhaustion, resting as he awaited the return of Tygron. Then he looked at the body underneath the crushing pillar and laughed.

* * *

Tygron was closer.

Kill or be killed, Mayhem told himself.

He couldn't stay hidden behind the desk for long. It had been a momentary bit of luck that Tygron lost sight of him while repositioning himself to jump down the rooftop hole. But the mutant was getting closer, and Mayhem knew he'd have to take action first if he wanted to get out of here alive. So he stayed quiet and still as he crouched behind the desk, listening for his adversary's approach. When he determined that Tygron was only a few feet away, he jumped up from behind the desk and took aim with his revolvers.

"Bye-bye," he said as he pressed the triggers.

Tygron quickly put his hands up in a blocking motion.

Mayhem fired his weapons.

With a concentrated effort, Tygron redirected the approaching bullets with an intense charge that made the hair on his head spike upwards. The bullets turned towards the metal gloves and stopped in mid-air, until Tygron stopped the flow of mutant power to his hands. Then he released another bio-electrical charge towards the guns in Mayhem's hands, rendering them white-hot with heat.

"Yow!" Mayhem shouted and dropped his weapons. Then his jaw dropped open for the second time that day: with a papery, ruffling noise, Tygron's claws and elbow-fins emerged for battle. "Jesus," the bounty hunter murmured.

In the next second, Tygron's razor-sharp claws were slashing at Mayhem. He somehow managed to block the killer claws and elbow-fins with his titanium baton, but the mutant fighter next dealt him a double-blow—a kick in the stomach, followed by a back-flip kick to the chin.

Mayhem spat a mouthful of blood and rubbed his jaw. He narrowed his eyes at Tygron, crouched on the floor and ready to attack. "Nice one, Wolfy, but it was your last shot," he said as he snatched one of his guns from the floor and aimed it at Tygron. The nimble wolfman raised his clawed glove to put up a magnetic barrier as before. But Mayhem fired at the fish tank at Tygron's side instead. After a crash of glass, a wave of water hit the floor, bewildering the mutant. But there was method to Mayhem's madness; he quickly leaped onto a desk and leaned over the side, then dropped his super-charged taser baton into the water.

750,000 volts rippled the water from the legs of the desk to where Tygron stood. He remained standing as he was electrocuted, his whole body vibrating so quickly that he looked like a blurred image—until the baton short-circuited and he fell into the puddle of water. He was breathing, Mayhem noticed, but unconscious. He could easily have finished him off there, but his main concern was getting the hell out of the building.

Once outside, he made a call to Higgins. The captain's cell phone was turned off, so he had to leave a message. His voice was trembling, he noticed with alarm, and after he finished the call and got into his Hummer, he realized his hands were still shaking.

* * *

Oh, God, the pain . . .

He knew he was not dead because of the pain. Underneath the massive red pillar, the Knight laid half-conscious, and the other half wanted to give up the ghost. He was beaten, he knew it; his mere "props" (as Sage had called them) could not defeat someone with that supernatural power.

He could not move. He tried, but it was hopeless. His gold visor was partially broken, exposing the area around his right eye. Compass showed him through his visual cortex that his bio-armor integrity was failing, due to the tremendous weight of the pillar.

The pillar . . .

So heavy . . .

That was when he realized he was holding up the pillar, just barely, though—just enough to keep it from crushing him to death. It was sapping what little strength he had left, and it was slowly sapping his will.

Still, it meant he had some strength left.

So what? he asked himself.

He'd never get out of this, he knew, so why even try?

Why?

He ached to know why.

What reason do I have to go on? Everything I've done has brought me nothing but pain and misery. Why the hell did I even try to start something like this? I should've just left this for the police . . . yeah, right, the police who think I killed Tony Lucci and his gang. Why did I even bother?

A strangely comforting warmth enveloped him, the cozy arms of Death told him he needn't feel pain any longer, to just close his eyes and sleep...

Then another voice shouted: *"Finish what you started."*

It jolted him awake. It was a familiar voice, someone he had let down, someone he desperately did not want to disappoint. He wept as he thought of Mr. Zimmer cradling his dead wife in his arms . . .

"Follow your heart and do what is right."

He knew that voice, too—his mother's, and then came another voice echoing in his ears: *"Reach beyond the break and hold on, hold on, hold on!"*

Yes, he wanted to, he wanted to so badly. But he had given it everything he had and now he had failed. He had tried...

He was no hero. He was a *pretend* hero, just as he had pretending to be Antorian by wearing an Antorian suit. Now he wore a different suit but it was still pretend, wasn't it?—just some "props" to give him enough edge to think that he was powerful, but he wasn't, not really. He was only Nygel. Nygel Spinner. And he was dying.

He closed his eyes.

"Finish what you started!"

It was Professor Zimmer's voice again, overlapping with itself: *"Finish what you started!"* repeating over and over again. But then he realized it was two different voices—a second voice echoing Zimmer's words—no, not quite; the overlapping words were slightly different, for some reason— *"complete what you have started"*—and now it spoke louder than Professor Zimmer's voice.

"You must complete what I have started."

Then he knew. It was a voice dimly remembered; it was the voice of Aracnus:

"I deputize you Seeker," the voice roared in his ears. *"You must complete what I have started."*

The words, spoken by Aracnus as he lay dying, resonated so powerfully that it awoke in Knight Seeker the strength and will to take action. It sprang to him suddenly like a shot in the arm, an untapped source he had all along but had suppressed—the strength and will of his Spycon self.

Several yards away, Sage grew tired of waiting for Tygron.

He realized he should have taken care of Mayhem when he had the chance, and entrusting the mutant with the task had been a mistake. Too much time had elapsed, and that was not a good sign.

As he passed the pillar that crushed his nemesis, Knight Seeker, a jarring sound behind him caught his attention. He turned to look and for a moment couldn't believe what he was seeing. The pillar that had fallen on Knight Seeker seemed to be moving—not rolling to the side, as might be expected by an unsupported pillar, but actually lifting upwards! He walked back to take a closer look.

Suddenly, a mighty thrust hurled the red stone pillar twenty feet into the air, and Knight Seeker jumped to his feet and pointed his sonic sword at the marble column.

"Full sonic shock," he yelled, and the blade activated with the gold claws quickly cupping the bottom of the blade. The energy built up and released by the sword could be heard for blocks around. When the enormous blue energy collided with the red pillar, all of its structure was obliterated and turned into harmless falling sand.

Sage was truly impressed by such a show of power.

"So, not quite as dead as I had thought," Sage said. "So much the better." He smoothly unsheathed the Soul Taker. As his adversary stepped towards him, Sage could see the determined eye of the Knight through the broken lens of the gold visor. The eye was orange in color, flashing brightly as the Seeker crouched to the ground a few feet away, his sword poised behind his right forearm. Sage gripped the Soul Taker with both hands and waited for the first move.

Knight Seeker swung towards Sage's head with a quick, precise movement of his blade. The warlord angled his sword to the side to block the attack. The Knight swung towards the other side of Sage's head, but yet again Sage blocked the blade.

Then he went on the offensive. Sage swiped viciously, the Knight deflected the Soul Taker with a mighty swipe of his own, then punched Sage square in the temple.

Sage swooned, his body listing to the side, but he came back immediately with a slash of his metallic clawed glove in the Knight's abdomen, cutting through his bio-armor.

Knight Seeker only glanced at the bleeding wound. The only way to win this fight, he knew, was to ignore the pain and give back everything he had. With cool precision, he launched a spike-bone into Sage's forearm, severing a tendon and making Sage drop the Soul Taker.

With the spike-bone firmly embedded in Sage's forearm, the Seeker swung him around his head like a wrecking ball, whipping his body into the remaining pillars. But Sage, though dazed, was not finished. As the Knight reeled him in like a fish to give him some more punishment, the warlord used his levitation powers to draw the Soul Taker back to his hand, and then swiftly cut the muscle strand attached to the spike-bone embedded in his forearm.

The searing pain of the severed muscle strand made the Knight scream. He involuntarily dropped his sword and the muscle strand shot back into his forearm.

It was the opening Sage needed. He raised his blade to make his final strike against the Seeker. "This ends now," he said as he swung the blade downward. But Knight Seeker quickly reacted by clamping the Soul Taker with both of his hands.

Sage's eyes widened at such an unanticipated move from his adversary.

Knight Seeker stood up as the warlord used all his demon strength to keep the hero down to the ground with his enchanted blade. But the Knight had another unexpected move: he kicked Sage in the stomach, sending him flying back ten feet. The Knight now had the Soul Taker in his hand and moved towards the fallen warlord, who now inched up to his feet.

"You feel the power of the Soul Taker? That thrilling power is yours if you join me. Admit it, Knight Seeker: you are a killer. Yes! You are very much like me. You can have anything you want. Just hand me the sword and I give you my word you will be a part of my empire."

In his voice was the merest hint of a man who realized his fate was in another's hands, and Knight Seeker had heard it clearly. "I'm not like you, Sage. I am a Seeker, a protector of the innocent. And the best thing I can do is to protect them from monsters like you."

Sage grinned a twisted smile. He didn't believe for a minute that Knight Seeker was a killer. At worst, he thought, he'd turn him over to the police, from whom he could easily manage an escape with his magic. But as Knight Seeker raised the Soul Taker and took aim to swing, the warlord realized he had been mistaken. He had only time enough to gasp in surprise as the blade came swinging down to his neck.

His head dropped and rolled across the roof before his body dropped. It kept rolling as Sage's hands thrust upwards—as if trying too late to catch the head before it fell—and then the hands dropped back to his sides, clenching and unclenching as his head knocked against the last standing pillar and rolled back.

The Seeker stood watching the rolling head, each revolution revealing a different look in the still-blinking eyes: contempt for Knight Seeker, then shock at seeing his neck spouting gouts of blood, then sadness upon watching his body fall with a thud to the wet asphalt rooftop, and then nothing as the eyes closed again for eternity.

The Soul Taker, still in the Knight's hand, grew warm and shining bright as souls awoke from the blade-crystal, then took leave of the sword as quickly as they had entered it. In a dazzling crisscross of soul-lights, they swirled around the Knight as if to honor him, and then shot up to the heavens in a blinding starburst. As the storm clouds parted to let them through the darkness, Knight Seeker knew it was over. Even Sage's body and sword at his feet were gradually fading away . . . and then they were gone.

The sudden silence and peace had a numbing effect, and he stood motionless for a long while. Then he bent over to pick up his sonic sword and his whole body screamed in pain. It awoke a new thought: where was Mayhem? Somehow the bounty hunter had managed to get away—at least for now. As he deactivated his sword and attached it to his side, he heard an unfamiliar voice coming up the stairs to the rooftop.

"Sage! Sage, where are you!"

It was Tygron—his mask now off, revealing a cat-like face. Knight Seeker hardly recognized him at first; the young fighter looked so different from his former brainwashed state—alive, focused, and very angry.

"He's dead, Tygron," the Knight told him quietly.

The young man stopped in his tracks and looked down at where Sage expired. It was a moment before he spoke, and when he did his voice was trembling with quiet rage.

"He forced me to kill anyone who stood in his way. I wasn't strong enough to fight off his power over me. I couldn't . . ." He lapsed into silence, then looked up to Knight Seeker, tears filling his eyes. "Thank you for freeing me from his hold."

"He was a powerful demon," the Knight said. "It wasn't you doing the killing—it was Sage controlling you. You have to believe that."

Tygron, alias Syre, nodded slowly, and with a parting smile of gratitude, he walked back to the stairwell housing and disappeared down the stairs.

There was a wail of police sirens on the streets below. Knight Seeker went to the ledge and looked down. It looked like the entire police force was taking this call.

"Compass, we're finished here. Create a rift-port home."

"You're forgetting your backpack, Seeker Spinner. You left it at the abandoned store on Third Avenue."

"Compass, you're amazing. Do you do windows, too?"

"Do windows'? This unit is not familiar with that expression."

"Skip it. Let's pick up my backpack first and then rift on home."

* * *

Captain Higgins' cell phone rang. He answered with a gruff "Yeah?"

"You get my call?"

It was Mayhem. Higgins stepped away from the other police, coroners, and paramedics to speak in privacy. "Yeah. It's a bloody mess. Sixteen bodies in Sage's office—their throats cut. Plus a small army of security guards and drug dealers in the lobby, all wrapped up in that sticky stuff."

"Yeah, I know. Did you get Sage?"

"Not a trace." Higgins paused and said, "No Knight Seeker, either."

"Yeah," Mayhem sighed. "Not for lack of trying. But I'll tell you this: you've got that guy all wrong. There's no way he was connected with the Lucci murders or the massacre at Dexter's last night. It was Sage. The Knight was beating the crap out of him and his guys."

"Uh-huh. So I should just take your word for this?"

"Hey, I wanted Knight Seeker bad, Higgins, just like you!"

Mayhem hung up and the line went dead. Captain Higgins put his cell phone away and sighed. He had mixed feelings he needed to sort out. Aside from a senseless massacre on the twenty-fifth floor, the war between the Lucci and Sage drug cartels appeared to be truly over. Did he have Knight Seeker to thank for that? Maybe, but he wouldn't know for sure until he got the vigilante in his office to clear up the story. And right now he was left with a lot of paper work and the damned media poking its nose into this mess . . .

"Excuse me, Captain Higgins." It was one of his deputies. "Sandy Castle is still outside, and she won't take no for an answer."

Higgins gritted his teeth. "You can tell Ms. Castle to drive back to Jersey right now, or I'll throw her in lock-up so fast, her head will spin."

* * *

"Damn it!"

"Let it go, Sandy," Max said for the third time. "Captain Higgins wouldn't give you an interview anyway, so what's it matter?"

"It matters," she snapped back, lighting up another cigarette in the van. "He would've given me the interview if I was a little more calm and collected and asked his deputies a little more nicely—"

"You don't know that," Andrew said. He was leaning his head on the back seat of the van. Traffic at the Lincoln Tunnel was at a stand-still. It would be an hour before they got back to the studio.

"And I *would* have been more calm and collected if my P.A. bothered to answer his damned cell phone so he'd know to show up for the scoop of the decade!"

Max shook his head. "Payne gave us the rest of the day off, remember? We just happened to be in town, and Nygel probably went to the movies or something."

Andrew murmured his agreement. "Yeah, give the guy a break, Sandy."

She puffed on her cigarette with fury, filling the network van with smoke. "It's not like he does that much anyway—just sits in the van to make sure the broadcast goes through. I can't stand incompetence."

Traffic started moving ahead. The car in front of them seemed to have fallen asleep, so Max gave his horn a blast. They drove the rest of the way back to the Rapid Action News office building in silence.

* * *

"A fraternity party?" Celine asked in disbelief.

Nygel nodded. It was the only excuse he could think of to explain the various cuts, scrapes and bruises on his face to his mother when he got home that night. She was horrified.

"Good Lord, Nygel. What kind of party was this?"

"I guess things got out of hand," he said with a shrug. Even shrugging was excruciatingly painful. Luckily he had on a long-sleeved shirt and sweat pants to cover up the other battle scars.

Celine just muttered to herself, "Kids," and that was the end of that discussion. "Your dinner's in the oven. You hungry?"

He was famished. After wolfing down his dinner, his friend James Booker called to see how he was doing. "Haven't seen you around much at work," he said. "Anything exciting going on?"

"I wish, Q," Nygel said, wishing just the opposite.

There was another important piece of unfinished business he absolutely had to take address. After pacing his bedroom floor for an hour, he finally worked up the nerve to call Kira Maru to ask her to meet him for lunch at the Mastoris restaurant in Bordentown, New Jersey, just outside of the Trenton area. He said he'd explain everything then.

"Well, that's all I wanted to hear," she said. Her voice sounded a bit distant, which was completely understandable, he thought. When he hung up the phone, Nygel had no idea what he'd tell her. And when the appointed day arrived, even as he walked into Mastoris and nervously greeted Kira at the banquette where she was sipping iced tea, he still was no closer to figuring out how to explain his odd behavior.

The waitress arrived to take their orders, giving him a few moments' reprieve. Nygel had no appetite but still ordered an iced tea and a cheeseburger platter. As Kira mulled over her menu, Nygel pretended to be interested in the news reports on the wall-mounted TV directly behind her. Then she ordered a grilled cheese and cole slaw, the waitress left, and the two were finally alone. Kira spoke first.

"Okay, Nygel, here's the thing," she began in what appeared to be a well-rehearsed speech. "You asked me out to dinner at Dexter's, I accepted, and we were having a pretty good time—at least I thought we were. Then you get up abruptly to go to the restroom . . ."

Nygel winced at the memory of that night: Kira stroking his cheek . . . the scent of her perfume on her wrist that drove him wild . . . his body temperature rising and something else rising, too, that forced him to bolt the table before his spike-bones ripped through his shirt sleeves . . .

". . . and you never come back. Nygel, I don't understand what happened. You just up and disappeared with no explanation, I kept calling and got no answer whatsoever from you. Is there something else going on that I should know about?" She put her hand up in a "hold on" gesture. "Let me rephrase that: I want to know what's going on. I did nothing to hurt you, but what you did—without any explanation—left me feeling really hurt. So . . ." She folded her hands on the table in an attitude of finality. ". . . I'm here and you're here, so if you have something to tell me, this is the time. Spill it."

Nygel spoke softly as he looked into her deep brown eyes. "Kira, I don't know if you'll understand this—if you'll ever understand this—but I'm not like most people, you know. I'm terrible about expressing myself and my feelings—maybe I'm afraid to let loose the real person I am, and it scares me. I don't want to hurt you."

He stopped and she waited for him to continue. "Then don't," she said.

Nygel turned his face away from her stare. She looked so beautiful and so innocent that he simply didn't know what on earth to tell her.

"All I can say is, I didn't ditch you."

"Yes, you did, Nygel—"

"Not intentionally, I mean. I wanted nothing more than to get back to the table and finish our date. But something came up—"

She rolled her eyes, having lost all remaining patience. "*What* came up, Nygel—*what*? If it's something embarrassing, you don't have to be specific, but you can at least categorize it for me, can't you? Okay, so you say you weren't trying to dump me, so maybe you were just being unbelievably thoughtless or unbelievably weird. I'll ask you one more time: *what happened?*"

Nygel hesitated, unable to speak, unable to look her in the eye. *Why?* he wondered. It would have been an easy matter to placate her, to just make up some plausible story about an anxiety attack or a bloody nose that embarrassed him beyond all reason. He could make up *something*, and it would only be a white lie, he felt; there would be no selfish intent or deception behind it, only his need to keep his Knight Seeker identity secret. *So why can't I do it?* he asked himself. Was it because that deep down, he didn't feel worthy of her love? Or simply that he didn't want to put her in harm's way ever again? Or could it be that he actually *wanted* her to know that he was Knight Seeker, despite the vow of secrecy he had made?

"Nygel," she said, demanding a response.

So he blurted out exactly what she didn't want to hear: "All I can tell you is that I didn't ditch you because I wanted to, or because I was having second thoughts about you. The fact is, I don't even know how to categorize my excuse, and there's a vitally important reason why I can't tell you. You'll just have to trust me on this, Kira."

She stared at him for a long moment, then reached across the table to touch his arm. "I'm sorry, that's just not good enough,

Nygel," she said softly. There were tears in her eyes, and that hurt him more than any punishment he had suffered in the hands of Sage or Mayhem or anything he'd ever feel, he knew beyond any doubt, and it was breaking his heart, too. "If we can't be completely honest with each other," she went on, "then there's no point in our continuing—"

Kira stopped abruptly, and a curious change came over her. It was a look of bewilderment, and then her eyebrows lifted with an expression of mounting realization. She was grasping his arm and had felt something underneath his shirt. It was the metal implant under his skin, and it took her only a second to remember it felt exactly like the metal implant she felt on Knight Seeker's arm that night he appeared in the tree outside her bedroom window. As she took all this in, her eyebrows lifted until they could lift no higher, and her brown eyes, still misted with tears, revealed that she understood everything.

"Kira?" he asked her, not comprehending the look on her face.

Suddenly she gasped and pulled her hand away—then just as suddenly, a smile of understanding and amazement spread across her face. Nygel had been so absorbed in her upset state and what had done to cause it, that he didn't understand the reason for the bewildering change that came over her so quickly. He didn't realize that in a matter of seconds, she understood everything.

"Kira, is there anything—"

The words died in his mouth. His attention had been diverted by the image on the wall-mounted television behind her. It was a late-breaking news story, the captions on the screen told him, coming live from the Fort Dix military base. A marauding tank was running over cars and crushing everything in its path.

"Kira, I'm sorry, but I gotta—" He got up quickly from the banquet. "Man, I can't believe I'm doing this to you again . . ."

Nygel didn't even have time to finish the sentence and he couldn't bear the look of shock on her face. He slapped a twenty dollar bill on the table, then dashed out of the restaurant and found a private spot behind a dumpster in the parking lot. There he transformed into his alter ego and rift-ported to Fort Dix to stop a crazed tank from destroying the entire base.

But that is another story.

Breinigsville, PA USA
12 October 2009
225690BV00002B/13/A